D1479155

The People of Taihang

THE
CHINA
BOOK
PROJECT Translation and Commentary

A wide-ranging series of carefully prepared translations of books published in China since 1949, each with an extended introduction by a Western scholar.

The People of Taihang: An Anthology of Family Histories
Edited with an introduction by Sidney L. Greenblatt.

Fundamentals of the Chinese Communist Party
Edited with an introduction by Pierre M. Perrolle.

Shang Yang's Reforms and State Control in China
Edited with an introduction by Li Yu-ning.

The Early Revolutionary Activities of Comrade Mao Tse-tung
Edited by James C. Hsiung. Introduction by Stuart R. Schram.

The Rustication of Urban Youth in China: A Social Experiment
Edited by Peter J. Seybolt. Introduction by Thomas P. Bernstein.

AN ANTHOLOGY OF FAMILY HISTORIES

The People of Taihang

EDITED WITH AN INTRODUCTION
BY SIDNEY L. GREENBLATT

INTERNATIONAL ARTS AND SCIENCES PRESS, INC. WHITE PLAINS, N.Y.

From The China Book Project. The People of Taihang is a translation of T'ai-hang jen-chia,
compiled by the "Four Histories" Editorial Committee of Southeast Chin District, Shansi
(Peking: China Youth Publishing House, 1964).

For Chün-fang and Ta-wei

When people see only what is under their feet, not what lies above the mountains and beyond the seas, they are likely to be boastful as "the frog at the bottom of a well." But when they raise their heads to see the immensity of the world, the kaleidoscope of man's affairs, the splendour and magnificence of the cause of humanity, the richness of man's talents, and the breadth of knowledge, they become modest.

"THE CENTRE'S INSTRUCTION ON LEARNING FROM EACH OTHER AND OVERCOMING COMPLACENCY AND DECEIT," December 13, 1963.

Contents

The People of Taihang

Acknowledgments

Very special thanks are due to Douglas Merwin, friend, col-
league and editor, whose patient encouragement and firm support have brought The People of Taihang to a Western audience.
I am also deeply indebted to the staff of International Arts
and Sciences Press for their aid in the labor of translation.
Variations in style and idiomatic usage complicated the task,
and they were handled with adroitness. I am also indebted to
Oxford University Press for permission to use a citation from
Jerome Chen's Mao Papers for the epigraph to this book.

My colleagues and students at Drew University played an
important role by extending their encouragement and proffering
their criticism so that I might sharpen an often unhoned perspective. Foremost among my colleagues in the China field
is my wife, Kristin Yü Greenblatt, my principal sounding board
and critic. Her insight into the workings of Chinese religious
and historical consciousness is a constant source of inspiration.

There is one to whom I owe a special debt of gratitude.
Fred Ablin, for years the guiding force of International Arts
and Sciences Press, oversaw the beginnings of this work. His
mission to build bridges of understanding through translation
has, since his passing, become our legacy. I can only hope the present volume contributes something of value to its continuation.

S. L. G.
March 1976

Introduction

The Taihang Mountains, the setting for the stories in this anthology of family histories, straddle the border between Shansi and Hopei. They rise abruptly from the great expanse of the North China Plains to create a formidable barrier, physical and cultural, over 3,000 feet in height — one link in a scarpment chain that begins at the edge of the Kweichow Plateau, thousands of miles to the southwest, and extends through the Great Khingan Mountains, which border on Outer Mongolia — as an old proverb puts it: "Door after door; gate after gate: mountains on the outside; mountains on the inside." (1)

In times past entire armies trod in and out of Shansi through the handful of river-cut passes that were the only access. Streams of peasant refugees from Honan and Hopei, pressed by flood, famine, drought and the oppression of landlords and officials, traveled these routes to find refuge in the very mountain fastness that harbored bandits, rebels and guerrillas, for whom the refugees were sometimes prey, sometimes recruits. And these outlaws, in their turn, used the same routes to return to the villages on the plains below, sometimes to raze them, sometimes to pillage them, and on rare occasions to mobilize them for planned change.

Shansi proper is a maze of mountains, subregional plateaus,

and rocky highlands which intersect with gullies, deep gorges, and loess canyons to make much of the region virtually impassable, if not uninhabitable. Only 3 percent of the land of Shansi is covered with natural vegetation; the remainder is rock and loess. (2) The climate of the region is as treacherous as the terrain. Cyclones are frequent occurrences and, partly owing to the high rate of evaporation in the highlands and the variability of rainfall, so are drought and flood. According to one source, every year between 281 and 290 A.D. was one of drought, and a drought in 298 A.D. drove over three hundred thousand refugees from Kansu, Shansi and Shensi into Honan and Szechuan. (3) More recently, in 1933, Shansi suffered a drought that lasted several years, and that was followed by floods. Drought struck again in the years between 1941 and 1943, and its impact is felt in the family histories in this book. In addition to drought and floods, Shansi also suffers heavy frosts and dust storms, and in the regions where the loess soil reaches its greatest depth (up to fifty feet), earthquakes have taken a heavy toll — some two hundred thousand people are said to have perished in the quake that struck Shansi and Shensi in 1920. (4)

It is in this harsh and often hostile setting that the people of Taihang live their lives. The impact of the Taihang Mountains on the region's social environment is registered in the stereotype by which Taihang's mountaineers are traditionally labeled. The people of the plains call them "Cow Skin Lanterns": dark on the outside, bright on the inside. (5) Like shepherd's lanterns held up to the dark on a windy mountainside, their light is flickering and dim. Thus are the inhabitants of Taihang supposed to be — timid, soft, and shrinking in appearance. But they are also bright within — frugal, diligent, with a strong capacity to bear up under hardship — a people steeled by the harshness of their environment. If there is a semblance of truth in this stereotype, as there is in most, then the people of Taihang must be regarded as unlikely participants in a program of rapid and immense social change. Yet for a moment in his-

tory these very people became the principals in just such a
program. That moment is relived in The People of Taihang. (6)
   Before moving to a specific discussion of this work it
would be well to examine the historiographic context from
which it emerged.

"Using the Past to Warn the Present"

> Disregarding my inadequacy, I have constantly
> wished to write a chronological history...taking
> in all that a prince ought to know — everything per-
> taining to the rise and fall of dynasties and the good
> and bad examples that can furnish models and a
> warning. (7)
>
>   Ssu-ma Kuang

   Chinese historiography has undergone considerable change
over the past century, in part because of the importation of
Western models of historical scholarship and in part because
of the elaboration of indigenous schools of historical criticism.
There remains, however, an element of contemporary Chinese
historical writing which cannot be understood without reference
to a more remote legacy, premodern in its origins, independent
of Western models in its development, and persistent in its effects. By the terms of that legacy, historians sought, through
their investigations of the minutiae of past events, to discern
the pattern of the Tao, the cosmic, moral force that gave frame
and meaning to the universe. By portraying its manifestations
in the practical activities of humankind, the stuff of chronologi-
cal history, they gave the Tao a visibly human form and voice,
pointed out its direction, and established those moments when
humans might take history by the hand and alter its course or
fail and so fall victim to blind fate. Each practical case was a
moral example at work, and given the view of historical change
as cyclical, each was a "model" and a "warning," a significant
and meaningful signal to an audience sharing the historians' ba-

sic vision of the world. This, in brief, was the moral paradigm
of Chinese history. (8)

The central importance of the moral paradigm to traditional
Chinese historiography is clear, but problems arise when it is
treated as an element in contemporary Chinese historical
work. (9) While there are moral dimensions to communist history, to what extent is the derivation from the moral paradigm
justified when the terms so basic to tradition have undergone
fundamental change and the institutions that once established
a context for that paradigm have disappeared? "Harmony," to
cite an example, is hardly consonant with "class struggle."

Chinese institutions have been altered, but it is entirely plau-
sible that new structures perform functions only partially dis-
tinguishable from those performed in the past. (10) Too much
weight has been given to the contrast between Chinese Communist ideology and classical Confucianism, with rather less attention paid to variants in the Confucian tradition, the hetero-
doxies of the past, or the multifarious forms communist ideology has taken. (11)

Documents such as The People of Taihang may lay claim to
a new vision of history, but as we shall see, such a claim must
be weighed against the actual form and content of the stories
composing the whole. To see why this is the case, we seek first
to place The People of Taihang in its appropriate genre, to examine the functions it performs, and finally to demonstrate the
influence of the moral paradigm on its contents.

"The People of Taihang" in the Context of the Four Histories Movement

The term "Four Histories movement" (ssu-shih yun-tung)
refers to a broad-based campaign within a campaign launched
at an unspecified date in 1962 as part of the Socialist Education
Movement, to collect, exhibit, compile and publish the histories
of families (and clans), villages, communes, and industries
(factories and mines). (12) In the course of the movement, which

was absorbed into the Great Proletarian Cultural Revolution in 1966, four histories editorial committees were established at all territorial levels of organization. Such committees functioned typically under the guidance of the propaganda departments and committees of local Party organs or, as in the case of factories and mines, under the direction of trade-union branches. Something of the size and scope of the movement can be gleaned from a 1965 report from Peking Municipality noting the compilation, between the fall of 1963 and January 1965 in that region alone, of over ten thousand "items" on family, village, and commune history communicated in a sum total of 70 million characters. (13) Most localities from which reports are available underwent a mobilization of comparable intensity.

While certain features of the Four Histories movement (its organization and the intensity of mobilization) permit its classification as a species of "pre-Cultural Revolution political movement," other features make its classification more ambiguous. Official directives marking the initiation of the movement and stages of its mobilization are notable for their absence. Though certain areas and organizations may have served as "experimental sites" (chung-tien) and models for emulation, there is little evidence of the systematic planning that generally accompanies major campaigns. Furthermore, the term "four histories" and the activities associated with their compilation predate the movement of 1962-66. Some of the best known works bearing the four histories label were produced in the late 1950s, and the systematic compilation of data on villages and industries for the volumes published in that period can be traced back to the initial stages of land reform in the late 1940s. If these and the innumerable unpublished essays that have accompanied them are incorporated under the four histories rubric, then the movement is most accurately described as a sporadic and recurrent mobilization, over a period of nearly thirty years, of Chinese historical consciousness and historical resources in a variety of forms and for a variety of purposes. The political campaign is only one of the forms it has assumed.

Variations in form are evident even within the confines of the movement of 1962-66. In some rural areas, the history of factories and mines was eliminated to constitute the "three histories." In urban areas, the history of streets and neighborhoods, and in People's Liberation Army units, the history of PLA companies were added to the usual four to constitute the "five histories." Such variations as these are minor, however, when they are placed in the context of the movement treated as a long-term, cumulative enterprise. In this case, differences in authorship, sponsorship, style, and function assume greater significance.

Shih Ch'eng-chih, who has written extensively on the Four Histories movement, groups the total range of documents into four types, which for our purposes are readily collapsed into two major categories. (14) The first is comprised of all those histories compiled by specialists working either as individuals or in collaborative field teams. Such specialized works, marked by their academic style, were produced largely under the auspices of the Chinese Academy of Sciences or its local branches, and they functioned to provide a data base supporting the formulation of new social policies, national defense, and economic construction. Since they were produced as part of a routine organizational process, it would be inaccurate to tab them "campaign" documents, though they were often timed to coincide with campaigns and campaign-related materials were well within their purview. This form of four histories documentation dominated activities of the early and mid-1950s and to a certain extent overlapped the second category.

In that second category belong all those histories compiled by semiprofessional personnel, college students, middle-school students, local and hsia-fang cadres working in collaborative field teams under the auspices of local Party committees. Through on-the-spot interviews and data-gathering, with peasants, cadres and factory workers as their targets, informants and co-participants, writers garnered information on "class sympathies," related "family treasures," dug out "roots of bitterness," and gathered "heart-to-heart confessions" and "family talk" in order to provide a moral education for a new generation of revolutionary successors. If campaigns were merely pertinent to the first, "academically styled," category of the four histories documents, they were intrinsic to the second, "popular," category, and where teams of writers operated essentially as outsiders engaged in investigatory work in the former instance, they were participant-observers often directly involved in the events they chronicled in the latter instance. The appearance of this form of documentation virtually coincided with the widespread implementation of rustication (hsia-fang) policies and the Great Leap Forward in the late 1950s. In the early sixties the Socialist Education Campaign and the Four Cleanups provided an additional impetus.

While these two categories of four histories materials can be distinguished in form and function, there is a considerable degree of overlap between them. The earlier, academically styled, histories sought to include interviews with workers, cadres, and peasants who were witness to the onerous feudal practices of the past. By digging out their "roots of bitterness" and drawing out their "class sympathies," the authors simultaneously established and embodied the grounds for a moral judgment against the old society and moral commitment to the new. And, by implication, they cast a "warning" before their readers by personalizing the attitudes and detailing the activities that lay at the base of a nefarious social order. Such interviews, judgments, and warnings were, however, placed either alongside or within a validated, "objective" textual framework. (15)

The moral judgments that are secondary to the earlier, academically styled, histories are primary to the histories of the second, popular, type, but the investigatory style that marks the first is never entirely displaced in the second. Most of the latter claim to be objective and representative surveys of workers, cadres, and peasants — empirically valid accounts of their values, attitudes, and actions. Thus, the two categories are not as distinct as they might otherwise appear.

If we follow Shih Ch'eng-chih's general schema, The People of Taihang clearly falls into the second category, though more than one set of authors was involved in its creation. In fact, according to an official account of its origin, The People of Taihang was the product of at least three groups of authors working in four separate stages under the joint auspices of the China Youth Publishing House (Chung-kuo ch'ing-nien ch'u-pan she) and the "Four Histories" Editorial Committee of Southeast Chin District in Shansi Province. (16)

In the first stage an unspecified number of "intellectual youths" were mobilized as part of the Socialist Education Campaign to conduct interviews and record family histories. Their collective efforts yielded a rough draft containing over seventy thousand family histories. In the second stage, the editorial committees, cooperating with a select group of authors, produced a research outline for further work on ninety-six model stories drawn from the first stage draft. This work was taken another step when, in the third stage, "comrades of higher literary and ideological levels" were selected to make improvements. For the fourth and final stage, a revised draft was circulated to branches, hsien committees, and the Southeast District Committee for approval.

This description of the production of The People of Taihang forms the final, brief paragraph of an article in which the primary focii are guidelines for the writing of Four Histories documents. According to those guidelines, writers of the Four Histories were to link their efforts to the Socialist Education Campaign, and to emphasize three stages (social suffering, revolutionary struggle, and the struggle between socialism and capitalism) in two periods: the democratic revolution and the socialist revolution. They were to (1) publicize the superiority of the socialist line, (2) expose the ugliness of the bourgeoisie and the demise of the capitalist line, (3) expose imperialist, particularly U.S. imperialist, crimes of aggression, and (4) continue to expose the evils of feudalism. (17)

The impression given by the guidelines and the description of the creation of The People of Taihang is that work of this kind was pursued systematically under established ideological criteria.

There is, however, good reason to treat such an impression with suspicion. First, the guidelines are extremely broad, allowing maximum leeway for local invention or for the importation of values not subject to ideological control. Second, the description of the creation of The People of Taihang provides an inadequate basis for a judgment of the character of the work. No dates are given. The criteria for the enormous task of winnowing ninety-six model stories from more than 70,000 originals are not offered. Indeed, no mention is made of the final reduction to seventeen histories. More important, though the article explicitly links the creation of The People of Taihang to the Socialist Education Campaign, only three of the seventeen family histories that make up the volume — "A Home Given By Chairman Mao," "The 'Millstone' Shoes," and "Revolutionary Mother Pao Lien-tzu" — refer explicitly to events after 1962. (18) Indeed, it is likely, given the variations in the style of composition and in the events to which the histories refer, that parts of The People of Taihang were compiled at two or possibly three different times: in the early 1950s, between 1958 and 1962, or on the eve of publication in 1964. Whether or not some of the documents derive from data collected in the early fifties depends on how certain of the histories are interpreted. Those which terminate in a discussion of land reform might well be reprints or revisions of materials collected in the early 1950s. (19) It is also possible, of course, that these materials were collected in the late fifties or early sixties under guidelines that limited their purview to events surrounding land reform. It seems unlikely, however, that either the authors or their sponsors would employ such a device and thus deliberately miss an opportunity to address salient, contemporary issues. What does seem likely is that the "comrades of higher literary and ideological levels" employed in the third stage of this document's production did more to affect its style than its content. Thus, while there is a claim to a new vision of history, that claim is too broad and too loose to serve as a basis for a final judgment on the work.

   Despite heterogeneity in styles and references, there is a
common thread that links the histories in The People of Taihang
into an organic whole. With few exceptions, each family history
begins with a genealogical account tracing the "roots of bitterness" to the familial origins of its principal character. Once
the conditions for thought and action are established, a biographical account is reconstructed to highlight the focal points
of the protagonist's preliberation career: his or her social
relations with class and state enemies, with class consociates*,
and ultimately with the fighters and cadres of the Eighth Route
Army. Each succeeding status, before the arrival of the Eighth
Route Army, marks a new encounter with the exploiting classes.
The experience of exploitation, coupled with the impact of war,
starvation, physical suffering, and psychological deprivation,
heightens tension and establishes a motivation for action. The
potential that underlies that motivation is transformed into sus-
tained, directed, and corporate commitment when individual
self-awareness and class consciousness are fused under the
stimulus provided by the Eighth Route Army and the Communist
Party.
   The denouement for some of the histories occurs with liberation, the "settling of accounts" and the redistribution of property during land reform. Others, however, add a brief epilogue
to describe the main character's performance in the course of
cooperativization and communization. For a few, such as "A
Home Given by Chairman Mao," "The 'Millstone' Shoes," and
"Revolutionary Mother Pao Lien-tzu," the denouement occurs
not with land reform but with the rebirth of class conflict in the
countryside during the sixties. These three histories are the
most concrete manifestations of the intent to link The People
of Taihang with the Socialist Education Campaign. They
contain explicit moral warnings against the recrudescence of
those bourgeois and feudal attitudes and behaviors that dominated the era prior to liberation. The moral lessons of the past
are thus used to "warn the present." These three histories

---

*See note 22 for a discussion of this term.

should not, however, be treated as exceptional cases, for they provide a context supported in one way or another by all the histories contained in the volume. For all of them the subject matter is the transformation of ordinary peasants, cadres, and workers into revolutionary heroes and heroines. Since heroism is central to all the histories and is made meaningful only when cast against the backdrop supplied by "ordinary" and by dis-approved behavior; any attempt to depict it entails an explora-tion of moral exemplariness — its roots and its development — and conveys a moral warning.

None of this, of course, determines the salience of The Peo-ple of Taihang to its readers. The fact that only three of the seventeen histories focus on the issues most pertinent to the Socialist Education Campaign suggests that it was of limited value as a campaign document. Yet, the dynamics of individual transformation and the meaning of ideology and morality are significant topics in their own right. The People of Taihang of-fers an unusual opportunity to explore such topics in depth.

"The People of Taihang" as Family History

In the introduction to "A Home Given by Chairman Mao," the editors remark that "home" and "history" are two indispens-able elements of a family history. Ku Hua-jung, the subject of the account had no "home" of her own. Her family history must therefore be treated as a story of continuous hardship in a suc-cession of "non-family families." These same remarks apply equally well to most of the "family histories" contained in this volume, which raises an interesting question. If ancestral "homes" were the sine qua non of family histories and clan ge-nealogies in the past, do the family histories in The People of Taihang represent a complete break with traditional conven-tions ? (20)

The answer is not simple. In an effort to develop an histori-cal format reflective of reality as poor peasants, cadres, and workers lived it, the writers of The People of Taihang devel-oped some conventions of their own that distinguish family his-

tories as they are portrayed here from their traditional counter-
parts. At the same time, a good deal of the old survives in the
new. In fact, the convention by which the status-honors of notable ancestors were listed in the traditional clan genealogy is
carried over into the family histories of poor and lower-middle
peasants in The People of Taihang. By this means clan members once deemed too low in status to be accorded recognition
in the clan and family records are given genealogical records
of their own; and this change is accompanied by a replacement
of what were formerly positive with negative status-honors.
Thus if civil service honors, the birth of a male heir, the birth-
day of an aged head of the household, auspicious signs and ceremonies, and newly acquired property contributed to the destiny
of the family in the traditional family history, the loss of jobs,
death, sale and abandonment of children, death in advance of
old age (resulting from frustration and mistreatment) and ig-
nominious burial for the heads of households, inauspicious
signs and ceremonies, the loss of property, and the accumula-
tion of debts decree a family's destiny in the new family history. In both, the fate of a family's successors is conditioned,
but not determined, by its history. Status-honors do not cumu-
late to produce a sage, and a history of frustration is not sufficient to create revolutionary heroism. Thus, except for the far
more variegated role allotted to women, the general format and
function of the traditional clan genealogy and family history is
maintained, but the contents are radical departures from tradition.

Ssu Ta-jen, the hero of "Yü-huang Temple in a Blizzard,"
entered his career as a sole survivor of a family of four. His
father died of exhaustion working for a landlord, his third
younger brother was sold, and his elder brother was murdered.
Ho Shou-i, whose family history is celebrated in "Under the
Iron Hoof of Japanese Imperialism," came from a family living
on the verge of starvation. His father had to leave home in an
attempt to secure a job and died of illness away from home.
His mother remarried, but debts, the marginal productivity of
the land, and the necessity of feeding additional children drove

her to death by starvation. Wang Ch'ün-lan, the heroine of "A Woman Farmhand," began her career as a maid-servant in the home of a rich peasant after her father died of overwork following a lifetime of service to landlords. Her ailing mother, pressed with the care of three children and her husband's debts, succumbed shortly thereafter.

The genealogical and biographical elements in the family histories of The People of Taihang are paralleled by the development of such symbols as the millstone shoes in the story of that title, the wheelbarrow in the history for which it serves as a title, the cave in "A Cave with Two Entrances," the miner's lamp in "An Honorable Family of Miners," and the locust tree in "The Tragedy of the People of 'Lucky Star Locust.'" When the authors are tracing the genealogies of peasant and worker families, they cast such symbols as if they were mute but living witnesses to the interminable scourges visited upon the oppressed. When the central characters of the stories manifest a spirit of activism, the symbols with which they are associated are sometimes treated as witnesses to the action or as the means for its prosecution, and when activists become revolutionary heroes and heroines, these symbols are venerated as monuments to the revolutionary careers their owners have forged: they are transformed from utilitarian objects into symbols of revolutionary self-transcendence. (21)

In a few histories, naming and renaming serve a similar function by either pointing up the loss of familial identity or by dissociating the process of naming from "fate." Ku Hua-jung, the heroine of "A Home Given by Chairman Mao," is surnamed Ch'eng to suit the tastes of her new "owners" and called Mei-hsiang, or "slave girl." Ch'ien Ma-fu, the central figure in "The Funeral for a Dog," is so named because of his parents' hopes for "immediate good fortune" (ma fu) but, as the authors note:

...in the old man-eat-man society, how could a man decide his own fate? Ch'in Liu-chiu's family did not get "immediate good fortune" just because his son was so named.

Ma-fu's birth brought immediate hunger instead.

In the story of Cheng Ch'ing-yin, the subject of "The Wheel-barrow," the renaming takes place as Ch'ing-yin's father lies dying after being kicked in the chest by a landlord. The father's last words to his son are a prelude to the settling of accounts in the course of land reform: "The animosity of our family is vividly [ch'ing] stamped [yin] on your heart...."

The replacement of status-honors, described above, is also evident in the treatment of filial piety. For the most part, the authors of The People of Taihang are content to contrast true filial affection and self-sacrifice among poor peasants and workers with the bestiality and deviousness of rich peasants and landlords in dealing even with their own kin. But the family history of "Revolutionary Mother Pao Lien-tzu" subjects the Classic on Filial Piety (Hsiao Ching) to a radical change that reflects neither the traditional model nor the conventions adopted in other family histories. Pao Lien-tzu not only washes the wounds of a People's Liberation Army man, she also pulls the quilts from the backs of her own children to put on Small Ch'en (an Eighth Route Army guerrilla) and uses cotton padding from the children's blankets to stuff Ch'en's single-lined jacket to protect him against the cold.

> She loved the wounded more than she did her own children, and they in return loved her more than they did their own mothers.

When "Mother Pao" is brought a seriously wounded man, too badly burned to fend for himself, she meets his every need, aiding him in his bowel movements and chewing food first and then passing it to him mouth-to-mouth. In this portrait of revolutionary mother Pao Lien-tzu, classical expressions of filial piety and the modern vision of comradely self-sacrifice conjoin in acts that transcend the boundaries of kinship.

The genealogical elements in these family histories occupy only a small portion of the writers' attentions; their principal concern is in the dynamics of transformation. These elements are important, however, because they set the pace for what is to come, and they demonstrate that traditional and Communist morality interpenetrate partly through the retention of the form and function of traditional models, infused with new contents, and partly through the recombination of elements common to both the new and the old.

"Speaking Bitterness"

The most important facet of the family histories in The People of Taihang is the development of their principal characters and the transformation of those characters into committed communists. The dynamics of development and transformation can, perhaps, best be seen in the light of social interaction, for it is in the relationships the subjects of these stories form with class enemies, class consociates (22), and the personnel of the Eighth Route Army that the attitudes and attributes underlying self-transcendence and transformation are revealed. Such attitudes and attributes define heroism and demarcate the boundaries separating heroes, villains, and ordinary human beings. (23)

In "The Funeral for a Dog," Ch'in Ma-fu is sent out by his family to work as a shepherd for landlord Li Ch'i-ts'ai. The wages Li promises are never paid. In describing the helplessness of the family in the face of the landlord's recalcitrance, the writer comments: "The meat was in the tiger's mouth, and power was in the man's hands." That phrase sums up the context within which the protagonists' relations with landlords and rich peasants take place. The latter confront the former with a monopoly of economic and political power, buttressed by their ownership of the land, access to money, and ties to the courts, the police, the puppet troops, the Japanese, and the Kuomintang. They are filled with a surfeit of venality, cunning and viciousness, and they maintain the ability and have the willingness to manipulate religious beliefs and superstitions to service their own immoral ends. In short, they are depicted as the dominant force over every nook and cranny of the social and political superstructure. By contrast, poor peasants and workers belong

to a subsociety that is atomized and victimized. Without outside
intervention, they have few resources with which to respond beyond their willpower, their labor power, and their number.
Given the tradition that demands their obedience in the face of
superior authority, the price of a threat to withdraw their labor
power, especially in the face of famine and misery, and the
atomization that cuts into the power of numbers, their principal
and first resort is to willpower. And in the initial stages of its
exercise, fear for one's own life and the lives of one's associ-
ates reduces willpower to unspoken defiance.

   The behavior of Wang Ch'ün-lan, the subject of "A Woman
Farmhand," is a case in point. As a child maid-servant in a
rich peasant household, she is whipped into submission. Her
first response is defiance expressed in sabotage: the breaking
of a chamberpot. When her rich peasant owner sells her in
marriage in order to place her husband in permanent debt, she
responds with unspoken defiance:

> ...she thought to herself, "Come back? Never! I'd rather
> die of poverty than come back to this Palace of Night-
> mares!"

When Liu Erh-mo, in "The Tragedy of the People of 'Lucky Star
Locust,'" is forced to witness his father escorting the funeral
of a dog because of the trickery of "Killer Liu," he swallows
his anger to prevent a worsening of his father's condition already exacerbated by the shame the elder man has had to swal-
low. "He stamped his feet and bit his lip and said nothing."
Ch'in Liu-chin and his wife having heard the conditions a landlord has set for saving their son's life "clenched their teeth"
in silence. (24)

   Silent defiance and hidden acts of individual sabotage — swallowing bitterness rather than publicly expressing it — reflect
the stranglehold of tradition and the atomization of peasant
life. (25) Swallowing bitterness can be the motive force behind
open rebellion; it can also lead to withdrawal (Li Yu-ch'eng's
elder brother in "The Poor People's Cave"), to attempted sui-

cide (Kao Ts'ai-yun in "The Story of Selling Oneself"), and death from shame and frustration (Liu Man in "The Tragedy of the People of 'Lucky Star Locust'").

These stories provide ambiguous cues to the process that mediates between silent defiance and open rebellion. In the case of Feng Wu-ch'ou, the principal figure in "The Fight," silent defiance and resistance deepen as exploitation grows, until the traumatic death of a younger brother forces him to cast off silence and assume the stance of an open rebel. Kao Ts'ai-yun, mentioned above, is herself the catalyst when her attempted suicide draws a group of hunters into open rebellion. For Hsiao Ping-ch'üan, the hero of "The 'Millstone' Shoes," the resort to open action stems from the fact that he shares his secret acts of resistance with a close friend, and that relationship establishes a nexus for social action.

There is even a muted hint, in a few of the histories, that open rebels are born that way. Wang Man-hsi of "An Honorable Family of Miners" demonstrates his congenital fearlessness in a childhood incident. An inborn intensity in fourteen-year-old Feng Wu-ch'ou of "The Fight" is so powerful that silent outrage slips over into direct action. By way of explanation the writers note that "children of a poor family mature early."

> He became so enraged that he tore chips out of the bricks of the k'ang and bit his lips until they bled.

Wu-ch'ou heaves firecrackers over the walls of a landlord's house.

Whatever the explanation, silent defiance becomes open rebellion only when both psychological and social prerequisites are met. The psychological prerequisite, in most instances, is the deepening trauma caused by exploitation and the consequent urge to vengeance; the social prerequisite is interaction among class consociates that cuts across barriers erected by class enemies and the atomization of village life.

There are instances in which a hero takes action that does not meet these prerequisites. Feng Wu-ch'ou refuses landlord

Feng Shou-heng's offer of a job, using the withdrawal of his labor power as a threat. Bereft of significant social support,
however, the threat falls on deaf ears.

Once established, interaction among class consociates creates a basis for concerted, corporate action against class enemies. Peasants refuse to pay rents, sabotage the flocks and
crops of landlords and rich peasants, and withhold legitimacy
from the latter's exercise of power. Now the withdrawal of labor power is buttressed by the power of numbers. But the superior forces class enemies can bring to bear continue to im-
pede the effectiveness of a new found solidarity, and moreover,
there are signs in these histories that a part of the threat to
such solidarity comes from within. In an effort to describe the
sources of activism in groups of class consociates, the writers
delve into the dynamics of fear, timidity, and caution. In so doing, they begin to unravel the knotty distinction between activists and ordinary human beings. (26)

In most of the histories where relations among class consociates are treated, traditional conventions of friendship and
brotherhood overlap conventions of comradeship. Some of the
most moving passages on the meaning of steadfast loyalty, gen-
erosity, and self-sacrifice are to be found in those histories
that stress the bonds of comradeship. "The Poor People's
Cave" and "Under the Iron Hoof of Japanese Imperialism" are
notable examples.

Traditional conventions receive slightly greater weight in
dyadic relationships such as the one forged between Ssu Ta-
jen, the subject of "Yü-huang Temple in a Blizzard," and his
friend Shen Hsiao-lai or between Hsiao Ping-ch'üan, in "The
'Millstone' Shoes," and Liu Ch'iu-shan, his closest friend. A
more unconventional dyad combining a modern commitment to
romantic love and comradeship is movingly described in the
marriage of Wang Ch'ün-lan, the heroine of "A Woman Farmhand," to Chiao Ho-shang, a former opera singer forced into a
life of poverty by an exploitive rich peasant.

Not all relations among class consociates are treated as relations among co-equals, as is made clear in a number of in-

stances. When Amah Chang entreats Ku Hua-jung, in "A Home Given by Chairman Mao," to admit falsely to acts of defiance and theft and to accept gifts from her oppressors and beg their forgiveness, she is roundly chastised by the heroine in whose interest her advice is offered. When Ch'in Liu-chin is faced with a landlord's unreasonable demands in "The Funeral for a Dog," some of the villagers vow death to the landlord and his allies. Others bind an outraged Liu-chin lest he "lose his life in vain." Liu Erh-mo in "The Tragedy of the People of 'Lucky Star Locust'" is faced with the same situation, and his "brethren" meet to discuss it. Some advise rejection of the landlord's demands; others reiterate their fears that a lawsuit will follow if the demands are not met. Still others recommend that he flee from the village.

These three cases are exceptions to the rule, but they are significant exceptions. Though bound by a single theme, they also differ. Amah Chang fears for Ku Hua-jung's safety, but her fear borders on timidity when it is expressed in terms of submission in the face of superior authority. The restraints the villagers place on Ch'in Liu-chin likewise reflect their fear for his safety, but they also imply something further: the fear of luan — of chaos — that is, the fear that Liu-chin's ungovernable rage and desire for vengeance will destroy both him and the cause he has come to espouse. (27) The advice given by Liu Erh-mo's brethren reflects their fear for his safety, their fear of luan, and their caution — caution, not fear, which reflects their lack of organization and the vagueness of their goals. Organization orders corporate action; goals legitimate it. Taken together, they provide a context for action and remove the obstacle to cooperation that particularism, expressed here in the form of personal vengeance, represents. (28) Liu Erh-mo and his friends are faced with a dilemma, and they lack the grounds for its solution.

While there are exceptions in a few of the histories, fearlessness, in the sense of freedom from concern for personal safety, does not distinguish an activist from an ordinary human being. It is more often a consequence of activism than a prerequisite

for it. But activists are definitely not timid. Ku Hua-jung takes
an affectionate but ideologically correct stance toward Amah
Chang.

Fear of luan, however, creates a behavioral dilemma — the
same dilemma that confronts Liu Erh-mo and his brethren.
What distinguishes the activist is the willingness to take action,
despite the threat to one's own life and limb, where others
would retreat. But when? To move too soon is to undermine
the foundations for corporate action already laid; to move too
late is to miss an opportunity history rarely offers. (29) Furthermore, an activist bears an immense moral responsibility
because his or her actions are now in the public domain, beyond
the range of silent defiance, and they will carry ordinary human beings with them.

The dilemma is not unique to the activists in The People of
Taihang. One could argue that it stems from the link between
action and moral choice in the Book of Changes, elaborated in
every nuance of interpretation to which that work has been subject over the centuries. (30) What is unique here is the approach
to the resolution of the dilemma, and that involves the element
we have labeled "caution." In this second stage of development
and transformation, however, resolution of the dilemma is not
possible. The histories in The People of Taihang testify re-
peatedly to the likelihood of failure, registered in the biogra-
phies of activist martyrs, so long as the conditions necessary
to resolve the dilemma are absent.

"Turning Over"

Only a few of the histories in The People of Taihang deal
with the final stages in the development and transformation of
a revolutionary hero or heroine. Most are content to mark the
transformation rather than describe it.

Where it is so marked, the arrival of the Eighth Route Army
and the exaction of retribution through the settling of accounts
in land reform simply remove the obstacles created by landlord and rich peasant power and expunge the need for personal

vengeance. The transformation of activists into committed revolutionaries is assumed, and there is no evidence of the back-
sliding, confusion, and recommitment that play such important
roles in William Hinton's classic study of land reform. (31)

Transformation is given a more complex treatment, however,
in those histories which seek to describe it as a process. In
every such case, Eighth Route Army and Communist Party cadres play a crucial role. The transformation of Wang Ch'ün-
lan of "A Woman Farmhand" is one case in point.

Ch'ün-lan, under the name of Wang Ch'ün-yeh, has a long
history of struggle and activism, but her transformation is
particularly marked when she encounters Comrade Jen Hsiu-
lan, a Party member who addresses a hsien-level meeting of
the Shansi Women's Salvation Association at which Wang Ch'ün-
yeh is present. With Comrade Jen's help, Ch'ün-yeh joins the
Party, and her new identity as a revolutionary is symbolized
by the adoption of a new name: "Wang Ch'ün-lan" (the last character in the new name is an adoption of the last character in
Jen Hsiu-lan's name). Wang Ch'ün-lan is now a member of a
revolutionary sisterhood. Jen Hsiu-lan's character is never
described, but her place in the transformation is central.

Li Yu-ch'eng of "The Poor People's Cave" begins his transformation when a strange and mysterious figure enters the cave
and introduces himself to its residents. He explains "many
things about the revolution" and urges Li to stay behind to organize the poor people for action against the Japanese. When
he leaves, the "spark of revolution" remains behind. As in the
case of Jen Hsiu-lan, there are no details about his character
or his background.

As author and analyst Joe Huang points out, an air of mystery
and anonymity is present in all forms of Chinese Communist
role-model literature dealing with Party cadres in land reform. (32) To a certain degree, it is explicable as a device to
sustain tension and lend support to charisma — a charisma that
is evident in Wang Ch'ün-lan's emulation of Comrade Jen. Yet
there is nothing about charismatic effect that could not be
served as well by a personalized portraiture.

More likely, given what has been argued thus far, the anonymity and mystery of the cadre role serves to point up the
significance of what the Party and the Party's message represents rather than who the people are who do the representing.
The partial disembodiment of the Party cadre stands in stark
contrast to the personalized portrait of the activist, and with
reason, for Party cadres bring to bear that experience of
organization — discipline in the pursuit of transcendent goals —
that the peasant activist lacks. The cadres too express "caution," but it is a caution born of their superior knowledge of the
conditions that underlie historical movement and change. When
they confront a peasant activist, vengeance disappears as a
primary motive; the cause of the revolution takes its place.
This, I would argue, is the resolution to the dilemma of choice.
Commitment to Party discipline and the historical experience
it contains provides an analytical and practical framework of
proven validity for the translation of group action into a successful social movement.

Striking parallels appear between The People of Taihang,
treated as role-model literature, and the morality book of traditional times. The T'ai Shang kan-ying p'ien, a sixteenth century work, is probably the best known of the genre. (33) In its
most famous tales, mysterious visitors confront aspirants to
sagehood with their superior knowledge of moral truth and phe-
nomenal reality to cause a transformation in the behavior of
the persons they address and to inspire self-transcendence.
Such tales can be read on two levels: as a literature of super-
stition describing the actions of the spirit world, or as meta-
phorical accounts of the workings of moral consciousness. (34)

Once transformation is accomplished, whether through the
stimulus of the Party or a leap in moral consciousness, heroes
and heroines become moral exemplars. Their behavior, most
clearly represented in "Revolutionary Mother Pao Lien-tzu,"
now appears in an objectified and reified state — immovable in
its moral perfection. The millstone shoes, the wheelbarrow, the
miner's lamp, and the locust tree — objects that once symbolized suffering and death — now, like their heroic owners, sym-

bolize transcendence and transformation. Heroes, heroines and
the objects with which they are associated come to stand as
moral legacies to guide the course of future generations. As
Hsiao Ping-ch'üan puts it in "The 'Millstone' Shoes":

> Good shoes will spoil your feet. Wearing patched shoes
> will harden your heels and help you stand firm on the
> ground.

The "patched shoes" bear a moral legacy which "haunts" these
otherwise mundane phrases from the realm of everyday reality
by infusing them with transcendent meaning. (35)

Epilogue: Morality, Ideology, and Social Reality

The parallel drawn earlier between The People of Taihang
and such morality books as the T'ai-Shang kan-ying p'ien [The
Treatise of the Exalted One on Response and Retribution — hereafter Treatise] is worth further consideration. What is it about
two works so widely separated in time and socio-cultural milieu,
so apparently disparate in content, that can justify such a parallel? (36) The Treatise is a Taoist-Confucian work; The Peo-
of Taihang is obviously a product of communist authorship. The
Treatise aims at the prolongation of life; The People of Taihang
aims at the training of a new generation of "revolutionary successors." Reward and retribution, filial piety and propriety,
merit and demerit are the key terms in the contents of the
Treatise; in The People of Taihang the central terms are class
struggle, comradeship, and rebellion. The Treatise is per-
meated by popular religious beliefs; The People of Taihang con-
demns such beliefs in the name of a popular ideology. One
could, as I did earlier, quibble with specific differences. Filial
piety is not entirely absent from The People of Taihang anymore than "struggle," in the sense of an inward striving for
self-cultivation and self-discipline, is absent from the Treatise.
But such an approach fails to identify what it is that legitimates comparison between these two works when each is taken as a whole.

The parallel is justified, despite the disparateness of contents, by similarities in form and function in essentially four
regards: (1) Both works convey moral "warnings" and exhorta-
tions to their respective audiences in order that the latter might
attain what the authors of these works would designate as emi-
nently practical ends: the prolongation of life in the case of the
Treatise and the training of revolutionary successors in the
case of The People of Taihang. (2) Both establish the salience
of the abstract moral principles they convey through a process
of concretization and personification. (3) Both works give substance to morally guided practical action by linking the province
of everyday meaning with the provinces of religious and ideological transcendence. (37) (4) In both cases the authors and the
sponsors look upon existence of each work as proof positive of
the intentions of its contents.

The last three of these four points are best taken first. Making an abstract moral value salient is perhaps the most readily
identifiable function performed by the Treatise and The People
of Taihang. To be specific, abstract values are expressed by
consociates who speak the language, employ the "typifications,"
are accounted for by others and do account for themselves and
their actions, express the "because-of" and "in-order-to" motives that we, if we share the "stock of knowledge" that consti-
tutes Chinese peasant culture, must take to be real. (38) The
degree to which these two works are structured to produce salience as it has been described is, in part, a measure of both
their common membership in the genre of role-model literature
and a measure of their differential location within that genre. Much
of the Treatise is composed of lists of acts and the degree of merit
or demerit they are claimed to warrant. This is concretization
without personification, and it is readily subject to the danger
of objectification and utilitarian calculation. But the parables
that form the commentaries in the Treatise and similar works
are both concretizations and personifications. They are concerned with a human being's inner world, not with external cal-
culae. (39) Looked at in these terms, The People of Taihang is
a major improvement upon the traditional morality book. Cal-

culativeness and exteriority most certainly have a place in
this work, but in a form that mutes their presence, re-
stricted to the stereotypic treatment of bad characters. One
could argue that the ideological elements in The People of
Taihang facilitate the establishment of salience more than religious elements do in the Treatise. Insofar as ideological norms
call for a recognition of the complexity of the interrelationships
between social conditions, motives, attitudes and actions, most
evident in the treatment of the behavior of class consociates,
characterization in The People of Taihang is freer of the kinds
of restraints religious convention imposed upon the writers of
the morality books. The same elements can, of course, also
facilitate rigidity in characterization as they do, once again, in
the case of the stereotyped traitor, landlord and rich peasant.

The third function is less easily described. In both the Treatise and in The People of Taihang the world of everyday and the
worlds of religious and ideological transcendence interpenetrate.
When, to use Alfred Schutz's phraseology, these "finite provinces of meaning" meet, mystery and awe predominate. The appearance of gods in the Treatise and mysterious comrades in
The People of Taihang make us aware that a transitional boundary between provinces of meaning has been crossed and alert us
to the "shock" that attends the crossing — "shock" because the
reality of everyday life is so taken for granted that it admits of
no other possibility. (40)

While both works attend to the existence of transcendent
worlds of meaning, The People of Taihang draws a finer distinction between the world of common sense and, in this instance, the world of ideological transcendence. Unlike ordinary
peasants, peasant heroes and heroines have an immediate grasp
of the significant as opposed to the ephemeral in the relations
they form, the work they undertake, their talk and their thought;
they carry, in short, a finer cognitive map. Their patterns of
"sociality" follow suit. Heroes and heroines appear less toler-
ant than ordinary men and women. They are not plagued with
doubt or ambivalence in the choice between enemies and friends.
They "see" the long-range consequences of choices of action

and affiliation. Their "time tracks" are not those of ordinary
men and women. With perhaps the one exception of Pao Lien-
tzu, their attitudes and actions do not adjust with changes over
time for they are virtually ageless and timeless — paragons of
what might seem to be Calvanist antitraditionalistic values. Yet
they remain linked to the world of everyday, in a state of "full
awakeness." (41)

The positing of such differences as these has the effect of increasing dramatic tension; it also affords an author a superb
opportunity to draw fine lines of distinction between the ordinary
and the extraordinary. But we would be on dubious grounds if
we argued that these are the principal functions performed by
the distinction between the world of everyday life and the world
of ideological transcendence.

The principal function of the distinction is best understood in
terms of the link forged between the unfolding pattern of historical events and the process of personal biographical "accounting." (42) While this linkage is also an element in the Treatise,
the two documents are, in this case, different in kind as well as
degree, for The People of Taihang is not only role-model literature; it is at the same time an historical document. Each phase
in biographical development is linked, sometimes in the most
artful ways, to environing historical conditions and events. Both
are selected from the infinite variety of historical and biographical possibilities. It is their meaning, taken in its total pattern,
that is effected by the existence of the world of ideological transcendence. To cross the boundary into that world is to have
emerged from the confining effects of historical conditioning to
grasp its meaning and exert a measure of control over its
course. It is compelling as a challenge, but more important,
it is imperative if meaning is to be given to the self-sacrifice,
doubt and ambivalence, to the false-starts and retreats that
checker a career, especially a career forged in so unordinary
a slice of everyday reality as the wartime period represented.

That it is a function as difficult to accomplish as to explain
is indicated by the trap some authors tended toward in an effort
to short-cut the complications otherwise involved. It is easier

to let heroes and heroines be born that way than to trace the intricacies of their emergence.

The fourth function is most easily ignored because it is itself so taken for granted. Members of the scholar-gentry, even emperors, vied for the honor of compiling and publishing morality books like the Treatise because that in itself was manifestation of the merit of which the morality books spoke. Thus participation in authorship and sponsorship of these works was deemed proof positive of the moral virtues morality books were to instill in their readers. That model is perfectly applicable to The People of Taihang. The very act of compilation and publication is itself proof of the moral-ideological commitment the contents of The People of Taihang can engender. It is a model for emulation, an objectified and reified collective moral experience, the moment it is completed, functioning as proof of its own efficacy.

If for no other reason this particular facet of The People of Taihang should alert all its readers, Western and non-Western, to the fact that The People of Taihang is an historical document of a very special kind inappropriately evaluated when it is analyzed in accord with "scientific" canons of historical research. It is clearly a moral-historical document, and its meaning depends on that recognition.

Now we are in a position to treat the first function. The People of Taihang is a moral document with a practical intention. Morality, ideology, and action are intimately interrelated in all facets of the work including its production. If this is true, however, of both The People of Taihang and such morality books as the Treatise, and if The People of Taihang differs from the Treatise primarily in terms of its historicity and its ideological elements, then it is likely that the parallel between them is accounted for largely by the continued vitality of the moral paradigm. In undertaking this explanation, I am not arguing that "ideology" is "washed out" by the continuing dependence of Chinese writers on traditional models. Rather, I am suggesting that ideology and morality are dialectically interrelated in an organic whole, their relationship changing with each new incre-

ment of experience. By stating it in this way, my intention is
to lay particular stress on the legacy of syncretism in the Chinese experience — a legacy that is seldom incorporated into
the treatment of contemporary Chinese thought and practice. If
there is any particular advantage that lies in syncretic form,
it is the leeway it permits in the negotiation of values and
value-priorities. Its flexibility detracts from dogma, though
stereotypy is fully accommodated, as the treatment of villains
and sometimes heroes demonstrates. (43)

That flexibility is partly reflected in the style by which The
People of Taihang was composed. It is a "mass-line" work con-
stituted, presumably, out of the relived thoughts, feelings and
actions of its subjects, reworked in accord with accepted ideological standards. Here, indeed, one would expect to find a
meeting ground between ideology and morality. One would also
expect to find contradictions reflective of the negotiatory process, and as we have pointed out, they are present in the differ-
ing explanations for the sources of rebellion and the causes of
transformation. We cannot, of course, know whether such contradictions are reflections of disagreements among subjects or
editors, but I think it is safe to assume that both contributed to
the making of this work.

It is, of course, one thing to say that The People of Taihang
is structured to depict reality and another to say that it suc-
ceeds. For one who adheres to the tenets of the phenomenological school in sociology, there is a third problem: the value of
asserting the existence of any ontological "reality." Yet, insofar
as The People of Taihang lays claim to historical accuracy and
insofar as the events it depicts can be, if only for a moment,
torn from concern with the morals of the present rather than
the past, what can we say about its rendering of peasant and
worker culture in the 1940s?

For one thing, negative exemplars as drawn in the pages
of The People of Taihang are more tarnished than they are
in documents of the period. There are no good landlords
and rich peasants in these accounts, despite the fact that
land reform regulations and associated documents exempt a

good number of both from the most exploitive behavior. (44)
Stereotypy is prominent in this respect. That does not mean
that there were no landlords and rich peasants who, in fact,
reached the heights of depravity described in The People of
Taihang. Such depravity recurred in many small, poverty-
stricken villages during the worst years of famine, occupation,
and civil war. (45)

Guidelines for the writing of the "four histories" are said to
have prohibited the depiction of the seamy side of peasant behavior. In The People of Taihang peasant and worker resistance
is given prominence; collaboration is deeply muted. Despite
the guidelines, however, the seamy side of peasant life during
the war years is not eliminated altogether. Peasant and workers
do not collaborate with either foreign or domestic enemies for
fun and profit, though judicial records of the period indicate
that there were some who did, but they are often forced to com-
ply with enemy demands or placed in an exceedingly difficult
position so that many of the nuances of collaboration are dealt
with. (46)

Other aspects of "reality" are more difficult to grasp. The
portraits of activists seem to suit the stereotype of the Taihang
people as "cow-skinned lanterns" rather well. From this point
of view, The People of Taihang may reflect both the special attitudes outsiders held toward them and their self-perceptions.
The ecological conditions of the region, the roles of social, religious, political, and economic institutions in the region seem
well represented in all important regards, but our principal
concern here is with role-modeling.

In general, I would regard The People of Taihang as a picture
of a reality. On a related matter, one can be far more firm.
The People of Taihang is, as should by now be clear, not "mere
propaganda," a pejorative label too often taken for granted.
That label is sometimes applied to indicate either that there is
no relationship between image and reality, or that the scientific
canons for description of reality are insufficiently met, because
the ideological or other blinders prohibit the disclosure of the
full-range of "real" behaviors. I have argued that there is no

case for the first charge. The other is more difficult to deal
with because it opposes one system of relevancies with another.
Stephen Uhalley, Jr., in his accounting of the Four Histories
movement, offers a judgment that demonstrates this point:

> It is a loss to history that the great amount of energy and
> organization being invested in this program could not have
> been more soundly motivated and more directed, so that
> materials of genuine value might be collected and preserved.
>   The peasants and workers of this transitional generation
> would, indeed, have much to tell, if objective, a-political
> questions could be put to them. Instead, to the degree that
> the movement is politically successful, it will serve only
> to obscure history. (47)

I find it difficult to conceive, as I believe the peasants and
workers featured in The People of Taihang would also, how a
very political experience would be tapped by a-political questions, how a moral vision of history could possibly yield practical results if it were politically unsuccessful. Finally, I would
find it impossible to understand how such commitment could be
generated for the production of this work were the materials
in it not of "genuine value."
   The final judgment on the meaning of The People of Taihang
rests, of course, in the perceptions of those who read and apply
it. That you, the reader, may judge for yourself, we now present The People of Taihang.

Notes

1) Jack Belden citing a January 1947 interview with Po I-po,
then commissar of the Shansi-Hopei-Honan Border Region, in
China Shakes the World (New York, 1949), p. 48.
   2) R. R. C. de Crespigny, China: The Land and Its People
(New York, 1971), p. 55.
   3) Albert Kolb, East Asia: China, Japan, Korea, Vietnam:
Geography of a Cultural Region (London, 1971), p. 200.

4) Kolb, East Asia, p. 200.

5) Belden, China Shakes the World, p. 49.

6) No history of Shansi on the eve of the Sino-Japanese War is complete without reference to Donald Gillin, Warlord Yen Hsi-shan in Shansi Province, 1911-1949 (Princeton, 1967). A general history of the Chin-Chi-Lu-Yü [Shansi-Hopeh-Shantung-Honan] Base Area can be found in James Pinkney Harrison, The Long March to Power: A History of the Chinese Communist Party 1921-72 (New York, 1972), pp. 301-373. For a more detailed account of the Eighth Route Army's penetration of the Taihang region, see Chalmers A. Johnson, Peasant Nationalism and Communist Power: The Emergence of Revolutionary China, 1937-1945 (Stanford, 1962), pp. 94-113. Early and contemporary accounts of guerrilla mobilization and the establishment of social order in the Taihang region include: Ke Han, The Shansi-Hopeh-Honan Border Region Report for 1937-1939 Part I (Chungking, 1940) and Wang Chien-ming, Chung-kuo kung-ch'an-tang shih-kao [History of the Chinese Communist Party], Vol. III (Taipei, 1965), pp. 331-357. For an account of the Chin-Chi-Lu-Yü Base Area in the 1940s, see Jack Belden, China Shakes the World, and William Hinton, Fanshan: A Documentary of Revolution in a Chinese Village (New York, 1966). A particularly valuable account of local mobilization as it pertained to judicial work is T'ai-hang ch'ü ssu-fa kung-tso kai-k'uang [General Condition of Judicial Work in T'ai-hang District], translated in Chinese Law and Government, Vol. VI, No. 3 (Fall 1973). Finally, biographical data on the principal figures involved in the Chin-Chi-Lu-Yü Base Area and their subsequent careers can be found in Donald W. Klein and Anne B. Clark, Biographical Dictionary of Chinese Communism, 1921-1965, Vols. I and II (Cambridge, Mass., 1971).

7) Cited in Arthur F. Wright, "Comment on Early Chinese Views," in John Meskill (ed.) The Pattern of Chinese History: Cycles, Development, or Stagnation? (Boston, 1965), pp. 3-4.

8) For one view of the moral paradigm see Wright, "Comment on Early Chinese Views," p. 3. Arthur Wright's inquiry into the characteristics of the moral exemplar in "Values, Roles and Personalities" found in Arthur F. Wright and Denis Twitchett (eds.),

Confucian Personalities (Stanford, 1962), p. 9, establishes a
relationship between characterization and paradigmatic frame
that bears comparison with the moral exemplars of The People
of Taihang. Readers are also referred to E. G. Pulleybank,
"The Historiographical Tradition," in Raymond Dawson (ed.),
The Legacy of China (New York, 1971), p. 160.

9) The late Joseph R. Levenson was an ardent critic of attempts to establish parallels between traditional and modern
Chinese thought and practice. See particularly Confucian China
and Its Modern Fate: A Trilogy (Berkeley, 1968), pp. 76-82;
110-115; 123-125. John Israel has revived that criticism with
special attention to recent events in "Continuities and Discon-
tinuities in the Ideology of the Great Proletarian Cultural Revolution," in Chalmers Johnson (ed.), Ideology and Politics in
Contemporary China (Seattle, 1973), pp. 3-46. The position
taken here is not that Levenson erred in pointing to the link
between thought and the socio-cultural milieu in which it is expressed or that Israel misstates the case against superficial
parallels. The objection is rather that both authors, insofar as
they regard the communist uses of history as evidence of its
"mumification," deny the transmissability of historical consciousness from one milieu to another and understate the enormous variety of forms that expression of that consciousness
can take.

10) On functional alternatives see Robert K. Merton, On The-
oretical Sociology: Five Essays Old and New (New York, 1967),
pp. 87-88.

11) Of the multifarious forms Communist ideology has assumed, role-model literature is the most ubiquitous, and it
often represents a rather different vision of history and ideology
than works authored either by professional historians or professional idealogues. Yet this work is seldom exploited for its in-
sights into either history or ideology. An exception is Mary
Sheridan, "The Emulation of Heroes," The China Quarterly
No. 33 (January-March 1968), 47-72. On the traditional side,
explorations of the influence of heterodox Neo-Confucian thought
and of Buddhism and Taoism on Chinese Communist ideology

are rare. For an early attempt to incorporate such elements
into the study of Chinese Communist ideology see David S.
Nivison, Communist Ethics and Chinese Tradition (Cambridge,
1954).

12) Few Western language works have been written about the
Four Histories movement, probably because of the limited attention given to it in the Chinese public press. An article entitled "The Four Histories Movement: A Revolution in Writing
China's Past," by Stephen Uhalley, Jr., appeared in Current
Scene, Vol. IV, No. 2 (January 15, 1966), 1-10. Uhalley's article
was reprinted as "Les'Quatres Histoires' En Chine" in Le
Contrat Social, Vol. X, No. 4 (July-August 1966), 219-225. A
month earlier an article entitled "Everyone A Historian" appeared in an English language Indian publication, China Report,
Vol. 2, No. 4 (June-July 1966), 22-26. While the China Report
version was anonymously authored and tendered no citations to
Western sources, the format of the article and the wording applied were obviously drawn from Uhalley's earlier article in
Current Scene. The wonder of it all is that despite the fact that
both the Current Scene and the China Report articles were based
on virtually the same limited Chinese sources, and despite the
fact that both articles used virtually the same descriptive language, Uhalley inferred the movement's dismal failure and the
China Report inferred its sterling success. This is fair testimony that "doing China" has been as important a common sense
set of rules for the making of inferences about things Chinese
as any set of scientific methods. How "doing" and "inferring"
are related can be found in Harold Garfinkel, Studies in Eth-
nomethodology (Englewood Cliffs, 1967), pp. 9- 10. More elaborate
demonstrations are in Harold Garfinkel, "Common Sense Knowledge of Social Structures: The Documentary Method of Interpretation," in Jerome G. Manis and Bernard Meltzer (eds.), Symbolic
Interaction: A Reader in Social Psychology (Boston, 1972), particularly pp. 356-357, and Peter McHugh, Defining the Situation: The
Organization of Meaning in Social Interaction (New York, 1968).

13) Chao Yu-fu and Li K'ai, "Shih-lun pien-hsieh ho yen-
chiu 'ssu-shih' ti chung-ta i-i — pien-hsüan 'Pei-ching ssu-

shih ts'ung-shu' ti chi-tien t'i-hui" [The Great Significance of
Compiling and Researching the "Four Histories" — Composing
Some Guidelines for the "Peking Four Histories Collection"]
Li-shih yen-chiu [Historical Research] No. 1 (1965), p. 1.
The categorization of works included in the Peking collection
goes beyond the usual "four" histories to include such special
topics as "the history of guerrilla struggles" (min-pin tou-
cheng shih), "the history of the struggle of peasant associations"
(nung-hui tou-cheng shih), "the history of landlord exploitation
and crime" (ti-chu po-hsiao shih ho tsui-o shih).

14) Shih Ch'eng-chih, "Shih-lun 'ssu-shih' yü wen-ke (I),"
Ming Pao Monthly, No. 72 (December 1971), 5-17, translated in
Chinese Sociology and Anthropology (CSA), Vol. IV, No. 3 (Spring
1972), 175-214; "Shih-lun 'ssu-shih' yü wen-ke (II)," Ming Pao
Monthly, No. 73 (January 1972), 37-43, translated in CSA, Vol.
IV, No. 3 (Spring 1972), 215-233; "Shih-lun 'ssu-shih' yü wen-ke
(IV, V)" Ming Pao Monthly, No. 73 (March 1972), 20-26; No. 76
(April 1972), 80-87, translated in CSA, Vol. V, No. 3 (Spring
1973), 6-52.

15) One of the best examples is Nan-yang hsiung-ti yen-ts'ao
kung-ssu shih-liao [Historical Materials on the South Seas
Brothers Tobacco Factory] (Shanghai, 1960), portions of which
are translated in Chinese Sociology and Anthropology, Vol. VI,
Nos. 1, 3-4 (Spring-Summer 1974; Fall 1973); Vol. VII, No. 1
(Fall 1974).

16) Chung-kuo ch'ing-nien ch'u-pan she [China Youth Publishing House], "Pien-hui ch'u-pan 'ssu-shih' ti i-hsieh t'i-
hui" ["Some Guidelines for the Editing and Publication of the
'Four Histories' "], Jen-min jih-pao [Peoples' Daily] (October 25, 1965), p. 5.

17) China Youth Publishing House, "Some Guidelines," p. 5.
Also in Uhalley, "The Four Histories Movement," pp. 5-6.

18) For a full treatment of the Socialist Education Campaign
see Richard Baum and Frederick C. Teiwes, Ssu Ch'ing: The
Socialist Education Movement of 1962-1966 (Berkeley, 1968).

19) Guidelines for the production of "four histories" documents called for the use of such original materials as "bogus"

court judgments, old title deeds, clan and family records, pre-
revolutionary local newspapers and rural surveys in order to
ensure authenticity and accuracy. Insofar as these materials
are directly reflected in The People of Taihang so are the values,
relevances and typifications prevalent at the time they were recorded. It is highly unlikely that such elements were edited
out at a later point in the production of the larger work. See
Chao Yu-fu and Li K'ai, "Shih-lun pien-hsieh ho yen-chiu
'ssu-shih' ti chung-ta i-i...," p. 12. Also Uhalley, "The Four
Histories Movement," p. 4.

20) An excellent review of the structure and functions of traditional clan genealogies can be found in Johanna M. Meskill,
"The Chinese Genealogy as a Research Source," in Maurice
Freedman (ed.), Family and Kinship in Chinese Society (Stanford, 1970), pp. 139-161.

21) "A symbol can be defined in first approximation as an
appresentational reference of a higher order in which the ap-
presenting member of the pair is an object, fact, or event within the reality of our daily life, whereas the other appresented
member of the pair refers to an idea which transcends our experiences of everyday life." Alfred Schutz in Helmut Wagner
(ed.), Alfred Schutz: On Phenomenology and Social Relations
(Chicago, 1970), p. 247.

22) "Consociates" is treated as a more appropriate term because it does not imply a co-equal relationship, yet it connotes
the possibility of face-to-face interaction between members of
the same grouping. While the term is drawn from Alfred
Schutz, the usage here is a modification of Schutz's understanding. Schutz would likely have used the term "contemporaries" reserving "consociates" for persons whose knowledge of one another derives from direct face-to-face contact;
they are "co-present" to one another. The contemporary Chinese notion of relationships between members of the same ideologically favored class connotes comradeship; "contemporaries" im-
plies a social distance greater than the Chinese usage intends. For
the accepted definition see George Walsh and Frederick Lehnert,
Alfred Schutz: The Phenomenology of the Social World (North-

western University, 1967), pp. 139-144. See also Herbert
Spiegelberg, "On the Right to Say 'We': A Linguistic and Phenomenological Analysis (1)" in George Psathas (ed.), Phenomenological Sociology: Issues and Applications (New York, 1970),
pp. 131-132.

23) A detailed treatment of the attributes and multiple func-
tions of both positive and negative role models can be found in
Orrin E. Klapp, Heroes, Villains and Fools: The Changing
American Character (Englewood Cliffs, 1962), esp. pp. 18-23.

24) See Richard H. Solomon, Mao's Revolution and Chinese
Political Culture (Berkeley, 1971), pp. 70-73.

25) Barrington Moore, Jr., Social Origins of Dictatorship and
Democracy: Lord and Peasant in the Making of the Modern
World (Boston, 1967), pp. 208-211.

26) The best treatment of this distinction and of the strain between collectivist values and individualism in heroes is Sheridan,
"The Emulation of Heroes," esp. p. 57.

27) On this point see Solomon, Mao's Revolution and Chinese
Political Culture, p. 103.

28) Joe C. Huang, Heroes and Villains in Communist China:
The Contemporary Chinese Novel As a Reflection of Life
(London, 1973), p. 28.

29) This is a fundamental theme that has its roots in the I
Ching: "... at the beginning of the world, as at the beginning
of thought, there is the decision, the fixing point of reference.
Theoretically any point of reference is possible, but experience
teaches that at the dawn of consciousness one stands already
enclosed within definite prepotent systems of relationships. The
problem then is to choose one's point of reference so that it co-
incides with the point of reference for cosmic events." "Ta
Chuan — The Great Treatise [Great Commentary]" in Richard
Wilhelm and Cary F. Baynes, The I Ching or Book of Changes
(New York, 1962), p. 302.

30) My sources for the dilemma of choice are Helmut
Wilhelm's interpretation of the dilemma inherent for the per-
ceiving actor in Change: Eight Lectures on the I Ching (Princeton, 1960), p. 22, and Max Weber's treatment of the dilemma of

action derived from the imperatives of the Protestant ethic in Max Weber, The Protestant Ethic and the Spirit of Capitalism (New York, 1958), pp. 110-112.

31) William Hinton, Fanshen: A Documentary of Revolution in a Chinese Village (New York, 1966), esp. "Counter Measures," pp. 161-178.

32) Huang, Heroes and Villains in Communist China, p. 48.

33) Dr. Paul Carus (ed.), T'ai Shang Kan Ying P'ien: Treatise of the Exalted One on Response and Retribution (La Salle, 1944). Of particular relevance is the story entitled: "The Spirit of the Hearth," pp. 110-124.

34) For this point I am indebted to Kristin Yü Greenblatt. Chapter 5 of her dissertation entitled "Chu-hung's Advocacy of Social Ethics: The Record of Self Knowledge" reviews the history of morality books (shan-shu) and analyzes the contents of three of the most eminent works in that genre: The T'ai Shang kan-ying p'ien, already mentioned, The Ledger of Merit and Demerit, a Taoist authored work, and The Record of Self-Knowledge, a revised and expanded version of the Ledger composed by Buddhist cleric Chu-hung. The point raised here derives from Chu-hung's conception of the "double truth." Kristin Yü Greenblatt, "Yün-ch'i Chu-hung: The Career of a Ming Buddhist Monk" (unpublished Ph.D. dissertation, Columbia University, 1973), pp. 197-198.

35) Clifford Geertz uses this imagry to describe how religious experience comes to "haunt" daily life for religious men who move between religious and common sense existence with high frequency. There is no reason why the same imagery should not be applied to ideological activists. "Proximate everyday acts come to be seen, if vaguely and indistinctly, subliminally almost, in ultimate contexts, and the whole quality of life, its ethos, is subtly altered." Clifford Geertz, Islam Observed: Religious Development in Morocco and Indonesia (Chicago, 1971), p. 110.

36) The exact origin of the Treatise is unknown though specialists argue that its author was probably a Taoist priest writing sometime in the eleventh century. New prefaces and commentaries were added in editions published and widely circulated

during the Ming and Ch'ing dynasties. The Carus and Suzuki
translation is of an eighteenth century edition. More recent accounts suggest that as recently as the 1920s, the Treatise was still
readily available in Manchurian bookstalls. See Greenblatt,
"Yün-ch'i Chu-hung: The Career of a Ming Buddhist Monk,"
pp. 169-170.

37) The term "provinces of meaning" represents Alfred
Schutz's redefinition of William James' "subuniverses" to suit
the phenomenological perspective. Each province of meaning
is finite and has its own cognitive style. "Moreover, each ... is
among other things, characterized by a specific tension of consciousness (from full awakeness in the reality of everyday life
to sleep in the world of dreams), by a specific time-perspective,
by a specific form of experiencing oneself, and, finally, by a
specific form of sociality." in Wagner (ed.), Alfred Schutz, pp.
252-253.

38) "What the sociologist calls 'system,' 'role,' 'status,'
'role expectation,' 'situation,' and 'institutionalization' is experienced by the individual actor on the social scene in entirely
different terms. To him all the factors denoted by these con-
cepts are elements of a network of typifications — typifications
of human individuals, of their course-of-action patterns, of
their motives and goals, or of the sociocultural products which
originated in their actions." Alfred Schutz in Wagner (ed.),
Alfred Schutz, p. 119. On "because-of" and "in-order-to"
motives see pp. 126-129.

For a supurb treatment of how literature may complement
social science through the creation of salience see Peter C.
Sederberg with Nancy B. Sederberg, "Transmitting the Non-
transmissable: The Function of Literature in the Pursuit of
Social Knowledge," Philosophy and Phenomenological Research,
Vol. XXXVI, No. 2 (December 1975), 173-196.

39) The Treatise of the Exalted One on Response and Retribution, or Treatise for short, begins with a statement of the doc-
trine of reward and retribution, lists acts of meritorious and
demeritorious nature and the number of years of life to be added
or subtracted. Then its principles are illustrated in an exten-

sive body of moral parables. In the Treatise the calculus of reward and retribution is very unsystematic though the intention
to provide such a system is clear. In the Record of Self-Knowledge, however, each recorded merit and demerit represents a
systematically assigned value, thus establishing a hierarchy of
valued and disvalued behaviors but at the same time extending
an open invitation to utilitarianism. Chu-hung, the author of the
Record, was well aware of the danger. See Greenblatt, "Yün-
ch'i Chu-hung: The Career of a Ming Buddhist Monk," pp. 207-
208.

40) See "Transitions" by Alfred Schutz in Wagner (ed.),
Alfred Schutz, pp. 254-255.

41) See "Paramount Reality" and "The Cognitive Style of the
Paramount Reality" by Alfred Schutz in Wagner (ed.), Alfred
Schutz, pp. 253-254. The term "time tracks" derives from a
different though related school of sociological thought, the So-
ciology of the Absurd. See "On the Time Track" in Stanford
M. Lyman and Marvin B. Scott, A Sociology of the Absurd (New
York, 1970), p. 190.

42) The classical treatment of "accounts" and the accounting
process can be found in "Accounts" in Lyman and Scott, A Sociology of the Absurd, pp. 111-143. See particularly, pp. 135-
143. Lyman and Scott attend to situational more than biographical aspects of the accounting process. For a usage more akin
to the one applied here see Jack D. Douglas (ed.), Understanding
Everyday Life: Toward the Reconstruction of Sociological
Knowledge (Chicago, 1970), p. 10.

The impact of accounting in The People of Taihang is such
as to add substance and integrity to the solutions actors arrive
at in resolving their dilemmas of choice. Arthur Wright inad-
vertantly struck this chord in his observation about Confucian
examplars that minatory and exemplary figures of the past
". . . were not treated simply as bundles of desirable or unde-
sirable traits. They tended to be viewed in relation to their
situations, their dilemmas, their choices and the circumstances
surrounding them were usually known." Arthur F. Wright,
"Values, Roles and Personalities," p. 9.

43) The concept of syncretism is largely confined to the study of religion and seldom applied to ideological systems. Even in the context of religious studies, the dominant approach is ideographic. One review, despite its brevity, has considerable import for the social sciences. See Helmer Ringgren, "The Problem of Syncretism," in Svens S. Hartman (ed.), Syncretism (Stockholm, 1969), pp. 7-14.

44) The provisions of the "Outline Land Law of China" and "The Agrarian Reform Law of the People's Republic of China" with reference to this point can be found in the appendices to John Wong, Land Reform in the People's Republic of China: Institutional Transformation in Agriculture (New York, 1973), pp. 282-296. Wong's coverage also includes the experience of land reform in southeast Shansi.

45) See Victor D. Lippit, Land Reform and Economic Development in China: A Study of Institutional Change and Development Finance (White Plains, 1974) for a reanalysis of data on exploitation derived from William Hinton's Fanshen. See also Moore, The Social Origins of Dictatorship and Democracy, pp. 190-191; 218-221.

46) See "General Condition of Judicial Work in T'ai-hang District," pp. 9-11. For a more general approach to the issue of wartime collaboration see John Hunter Boyle, China and Japan at War, 1937-1945; The Politics of Collaboration (Stanford, 1972).

47) Uhalley, "The Four Histories Movement," p. 10.

The People of Taihang

Foreword

In the course of the great Socialist Education Movement, our Southeast Chin District consciously mobilized youth to inquire into the family histories of the poor and lower-middle peasants and organized the masses to discuss and write family histories so as to raise the class consciousness of youth, enable them to remember bitterness and think of sweetness, and further the goal of their revolutionization. The People of Taihang is an anthology of family histories of the poor and lower-middle peasants which have been selected from more than 70,000 family histories. It is an indictment against the old society as well as a eulogy to the new society. It is vital material for class education of the young and a legacy for the education of our offspring.

The Southeast Chin District was one of the old base areas of the War of Resistance Against Japan. Located in southeastern Shansi Province, this district has an area of 23,630 square kilometers, with about 8 million mou of farmland and a population of 3.09 million. Under its jurisdiction are one municipality and sixteen hsien. The Taihang, T'ai-yüeh, and

3

Chung-t'iao mountains rise in this district. The Chin, Chang, and Tan rivers run through it to form the majestic and strategically important Shang-tang Basin. The Southeast Chin District is rich in mineral deposits. Its land is fertile, and its people are diligent. But, before liberation, under a long period of control and exploitation by the landlord class, Chiang Kai-shek, and the Yen Hsi-shan reactionaries, the productivity of this district was extremely low, and the broad masses of the people in this district lived in hunger and cold. Here is an old poem:

> The land is heaped with dried bones,
> People's tears have formed a river.
> There are many orphans in Lu-chou.*
> Aged rustics weep when they remember their
>   deceased relatives.
> How many wandering souls there are!

This is really a description of the life of the people of the Taihang Mountain region in the old society. The facts recorded in The People of Taihang are similarly a glimpse into the experience of the hardships suffered by the laboring people of the Southeast Chin District. Indeed, the old society was a paradise for landlords and reactionaries, but an inferno for the laboring people.

However, the more brutal the oppression, the stronger the resistance. The people of the Southeast Chin District did not want to live like cows and horses or let others decide their destiny. In the old society they did not shy away from violence or fear sacrifice, but carried on a heroic, relentless struggle against generations of reactionary rulers at a great cost in lives, leaving many inspiring traces. For example, in 1524 (the third year of Chia-ching of the Ming dynasty), a rebel force fifty thousand strong, led by Ch'en Ch'ing of a peasant family in Lu-chou, rose up against the Ming rulers and began

---

*Lu-chou was the old name of Ch'ang-chih in Shansi. — Tr.

a massive antifeudal armed struggle. The rebel force captured
present-day Lin hsien in Honan Province, marched to the north
as far as present-day Tso-ch'üan hsien in Shansi Province, and
controlled the whole Shang-tang area, gaining a resounding
fame that endured five or six years. The heroic record of the
rebel force is still remembered by the people in this area.
As for small-scale spontaneous struggles, the books do not
record victory. These struggles failed because of the limitations of historical conditions — because at that time there was
no advanced proletarian party leadership. In the past several
decades, with the brilliant leadership of the Chinese Communist
Party and Chairman Mao, the heroic peoples of the Taihang
Mountains, together with the whole Chinese people, through
the Anti-Japanese War and the War of Liberation, struck down
imperialism, feudalism, and bureaucratic capitalism, achieved
a revolutionary victory and a real liberation. In the course of
revolutionary struggle, the people of the Taihang Mountains,
under the leadership of the Party, joined the army, supported
combat troops at the front, worked as stretcher bearers, trans-
ported supplies, made mines, collected intelligence on the
enemy, and fought the enemy in coordination with the regular
army, leaving a glorious revolutionary legacy. After the victory of the revolution, the people of the Taihang Mountains
actively responded to the call by the Party and Chairman Mao
by organizing themselves, developing production, and taking
the road of cooperativization. Following communization, under
the brilliant rays of the Three Red Flags, they rose with even
greater vigor and made great strides in their speedy advance
along the broad road to socialist revolution and socialist construction. The Southeast Chin District today has become a
paradise for the laboring people. Note how the people sing the
praises of their new life and lyricize their revolutionary aspi-
rations:

> The glorious traditions of the people in the majestic
>   Taihang Mountains have been handed down
>   through generations;
> They are diligent and brave and fear no hardships.

Thousands and tens of thousands of heroic fighters and
   model revolutionaries were born in this place.
The three big mountains* have been struck down;
The people have enthusiastically embraced socialism.
What a scenic spot the Shang-tang Basin is!
The people's communes are shining with success.
Bald mountains and hills have put on new costumes;
Pines, cypresses, and fruit trees grow abundantly.
Wasted slopes have become terraced fields and sandy
   banks and gravelly beaches have been turned into
   farmlands;
Villages in mountains and rural areas can be reached by
   telephone;
Cities and towns are linked by highways.
Tall chimneys can be seen everywhere so that the people
   of Yin-ch'eng** can no longer boast of their industrial
   production.
The red sun shines over the Taihang Mountains,
The Three Red Flags fly in the wind.
Future generations will always remember Chairman Mao
   and the Communist Party,
And they will not forget class hatred and will give full
   play to the traditions of revolution.

In the Socialist Education Movement we have found that the
great majority of people of the older generation who personally
suffered the bitterness of class oppression and exploitation
and stood the test of the class struggle have heightened their
class consciousness and strengthened their revolutionary will.
However, there is also a minority who do not want to recall or
think about, much less talk about, their hardships in the past,
and some, because of the passage of time, have gradually mud-

---

*Imperialism, feudalism, and bureaucratic capitalism. — Tr.
**The town of Yin-ch'eng in Chang-chin hsien used to be re-
nowned for its handicrafts. The town won the title of "Ten-
thousand li Yin-ch'eng" because its handicrafts were sold
throughout China.

dled their memories of past events and have gradually forgotten class hatred. Thus, members of the older generation have to refresh their memories of the past. As for young people and adolescents, they are "doves of peace" who "have not suffered exploitation by landlords and rich peasants, witnessed the massacres by the Japanese imperialists, or experienced land reform." "Who knows what the past was like?" If they do not understand the past, then they cannot understand the present. Chairman Mao has taught us: "Because they lack political experience and experience of social life, many young people are not good at making a comparison between old China and new China and have difficulty in deeply understanding how our people overthrew imperialism and the Kuomintang reactionaries in their arduous struggles and how our people established a beautiful socialist society after so many years of hardship and toil." We can see that to carry out education in class struggle among youth enables them to adopt a firm proletarian stand, to acquire a Marxist-Leninist class viewpoint, to inherit and develop the Party's revolutionary traditions, to always stand firm in the winds and waves of class struggle at home and abroad, and to carry through revolution to the end in such extremely important areas. Class struggle is long-term. Children grow up to be adults step by step. What is understandable to the present generation of young people may not be understood by the next generation of young people. Hence we must make long-range preparations for providing class education for succeeding generations of children and grandchildren. This is a strategic task that stands before us. According to our understanding of the socialist education movement, lecturing on village histories, family histories, communal and factory histories is a good, effective method for educating youth. In order to rescue these precious and vital materials for class education from oblivion and in order to hand them down to future generations, we have specially selected this anthology from a great volume of family histories for young people's reference. We hope that it will help young comrades to revolutionize further, to continue to write glorious records of proletarian families, and to add new glories to these family records.

Owing to limitations of time and limited cultural level, shortcomings and errors have been difficult to avoid. Corrections by the readers are welcome.

> Chao Chün, Secretary
> The Chinese Communist Party Committee
> of the Southeast Chin District in
> Shansi Province

The City of Ch'ang-chih
October 1, 1964

A home given by Chairman Mao

This short story is the family history of Ku Hua-jung, an old woman from Hsi-wu Village in Li-ch'eng hsien, Shansi Province. "Family" and "history" are the two indispensable elements of a family history. As for Auntie Ku, who is fifty-one years old, her experience over the past fifty-one years can of course be written into a "history," but hardly into a "family history," because for half her life she had no home of her own. Although she lived in four other homes at different times, she had no home she could really consider her own. How anyone could be called upon to write a family history for her is a difficult problem. However, she did have stories of how she had to leave her own home in order to survive and how she suffered scoldings and beatings in the homes of others; and how she suffered extreme hardships in those "nonfamily families" can be regarded as her "family history."

Leaving Home

Ku Hua-jung was born in Shan-chuang Village in Wu-an hsien, Hopei Province. In her fifth year, floods struck her village

---

Han Wen-chou, Yao Lung-ch'ang, "Mao chu-hsi kei-le i-ko chia."

and destroyed all the farmlands. What would her family, a
family of ten, live on? They ate tree bark and wild plants; in
the winter months they couldn't even find wild plants. Sometimes they had no fire going for several days. Hua-jung's father
was so worried that he got no sleep at night. His six children
were just skin and bones and would soon starve to death. One
night, after going to bed, Hua-jung overheard her father saying
to her mother:

"Life is becoming difficult. We'll starve to death! It doesn't
matter if you and I die of hunger. We're so old. We've never
eaten well — we've had poor food for years; we've never been
well dressed — we've worn shabby clothes most of the time.
But what about the children? Are we supposed to let them
starve to death?..." Then she heard her mother say:

"If things stay this way, the next few days we'll be neither
dead nor alive! You must find a way to let the children
escape!..."

Hua-jung was too young to understand matters of life and
death. While the adults were talking she fell sound asleep.
The following day, shortly before dawn, mother woke Hua-jung
and her third elder sister, Jung-hua: "Jung-hua! Hua-jung!
Get up. Hurry!"

Hua-jung saw that it was still not daylight, and she did not
want to get up. "Why are you calling us when it's still so dark?
I don't want to get up."

"Get up, Hua-jung," her mother said, "a letter from your
aunt has come. It says that she's ill. You and third elder sister should visit her. There are things to eat at auntie's house.
Won't that be better than staying at home? Come on, get up."

Hua-jung was very happy when mother told her she was going
to visit her auntie. She jumped out of her bed and began to put
on her clothes, then she ran over to her third elder sister.
"Third elder sister, mother wants us to go visit our auntie.
How come you're still not up?"

Jung-hua got up too. The two sisters put on their clothes.
Mother was busy lighting a fire in the cooking stove and setting the pot on the stove. She measured half a bowl of corn

flour from the last two catties of corn meal they had.
When Hua-jung saw this, she felt it was strange and thought to
herself: "Every day mother says we have to save the two catties of corn meal for the New Year. Why is she going to use
it today?" Then, she asked mother: "Mother, didn't you say
we had to save the corn meal for the New Year? Why are we
going to use it today? Don't we have to wait till the New Year
comes?" Hua-jung looked at her mother's face. Her mother
burst into tears. "You two will have to travel a long distance.
You can't walk for hours with nothing in your stomach. We
still have enough corn meal left."

Hua-jung was satisfied with the answer given by her mother
and stopped asking questions. After the two sisters finished
their corn gruel, father borrowed a young donkey from the
next-door neighbor and told them to get ready for the journey.
When she saw the donkey, Hua-jung asked: "Father, why is it
necessary to ride a donkey to go visit our auntie?"

"It has just snowed," said father. "It'll be hard to walk on
the road, so you'd better ride a donkey."

While he was saying this, tears trickled from father's eyes.
When Hua-jung turned to look at her mother, she saw tears
streaming down her cheeks. Hua-jung said to herself: "Father
and mother never wept when we visited our auntie before. Why
are they crying this time?" Mother wiped away her tears and
said to Hua-jung: "Now it's time to start your trip. Be a good
girl when you stay at your auntie's house. Listen to the adults.
Be sweet and diligent. At night be careful of the lights —"
Before she finished, she started to wail aloud.

"Mother, why do you keep on crying? It's not as if we won't
come back."

Mother wept even more bitterly when she heard Hua-jung's
words.

Father hurriedly helped the two girls get up on the donkey's
back; when he cracked the whip on its rump, the donkey started
off at a gallop.

It was a December morning after the snow. The northwesterly wind roared. On the donkey's back Hua-jung and Jung-hua

shivered in the cold.

"Third elder sister, it is really cold!" said Hua-jung.

"I'm freezing to death," Jung-hua complained.

Father broke in, "Girls, are you cold? Well, let's hurry up. You won't feel cold when you reach your auntie's house."

While he was talking, suddenly Jung-hua noticed that they were taking the wrong road. She whispered to her younger sister: "Hua-jung, the village where auntie's house is is over there, but father has driven the donkey this way. Why?"

"I remember this is not the road to auntie's," said Hua-jung as she looked around.

"Father must have lost his way."

"Oh, no. Father is a grown-up. How can a grown-up lose his way?"

"Let's ask father about it."

"Father, this is not the road to auntie's house. You're a grown-up; how come you've lost your way?" Hua-jung said to her father.

"Don't you know your auntie has moved to another place? Don't worry. I know the road," said father.

The two sisters stopped arguing with their father after they were told their aunt had moved to a new place. On the back of the young donkey, they talked to each other about what they would like to eat and what kinds of games they would like to play after they arrived at their auntie's house. They were very happy. But their father did not utter a word. Suddenly Hua-jung turned to see her father wiping away tears as he walked behind the donkey. Hua-jung thought to herself: "Why is father crying while he walks? Is it because he doesn't want to walk?"

"Father, you'd better ride the donkey. We'll walk," said Hua-jung.

"No, I don't want to ride," said father as he wiped his tears away quickly.

"Are you sure you don't want to ride the donkey? Then why are you crying?"

"Grown-ups always shed tears when they walk on a cold day."

"When I grow up to be an adult will I also cry when I walk

on a cold day?"

"Yes, you'll do the same thing everyone else does."

Hua-jung did not understand why grown-ups cried when they walked on cold days. She gave it some thought. At about noontime they entered a village. Father suggested that they take a rest and find something to eat before resuming their journey. He helped his children get down from the donkey. Then they entered a house. There was a woman in the house who was very friendly to them. In a little while she carried out two bowls of soup. The girls were very hungry, and they gulped it down. Just at that moment, a man came in. He exchanged some words with father. Father put his hand under his gown and the man extended his to shake father's under the gown.* The two little girls could see their hands in motion under the gown. Hua-jung could not understand what her father and the man were doing. She whispered to Jung-hua: "Elder sister, what is father doing holding that man's hand under his gown?"

"Who cares? Perhaps he wants to keep his hands warm," Jung-hua answered.

Jung-hua saw the man give her father some money. She lost no time in telling her sister. "Hua-jung, I think father has sold us to that man!"

"No, father would not sell us" said Hua-jung, who couldn't believe what her sister had told her.

In a moment, father came back and said to Hua-jung: "Jung-hua and I are going out to get some cakes for you. Hua-jung, stay here till we come back."

"If my elder sister goes, I want to go too," said Hua-jung.

"Your elder sister is already eight. She's older than you, and I want her to go with me. You're a little girl, and you may catch cold if you go out."

Hua-jung saw father and Jung-hua quickly leave the house. She hoped her father would come back soon, bringing her some cakes. But her father did not come back. Later, she heard a

---

*This was, and may still be, the way prices were fixed in business transactions in some rural areas of China. — Tr.

knock at the door. Thinking that her father was coming back
with the cakes, she went to open the door. When the door
opened it was not her father but a big man of heavy build.
Hua-jung stepped back from the stranger. But the big man
came up to her with a cake in his hand. He asked her: "Do
you want a cake?"

Hua-jung was too anxious to look for her father to think about
having cakes. She told the big man: "I want to find my father.
I want to find my father."

"You want to find your father? All right, come with me. I
know where he is."

Anxious to see her father, Hua-jung left with the big man,
walking behind him. They came up to a handsome looking
house with a large courtyard. He led her into the house and
inside she saw an old, fat woman sitting on the k'ang.*

"Where's my father?" Hua-jung asked immediately.

"Your father sold you to us. Where do you think he's gone,"
the old, fat woman replied coldly.

A shudder passed through Hua-jung when she heard that she
had been sold by her father. She let out a screech, demanding
to look for her father. As she cried, she ran for the door, but
the old, fat woman dragged her back again and slammed the
door shut.

In the Home of "The Living King of Hell"

Hua-jung had a long and bitter cry after the disappearance
of her father and sister. A five-year-old child, after all, is
not very mature. She cried for a while, and then stopped. By
dinner time, when Amah Chang brought her a bowl of rice
gruel, she was glad to have something to allay her hunger.
But no sooner had she eaten a mouthful of the rice gruel then
she thought of her father and sister, stopped eating, and began to
cry again. The old, fat woman cursed her: "What are you
crying about? Is your father dead? Is your mother dead?"

---

*A brick bed warmed by a fire. — Tr.

Hua-jung didn't dare cry anymore.

"Hey! What's your family name?" the old, fat woman asked.

"Ku is my family name," Hua-jung answered, wiping away her tears.

"And what's your first name?"

"Hua-jung."

"From now on, you'll no longer be called Ku in our home. Our's is the Ch'eng family and Ch'eng will be your surname hereafter. We'll have to change your first name too. From now on, you'll be called Mei-hsiang."*

Hua-jung did not care whether her name was changed or not. When she thought of her father and sister she began to cry again. Annoyed by the little girl's crying, the old, fat woman scolded her and told Amah Chang to take Hua-jung to the kitchen.

Amah Chang questioned Hua-jung and tears of sympathy trickled from her eyes. "To be separated from your mother so young and handed over to others is such a pity! My fate has been bitter and your's is unlucky too!"

Hua-jung cried even more bitterly when she heard her mother mentioned. The old, fat woman shouted from her room: "Amah Chang, what is that little thief crying about?"

"She misses her mother," Amah Chang replied.

The old, fat woman cursed: "She misses her mother, does she! She comes to our house and eats our food. Well, she's not allowed to miss her mother and she's not permitted to cry. If she cries anymore, see if I don't dash her to bits!"

Hua-jung was not only separated from her mother, she was deprived of the right to live with her, and she didn't even have the right to miss her. She cried bitterly. The old, fat woman lost her temper. She came out of her room, shouting in the hallway: "Mei-hsiang, come over here!"

Hua-jung was still crying. She hadn't come out, and the response that was expected of her was not forthcoming. The old, fat woman scolded her again: "Mei-hsiang, I'm talking to

---

*Mei-hsiang means "slave girl." — Editor.

you. Why don't you answer? What airs you put on!"

Only then did Hua-jung speak up: "My name is Hua-jung, not Mei-hsiang!"

"Shut up, you brat! What an obstinate child you are! If you dare talk back again you'll be sorry! You came to the Ch'eng family today. You ate our food, so now your name will be Mei-hsiang!"

Hua-jung dared not cry any more.

The following day, when it grew light, the old, fat woman called Hua-jung to her room and gave the little five-year-old girl chores to do. She had to sweep the floors, clean tables, serve food, and set out the chamber-pots every day. The old, fat woman immediately handed a straw broom to the little girl and said: "Sweep the floor for me."

Hua-jung was, first, too young to do the chores. Second, at her own home there were three elder sisters at her mother's side to do the household chores. Of course she couldn't do these things, but she thought it would be about the same here as it was at her mother's. If there were tasks she couldn't do, she should say so. So she said: "I don't know how to sweep the floor."

"You mean the only thing you know how to do is eat? If you eat the Ch'eng family's food, you have to work for us. Sweep up!"

Hua-jung was afraid of her. She had to go sweep the floors. What would a five-year-old child know about sweeping floors? So she touched one place and missed another, making a mess of it. Ch'eng Yung-yüan, the young master of the Ch'eng house — the big man who bought Hua-jung — came in, saw the job she was doing, and kicked her in the behind. He scolded her: "Look at how you've swept the floor! You're just a useless bitch who wastes food. The dirt you left untouched, are you going to eat it today or tomorrow?" So saying, he kept on kicking her until little Hua-jung had to go back and sweep it again.

On the third day, the old, fat woman told Hua-jung to sleep in a room in the west wing of the house. If a five-year-old girl had slept beside her mother, she would have worried about her: afraid she'd get cold, she'd wake up and cover her; afraid she'd get burned, she'd check the fire. But now, who was going to take care of her? Little Hua-jung slept till midnight but she kicked her quilt into the brasier. Then she felt pain in her legs. Wakened from her dream, Hua-jung found that the burning quilt was near her legs. She was frightened. Immediately she said to herself: "I've burned the quilt. Tomorrow, when the young master finds out, he will beat me to death." She tried to put out the fire, wringing the burning quilt with both hands and then trampling on the burning quilt. Her hands and feet were burned. She didn't know what to do. She cried in a low voice: "Father, put out the fire! Mother, come quickly —" But her father and mother were not living with her. She was all alone. Suddenly she saw a teapot near the brasier. She desperately poured the tea on the burning quilt and finally put out the fire.

Hua-jung wept for hours when she thought that she would have no quilt to keep her warm and that she would be soundly beaten the following day. The next morning, the young master of the house got the news of the fire in Hua-jung's room. He sent for Hua-jung. As soon as the little girl entered his room, he gave her a slap in the face and cursed her:

"You cheap scamp! Who told you to burn the quilt?" Ch'eng Yung-yüan shouted at Hua-jung.

"I was asleep. I didn't know the quilt caught fire," said Hua-jung, crying. The young master was angry.

"You burned the quilt. Are you trying to tell me that this was not your fault?"

"Beat her! Slap her in the mouth!" shouted the old, fat woman.

The young master slapped Hua-jung in the face several times. Blood trickled down. The old, fat woman was still not satisfied. She said: "You beat her too lightly. Slap her harder! Slap her harder! She burned my quilt. One of these days she may burn down my house."

The young master went out. A few minutes later, he came back with two large brick tiles in his hands. He threw down the tiles, smashing them to pieces. Then, with an axe he broke

these pieces up into smaller pieces the size of peach pits.
Pointing to a heap of these small, jagged pieces, he said to Hua-
jung: "Kneel on them!"

Looking at the heap of broken, jagged tiles, Hua-jung thought
to herself that it would be very painful to kneel on them. The
young master grabbed her and forced her to kneel on the broken tiles. Her knees hurt so badly that she could not keep the
upper part of her body upright. She screamed loudly. The
young master told her to straighten up her body. Then he put a
slab of earth on her head and poured a bowl of boiling water
into a bowl resting on the slab. He said to Hua-jung: "If you
dare move and break my bowl, I'll pull out your sinews and
flay off your skin." As soon as he finished cursing he picked
up a whip and beat her. Hua-jung could not bear the thrashing.
When she moved to escape the whip, the bowl fell from her
head. The young master whipped her more fiercely. Amah
Chang came to plead for Hua-jung, saying: "Madam and young
master, please let her off this time! Of course, she should be
flogged for her error. But she is only five years old. How
can she endure such punishment!"

"If I let her off this time, she'll only be spoiled next time,"
said the young master. Then he whipped Hua-jung several
more times. The little girl cried but did not utter a word.
Amah Chang felt both pity and anger. "You silly little girl,
can't you plead for mercy? Mei-hsiang, say quickly that you'll
never dare do it again."

Hua-jung pleaded for mercy as Amah Chang told her to. The
young master flogged Hua-jung a few more times before he let
her go.

For the following year, Hua-jung was not allowed to have a
quilt so she had to sleep with her clothes on. In winter, she
had chilblains all over her body and her feet festered. But to
whom could she state her grievances?

After she suffered this beating, Hua-jung's wounds had still
not healed when the New Year arrived. Others were dressed in
their best and happily celebrating the New Year, while little
Hua-jung wept in her room by herself because her wounds hurt

and because she missed her parents.

"Amah Chang, I really don't want to stay in this home. I want to go back to my parents," Hua-jung quietly told Amah Chang.

"Silly girl, you think the young master will let you go? I'm afraid you'll have to endure such suffering," said Amah Chang.

"If he doesn't let me go, I'll get away secretly."

"You won't have a chance. If he catches you and brings you back he will certainly give you a good beating."

When she thought about the possibility of being flogged, Hua-jung abandoned her plan to escape. She stayed reluctantly in the house of the Ch'engs.

On the fifth day of the first month, when the Ch'engs made offerings to the statues of the gods of heaven and earth in the yard, they found that two of the sesame candy bars which were offered in sacrifice were missing. Ch'eng Yung-yüan, without any reason, decided to interrogate Hua-jung. He called Hua-jung over. As soon as the little girl entered his room, she saw a red-hot metal poker in the fire. She was scared to death as though she had entered the Palace of the King of Hell. Ch'eng Yung-yüan was furious.

"Mei-hsiang, you have done it again!"

Hua-jung didn't know what he was referring to. "What did I do this time?" Ch'eng Yung-yüan whipped her straight off.

"Are you still pretending? Who told you you could eat the candy offered to the Gods of Heaven and Earth?"

When Hua-jung heard this, she felt greatly wronged.

"I've never even seen it," retorted Hua-jung. "How could I have eaten it?"

"Are you still insisting?" He whipped her twice more.

"I didn't steal the candy. Why do you continue to beat me?"

The old, fat woman saw that Hua-jung was talking back. "Yung-yüan, burn this low scamp with the red-hot poker!" the old woman ordered.

"You dare to talk back! Today, let's see who's the stronger."

Immediately Ch'eng Yung-yüan picked up the red-hot poker and branded Hua-jung's back. She cried out, "Ah Ya!" and fell to the ground. Ch'eng Yung-yüan kept on asking the same question: "Did you eat it?"

Hua-jung didn't know how to tell lies. Even after suffering such pain, she still insisted that she did not eat the candy. Ch'eng Yung-yüan branded her back several more times. She rolled on the ground, her body wracked in pain, crying, "Ma! — Tieh! —" Amah Chang was alerted by her cries and came over. When she saw pitiful little Hua-jung still insisting that she hadn't eaten the candy, she said to herself: "What a strong-willed child! She still talks back after such torture. But it's not the time to talk back." Then she said to Hua-jung: "Mei-hsiang, don't talk back. Tell the young master you ate it, and he won't beat you again."

Hua-jung listened to Amah Chang's advice and stopped her screaming. Ch'eng Yung-yüan took Hua-jung's silence as a sign of admission, so he stopped beating her and asked in a low voice: "With how many mouthfuls did you finish the two candy bars?"

Since Hua-jung hadn't eaten them of course she could not answer his question.

"Who told you you could eat them? I've never seen such a slut who would steal the food offered at New Year's time. So today I'm going to beat you to death!" said Ch'eng Yung-yüan as he began to flog Hua-jung again. Unable to bear the sight of another cruel thrashing, Amah Chang said boldly: "Young master, why are you beating her again? She has come to this home for survival not for death. You shouldn't do such a thing!"

"What are you going to do about it? I'm going to beat her to death," shouted Ch'eng Yung-yüan as he started to whip Hua-jung again. Knowing that the little girl would never last the cruel flogging, Amah Chang changed her approach and pleaded: "Young master, you spent good money to buy Hua-jung. If you do damage to her she'll be unable to wait on you. Then won't you feel that you've spent twenty strings of cash for nothing?"

As soon as money was mentioned, Ch'eng Yung-yüan thought to himself, "It's true that if I beat her to such a state, then what's the use of the money I spent to buy her." Only then did he stop.

In the less than ten days since her arrival at the house of the Ch'engs, Hua-jung had undergone all the cruel sufferings the world could offer. She didn't want to stay there, but she had to, and she lived this way, in fear of the leather whip, for twelve years.

When Hua-jung was seventeen years old, Ch'eng Yung-yüan saw that she had grown up to be a pretty girl, so he wanted to make her his concubine and asked an old kinswoman to act as a go-between. Hua-jung had always regarded Ch'eng Yung-yüan as her mortal foe. Of course, she didn't want to marry him, and she flatly rejected the proposal.

The woman still tried to persuade her. "Don't be silly! The young master owns houses, land, and several shops. Besides, he has maidservants. If you marry the master, won't you be able to enjoy these blessings?"

"The houses and land are theirs. I don't care," Hua-jung replied coldly.

After the go-between told Ch'eng Yung-yüan's mother of Hua-jung's rejection, the old, fat woman came in person to talk with Hua-jung about the marriage.

"Hua-jung, is there any reason for you to refuse to marry the young master? We're rich people. As you can see yourself, our wardrobes are full of clothes, and our chests are full of money...."

Hua-jung didn't want to listen to her patter. "I know you're rich. If you weren't rich, you wouldn't have so many maidservants, and how would you dare beat people?"

The old, fat woman was rebuffed, and she went away cursing loudly. When she returned she told Ch'eng Yung-yüan, and he was furious. "It is really true that rotten dog meat should never be weighed on a scale. Today I'll put my power to use." Seized by a fit of anger, he stormed into Hua-jung's room. He hung her up with a strong rope from the beam across the room and flogged her with a whip. Hua-jung knew that he had come to flog her because she had refused to marry him. She cursed: "You're a living demon! All right, flog me. You'll prove yourself a coward if you don't beat me to death!"

The more Ch'eng Yung-yüan flogged her the more furiously she swore at him. The old, fat woman overheard from outside and realized that there was no way of turning back. In a second, she decided on a plan to sell this "low scamp" to someone else. She entered the room and bade her son let Hua-jung down, cursing until she left in anger.

In a discussion immediately afterward, the mother and son reached the conclusion that Hua-jung had grown up to be an obstinate girl and that it would be advisable for them to sell her to some-one else. The following day, Ch'eng Yung-yüan went out to find a new master and sold her to Chao Ying-lai, a rich man of Chao Village, to be his wife. Upon hearing this news, Hua-jung told herself: "It would be much better to go away than to be a maidservant in this cursed house of the living King of Hell."

One evening, Chao Ying-lai sent someone on a donkey to take Hua-jung. The old, fat woman called Hua-jung to her room and said insincerely: "I've found a husband for you. Today you can go to his home. You've lived here for twelve years. You can count our home your own. If the Chao family mistreats you, come back to us. We'll help you."

Hua-jung, as she gave the old, fat woman a contemptuous glance, said rudely: "After I go to the Chao's, even if I'm sliced up a million times, I won't come back here!"

"Don't be obstinate — It's already late. Hurry up! Eat something before you go."

"I don't want to eat. I've had enough of your food!"

The fat woman, seeing her so fierce, said angrily: "Yung-yüan, let her go right away. Hurry up! I don't want to see her again."

"I've wanted to leave for a long time, and I don't want to see you again!" Hua-jung retorted while giving the old, fat woman another contemptuous glance.

Knowing that the old, fat woman had put some money in a red envelope for Hua-jung as a wedding present, Amah Chang said to Hua-jung: "Why don't you kneel down and kowtow to the old mistress to show your gratitude before you go? Come on, kneel down —"

"Kneel down to her? I've been forced to kneel enough in this house. I won't do so this time! " said Hua-jung.

"Hua-jung, since you're going to leave this house pretty soon, you needn't be so stubborn. The old mistress has a wedding present for you. How come you don't want the money?"

"What would I do with the few dollars she'd give me? I've worked here for the past twelve years. There wouldn't be enough to cover one month's salary.

Hua-jung left the house of the Ch'engs by the front door without looking back.

What Kind of "Home" Is This?

Chao Ying-lai was a rich man. He had sold his wife before he married Ku Hua-jung because they didn't get along. His mother originally knew only that Hua-jung was a girl from a poor family. She didn't know that Hua-jung had been a maid-servant. Later, after she had heard about it, she asked Chao Ying-lai:

"Ying-lai, who told you to marry a maidservant?"

"Auntie told me. I didn't know she had been a maidservant! "

"Aren't you afraid that outsiders will laugh at us ... the kind of people we are for taking in a maidservant? How come you didn't think about that?"

"It's too late. I've already married her. But it can be taken care of easily. I'll sell her again if it doesn't work out. . . ."
That was Chao Ying-lai's intention.

Only a few days after Hua-jung's arrival at the Chao home, Chao Ying-lai changed his attitude toward her. He didn't open his mouth unless to curse her or raise his hand except to beat her. He cursed Hua-jung for being a maidservant who had brought shame on his family.

On New Year's a beggar woman came to beg for food. Born to a poor family, Hua-jung understood the misery of hunger. She pitied the woman and gave her a piece of corn bread. Fearing that the poor woman would be caught with the corn bread, Hua-jung told her to leave the house quickly and eat it after

she got out of the house.   But the woman was too hungry
to wait.   She started eating the corn bread in the courtyard
and she ran right into Chao Ying-lai as he was coming
home.

"Who told you to give food to that beggar? Is she your mother
or your grandmother?"

"She was so hungry. Don't you feel any pity for her?" asked
Hua-jung.

"Hang it! If you want to be kind to her, give her your things,
but not our things."

"I gave her my corn bread. What's wrong with that?"

"Shut up! Since when is this your home?"

"Of course it's my home too. You married me!"

"What's this? Since when is a low class servant a human
being?"

"If I'm not a human being, what do you think you are, a pig
or a dog?"

Hua-jung's abusive words aroused Chao Ying-lai's anger.
"You wait and see!" He picked up strong rope and dipped it
into a large earthenware vessel filled with water.   Then he
used the water-soaked rope to beat her over the head. Hua-
jung was covered with blood. She had hoped that her marriage
to Chao Ying-lai would put an end to her suffering. Now she
found that Chao Ying-lai was as diabolic as the King of Hell,
Ch'eng Yung-yüan.   She thought to herself: "No matter where
I go it seems I can't survive. I might as well let him beat me
to death."

In an even louder voice, she cursed him: "Chao Ying-lai,
beat me to death if you have the nerve to do so!"

"You think you're going to live?" said Chao Ying-lai, "You're
dreaming!" After awhile Chao Ying-lai got tired. He stopped
thrashing her and left.

Two days later, a kinswoman came to invite Hua-jung to
spend a few days in her house. Hua-jung wanted an opportunity
to get away for awhile. She told her mother-in-law of the invitation and got Mrs. Chao's permission.

As soon as they were out of the village, the kinswoman told
Hua-jung: "I think I should tell you the truth. We're not going

to my house. Chao Ying-lai has sold you to a man in Li-ch'eng for 280 yuan...." After she heard this startling news, she felt as if she had been struck by a thunderbolt and she was stupefied. Half the day had passed before she came to herself again. Through her sobs she said: "What am I living for! I'm only eighteen, but I've been bought and sold like a commodity. What kind of a life is this!"

The kinswoman said a few words to show her sympathy toward Hua-jung. Suddenly, Hua-jung said to herself: "It may be better for me to leave the house of the Chao's. Not everyone is as brutal as Ch'eng Yung-yüan and Chao Ying-lai."

After she made up her mind to leave, she suddenly remembered that she hadn't taken her clothes so she went back to get them. But she was stopped at the gate of the house by Mrs. Chao.

"A sold woman is like water spilt on the ground. What do you think you're doing coming into my house?" said Mrs. Chao.

"All right, I won't go in. You can wear my clothes when you go to the coffin!" Hua-jung retorted.

In this way Hua-jung left the home which was actually not a home at all.

Still No Home

Ku Hua-jung left the Chao's and went to Li-ch'eng hsien in Shansi Province with a go-between (i.e., a person who sells people to others), and he sold her to Li Yung-chü, a rich man in the village of K'uan-chang-shan, to be his wife. His family was very large, consisting of eighty persons. After Hua-jung arrived, she was entrusted with a large pot for making bean curd, and she had to prepare food for eighty people every day. She was often insulted by her mother-in-law for her improper preparation of the food. That was all right, but after one year or so, Hua-jung gave birth to a girl, and her husband suddenly died of an illness. Her mother-in-law attributed her son's death to Hua-jung. She said that Hua-jung was an "evil comet"*

---

*A comet was believed to be a sign of bad luck. — Tr.

and a "family breaker." After Li Yung-chü died, Hua-jung
wasn't beaten much. She had a child and she did not want to
marry again, but every day her mother-in-law abused her by
calling her the "evil comet." She was still only nineteen. When
would she ever be delivered from all this?

Li Yung-chü's mother began to show her unwillingness to keep
the "evil comet" in her house. Hua-jung knew that her mother-
in-law wanted to sell her, and she was anxious to leave the
house of her deceased husband. One day, a relative, Li Hsiao-
yüan, brought another man to see Hua-jung. Li Hsiao-yüan
told her that he would like to arrange a match between her and
the man, but she rejected the proposal because the man was
already over forty. Later, Hua-jung had another proposal of
marriage from a young man named Wang Shou-ch'eng, and she
accepted.

One night, Wang Shou-ch'eng came to meet his bride. Hua-
jung was glad that she would soon leave the house of the Li's.
Carrying her child in her arms, she left, but as soon as she
emerged from the house, her mother-in-law put a red-hot
metal poker into a bowl of vinegar, and the acrid vapor caused
by the heating of the vinegar attacked her nostrils. Then her
mother-in-law threw the bowl out the front door and smashed
it.

"What's she doing?" Hua-jung asked some people standing
nearby.

"She is seeing off an 'evil comet,' " they replied.

Upon hearing this, Hua-jung became so mad that she was
short of breath. She swore at Mrs. Li: "Perhaps you can see
off an 'evil comet' but this 'evil comet' will not die away. It
will vex you until your death!"

Hua-jung arrived at Wang Shou-ch'eng's home in Feng-ling-
shan Village. The maid of honor accompanied her to an altar.
When the bride and bridegroom were about to worship the gods
of heaven and earth, Hua-jung found that the bridegroom was
not Wang Shou-ch'eng but the middle-aged man whom she had
rejected. When she realized that she had been taken in, Hua-
jung did not join the bridegroom to worship the gods of heaven

and earth. She ran to the bride's room and wept. The bridegroom came into the room.

"Please, don't weep. This is my fault. Please understand
me! I've been compelled to do this because you rejected my
proposal. I know I'm too old for you," the bridegroom
apologized.

"I don't want to marry you. I don't want to talk to you. I
want to marry Wang Shou-ch'eng. I'll go to his home..." said
Hua-jung as she wept.

"Please, don't go. I'm Wang Shou-ch'eng."

Hua-jung realized that she had been cheated, so she said
nothing more but only continued to cry.

Making Her Home in Desolate Temples

Wang Shou-ch'eng was a kind and honest man. Every day,
after returning from his work in the fields, he helped Hua-jung
take care of her child and wash the cooking pots. He was very
kind to her. He was the first kindhearted man Hua-jung had
met in her twenty-odd years of life. Because they were very
poor, Shou-ch'eng went out every day to find part-time jobs to
feed her and the baby. She was very happy, so she said to herself: "I've met many rich people in the past. None of them
treated me as a human being. Wang Shou-ch'eng may be poor,
but he is kind." Hua-jung made up her mind to live with Wang
Shou-ch'eng.

About eight years later, Hua-jung was already a mother of
three children. It was then that the Japanese aggressors came
to the Taihang Mountains. They slaughtered people and
burned down houses in Li-ch'eng after they occupied the town.
The Japanese devils launched a sweep-up operation in the Taihang area. During the operation, they arrested Wang Shou-
ch'eng and took him away with them. Day and night, Hua-jung
worried about her husband's safety, hoping that her husband
would come back safely. But Wang Shou-ch'eng did not come
back. He was beaten to death by the Japanese bandits. Hua-
jung cried when she heard of her husband's death. The Jap-

anese bandits also took away what few pecks of grain Hua-jung
had left. Her children cried for food every day. Finally, she
took them to neighboring villages to beg for food.

Ku Hua-jung and her three children became vagabonds. During the day, they begged for food from door to door. At night,
they slept in desolate temples, providing they could find any.
For three years they lived as vagabonds. In 1942 the Taihang area was stricken by a drought, and famine followed.
Many people had nothing to eat and begging for food became
impossible. Hua-jung's three children were so hungry and weak
they were unable to walk. Mother and children sat by the roadside. Hua-jung wept bitterly as she embraced her children. A
passerby came up to her and asked her if she was in trouble.
After hearing Hua-jung's story he said to her: "If you have no
objection, I'll find a husband for you. I think this is the only
way for you to avoid starvation."

"I'd rather die than marry again. If I marry again, I'll
probably have to suffer for a few more years. I've suffered
much at the hands of rich men. I only wish I would die soon,"
said Hua-jung as she shed her tears.

"Then, how about giving your children away? They should
have a chance to get away with their lives."

The suggestion made by the passerby reminded Hua-jung of
that sad time when she was sold by her parents in her early
childhood. She said in tears: "My parents sold me when I was
a little girl. Since then, I've experienced untold suffering. How
can I sell my children? I want to live with them. As long as
I can beg a mouthful of food, the children will have at least
half a mouthful.

Knowing that Hua-jung would not sell her children, the man
took leave of her.

Hua-jung and her children finally arrived at Ch'ih-yü-shan.
They were near starvation. Hua-jung said to herself: "The
poor children haven't been well-fed or well-dressed since
they were born. I can't let them die of hunger without doing
anything to save them."

In order to save the lives of her children, Hua-jung decided

to marry again. At Ch'ih-yü-shan there lived a man named
Yang Ts'ang. He was a poor farmer and had no wife. With the
help of a go-between, Hua-jung married him. Yang Ts'ang
owned only half a <u>mou</u> of land. Now, a family of five could
hardly be supported by such a small plot. Even though they
weren't starving, it was very hard to make a living.

A Home Given by Chairman Mao

Yang Ts'ang's family was on the verge of starvation. But
when the Eighth Route Army, the people's army led by Chairman Mao, came to Li-ch'eng <u>hsien</u> in the Taihang area, their
lives were saved. They moved to the village of Hsi-wu, and in
the course of the Land Reform movement, Ku Hua-jung was
the most active in the struggle against landlords. Her family
obtained a plot of land, a house, some farm implements, and
some food. Now Ku Hua-jung had a home of her own. She was
very happy. Day and night she repeated the words: "If it were
not for the help of Chairman Mao and the Communist Party,
I'd not have been able to live such a happy life." Thus Ku Hua-
jung faithfully followed Chairman Mao's teachings and tried to
step out in front at every opportunity. When the Party called
on women to take part in labor, she was the activist in Hsi-wu
Village. When the Party called on farmers to organize themselves into mutual aid teams, she was one of the seven poor
farmers in Hsi-wu's first mutual aid team. She was among
the first group to join the agricultural cooperative in her
village.

Ku Hua-jung lived half her life without a proper home, and
she obtained a home only through land reform. She valued her
new life. She worked hard and practiced frugality. She threw
herself into household matters for she hoped that her family
would thrive. She devoted herself to the agricultural cooperative and the people's commune after she joined this great
communal family. In order to defend the interests of the
people's commune, she worked hard and mercilessly struggled against those who harmed the collective interests of the

commune members. At one time, when Ku Hua-jung and several other women were weeding in the field, she found that San Ch'e and Hsiao Huan did not work energetically. She bluntly told them: "San Ch'e and Hsiao Huan, you've done a poor job. You haven't dug up the weeds near the growing crop. Don't step on the young plants! If everyone does as poor a job as you have, our commune will have nothing to reap and will be unable to support industry."

San Ch'e admitted her mistake and went back to her work. But Hsiao Huan angrily told Hua-jung: "I'm not digging up weeds in your field! You'd better mind your own business."

"Hsiao Huan, are you crazy? The land owned by our commune belongs to all of us. Don't we have to keep it in good shape? If you cheat others, you also cheat yourself." Hua-jung saw she wasn't listening, but she couldn't help trying to persuade her.

"I know what I have to do. I don't need your instructions."

"Then, why did you do such a poor job? Ability is measured by performance. Eloquence will never help us produce foodstuffs."

Some people thought that Hua-jung had quarreled with Hsiao Huan over an unimportant thing. They said to Hua-jung: "She's young and obstinate. Leave her alone. If the production is unsatisfactory, you won't be the only one to lose. You don't have to make her mad."

"I don't mind if I lose anything, but we can't deceive the whole group. (Turning to Hsiao Huan) Hsiao Huan, are you going back to work? If you're not, I'm going to go see the team captain," said Hua-jung.

Knowing that her attitude toward work was wrong, Hsiao Huan went back to her work reluctantly, muttering to herself all the while.

On another occasion, a piglet kept by Hua-jung's team of seven ran into rich farmer Hua T'ung-fa's yard and ate the chicken feed he had left for his chickens. His wife didn't cherish the collective's property. She picked up a hook and broke the piglet's back with it. The piglet died after it returned to the

pigsty. Hua-jung and her neighbors knew the cause of the piglet's death. But they thought that the death of the piglet was
not serious business, so why should they provoke a next door
neighbor they saw every day. So the person who killed the piglet was not found out.

However, during the socialist education movement last year,
Hua-jung's class consciousness was further heightened. She
said to herself: "I don't regard Hua T'ung-fa as my neighbor.
He is a rich farmer. We didn't inform on him simply because
he was our neighbor. We've been nice to our neighbors, but
we've ignored the interests of the people's commune. If others
don't want to get involved, I'll inform his wife. If one doesn't
care and is afraid to provoke others, Chang San will kill the
commune's pig today, and Li Szu will kill the commune's goat
tomorrow. Then how will the commune be able to operate?"
She reported to the team captain the fact that Hua T'ung-fa's
wife killed the piglet. An investigation was soon conducted,
and Hua T'ung-fa's wife was ordered to make amends for the
loss to the commune.

Hua-jung is enthusiastic in defending the interests of the
commune. She is a patriot and also a good member of the
people's commune. When the unified purchasing and unified mar-
keting system was implemented in 1953, she sold 1,200 catties of
grain to the state. Some cadres had advised her to keep more
grain for the consumption of her family. But she disagreed.
She told them: "What function would be served by keeping it
at home? We sell our grain to the state for the purpose of
supporting industry. There's an autumn every year; why fear
that there won't be food enough to eat? We're not living in the
old society. In the old society, girls of poor families often
became maidservants in landlords' houses because their families were threatened with starvation. Such days will never
return!"

CHANG JU-YÜN, KUO SHIH-KANG AND LI CHIA-MING

The tragedy of the people of "Lucky Star Locust"

Yü-k'ou Village is located thirty <u>li</u> south of Ch'in <u>hsien</u> in Shansi Province. In this village lives an old shepherd named Liu Erh-mo. A "five-good" commune member, he is sixty-seven years old this year. Starting at age seven, he has already worked as a shepherd for sixty years. People, concerned about him, have advised him to retire, but he is unwilling to do so. Every day he drives his flock of sheep to pasture, and the sounds of the song "The Communist Party Is Our Benefactor" fill the mountain fastness. Every time people hear him sing the song, they say in admiration, "That poor wretch is getting younger and younger."

Indeed, Liu Erh-mo was a "poor wretch" in the old society. The story of the misery suffered by this "poor wretch" in the old society would take forever to relate. But let us start with the locust tree in his yard.

Chang Ju-yün, Kuo Shih-kang, Li Chia-ming, " 'Chi-hsing huai' jen-chia ti pei-chü."

The "Lucky Star Locust" and the "Three-Locust Hall"

In the old society the reactionary ruling class, in addition to establishing a set of mechanisms for its rule, constantly utilized such feudal superstitions as fortune-telling and geomancy to benumb and enslave the laboring people spiritually. The reactionary ruling class hoped that with superstitions it could suppress the laboring people's fighting spirit and continue exploitation and oppression to its own advantage. Liu Yao-hai, a rich man in Yü-k'ou Village, was an old hand at manipulating these supersititions. He owned herds of cattle and flocks of sheep, fertile farmlands, and a sixty-room mansion. In his courtyard were three old locust trees with leafy branches that filled the courtyard with shade. People who looked up at them from the ditch below could see only the dense darkness of their shade. In order to deceive the masses of the people, Liu Yao-hai said that the three locust trees were a symbol of the "geomantic life" of his house, and he separately named the trees "Locust of Kindness," "Locust of Righteousness," and "Locust of Propriety." Three large characters — San-huai t'ang [Three-Locust Hall] — were painted in blue on a yellow background over the gate. Although Liu Yao-hai always put on his best smile when he created rumors about the "geomantic vitality of graves," the poor people knew his real face. They whispered deprecatory words about him behind his back: "He has a jackal's heart, although he has a man's head and is covered with human skin." They nicknamed him "Killer Liu" and called the "Three-Locust Hall" the "Three-Evil Hall." *

In 1925, for some reason, the branches on the three locust trees in Killer Liu's courtyard started to wither away from north to south. In order to protect the "geomantic vitality" of his house, he built an annex named the "Locust Protector." The wings of the building provided protection for the "Locust of Propriety," the oldest and weakest of the three trees. But this did not help. Killer Liu thought: "Could this mean the end of the 'geomantic vitality' of

---

* 槐 (locust) iş pronounced huai in its second tone, while 坏 (evil) is pronounced huai in its fourth tone. — Tr.

our house of Liu? Perhaps someone has ruined the 'geomantic vitality' of our house." When he looked to the north, he saw a locust tree in Liu Man's courtyard; its branches reached to the sky and its verdant shade filled the courtyard, making Liu Man's property geomantically more prominent than Killer Liu's. Killer Liu did a double take! Then an "explanation" came to his mind: "I let this riff-raff steal the 'geomantic vitality' of my house. I have a plan: this locust of Liu Man's must come down! What is more, this locust can be turned into silver."

Liu Man was none other than this Liu Erh-mo's father. He was timid by nature. He worked for landlords when he was young. He worked hard, but he could hardly support his family with his scanty income. At that time, Erh-mo's grandfather was still living. He was an old man who had seen nothing but poverty and suffering all his life. He began to believe in superstitions. He heard somewhere that the locust tree was a symbol of the lucky star. One day, cherishing a lovely hope, he got hold of the seedling of a locust tree. Pointing at the young plant, he told Erh-mo's grandmother: "Plant it at a 'lucky star' spot in our yard. Let's try our luck. If it grows up, our family will prosper. If it doesn't grow up, we'll be out of luck." She planted the seedling in the southeastern corner of their yard and watered it every day. The young plant thrived. The old couple were very happy, believing that the young locust tree had been planted on a "lucky star" spot. Several years later, the "lucky star locust" had grown into a tall tree with a canopy of leaves.

In spring, the locust tree put forth its tender shoots, which were delicious leafy vegetables. In summer, it produced clusters of delicate snow-white blossoms from which they prepared fragrant and sweet locust flower cakes. On hot days, the locust tree was a gigantic green parasol under which the family loved to sit and eat their meals, enjoy the cool of summer evenings, and listen to grandmother tell stories about the history and the promises of the "lucky star locust." Therefore, everyone in Erh-mo's family regarded the "lucky star locust" as their precious tree and hoped that it would bring blessed days to them.

However, the "lucky star locust" did not bring Erh-mo's family any such "good fortune." On the contrary, they became more and more wretched. Erh-mo's grandfather, who had brought the "lucky star locust" to their yard, did not even have a tattered mat when he went to his grave.

Erh-mo's father, Liu Man, had worked for a landlord from his youth. Working from dawn till dusk, bit by bit, he scratched a two-<u>mou</u> wasteland on a thorn-covered sandy slope into a patch of field; but the crop harvested from the land was not even sufficient to pay the exorbitant taxes, which were "as many as the hairs on a cow," levied by Yen Hsi-shan. There were many people in the family, and even grass roots and tree bark were insufficient to feed them. Liu Man was compelled cruelly to send Erh-mo's eleven-year-old sister to a rich man's home as a child-wife*, to send Erh-mo's eldest brother to work in Ch'in-yüan <u>hsien</u> as a farmhand, and to send Erh-mo's second elder brother, Yü-hu, and his third elder brother, Mo-hui, to tend sheep in neighboring villages. Liu Man and seven-year-old Erh-mo tended sheep for landlord Liu Yao-hai in Yü-k'ou Village.

Liu Yao-hai suspected that Erh-mo was too young for this job: "Can this brat tend sheep? Let him eat grass for a couple of more years." Then, Liu Man sent Erh-mo to Ch'en-chia-kou to "seek the rice bowl." By the time he was nineteen, Erh-mo had turned out to be a good shepherd, so Liu Yao-hai sent someone to fetch Erh-mo back to take care of his sheep.

Soon after Erh-mo had returned to Yü-k'ou Village, Liu Yao-hai "promoted" him to "foreman of the shepherds." "Erh-mo, just do a good job and you'll be well rewarded for it. I'll find a good wife for you."

However, every time Erh-mo asked for his wages, Liu Yao-hai said with an air of "solicitation": "Erh-mo, what a shame it is to waste all your earnings. I'll keep the money for you and pay you interest! If there is a wedding ceremony or a funeral in your home, I'll give you every cent of your pay and the interest."

On this "Shepherds' Day" (the sixth day of the sixth month on

---

* A child-wife is a girl who, for reasons of poverty, is brought up in the home of her fiancé. — Tr.

the lunar calendar), Liu Yao-hai "expressed his appreciation" for the work of his shepherds by giving each of them three tiny loaves of steamed bread. Thinking of his sick grandmother at home, who did not get enough to eat or drink, Erh-mo decided to save the bread for her. Putting the three tiny loaves in his pockets, without a taste for himself, he went back up the mountain to herd the sheep. After the sun had set in the west and he had driven the sheep to fold, he hurried home.

As soon as he came to the yard, Erh-mo heard people weeping in the cave in which the Liu family lived. The crows in the "lucky star locust" were flying about and cawing in confusion. He rushed into the cave and saw his father and mother prostrate, weeping at the side of his grandmother. A small flickering oil lamp threw a dim light through the cave. In the lambent light he could see his grandmother's rigid body lying on the k'ang. He ran to the k'ang and cried bitterly over his grandmother's body. Then, he fell into a dead faint.

When Erh-mo came to his senses, the cave was filled with his poor relatives. His parents were discussing the grandmother's funeral with them.

"I'm afraid we'll have to sell our land!" said Liu Man. Erh-mo's mother objected: "The land is our life. We hoed every inch of that land to make it tillable. How can we go on if we give it up?"

The relatives said: "Don't sell it. We'll get together to help you —" Before they could finish, Erh-mo leapt up in anger: "I know you people are also poor. Please, don't trouble yourselves about helping us. We don't have to sell our land. I'm going to Liu Yao-hai for my pay!"

Erh-mo rushed out of the cave. Fearing that his son might get into trouble, Liu Man called after Erh-mo, "Erh-mo, come back! Come back!" But Erh-mo did not respond, so some of the people helped Liu Man to the house of Liu Yao-hai.

Erh-mo burst into "Three-Locust Hall" and entered Liu Yao-hai's office. Beneath the blood-red light of the lamp, Liu Yao-hai was reckoning on an abacus.

"Manager! My grandmother died. Now, give me my pay!" Erh-mo demanded.

Liu Yao-hai turned his crafty eyes toward him and with a

cunning smile said: "Hey, Erh-mo, you've come at the right time. I've been reckoning accounts. I want to settle the accounts with you!"

After leafing through the pages of accounts, Liu Yao-hai went on to say: "You've herded sheep for me for nine years. In the past nine years, ten sheep, including eight ewes, died. As you know, a ewe breeds one lamb a year, and it takes two years for a lamb to grow up.... So, you owe me at least thirty sheep...."

"No shepherd can prevent sheep from dying. This is just nonsense! Give me my pay," Erh-mo shot back, taking two steps toward Liu Yao-hai.

Liu Yao-hai winked at his lackey, Yang Wu-erh.

"Are you looking for trouble?" asked Yang Wu-erh, as he flourished a stick.

Just at that moment, Liu Man rushed in and pleaded with Liu Yao-hai.

"Please, give us some money or lend us a coffin first. We can settle the accounts later."

Liu Yao-hai squinted his eyes and said: "We at 'Three-Locust Hall' admire virtuous conduct. We have coffins and grave garments. But we can't give them up for nothing."

"I have no money. I can only mortgage my two mou of land."

Liu Yao-hai signaled with his eyes. Knowing what his master was thinking, Yang Wu-erh said: "Liu Man, nobody wants your infertile land. Besides, it comprises only two mou. If you really need the money, you'd better mortgage the 'lucky star locust' in your yard."

When Erh-mo's father heard the "lucky star locust" mentioned, he felt as if his heart had been plucked out. He abandoned the idea of borrowing money from Liu Yao-hai and took Erh-mo home. Then he talked the matter over with his poor neighbors. The following day, Erh-mo's grandmother had a pauper's funeral.

For three days after his grandmother's death, Erh-mo was very aggravated. He leaned against the "lucky star locust" and spoke to himself: "Lucky star locust, lucky star locust! He hasn't paid me a penny for my nine years' work. Now, he has

the impudence to say that I owe him thirty sheep. You tell me.
Is there a Heaven?"

On the fourth day, Erh-mo quit working for Liu Yao-hai
and began to tend sheep for Liu Chiang-hai in Ch'en-chia-kou.

The death of Erh-mo's grandmother had provided no opportunity for Killer Liu to seize the "lucky star locust." Besides,
he had lost Erh-mo, a good shepherd. Hence, he had a grudge
against Erh-mo and tried to find an excuse for insulting Erh-
mo's family.

The "lucky star locust" brought no lucky star to Erh-mo's
family. On the contrary, it planted the seeds of misfortune for
his family.

Five "Yu-tzu"

In the old society there were "wolves inside and outside the
ditch." Erh-mo herded Liu Chiang-hai's sheep for more than
a year, and he was as poor as he had ever been. He had no
money even to pay for medical treatment for his ailing father.
His father's worsening health intensified his grief, and he often
sat on the mountainside in a stupor. His friend Li Erh-mao,
who had tended sheep with him since boyhood, said to him:
"Brother Erh-mo, grief won't help a bit. There's always a way
out."

"All roads lead to death!" Erh-mo said indignantly.

After a while, Erh-mao said: "Brother Erh-mo, I've heard
that fox poisoning is profitable work. A fox fur can be sold
at 500 to 600 cash. Isn't poisoning foxes a way out?"

"But what do I use to pay for 'yu-tzu'?"

"We'll think of a way to borrow some money."

A "yu-tzu" is a poison coated with fat to attract foxes, which
resembles a walnut. After eating this poison, a fox is dead before it goes a hundred paces. Hence, people also call "yu-tzu"
the "hundred-pace pill." Hunters in Ch'in hsien often use this
deadly poison to kill foxes.

Erh-mo sold almost all of his personal effects, even his
tattered cotton shoes, for only sixty copper coins and bought

two "yu-tzu." Erh-mao bought three more with the money raised by pawning his overcoat.

That night Erh-mo was so excited that he could not sleep, and his eyes were open till dawn.

When he heard the cock crow, Erh-mo leaped out of bed, threw on his clothes, carefully felt the five "yu-tzu" in his pocket, and set out up the mountain. All of a sudden, he ran into Liu Yao-hai's lackey, Yang Wu-erh. Yang Wu-erh smiled falsely and told Erh-mo, "The manager has asked to see you." Erh-mo's heart jumped and he wondered why Liu Yao-hai had sent for him so early in the morning. He suspected that this was some kind of a trick.

This time Liu Yao-hai greeted Erh-mo with a big smile and invited him to take a seat.

"I've heard that you want to go up the mountain to poison foxes. Wonderful. A fox fur is worth 500 to 600 cash. Indeed, this is a wonderful idea! But you can't make money if you pay a high price for fake drugs," observed Liu Yao-hai.

"No, these can't be fake," said Erh-mo, taking the five "yu-tzu" out of his pocket.

"Oh, Erh-mo, you don't know how cunning those city people are! They specialize in deceiving us country bumpkins. I'm a good judge; let me see, and I'll be able to tell whether they're fake...," said Liu Yao-hai, snatching two "yu-tzu" from Erh-mo's hand.

When he seized the "yu-tzu," Liu Yao-hai's expression changed: "Our big spotted dog died last night from some unknown cause. Now, I see that you poisoned it with your 'yu-tzu.' What kind of thief are you!"

It happened so suddenly that Erh-mo still did not realize what was going on when lackey Yang Wu-erh dragged a dead dog into the room. "Look, what do you call this!" At that moment, Killer Liu quickly hid the two "yu-tzu." After casting a glance at the dead dog, Erh-mo protested: "I did not kill this dog...."

Killer Liu's eyes widened and he interrupted Erh-mo: "You still don't admit it? You say you didn't poison it? I ask you:

you bought five 'yu-tzu,' yet haven't yet been up the mountain. How is it that there are only three 'yu-tzu' left?"

At this point Erh-mo finally looked at Killer Liu's hands, but he saw only two open hands — there was no sign of the "yu-tzu." Erh-mo was very angry and shouted at Killer Liu: "You have the impudence to swindle me out of my two —" Before Erh-mo finished his charge against Killer Liu, Yang Wu-erh had raised a stick to threaten Erh-mo.

"Erh-mo, confess! I'll thrash you to death if you don't confess," Yang Wu-erh warned.

Erh-mo's father knew that it boded no good when he got word that Killer Liu had sent for Erh-mo. Sick as he was, he hurried off to Killer Liu's house. When he saw what was happening, he feared that Erh-mo might be beaten, and he went so far as to apologize to Killer Liu. But Killer Liu could not have cared less.

"Your son Erh-mo poisoned my best dog. An old saying has it that to strike the dog is to abuse the master. He refuses to admit killing my dog and he hurls abuse at me. He should be charged with a third-degree crime. It is not wise to abuse Liu Yao-hai. Nobody can abuse me, the master of 'Three-Locust Hall.' I won't let it go at this. You have two choices: either you escort my dog's funeral and worship my dog as your ancestor, or we have this dispute settled by the hsien government. We have the testimony of a witness and material evidence. Do you deny it or not?"

Hearing this, Erh-mo clenched his teeth in anger. He jumped to his feet and was about to fight Liu Yao-hai to the bitter end. But Liu Man stopped Erh-mo, fearing that his son might be beaten. He staggered when his son tried to break free of him. But he held on for dear life, and in a few seconds, Erh-mo ceased to make any further effort to rush at Liu Yao-hai, for he knew that a fight would cause his ailing father's condition to worsen. He stamped his feet and bit his lip and said nothing.

A Gross Insult That Can Never Be Forgotten

Erh-mo's poor brethren were indignant over Liu Yao-hai's demand that Erh-mo escort the dog's funeral and worship the dead dog as his ancestor. Some of them thought that Erh-mo should not accept the demand. Others feared that Erh-mo would lose a lawsuit if he refused to do what Liu Yao-hai had demanded. Still others suggested that Erh-mo leave the village to escape trouble and bide his time. Finally, they reached the conclusion that the best thing was for Erh-mo to leave the village. But Erh-mo was unwilling, fearing that if he went alone, his family would suffer. In view of the urgent situation, Erh-mo's friends pushed and pulled him out of the village, no longer concerned with whether he was willing or unwilling.

After hearing that Erh-mo had "run away," Killer Liu maliciously said, "The monk has run away, but the temple is still there." Immediately he ordered lackey Yang Wu-erh to tell Liu Man that he was to conduct the dead dog's funeral.

At his wits end, Liu Man sold his two mou of land. He asked Chang Yao-sheng, a rich man of Ch'in hsien, to act as mediator. In order to get his mediation, Liu Man paid Chang Yao-sheng many compliments and presented him with two silver dollars. Chang Yao-sheng "reluctantly" accepted the role of mediator and promised that he would try his best to settle the dispute. In order to stand in Chang Yao-sheng's good stead, Killer Liu agreed to a funeral banquet on a smaller scale. However, he insisted that the other conditions, that Liu Man escort the dog's coffin and worship the dead dog as his ancestor, stand.

As news of this matter spread, it aroused indignation among Erh-mo's poor brethren. Among them was Liu Ssu-ch'eng, a man with an "explosive temper." He led forty-odd shouting and cursing young men to Killer Liu's main gate.

When Killer Liu met the angry men, a cold perspiration streamed from every pore of his skin. He said defensively: "Kinsmen, sit down, please. We can't discuss matters till each of us takes a seat, can we?" said Liu Yao-hai, who pretended to be calm.

"Why do you want Erh-mo's family to escort your dead dog's coffin and worship it as their ancestor?" Liu Ssu-ch'eng thundered at Liu Yao-hai.

Liu Yao-hai smiled craftily: "Oh, so that is what this is all about. Erh-mo poisoned our big spotted dog, and there is material evidence and the testimony of a witness to prove it. Isn't it reasonable for me to ask him to bury the dog? As for worshiping the dead dog as their ancestor, these were words spoken in anger. Of course, I didn't mean it. No one in our family has ever done such a malicious thing. However, Erh-mo should not get away with poisoning my dog. That dog guarded my main gate for more than ten years. As they say, 'man and beast are one family.' He was loyal to me — I can't stand idly by when he has been killed wrongfully —" He stopped and stared cruelly at Erh-mo's father (who had just come in with the group led by Liu Ssu-ch'eng). Erh-mo's father, a timid old man, was cowed by Liu Yao-hai's angry stare, and could not say anything.

"As for the dog's funeral, I want Liu Man to consult his conscience — just so Liu Yao-hai's face is in no way diminished."

Liu Yao-hai fastened his angry eyes on Liu Man. Knowing that if he refused, Liu Yao-hai would try to kill Erh-mo, Liu Man replied, "I'm afraid I have to do so!"

"Kinsmen, you are all witnesses. Liu Man has made the promise with his own lips," said Liu Yao-hai to the group led by Liu Ssu-ch'eng.

Then Liu Yao-hai turned to Liu Man: "It should be a decent funeral. If you don't have the money for it, I'll lend you money and boards for a coffin. Since Erh-mo is away from home, tell his brother Mo-hai to return to escort the funeral...."

"What! What!" the men shouted angrily.

At this point Yang Wu-erh hurried back from outside and whispered in Liu Yao-hai's ear.

"Yes, I know," Liu Yao-hai said in a voice loud enough for everyone to hear. "Tell the farmhands to clean the house and courtyard and prepare fodder for horses, and make ready the welcome!"

Then he turned to the crowd: "Kinsmen, please go home. We've just been informed by a man from the <u>hsien</u> government that my second son will lead a unit of the security force to our village on business tonight. I have to make preparations for a reception. Excuse me!" He waved to the crowd, fixed Liu Man with an angry stare, and went back into the house.

Liu Yao-hai's second son was a district chief. He had soldiers and influence and was on good terms with the high-ranking officials in the <u>hsien</u> government. When the young men led by Liu Ssu-ch'eng heard that he was coming with his soldiers, their hearts sank. Impetuous Liu Ssu-ch'eng wanted to call Liu Yao-hai to come out again. But when he saw the young men going away in two's and three's, and Liu Man with his attitude of "let it lie, avoid a major incident," Liu Ssu-ch'eng left "Three-Locust Hall," highly agitated.

As soon as Liu Man got home, he sent his wife and Mo-hai's wife out of Yü-k'ou Village to hide from the soldiers, and he dispatched a man to the neighboring village to tell Mo-hai not to come back. Liu Man had made up his mind: "If a calamity comes, let it befall me. I'll not let my son and daughter-in-law suffer it."

Liu Man gave Killer Liu all the money left from the sale of the land. The following day, Killer Liu had a "funeral shed" set up in his courtyard and inside was placed a tablet for the spirit of the dead dog, whose inscription read: "Tablet of the Spotted General, Guardian of Three-Locust Hall." Sacrificial offerings were placed before the dog's coffin.

A funeral banquet was served in the hall. The smiling Liu Yao-hai invited rich landlords and the village headman to sit at the tables.

A little before noon, Liu Yao-hai told Liu Man to perform the rite of three bows and nine prostrations before the dog's coffin. Liu Man refused on his life to do so. Yang Wu-erh and other lackeys forced Liu Man to perform the rite.

Liu Yao-hai's four farmhands carried the dog's coffin. His lackeys forced Liu Man to wrap a white cloth around his head and walk behind the dog's coffin. Liu Man staggered along,

tears streaming down his face. He was not weeping for the dog
but for the poor man being insulted so.

A short distance from "Three-Locust Hall," a group of young
men, led by Liu Ssu-ch'eng and armed with hoes, picul sticks,
and clubs, charged into the mourners. After receiving a blow
on the back, Yang Wu-erh escaped. Liu Yao-hai, the village
headman, and the rich landlords tried to hold them off, but this
made Liu Ssu-ch'eng and his friends even more angry. Liu
Yao-hai rushed off toward home with Liu Ssu-ch'eng and his
friends hard on his heels, shouting, "Hit him! Hit him! Hit
him!" After chasing him all the way to his gate, they turned
back. There were only two mourners on the spot. Liu Ssu-
ch'eng and the others started to smash the dog's coffin with a
hoe, but Liu Man and the village elders, fearing the consequences, quieted them down and sent them home.

After this, Liu Yao-hai had a bitter grudge against Liu Ssu-
ch'eng, and that night, he came up with a sinister scheme against
him. He sent for farmhand Liu Shui-hai, who had buried the
dead dog. "Shui-hai, you've tended my cattle for twenty years
without mishap. I trust you in everything. I know it's very
damp in the barn. The dampness is not good for your health.
I've got an idea. Tonight, you go dig up the dog's coffin and
skin the dog. You can use the dog's fur as bedding. By the way,
don't forget to bring back the coffin." Shui-hai, a simple-
minded man, did not understand, and he asked: "Manager, didn't
you say that 'man and beast are one family'?" Liu Yao-hai
scolded him: "Don't be silly! We keep pigs for meat and dogs
for fur. Do you get me?" On that night, Liu Shui-hai accomplished the mission assigned to him by Liu Yao-hai. Liu Yao-
hai told Liu Shui-hai to keep the matter a secret, and he ordered
Yang Wu-erh to spread the rumor that Liu Ssu-ch'eng had broken
into the dog's grave, that Liu Yao-hai would sue at court, and
that Liu Ssu-ch'eng would be shot to death by the authorities of
the security force. As for the dog's coffin, Liu Yao-hai sold it
to a poor man for an exorbitant price.

The condition of Erh-mo's father became worse immediately
after the humiliating insult. He constantly vomited blood, and

his face became pale and his eyes sank in their sockets. He lay on the k'ang with his eyes open all night.

Early the next morning, Liu Yao-hai sent his lackey Yang Wu-erh with a message: "The manager balanced accounts last night and discovered that the money you gave him was insufficient for even a portion of the funeral expenses. He knows that you're unable to pay all of the expenses. He wants you to clear up your debt by offering him the 'lucky star locust' and by letting you take the spotted general's place in guarding his gate." Then, Yang Wu-erh dragged Erh-mo's father to "Three-Locust Hall."

On the third morning, a squad of "gray dog troops" arrived from Ch'in hsien. Liu Yao-hai gave a reception in his courtyard to welcome the "gray dog troops." After wining and dining them, he bribed them. He sent Yang Wu-erh to help the troops arrest Liu Ssu-ch'eng and other "troublemakers." However, Liu Ssu-ch'eng and the others had already hidden outside the village, and they could not be found. Meanwhile, Liu Yao-hai, taking advantage of the situation, ordered his farmhands to fell the "lucky star locust." They sawed and chopped, and it fell before noon.

After the departure of the "gray dog troops," Liu Yao-hai told Liu Man: "Liu Man, the security force authorities want to build a bridge. By the order of the security force, our farmhands have cut down that locust in your yard." When Liu Man heard that his "lucky star locust" had been destroyed, he felt as if his heart had been torn out. Forgetting everything, he rushed at Liu Yao-hai. But he was stopped and driven out the gate by Liu Yao-hai's lackeys.

Later, Liu Yao-hai persistently demanded that old Liu Man take the dead dog's place in guarding his gate. All Liu Man could think was that this world was a place for the rich, and there was nowhere for a poor man to go. Heartbroken and weary, he left this world, dying of humiliation.

Hearing of his father's death, Erh-mo hurried home thirty days later. His father had already been buried. After his older brother Mo-hai had related to him the cause of their father's death, Erh-mo was speechless. He picked up a vegetable knife and rushed out. Mo-hai seized Erh-mo in his arms and held him back: "As if this isn't enough! Do you want to throw away your life too?" Gnashing his teeth until he bled, Erh-mo laid down the knife. On that night, the brothers went to their father's grave and sat there in silence till morning. Fearing that Liu Yao-hai would do further harm, Erh-mo left Yü-k'ou Village at dawn.

The Old Locust with New Branches

Erh-mo continued his wanderings through the outside world. He again returned to Yü-k'ou Village in the spring of 1938. By this time, the Japanese invaders had occupied Ch'in hsien, and a puppet administration had been set up in Yü-k'ou Village. Liu Yao-hai's second son had been made commander of the puppet garrison force in Ch'in hsien. Erh-mo's home? The cave was in ruins. His mother and his third elder brother Mo-hai had died of hunger somewhere several years earlier. Mo-hai's wife had returned to her parents' house; his eldest brother had been shanghaied in Ch'in-yüan hsien by Yen Hsi-shan's army and was shot when he deserted. His second elder brother, who had stayed in a neighboring village for several years, had wandered away to heaven knows where, and he was probably dead too.

Erh-mo lived alone in the cave. He did not eat. Indeed he did not want to eat. All day long, without crying, without talking, with his father's elm pipe in his mouth, he sat on the broken k'ang with his back against the wall of the cave and his arms crossed. Occasionally a deep sigh escaped him and his eyes blinked, that was all. When his friends talked to him, his only answer was a moan. When they told him how Liu Yao-hai had the "lucky star locust" sawed into planks and how Liu Yao-hai had made a lot of money by selling the planks, Erh-mo stared straight ahead in silence, whereupon everyone said: "Liu Yao-hai has made this wretch an idiot!"

It was getting warmer day by day. Erh-mo sat on the large

stump of "lucky star locust," lost in thought. Sometimes, he wandered alone at night in the bleak mountains nearby. Once, he was away from home for many days, and nobody knew where he had gone. He had heard that the Eighth Route Army had come to Ch'in hsien and that it would avenge the poor people. He had gone to look for this avenging Eighth Route Army! But he failed every time, and when he returned he would sit on the stump of the "lucky star locust" to resume his reverie.

One night he was sitting on the stump as usual, looking at the moon and stars until they started to fade and the eastern hills grew light. He was very tired and decided to go back to the cave to sleep. When he put his hand down to get up from the stump, it suddenly brushed against something soft and damp. "Ah!" he said in surprise. "Ah, 'lucky star locust' has put forth a bud!"

This tiny bud, not three inches long, seemed so fresh in the morning sunshine. It seemed to have boundless life. Erh-mo felt along the whole plant. He felt a warm feeling of spring spread through his whole body like an electric current. His frozen heart thawed; his dead eyes glistened with hope.

The next day Erh-mo began to clean the cave and yard. He built a little wall of broken bricks around the young "lucky star locust" bud and carefully surrounded it with soil, straw, and fallen leaves. Hence, like the young bud of the dying locust tree, his long-cherished hope of liberation grew.

Ch'in hsien was liberated in 1946. Liu Erh-mo saw the daylight again and joined the Peasants' Association. In the Land Reform movement, he obtained land and a house. The poor locust tree which had been handed down from his grandfather began to see happy days.

At the big struggle rally against Liu Yao-hai in 1947, Liu Erh-mo aired the grievances of himself, his parents, and his grandparents and accused Killer Liu of vicious crimes. At the request of the masses in Yü-k'ou Village, the revolutionary government suppressed villainous landlord Liu Yao-hai and eliminated the grievances of Liu Erh-mo, his parents, his grandparents, and the whole village.

After the birth of New China, Liu Erh-mo became active, energetic, and eloquent. He played a positive role in the mutual assistance teams, the elementary cooperatives, the advanced cooperatives, and the people's communes. Now, already sixty-seven years old, he is unwilling to retire. As always, he tends sheep for a production brigade. He often says, "I'm living such a wonderful life — how can you ask me to sit still!"

And what about that "lucky star locust" in his yard? Over the past twenty-odd years, the young bud coming out of the old stump has grown into a big, leafy tree taller and more vigorous than its predecessor.

Old Erh-mo has learned many things under the leadership of the Party. Unlike his grandparents and parents, he does not pin his hopes on the "geomantic life." However, he feels deeply for the "lucky star locust" in his yard. Therefore, when he returns from work, every time the branches of the "lucky star locust" rustle in the breeze blowing from the mountain, Erh-mo eloquently tells his own children: "Listen! Your old great-grandmother is retelling the old stories of the 'lucky star locust.' Children, keep these stories in your minds!"

The story of selling oneself

Kao Ts'ai-yün was born in Wu-li Village, Tun-liu <u>hsien</u>, Shansi Province. She lost her mother before she was two years old. When Tun-liu <u>hsien</u> was stricken by a famine in the spring of 1927, her father, Kao Tseng-wen, took her to escape for their lives. He carried a pole with a large bamboo basket at either end. He put Ts'ai-yün in one basket and a shabby quilt in the other. On their journey they almost starved, and it was with great difficulty that they finally reached Ts'ao-chia-shan in Ta-ning <u>hsien</u>. A stranger in a strange land, Kao Tseng-wen could not find work to his liking. The best he could do was to take a job tending sheep for a landlord named Wang Wan-ch'un.

Ts'ao-chia-shan is a mountain village in a deep forest, and there are many wolves. They often venture forth to attack people and livestock. One day, when Kao Tseng-wen was tending sheep on a grassy mountain slope, a wolf suddenly burst down the mountain into the flock and carried a sheep away in its jaws. Kao Tseng-wen returned to report the accident, but before he could finish his story, the landlord took his shepherd's staff away from him and thrashed him with it. As he beat him,

---

Kao Feng, Chang Tso-pin, Lang Ch'eng-hsin, "Mai shen chi."

he swore at him: "I'm just wondering why the wolf didn't eat you! I'll beat you to death, you poor devil! Your death means less than that of my sheep. Hurry up and get lost!" shouted Wang Wan-ch'un at Kao Tseng-wen.

After a cruel beating, Kao Tseng-wen was fired and sent packing without his wages. Carrying the shabby quilt and holding Ts'ai-yün's hand, he left the house of Wang Wan-ch'un in the biting wind. His eyes were filled with tears and his blood was stirred by indignation and hatred.

After hiking more than twenty li on the mountain path, father and daughter reached Chiang-chün-mu, a small village with but a few scattered houses. They finally collapsed in a deserted cave.

One day Ts'ai-yün's father went to draw water from Chiang-chün Spring near the village. Suddenly, the son of the landlord Wang Wan-ch'un, Ch'üeh Lao-erh, appeared. First, without a word, he struck Kao Tseng-wen's head with a club; and then he cursed him.

"I thought you'd been fed to the wolves. But you're still alive. This spring belongs to my family. Have you paid the tax for drawing water?"

"This water flows from the mountain. It's come into the possession of your family?" Ts'ai-yün's father retorted.

Perplexed for an answer, Ch'üeh Lao-erh kicked Kao Tseng-wen's brimming water bucket over and then kicked him in the chest. Picking up his empty water bucket, Kao Tseng-wen left Chiang-chün Spring. He felt a sharp pain in his chest, and after getting home, he vomited blood. His condition worsened daily.

On the evening of the twenty-third of the twelfth lunar month, Aunt Ch'ao, a kindly neighbor, gave Ts'ai-yün a half pint of rice, from which Ts'ai-yün prepared a bowl of rice gruel for her father. She took it to his side.

"Father, how about drinking some rice gruel?"

"This —" Kao Tseng-wen tried to say something while forcing his eyes open to look at his daughter.

"Yes, Aunt Ch'ao gave us some rice. You eat some!"

He took Ts'ai-yün's hand.

"My child, don't worry about me. I'll feel better. By the way, you have to do what Aunt Ch'ao tells you —"

Before he could finish, Ts'ai-yün's father clamped his jaws shut and closed his eyes and breathed his last. Ts'ai-yün screamed, "Father! —" The rice gruel spilled over the k'ang. Clinging to her father's body, she cried bitterly.

When they heard the sound of crying, Chiao Lao-erh, Aunt Ch'ao, and Niu Tieh-chu — Ts'ai-yün's poor neighbors — ran into the cave. Aunt Ch'ao embraced Ts'ai-yün and tried to comfort the sobbing girl.

Ts'ai-yün clung to her, crying: "Aunt, I don't know how to get money for my father's funeral."

"Her father never had a good day in his life. He can't be almost naked like this when he is going to be buried," said Chiao Lao-erh when he looked at Kao Tseng-wen's thin cotton wadded trousers.

As he talked, he took off his own plain trousers (which were much better than Kao Tseng-wen's) and put Kao Tseng-wen's legs into them. Thinking of her father's miserable death, Ts'ai-yün wept over his body again.

"Ts'ai-yün, don't cry. We'll try to get some money for your father's funeral," said Aunt Ch'ao, wiping away her tears with her sleeve.

Chiao Lao-erh turned to Aunt Ch'ao: "Please, stay here and take care of Ts'ai-yün. Tieh-chu and I will go to get some money and a mat. Even if we were poorer than we are, we couldn't let Old Kao be laid to rest like this."

When Chiao Lao-erh and Niu Tieh-chu went out, it was already midnight. In this isolated little mountain village, wild beasts often came out of hiding. Fearing that Kao Tseng-wen's body might be attacked, Aunt Ch'ao and Ts'ai-yün gathered some firewood and made two fires in front of the cave and also hung a broken bell over its entrance. Aunt Ch'ao brought a white cloth from her house and told the girl to wear it on her head as a sign of mourning.

It was a gloomy night. The feeble flames of the fires flickered in the cold wind. Now and then, the broken bell clanged in a deep tone.

Ts'ai-yün stopped crying and wiped her tears. Looking at her father's body, she said: "Aunt Ch'ao, my father endured many hardships to bring me up to be an eleven-year-old girl. He would go hungry himself so that I could eat. I never had a chance to show my filial piety. ... If Uncle Chiao can borrow some money for my father's burial, I'll pay back the debt by helping him cut firewood during the day and helping you spin thread at night. But I wonder whether Uncle Chiao can borrow some money." She began to weep again.

"Don't worry! He will borrow money for your father's funeral," Aunt Ch'ao comforted Ts'ai-yün.

But when it grew light, Chiao Lao-erh came back empty-handed. He had been to several neighboring villages, but they could not help him.

The following morning, Aunt Ch'ao went out to try her luck. She also came back empty-handed. Niu Tieh-chu went to his aunt's house to borrow money for Kao Tseng-wen's burial, but he too failed.

A greedy dog has a sharp nose. Wang Wan-ch'un's son, Ch'üeh Lao-erh, heard of Kao Tseng-wen's death. He knew that Kao Tseng-wen had an attractive daughter. He sent for his lackey Kao Shih-t'ou and told the latter of his sinister scheme. Then, he sent Kao Shih-t'ou to Chiang-chün-mu on a special mission.

Kao Shih-t'ou was a man with a kind face but a cruel heart. He came to Ts'ai-yün's cave and told her in his artful way: "Ts'ai-yün! When a man dies, he cannot be cried back to life — better that you think about your father's funeral!" Ts'ai-yün did not make a sound.

"When people are poor, there's no solution," observed Aunt Ch'ao.

"There is a solution," said Kao Shih-t'ou.

At this point, Kao Shih-t'ou winked at Chiao Lao-erh and Aunt Ch'ao and went out of the cave. The two took the hint and followed him and he spoke to them softly.

"A man named Li, who is not badly off, lives near the foot of East Hill. He asked me to find a good wife for his second son. I think Ts'ai-yün is qualified. If she accepts the proposal, she

will have a place to live and she can get the money for her
father's funeral. Is this not killing two birds with one stone?
Aunt Ch'ao, what do you think about it?"

Aunt Ch'ao thought and thought: "Ts'ai-yün is a good girl who
is intelligent and competent. Although she isn't my child, to
send her off would break my heart and dishonor me to her father.
But when people are poor, it's a dead end. It isn't living when
you can't even borrow the money to bury your own father's
naked corpse." So she said: "If we know for sure that the child
will be unharmed, the arrangement of a match may be advisable." Chiao Lao-erh also thought that it might be a way out.
After a consultation among the three adults, Aunt Ch'ao told
Ts'ai-yün about the proposal.

"Child, what do you think about this proposal?" asked Aunt
Ch'ao.

"I'll suffer any hardship in any place if I can only get the
money for my father's funeral," replied Ts'ai-yün.

"In that case, Shih-t'ou, you go tell Mr. Li of Ts'ai-yün's
acceptance and bring the money to her first. I'll send Ts'ai-
yün to the house of the Li's after we bury her father," said
Aunt Ch'ao.

"Auntie, as you well know, people have to see what they're
buying before they pay for it," said Kao Shih-t'ou, making a
face.

"Well then, Ts'ai-yün, go take a last look at your father before you go," said Aunt Ch'ao.

Again clinging to her father's body, Ts'ai-yün wept bitterly.
Carrying the old, shabby quilt which she had shared with her
father for the last ten years, she was ready to leave. Aunt
Ch'ao gave her a baked corn cake and said in tears: "Child,
take it and eat it on your journey." She wiped her tears away
with her dress. "Behave yourself when you live in the house
of the Li's. It won't be like it was when you were with your
father...." With tears in her eyes, Ts'ai-yün said good-bye
to Aunt Ch'ao and her other friends.

Ts'ai-yün had wandered everywhere in this region with her
father, so she was no stranger to this mountain road. Kao Shih-t'ou

had told her that they were going to the foot of East Hill; then
why were they going this way? The farther they went, the more
suspicious she became. On and on, Kao Shih-t'ou finally brought
her to Ts'ao-chia-shan. Kao Shih-t'ou led Ts'ai-yün to the flagpole in front of landlord Wang Wan-ch'un's house. Ts'ai-yün
finally realized that she had been tricked. Recalling that this
was where her father had been beaten by Wang Wan-ch'un with
a shepherd's staff, Ts'ai-yün cried, leaning against the flagpole.
She refused to enter this dark and scary prison. But it was already too late. Kao Shih-t'ou grabbed her by the arm and
dragged her in to see Wang Wan-ch'un.

Wang Wan-ch'un was counting his silver dollars in his room.
Seeing Ts'ai-yün at the door, he put the silver dollars on the
desk and said with a cunning smile: "Come in, little lady. Don't
you want money for your father's burial?" Ts'ai-yün stood
silently at the door and dared not enter the room.

"I'll keep the thirty yuan for you as a deposit," said Wang
Wan-ch'un as he showed Ts'ai-yün the silver dollars and then
put them into a safe. "Shih-t'ou will send the other thirty yuan
to your friends to take care of your father's burial."

After exchanging a knowing glance with Wang Wan-ch'un,
Kao Shih-t'ou put the thirty yuan into his pocket and went out
smiling and nodding his head. From then on, Ts'ai-yün was
like a lamb in a tiger's den, and she became Wang Wan-ch'un's
slave girl.

The following day, Wang Wan-ch'un's wife, known as the
Tigress, ordered Ts'ai-yün to fetch the water. With large
water buckets on her back, Ts'ai-yün left the house before
dawn. Ts'ao-chia-shan is the highest mountain in Ta-ning
hsien. Landlord Wang Wan-ch'un's house was on the top, and
the path from the top to the bottom was fifteen li long. If one
descends the mountain on this path, two li beyond the end is
Chiang-chün Stream. Ts'ai-yün filled the buckets and started
to climb the hill with the buckets in her hand. On the steep slope
she came back up the mountain, step by step. Halfway up the
mountain, she encountered Chiao Lao-erh coming from another
direction.

"Uncle, is my father buried?" asked Ts'ai-yün.

"Child, that's what I've come to talk to you about. No, he is not buried yet. I've already asked carpenter Sun to make a coffin for your father. As for the money, Kao Shih-t'ou said that you had taken it!'"

"Wang Wan-ch'un bought me with sixty yuan, but he only gave me half. Last night I saw him with my own eyes give thirty yuan to Kao Shih-t'ou to pay for my father's funeral. Why did he take the money and not give it to you?"

Chiao Lao-erh heaved a sigh and said with hate in his voice: "Ah! Those two have been colluding all along to cheat us! My child, never forget this hateful thing."

Ts'ai-yün fainted away in shock and disappointment. Chiao Lao-erh finally revived her and soothingly said: "Child, vexation won't get you anywhere. I'm sure the two bastards will die a violent death. As for your father, I'll go back and think of something with the others. We'll get money even if we have to break our cooking pot. By the way, tell Wang you need a day off to go home and escort your father's coffin to the grave."

It was perfectly natural that on this day Kao Tseng-wen's only daughter should attend to his funeral. Why shouldn't she be allowed to bury him? But as hard as Chiao Lao-erh argued, it was no use. The Tigress said: "She was sold into my house. Since when can she say 'go' and then 'go!'"

"You say she has been sold into your house, but we haven't seen a penny," retorted Chiao Lao-erh.

"Your words are against your conscience. You can ask Ts'ai-yün," roared the Tigress, while scowling at Chiao Lao-erh and pounding on the table.

"When did you give me the money?" Ts'ai-yün spat back at her.

The Tigress picked up a broom and hit Ts'ai-yün with it.

In short, Ts'ai-yün was not even permitted to witness her father's burial.

Although Ts'ai-yün was young, she was forced to cook, wash clothes, draw water, and turn a mill every day. She worked from cockcrow to midnight, and she was badly fed. One day, a few tiny loaves of steamed bread were stolen by a cat. These tiny loaves were sacrificial offerings to the ancestors of the Wang family. The Tigress accused Ts'ai-yün of stealing them. Then, the Tigress had Ts'ai-yün hung up and flogged her, first with a stick until it broke, then with a pair of metal chopsticks until they bent, and then with a leather whip, until she was forced to confess.

Hers was a bitter lot, with nothing but misery.

As the 1932 Spring Festival drew near, the Tigress forced Ts'ai-yün to grind two piculs of flour out of wheat in seven days and spin four ounces of thread out of cotton every night. How could a fourteen-year-old girl, thin as a stick and poorly fed and unable to sleep soundly, shoulder such a heavy work load? On the sixth day, Ts'ai-yün was exhausted when she turned the mill. The Tigress knocked her down and beat her. Ts'ai-yün could not stand it and screamed, "Help! Help!" Then, the Tigress put hay into her mouth and beat her with a brick, each blow leaving a bloody bruise. Ts'ai-yün fainted away. The Tigress said, "She's faking. Bring some water!" And she had cold water dashed on Ts'ai-yün's face. As soon as Ts'ai-yün came to, she was forced to turn the mill again.

In the summer of her seventeenth year, Ts'ai-yün was taken ill. She lay in the barn, unable to rise. The Wangs not only did not want to give her food, they even forced her to go up the mountain to cut grass. She was hungry and thirsty. Having no choice, she had to eat wild plants and drink water from a brook. She was sick like this for more than ten days.

Before Ts'ai-yün had recovered completely from her illness, the Tigress again forced her to cut firewood. Most parts of Ts'ao-chia-shan were covered with thorns. The red-graveled path through the thorns had been trodden out by Ts'ai-yün in the previous seven years.

It was drizzling steadily that day. Carrying the load of firewood on her back, Ts'ai-yün climbed the hill with faltering steps. Exhausted, hungry, and thoroughly soaked, she fell to the ground and lost her senses.

It was raining hard when Ts'ai-yün regained consciousness.

She dared not linger any longer. As she shouldered her load, she discovered that a bundle of firewood had fallen down the mountain. She was too fatigued to go down and come up again with that bundle. Just at that moment, a young man of Ts'ao-chia-shan passed by on his way home from his job as a day laborer. He carried the bundles of firewood for her and accompanied her to the entrance of their village.

When Ts'ai-yün entered the house, without waiting for her to say a word, the Tigress gave her a slap in the face.

"Where have you been that you're getting back just now!" the Tigress scolded Ts'ai-yün.

"I was walking —" Ts'ai-yün tried to explain.

"Shameless bitch! I know you were trying to allure men at the roadside," the Tigress cut in, while giving Ts'ai-yün another slap in the face. From the outside of the gate, Ch'üeh Lao-erh overheard his mother's scolding. His licentiousness aroused, he came in and said to the Tigress: "She is stubborn. It is no use thrashing her." Then, he told Ts'ai-yün, "Why aren't you hurrying to the barn to feed the donkeys?" Controlling her temper, Ts'ai-yün returned to the barn. She was so tired that she lay down on the hay. Ch'üeh Lao-erh followed her into the barn and raped her. . . .

Ts'ai-yün wept bitterly in the dark barn. The past events — her father's death from kicking, the collusion between Wang Wan-ch'un and Kao Shih-t'ou, fatigue, hunger, flogging, insult — flashed across her mind. Finally, she had a vague and confused recollection that she had a cousin in her native town — Wu-li Village. She told herself: "I must leave this cage and find him. That is the only way I will survive." With this plan in her mind, her strength began to return, and clenching her teeth, Ts'ai-yün cleared the back wall and escaped.

It was raining hard on the night of her escape, and the road was slippery. Ts'ai-yün, barefoot and hungry, went straight over the mountains, avoiding main roads and villages and seeking narrow paths. She walked for seven days and seven nights before finally reaching Wu-li Village in Tun-liu hsien.

When Ts'ai-yün entered her cousin's house and called out,

"Brother!" her cousin Kao Tao-yüan did not recognize her.
She was disheveled, haggard, and emaciated. Ts'ai-yün announced to him: "I am Ts'ai-yün, who ran off to Ta-ning hsien
nine years ago! And she told how her father had died, how she
had sold herself, and how she fled from the Wang house. The
cousins hugged each other and wept bitterly.

A few days later the Tigress heard the news and set out for
Wu-li Village on donkey back, accompanied by a servant. Before they entered the village, her donkey's braying could be
heard throughout it. When Ts'ai-yün heard this familiar sound,
she was terrified, knowing that the Tigress was coming.

With her parasol open, the Tigress came riding up to the gate
of Kao Tao-yüan's house on her braying donkey. She dismounted
and hollered out:

"Kao Tao-yüan, return her to me!"

Kao Tao-yüan casually replied: "Return who?" as he came
out of his house.

"Return Ts'ai-yün!" the Tigress said in an even sharper
tone.

"Are you referring to my uncle's daughter? Isn't she working in your home? Why do you come to ask me about her?"

"Don't play dumb with me! Are you going to return her to
me or not?"

Ts'ai-yün trembled in fear as she hid herself behind a pile
of firewood in Kao Tao-yüan's kitchen. She made up her mind:
"I'd rather die than return to Wang Wan-ch'un's house." When
Ts'ai-yün heard the Tigress order her servant to search the
house, she thought: "To go back with her is worse than death,"
and she sneaked into the backyard and jumped into a well....

The Tigress could not find Ts'ai-yün in Kao Tao-yüan's
home, and she threatened to bring a lawsuit against him. Indignant at the Tigress's actions, Kao Tao-yüan's kinsmen and
friends closed in on her.

At this moment Sung Yu-chih, Luan Shang-shu, and ten-odd
other hunters were just returning from the mountains. After
hearing the news, they hurried to Kao Tao-yüan's house. Sung
Yu-chih shouted in a booming voice: "Hold it!" Although the

Tigress, a few yards away from Sung Yu-chih, was somewhat frightened by his thunderous voice, she shouted back: "Is this a revolt? I'll deliver all of you to the hsien government!" Sung Yu-chih jumped on the roller of a mill. Immediately he cocked his homemade rifle and fired off a shot. The Tigress stood agape with astonishment.

"Now, I'll tell you the truth: I have her here. Abandon the idea of taking her back as your slave!" Kao Tao-yüan warned the Tigress.

Then Sung Yu-chih fired another shot into the air. When the Tigress realized that her servant had already disappeared, she mounted the donkey and fled.

It was already dark. With torches in their hands, Kao Tao-yüan's kinsmen and friends looked for Ts'ai-yün. But they could not find her. Kao Tao-yüan and Sung Yu-chih went to the backyard and cried: "They are gone. Ts'ai-yün, come out!"

The well into which Ts'ai-yün had jumped was a dry one, and its bottom was covered with grass. Ts'ai-yün had lost consciousness as soon as she jumped into it.

Now, Ts'ai-yün regained consciousness. When she heard her cousin call her, she answered: "Cousin Tao-yüan, I'm here." Kao Tao-yüan and other men went to the well, while they kept calling, "Ts'ai-yün! Ts'ai-yün!" But there was no answer. Ts'ai-yün, who had come to, had fainted again. By torchlight, they saw a dark shape in the bottom of the well. Sung Yu-chih found a strong rope. He asked the others to lower him down by rope, and they finally got Ts'ai-yün out.

Although she soon heard that Ts'ai-yün was in her cousin's home after having been rescued from a well, the Tigress dared not to molest Ts'ai-yün, for she knew that the poor people in Wu-li Village were of one mind. Thus, Ts'ai-yün's seven years of hell came to an end. She helped her cousin and his wife in farming, spinning, and raising silkworms. In 1938 she married the man who had saved her, the hunter Sung Yu-chih.

After their marriage the young couple worked hard to improve their livelihood. However, in the darkness of the old society, you broke your back with work but still went ill fed and ill clothed.

Gaze at the stars, gaze at the moon, how easy it is to see the Communist Party. Ts'ai-yün saw the daylight again, and she was purged of her suffering. In the Land Reform movement, her family obtained land, livestock, and a house. The livelihood of her family was further improved by the collectivization and communization of agriculture.

Ts'ai-yün is over forty now. She has a family of ten. Five of them are "five-good" commune members. Every time she talks with her husband about their happy life of the present, she invariably says, "If it were not for the Communist Party's help, I would have stopped being Ts'ai-yün long ago."

Land

I

It was already dark after the end of the struggle rally against landlord Liu Te-ch'ing. As people gradually drifted away from the rally site, I stayed there, squatting on the ground.

"...Six <u>mou</u> of fertile land and a seven-room house to Li Chin-pao's credit...."

"Six <u>mou</u> of fertile land...."

These words announced by the president of the Peasants' Association were still ringing in my ears.

Could it be true? Would that six <u>mou</u> of land belong to me?

As I stood up to leave, my legs felt light as air under me. Before I knew it, I was already in Liu Te-ch'ing's courtyard. Looking at the big house, its brick wall, and the stone steps leading to the front door of the house, I thought to myself of the many poor people with whose blood and tears this house was built! I recalled that many years before, my mother took me to this place to present a gift to the Liu family and we dared not enter this house. But now the owner was named Li! The pattern of the bricks of the wall could not be seen in the deepening darkness. I touched the wall with my hand, and I found

---

Yüeh Feng, Wang T'ien-ch'i, "T'u-ti."

that the warmth of the sun of the day still lingered.

I came out of the courtyard and with one breath had run to the land in Ch'ao-chia-fen. The six mou of land was covered by growing wheat that Liu Te-ch'ing had already sowed. Now even those straight young sprouts had been distributed to me. I walked around this fine tract of land, which was level and extensive. I took a handful of the unfrozen soil from the land and could feel its richness. In my heart I thought of this land — for which my grandparents and parents shed how much blood, how many tears. How much they toiled and how much they suffered without seeing any gain for themselves. But now this land had come into my hands. I plucked two young wheat plants and chewed them. The leaves of the plants after the frost tasted rather sweet.

On the day we moved into Liu Te-ch'ing's house, my mother sent my younger brother to buy a portrait of Chairman Mao and put it on the wall facing the front door. Then she asked a literate friend to write a pair of matching scrolls to go on either side of the portrait.

"How about 'joyfully engage in production' and 'happily plan good harvests'?" he asked as he picked up his brush.

"Good!" my mother said. "But I was thinking of parallel sentences: 'poor people always remember Chairman Mao' and 'tenant farmers never forget land troubles.'"

"Look," he said. "Now that you own land and a house, there should be happy words. Why put up words of 'troubles'?"

"We should not forget our past hardships," my mother said with a long sigh.

I asked him to write the parallel sentences as my mother wished, since they came from deep in her heart.

Indeed, my grandparents and parents underwent much sufferings. Their stories of suffering are endless.

II

I was born in the northern part of Ch'ao-lao-an Village, Lin hsien, Honan Province. As soon as I was able, I began to

follow my mother to the fields. She went in front digging up
the earth. I came behind breaking up the clods. Every day, by
noon, my mother sat on the ground, so tired that she did not
even want to eat. She only drank water in huge gulps. As usual,
I massaged her back, waist, and legs. Once I asked her, "Why
doesn't my father show up to help us till the land?" Immediately, her eyelids reddened, and I never dared ask that question again.

Every time it rained there were leaks in our thatched roof.
We were busy rolling up our mats and preventing our pillows
from getting wet, but nothing kept dry. In the confusion, my
grandmother usually started complaining about my father.

It was a rainy day. Our thatched roof was leaking badly. My
grandmother was in a fret.

"I've told your husband a hundred times that he should find
some time to repair the roof, but he won't listen! He is a
farmhand employed on a regular basis, but he is not a slave of
the Yangs. As his father said as he was dying, never hire out
to the Yangs. Never fill the rice bowl of that house. Ha! But
he won't listen! Has he forgotten how his father died? The
Yang house killed him with overwork and anger. And he went
to his grave with nothing.

"Little Chin-pao, whenever you and your younger brother
argue, remember what your grandfather said. Don't go to the
Yang house. Don't fill the rice bowl of that house," said my
grandmother, hugging my brother and me.

"Of the twenty or thirty families in this village, which one
doesn't till the Yangs' land? If we don't till, what will we eat?"
my mother explained.

"Does the rice of the Yang house taste so good? Sooner or
later, bad things will happen!" my grandmother warned.

After it was all said, my grandmother began to weep, my
mother began to weep, and my younger brother Yin-ao and I
also began to weep. And that rain was still falling through our
thatched roof.

Later, I was told that my ancestors had passed down two
mou of land. After the birth of my father and his two brothers,

grandfather could not support his family with the meager income from the crop on this small plot. Although he should never have done it, he leased several mou of land from the big landlord Yang Chen-kang. He worked hard, the suffering increased, and the back taxes accumulated into a large debt. Yang Chen-kang had the nickname of "Black Snake," and this venomous viper coiled around our family. He wanted to recover the debt by seizing our two mou of land. My grandfather could never give up that land, so he had to work for Yang Chen-kang and pay back his debt with his wages. He toiled for more than twenty years, but he was unable to clear the debt. When my grandfather died, we still had that two mou of land, which was still insufficient to feed us. Like my grandfather, my father leased a plot of land from Yang Chen-kang. The same things happened again. My father incurred a debt and had to work for Yang Chen-kang and repay his debt with his wages. And so we slaved for the Yang house from one generation to the next.

After the birth of my second younger brother, Ch'üan-pao, which meant another mouth to feed, my mother worried all the more. One night, my father returned from work and stood by the k'ang and stared at me and my two brothers. He said: "One generation after another! Will they too have to lease land, run up debts, and forever be trampled under the feet of others?" My mother thought he looked strange, and asked about it. But he would not say anything. At that time, my father often got together with some of his poor friends. Often he did not come back until midnight. We did not know what he was up to. As soon as someone called him from the yard, he hurried off. This added much to my mother's worries. She feared something would happen.

When you fear something will happen, it always happens.

In the fall of 1928, Chiang Kai-shek sat in his court in Nanking and he began to brutally suppress revolution. At this time, Yang Chen-kang was the district chief for the Kuomintang. Many people were apprehended and murdered by his band of men, armed with rifles and knives. Early on the morning of December 20, someone knocked at the door and cried: "Oh no,

Chin-pao's father has been murdered!" Immediately, my
mother pulled me and carried my younger brothers to the river
bank. Oh god! My father's body was there. His throat had
been slit, his abdomen had been ripped open, and his bowels
had come out. My mother wept hysterically over his body. I
was then six, Yin-pao was four, and Ch'üan-pao was not yet
three months. We too wept. My grandmother rushed over, and
she sat on the ground and wailed. There was not one of our
fellow villagers who were standing around us that did not weep.
They finally managed to get my grandmother and mother home.
Shortly after we got back, Yang Chen-kang came to express his
condolences.

"What a shock! Old Li is dead. Hasn't the murderer been
arrested? As the district chief, I promise you the murderer
will be arrested. Old Li and I have been friends for more than
twenty years. I can't stand idly by. I'll loan you some money
for his funeral and some boards for his coffin," said Yang
Chen-kang with false kindness and piousness. My grandmother
and mother thanked him for his offer but told him that we would
be unable to pay back the debt. Yang Chen-kang scowled at
them and said: "You think I'll blackmail you?!" They were so
frightened they could not say a word.

A few hours later, Yang Chen-kang's servants brought ten
yuan and some thin boards to my mother. One of the servants
asked her to sign a paper, which stated: "...equivalent to five
piculs of grain. If I cannot pay off the debt and interest by next
fall, I will surrender my two mou of land at the south of the
village to the Yang family."

Yang Chen-kang had said that he wanted to arrest the culprit,
when in fact the culprit was Yang Chen-kang himself. My father
and his friends had aroused his suspicion. He was fearful lest
the poor people in the village unite against him. He decided to
"show his strength by making the first move." In order to kill
one to warn a hundred, he ordered one of his lackeys to murder
my father. He also planned to seize our two mou of land.

When grandmother heard this story, she grew both angry and
vengeful. Her heart was overflowing with the death of her hus-

band and her son, but she could not even tell the world. She lay on the k'ang mortally sick. She died a few days later.

My brothers and I helped mother till our land. We worked from before dawn till after dusk. We were cultivating two plots of land: one was our own two mou of land; the other was the four mou of land which my father had leased from Yang Chen-kang. Sometimes, kindhearted neighbors herded their cattle over, stopping by to help out. One of them said: "If you reap a good harvest, you'll be able to pay back your debt. But I'm afraid you'll still have the food problem."

"I'll clear up the debt even if we starve or die of exhaustion. The two mou of land which has been handed down through generations is our roots. I can't give it up," my mother said with determination.

Who would have imagined that God himself would have his eyes closed to us? It did not rain for more than three months, and the wheat sprouts were becoming yellow and wasted. My mother's hopes for paying off our debt were crushed, and she fell sick from worry.

After the autumn harvest, Yang Chen-kang seized our two mou of land and took two large earthen vessels and a large wash basin away from us, which in no way diminished our debt. Yang Chen-kang also sent someone to fetch me back so that I could work for him as a shepherd and thereby work off our debt with my wages. My mother was infuriated and she swore at the man: "Black-hearted black snake! You taxed us for using a few mou of your land. You tortured my father-in-law to death. You murdered my husband. You seized our land. Now, you're going to lay your hands on my son!" She recalled my grandfather's words: never make a living by filling the rice bowl of the Yang house. But if she did not send me, they would have no mercy. So, Mother finally sent me off to him with her tears.

Yang Chen-kang's house was located in the southern part of Ch'ao-lao-an Village. The big sentry tower attached to his house could be seen from afar. As I entered the gate, I could see his guards in their quarters — they were all fierce and mean-looking. A strong rope was hung from an old locust tree in his backyard. A few days after I started working for Yang Chen-kang, my uncle was seized and taken to the backyard. He too had leased a plot of land from Yang Chen-kang. Yang Chen-kang wanted to seize my uncle's land because he could not pay the rent, but my uncle refused to give up his land. Yang Chen-kang's lackeys hung my uncle up from the locust tree with that strong rope and flogged him with a whip. He was covered with blood, but he still refused to give up his land. Then, Yang Chen-kang showed his "benevolence" by dropping his demand on my uncle's land. Instead, he wanted my uncle to make repairs on his house. My uncle had never done this sort of work before. Before long, he fell from the roof and died.

Another uncle of mine also died a tragic death. He was secretly murdered over some quarrel with one of the Yangs' lackeys. He was buried under a cliff, and his body was not discovered until the earth was washed away by a torrential rain. Knowing that it was hopeless to try to make a case to avenge his murder, his four sons and their mother gave up their house and left the village for Shansi. My aunt died of cold on the journey.

Many families in the village similiarly leased land from Yang Chen-kang and were consequently ruined by him. I was a young boy, and the tragic stories made me mad but also scared me. Whenever I saw Yang Chen-kang, I ran away. One day, however, I ran across him as I was bringing the sheep back, and he had a couple of his bodyguards with him. I dared not flee lest the sheep scatter.

Yang Chen-kang's eyes bore down on me.

"Have you learned how to tend sheep? Show me your shepherd's whip!" said Yang Chen-kang, snatching the whip from me and thrashing me on my back and legs until they burned with pain. "I'll flog you to death, you little bastard!"

"Why do you flog me and call me names?" I retorted angrily.

"Why?! It's because you're your father's son," said Yang Chen-kang, while giving me another flogging.

He threw my shepherd's whip to the ground and went away laughing loudly.

My back was badly swollen, and I could not lie down to sleep that night. It was half a month before it healed. After being flogged twice in three days, I fled home, no longer able to bear this crime. Embracing me and crying, my mother said: "Son! Ours is a cruel fate!" What is fate? Is it that evil people can beat and kill others while good people are afflicted? I refused to recognize such a fate!

"The Yangs are our enemies. Grandfather was right. We should not fill their rice bowl," I said.

"Since we can't keep ourselves alive in this place, let us too go to Shansi," said my mother.

III

In the spring of my eighth year the whole family fled to Shansi. My mother held my youngest brother Ch'üan-pao in her arms and carried our shabby clothes on her back. My younger brother Yin-pao and I carried baskets and jars, between two dog sticks. We begged as we went along. In the farming season, we worked as part-time farmhands. After the harvest season, we collected corn, grain spikes, and decayed sesame seeds that had been left behind. After passing through P'ing-shun, Hu-kuan, and Ch'ang-t'ai hsien, we finally arrived in Pei-chia Village, Ch'ang-tzu hsien, Shansi Province. In the village there were several families who had also come from Lin hsien. They helped us settle down and lease a plot of land. My mother shuddered at the thought of leasing land, but we had to make a living. We brothers could tend cattle for landlords, yet our scanty wages would be insufficient to support our family, and we would suffer flogging again.

So, against her inclinations, my mother leased four mou of land from a big landlord named Liu Te-ch'ing. The rent for each mou was six pecks of grain (a peck of grain weighing fifteen catties). Under normal conditions, the average annual crop per mou was about one picul. Mother explained to me that if we worked hard we might be able to reap 1.2 or 1.3 piculs of grain per mou. However, when we went down to take a look at the land, we were startled by its barrenness. It was covered by wild grass in which wolves could hide and by spiked weeds. With a hoe I dug six inches deep into the earth. It was not the red soil which is good for crop growing, and there were sand and gravel in the soil. Then, I dug a deeper hole and I found that the roots of the grass reached down more than one foot into the ground. How could we grow crops in this barren land? However, the lease had been signed. We had to cultivate it. Alas, it was as hard as the skin on a skull.

Every day, all four of us, mother and sons, dug up the roots of the grass from dawn to dusk. Blood blisters appeared on our palms. Little Ch'üan-pao was only five years old, yet he could pick pieces of sand and gravel and throw them away. At night, after my brothers and I went to sleep, mother spun thread to get some extra income, often working all night. In early morning, Yin-pao and I went out to gather manure to spread on the field. The blood and sweat we shed that spring paid off; our crop grew well. In the autumn harvest, we reaped eight pecks of grain per <u>mou</u>. Mother said to us: "Now you kids will have some hearty meals."

Shortly after the harvest, Liu Te-ch'ing and his men drove up in a big cart pulled by a mule. Our neighbors helped mother prepare a good meal for the master. We presented 2.4 piculs of grain to Liu Te-ch'ing. He measured the grain with a <u>tou</u>* which he had brought from his house. How strange! The 2.4 piculs had become only 2.1 piculs.

"Mother, I'll go to borrow a <u>tou</u> and we'll measure it again," I said.

"Come back here!" said Liu Te-ch'ing angrily. "It's an established rule that when I am repaid rent in kind, the grain is measured with my <u>tou</u>."

"I'm afraid your <u>tou</u> is not regulation. It's unfair."

"Your meager rent in kind won't repay the trouble of making a larger <u>tou</u>," he said, getting angrier.

"I'll go borrow one and then we can compare the one with the other."

---

*<u>Tou</u> is a dry measure, often called a peck in translation. — Tr.

Liu Te-ch'ing was speechless with anger. He stood up and
made a threatening gesture toward me. Some of our neighbors
held him back and advised my mother to give him two more
pecks of grain. That closed the matter.

After six months of hard work, we had less than six pecks
of grain left after paying the land rent, meaning that each of
the four of us had only about twenty catties. We would not even
be able to make it through the winter. Moreover, officials from
the government came wanting money or wanting grain. And the
village authorities wanted this tax or that tax. My mother said
with a deep sigh, "No matter where we go, we poor people have
no way out!"

As the New Year drew near, Liu Te-ch'ing came to the village to press for his rent and to press his debts. He came up
to our door.

"Hey! Family of old Li, I want to farm that plot of land myself. You find something else." My mother invited him to come
in and sit down, but he would not.

"If we can't farm it, we can't farm it. Anyway, no matter
how much we weary ourselves over it, we can't make it pay,"
I told my mother.

"But we've dug up roots of grass. Besides, the soil is improved. The land will yield more food next year. Why does
he want to have the land back?" Mother complained.

Having heard of the news, our neighbors came to ask Mother:
"You haven't offered Liu Te-ch'ing a New Year's gift? If you
don't give him a gift on New Year's and other festivals, he will
take his land back." The best my mother could do was borrow
five catties of wheat flour and buy two catties of meat. My
youngest brother Ch'üan-pao, not understanding, clamored to
eat the meat. My mother spanked him, but she herself cried
after it was over.

Mother and I entered the main gate of the Lius' house. As
soon as Liu Te-ch'ing saw that we were bringing presents, he
hurried forward. He kneaded the flour to see if it was of a
fine texture. He examined the pork to see if it was fresh. He
finally said: "A present, handsome or humble, is a token of

gratitude to a master. If you want to continue your lease on that four <u>mou</u> of land on the back bank, I have no objection. Work a little harder and apply a little more manure and till it well. Fertile land is beneficial to you and me."

We had to send gifts for each of the eight festivals and each of the four seasons.

We offered Liu Te-ch'ing glutinous rice dumplings at the Dragon Boat Festival, moon cakes at the Mid-Autumn Festival, and meat and flour at New Year's. Every time we offered him presents, we had to go hungry for a few days.

The following year, we applied to the land as much manure as we could possibly gather. We went back and forth, carrying it to the field. The soil grew rich and changed its color. We had a comparatively good harvest that fall. We paid our rent and had a few good meals. My mother told us: "Fight on! August Heaven does not turn its back on misery!" Then, spring came. Again, we applied much manure to the field. Just before we started turning up the soil, Liu Te-ch'ing came to our field and said: "Family of old Li, this year I want to farm this plot of land myself. You find something else." My mother was startled and wondered what to do.

"Master Liu, I'm not in arrears with my rent and I offered you presents for the seasons and the festivals.... My whole family has worked to improve this soil. You cannot repossess it," my mother protested.

Liu Te-ch'ing laughed: "You have no right to make that decision. The land belongs to me. I can cultivate it at any time I want. Tomorrow, I'll send my men to turn up the soil."

Seeing through Liu Te-ch'ing's sinister scheme, I was about to rush on him and take a few bites of him. Convinced by the flattery of a friend of a friend of my mother's, Liu Te-ch'ing finally agreed to lease us another plot.

The land comprised a rounded plot of seven <u>mou</u>. It did not have many weeds or much gravel, but it was covered with thorns. Besides, it was very marshy. When it rained hard the land became so soggy you could not go into it. My mother feared that we could not farm all seven <u>mou</u>.

"Obviously, he's out to harm us. He wants us to dig a drain-age ditch for him. If we want to farm this land, be it one <u>mou</u> or seven <u>mou</u>, we have to dig a drainage ditch," I said.

My mother got angry: "If you don't rent land, you can't sur-vive. If you do rent land, your fate lies in the palms of your landlord's hands."

The four of us, mother and sons, dug a drainage ditch in the field and leveled the ground on both sides of it. When everyone else was sowing seed, we were not yet turning up the soil. It would soon be too late. Fortunately, our neighbors came to help out, and we soon finished the plowing work. The following year, Liu Te-ch'ing repossessed this field too when he saw how nicely it had taken shape.

For thirteen years we cultivated the land leased from Liu Te-ch'ing. But during this period our leased land changed six times. Every time we had improved the soil of Hon-an, Hsiao-yen, Hsi-ling, Hao-ch'iang, and the other plots, he took the land back. If he did not keep it for himself, he leased it to another tenant farmer for a higher rent.

The ten <u>mou</u> of land at Hao-ch'iang was the worst that Liu Te-ch'ing leased to us. This tract of land had been leased to a farmer named Wang. In one year he had to sell a cow and a donkey to clear up his debt arising from the land lease. The land was covered by weeds whose roots stuck deep into the soil and which even resisted the plow. Liu Te-ch'ing said that he would lease this plot to us for lower rent — 4.5 pecks of grain per <u>mou</u>. We three brothers, older now and stronger, struggled to dig up the weeds, but we could not dig up all the roots. When the young plants of grain grew up, the weeds sprang up with them. That autumn we reaped a total of only four piculs of grain from the ten <u>mou</u>, which was not even enough for the rent. We asked Liu Te-ch'ing to lease another tract of land to us, but he flatly refused. The harvest in the following year also fell short of what we needed for the rent. In the third year, 1943, there was a great famine. We had not a scrap to eat. Yin-pao and I left home. I became a field hand employed on a temporary basis, and he became a blacksmith.

The greater the famine, the happier the landlords. Of course, Liu Te-ch'ing was no exception. He called up debts and demanded rents. If someone had a little land, it became the Lius'. If someone had a house, it became the Lius'. He raised the price of rice even higher — seven hsien-yang per peck. That year the house of Liu made a fortune. He boastfully told others that he owned land all along the road between Ch'ang-tzu hsien, P'ing-shun hsien, and Lin hsien, and that he need not step on the land of others when he went out. We had neither house nor land. Yet, Liu Te-ch'ing did not leave us a single room or an inch of land. On a day in December, he brought his men and forced his way into our home. When he could find nothing valuable except five pints of chaff and three pints of corn, Liu Te-ch'ing tried to take the shabby quilt which warmed all four members of our family. My mother and Ch'üan-pao desperately held it. His lackeys beat them and threw them to the ground. Then, they took our quilt, chaff, and corn away. Nothing was left in my home. Even those baskets and jars that we had brought from our old home were smashed. My mother was so upset that she fell sick and could not get out of bed. Every time I went home to see her, she recited to me: "Not filling the rice bowl of the house of Yang, we filled the rice bowl of the house of Liu. What's the difference? Leasing land is like walking on the blade of a sword."

When we could not go on, I went to An-tse-shan to herd someone's cattle and plow someone's land. Those were not happy days. But our whole world changed after the Eighth Route Army came to that place. Landlords no longer dared beat people working for them. With the intervention of the work teams, the landlords dared not be unreasonable. For the first time in my life, I could breathe freely. Members of the work team came to see me and chat with me. Seeing that I was barefooted, they told me that I should ask my employer to give me shoes, whereupon my employer reluctantly had a pair of new shoes made for me. He gave me a two-yuan raise when they said that my pay was too low. I saw with my own eyes the rallies that were held there, rallies at which they struggled against dishonest land-

lords until they owned up to their crimes. I also heard of a
new policy being propagated: tenant farmers could unilaterally
cancel land leases, and the landlords would not be allowed to
repossess the leased land; land rents were lowered across the
board. I could not keep back my tears. Truly, the Communist
Party is the savior and benefactor of poor and miserable people. Had the Eighth Route Army come to Ch'ang-tzu a few
years earlier, would my mother now be bedridden? Had it
come to Lin hsien ten-odd years earlier, would my father have
been murdered by Yang Chen-kang?

I found a comrade from the work team, and said: "Please,
go to Ch'ang-tzu quickly. The people there simply cannot survive."

The comrade from the work team grasped my hand and said:
"Right. Ch'ang-tzu will be liberated. The whole country will
be liberated."

He also told me that a land reform program was going to be
implemented and that the landlords' land would be redistributed
among the poor and they would no longer have to pay land rents.
I was beside myself with joy.

The Eighth Route Army became stronger and stronger every
day. Liu Te-ch'ing was so scared that he stayed home, not
daring to show his face. The poor people eagerly awaited the
Eighth Route Army every day. Before long, the Japanese aggressors surrendered, and our region was liberated.

IV

Land Reform, struggle against landlords, and the redistribution of land were carried out immediately after the liberation.
Our family obtained good land and moved into Liu Te-ch'ing's
house. Looking at Chairman Mao's portrait and the pair of red
scrolls, my mother said: "Chairman Mao! Chairman Mao! If
it were not for your help, we poor people would have died. How
long our ancestors have waited for this land. But it is only now
that we finally have our own land." Then, she told us brothers:
"Obey the orders of the Communist Party and Chairman Mao.

Never ever forget the hardships we suffered when we leased land." When the village authorities called on young people to join the army, without waiting for anyone else to mobilize, my mother let my youngest brother Ch'üan-pao join the army.

~Now that we were farming our own land, we worked even harder. Our crops grew well, and we did not have to pay land rent with our autumn harvest. This made our farming work finally pleasant.

In August of 1950, I had the honor of becoming a member of the Chinese Communist Party. After joining the Party and being educated by the Party, many truths became evident: collectivization was the only way to eliminate exploitation and poverty. In a village some ten li from ours, because of difficulties caused by a natural calamity, some farmers sold the land that had been distributed to them during the Land Reform movement. Again, they leased plots of land from other farmers. They simply "went down the same old road!" Therefore, the Party called on farmers to organize themselves into mutual assistance teams, and I actively participated. In 1952, we organized a cooperative, and I was the first to join. In the first year, our cooperative had only thirty-odd households, seven domestic animals, and a little more than 300 mou of land.

"Chin-pao! It has been a long struggle for your family to get the six mou of land. Now, as soon as you join the agricultural cooperative, your land is no longer yours," someone said.

"You're right that the six mou of land is no longer mine, but you don't see that the cooperative's 300 mou of land also belong to me. Furthermore, it is only by becoming part of the cooperative that my six mou is safe. If I didn't, who knows, in a few years it might be seized by someone else," I explained.

After collectivization the scale of our cooperative grew rapidly, and the foodstuff production also increased rapidly. Our average annual production per mou had been only 180-190 catties. However, by 1963, after several years of intelligent management, our average annual production per mou reached 613 catties. This was a yield I had never even dreamed of!

After the changeover to a people's commune, our cooperative

acquired tractors. With these tractors, we leveled raised paths [that used to mark the boundaries between small plots] through the fields, transforming countless small plots into a vast tract of farmland. The production team sent me to help out as a tractor operator. How happy it makes me to look from the seat of the tractor out over this seemingly endless expanse of farmland.

"Old Li! Now that it's a vast farmland, can you tell which part of it is your plot?" tractor operator Comrade Yang jokingly asked me.

But my answer was perfectly serious.

"Old Yang, in the past, our family did not own even a tract of land the size of the palm of your hand. And now? Just look around you. This vast farmland you see belongs to me. And it belongs to everyone."

A cave with two entrances

Aunt Yang Chan-mei, sixty years old this year, is a "five-good" commune member of the Wang-chai Production Brigade of the Wang-chai Commune in Ch'in-shui hsien, Shansi Province. The following is a portion of her family history.

Hsü Yin-yüan, Yang Chan-mei's husband, worked for a landlord named Li Shih-chün as a farmhand because he owed him seventy-two strings of cash. He hoped that by working steadily for Li Shih-chün, in a few years he could clear his debt with his wages. However, his wages were so scanty that every year when he figured his accounts he found that he had only enough to pay the interest on the seventy-two strings of cash. Yang Chan-mei took care of their children and cultivated a four-mou plot of barren land on a slope. She and her four children lived in abject poverty.

There was a drought in the spring of 1937. That fall they reaped a scanty crop of corn, and even though they went out to pick wild vegetation, they soon ran out of food. With each passing day of winter, the situation grew worse. All day long, the children wailed with hunger. Hsü Yin-yüan was

---

Chung-kung Ch'in-shui hsien wei pan-kung-shih, "Liang-kung yao."

compelled to borrow money from Li Shih-chün again.

Li Shih-chün was the villainous landlord of Wang-chai Village. In addition to exploiting the toil of poor peasants and making them pay high land rents, he robbed their sweat and blood with his policy of "partnership in breeding livestock." This so-called partnership in breeding livestock meant that he split the cost of buying domestic animals and shared their ownership with the poor peasants, who needed the livestock but did not have enough money to buy them. After the stock were purchased, the peasants were responsible for caring for them, and Li Shih-chün could use them at any time he wished. Whenever an an-imal produced young, they were divided equally between the two partners. If a peasant could not continue the "joint care," Li Shih-chün would force the peasant to sell the livestock to him at a depressed price. Through this practice, Li Shih-chün owned more than 100 head of livestock. The increasing number of livestock naturally created a need for more barns. Figuring that building new barns would be too costly, he used every scheme he could think of to seize peasants' living places to ac-commodate his increasing herd of domestic animals.

Li Shih-chün was delighted when Hsü Yin-yüan came looking for him. He thought to himself, "Here is a good opportunity."

He spoke slowly: "Oh, you've come to borrow money. There will be no problem as we've known each other for many years. However, I haven't yet seen a cent of that seventy-two strings of cash you owe me. I haven't called up the debt because I know you're poor and you've got a big family to support. Be-sides, you're tending my sheep. Now, you want to borrow mon-ey from me again. Let's make this perfectly clear: you can borrow the money, but this time I want something from you as a pledge for the loan."

Hsü Yin-yüan was so poor that he could no longer sustain his family. What could he possibly have that would do as a pledge?

He said entreatingly: "Master, we really have nothing to offer you as a pledge.... Please, lend me some money! I promise to pay you back after next year's harvest."

Li Shih-chün closed in: "You have a cave with two entrances, don't you?"

Immediately Hsü Yin-yüan knew that Li Shih-chün wanted
him to place a mortgage on his cave. He realized that if he
placed a mortgage on his cave, he risked eviction and the pros-
pect of his family's being homeless. If he refused to offer his
cave as a pledge, there would be no way to get through the
crisis confronting him. He finally came to a conclusion, thinking, "When the pot leaks, you have to plug the hole." He had
to keep his family from starvation. So he hardened his heart,
promised to pledge his cave, and asked Li Shih-chün to lend
him thirty strings of cash. Li Shih-chün prepared a mortgage
deed which stated that the owner of the deed would automat-
ically get possession of the cave on mortgage if the debtor
failed to pay off the mortgage within two years of the signing
of the contract and that the debtor should pay the owner of the
deed an annual interest of 30 percent on the loan. Having no
choice, Hsü Yin-yüan put his signature on the mortgage deed.

In order to pay off the mortgage on their cave, Hsü Yin-
yüan and his wife worked even harder than before and lived a
very frugal life. Every day, Hsü Ying-yüan tended Li Shih-
chün's sheep, and Yang Chan-mei, in addition to working their
four-mou plot of land, sold eggs and saved enough money to
buy a large earthenware pot. Early every morning, she prepared ho-tsu-fan* and sold it on the roadside near the entrance of the village. Nevertheless, by the end of the year they
had only put aside a couple of strings of cash — another year
like this and they would never be able to buy back their mortgage.

In order to alleviate their burdens and give their eldest
daughter Hsiang Hsiang a way out of all this, the couple be-
trothed her to Chang Lin in Wan-li Village. Chang Lin's father
gave Hsü Yin-yüan a bolt of native cotton cloth as a gift.

At this time, because his herds were constantly increasing,

---

*Ho-tsu-fan is a porridge made with bean noodles, millet,
and greens. — Tr.

Li Shih-chün was thinking about seizing Hsü Yin-yüan's cave
before the expiration of the term of the mortgage deed. Knowing that Hsü Yin-yüan had received a gift for his daughter's
betrothal, Li Shih-chün sent two of his servants to Hsü Yin-
yüan to call up the debt. The servants told Hsü Yin-yüan that
since he had received a lot of money for selling his daughter,
he must immediately pay off the mortgage on his cave. Hsü
Yin-yüan and his wife tried to explain, but the two sons of a
bitch refused to listen to the couple and began to search the
cave. Cooking pot and bowls were overturned. When the two
came upon the bolt of native cotton cloth sent by the Chang
family, Yang Chan-mei and her husband rushed forward and
firmly grabbed one end of the roll of cloth. While they were
struggling over the roll of cloth, one of the bastards unleashed
a string of invectives against Hsü Yin-yüan. Indignant, Hsü
Yin-yüan gave him a push. On purpose, the man fell over a
stone block at the door, to make it look as if he had been knocked
down by Hsü Yin-yüan. The other one shouted: "You have the
nerve to hit him!" and knocked Hsü Yin-yüan to the ground.
The two intruders got away with the bolt of cloth before Hsü
Yin-yüan could get up.

   Hsü Yin-yüan went to Li Shih-chün to appeal to reason, but
Li Shih-chün refused to return the cloth or make the cloth a
partial compensation for Hsü Yin-yüan's debt. Instead, he
charged Hsü Yin-yüan with repudiating his debt and beating
his servants. He demanded that the couple apologize for their
rude acts by giving a party and that the Hsü family move out
of their cave immediately. Of course, Hsü Yin-yüan rejected
this demand. Although the two argued for a long time, no settlement was reached. Li Shih-chün told one of his lackeys to
throw Hsü Yin-yüan out of his house, and he promised to bring
a lawsuit against Hsü Yin-yüan before the hsien government.
Li Shih-chün had connections with the judicial section of the
puppet hsien government in Ch'in-shui. A few days later, the
judicial section of the hsien government dispatched a runner
to Wang-chai Village to summon Hsü Yin-yüan to appear before the court in Ch'in-shui. Hsü Yin-yüan and his wife were

simple and honest persons. Thinking that a hsien yamen was a place where reason prevailed, a place that would not oppress the poor by deciding on giving their cave to Li Shih-chün, the couple went to the judicial section full of hope. During the hearing of the case, the judge spoke in mandarin, and the couple had a hard time understanding what he said. This judge was even more unreasonable than Li Shih-chün had been. He inferred that since Hsü Yin-yüan had failed to pay off his debt of 72 strings of cash for so many years, he would be unable to clear up his new debt of 30 strings of cash before the expiration of the terms of the mortgage deed. The judge told Hsü Yin-yüan that the interest on the loans would be reduced if he transferred to Li Shih-chün the ownership of his cave and the land on which the cave stood. Hsü Yin-yüan refused to give up his cave and land and promised to find ways to pay off the 30 strings of cash before the expiration of the term of the mortgage deed. When Hsü Yin-yüan told him what Li Shih-chün's servants had done, the judge's face hardened, and he said to Hsü Yin-yüan: "You and your wife beat and wounded Mr. Li Shih-chün's servants. I'll make a decision on this matter after examining their wounds." Li Shih-chün jumped up to ask the judge to order Hsü Yin-yüan to immediately clear up his debts of a total of 102 strings of cash as well as the interest amounting to 50 strings of cash. Li Shih-chün said that if Hsü Yin-yüan could not clear up his debts, he would accept the Hsü family's four-mou plot of land as a pledge. The judge nodded as he listened to Li Shih-chün make the request. As it dawned on him that his land would be taken away from him, Hsü Yin-yüan uttered an exclamation of shock. The judge pounded at his desk and charged Hsü Yin-yüan with "disrupting the court." Then, he ordered the court policemen to throw Hsü Yin-yüan down to the ground and give him a sound thrashing with clubs. Finally, it was the judge's decision that Hsü Yin-yüan should transfer the ownership of his cave and two mou of land to Li Shih-chün.

After being evicted from their cave, the Hsü family spent the winter in a shack built on the bank of a dry riverbed near

Wang-chai Village.

Hsü Yin-yüan already had consumption from too strenuously tending Li Shih-chün's sheep. The losing of the lawsuit aggravated his condition, and his wracking cough never stopped. In 1940, he contracted typhoid and became bedridden. In order to pay her husband's medical expenses, Yang Chan-mei sold their youngest son Hai-huei to a middle peasant named Ma Hsi-liang. However, the money she got from the sale of her son could not save her ailing husband's life. Hsü Yin-yüan died before long.

Although Yang Chan-mei was down, she was not out. She saw things more clearly now: landlord Li Shih-chün was the mortal enemy of her family; the hsien yamen was not a place where reason prevailed; the hsien yamen was hand in glove with Li Shih-chün. She harbored bitter hatred for them. But what could she do about them in the old society? She could only give vent to her bitter frustrations by telling the poor people in her village of her sufferings and cursing Li Shih-chün.

Li Shih-chün, knowing there was nothing Yang Chan-mei could do, told his lackeys to spread rumors that she was a witch, that she had strangled her husband and sold three of her children, and that anyone who kept company with her would have bad luck. Li Shih-chün was trying to use the villagers' superstitions to divert their attention from what he had done to the Hsü family and his attempts to isolate and get rid of Yang Chan-mei. But the poor people in the village did not believe the rumors because they knew the cause of Hsü Yin-yüan's death and the circumstances of the sale of Yang Chan-mei's child. Only a few rich peasants, to please Li Shih-chün, spoke ill of Yang Chan-mei behind her back and sowed seeds of discord between her and the other villagers. Because of drought in the previous two years, Yang Chan-mei could not make a living by cultivating her two-mou plot of land. Thinking that her family would be unable to live on in Wang-chai, she took her eldest son and youngest daughter and fled to southern Shansi....

In 1944, Yang Chan-mei returned to Wang-chai following the liberation of Ch'in-shui. During the Land Reform, an eight-room house, a ten-<u>mou</u> plot of fertile land, and an ox were distributed to her. In the same year, she married again. In the mutual assistance team and the people's commune, she actively responded to the calls of the Party. She was selected as a "ten-year meritorious commune member" on October 2, 1962, which marked the tenth anniversary of the people's commune in Wang-chai. She was old, but she always participated in the study of culture and often asked young people to read newspapers to her. She told them: "If we don't study hard, how can we have socialist construction? Besides, I want to be a tractor operator." According to a decision by the brigade Party branch in Wang-chai, commune members of old age, in consideration of their age, would be excused from attending evening meetings, and they would later be informed of proceedings of the meetings by their neighbors who attended the meetings. However, old Aunt Yang Chan-mei would not hear of it. She attended every evening meeting. When others tried to persuade her not to attend evening meetings, she always said with a smile: "Each of you has two legs, and so do I. I walk a little slower than you do, that's all!" Chang Fang-i, the branch secretary, also urged old Aunt Yang Chan-mei not to attend evening meetings and promised to personally tell her afterward what was discussed. She did not want to bother him, so she asked a friend of hers to buy her a small kerosene lamp in the town of Ch'in-shui. She told her friend, "Now I can attend those evening meetings."

In the spring of 1958, Hsü Hsiao-hu, Yang Chan-mei's eldest son, came back to Ch'in-shui to visit his mother. He told his mother and stepfather that when they were ready, he would take them to Peking to see the sights. Yang Chan-mei and her husband Kao Chen-hung were so excited that they did not sleep a wink on the three-day trip.

On the night of their arrival in Peking, Hsü Hsiao-hu said to the old couple: "Father and mother, you haven't had a sound sleep for three nights. You'd better go to bed early tonight. We'll go to T'ien-an-men tomorrow." But they were not sleepy. They would not go to bed until Hsü Hsiao-hu had given them a

detailed description of T'ien-an-men. It was already midnight,
and the traffic noises gradually subsided. Old Aunt Yang Chan-
mei could not sleep. Landlord Li Shih-chün's seizure of her
cave and her cloth, the oppression of the poor by the hsien
government, Hsü Yin-yüan's death from frustration and anger,
the wandering and begging of herself and her children passed
before Yang Chan-mei's eyes. She turned over in bed and
found that her husband, his eyes open, was also deep in thought.
Then, the old couple started talking. They talked about everything from past to present. And the more they talked about
how fortunate they were to be able to visit Peking, the more
excited they became. Before they knew it, the first light of
dawn was upon them. They got up and put on their clothes,
ready for the trip to T'ien-an-men.

Hsü Hsiao-hu led the old couple to T'ien-an-men in the early
morning. Old Aunt Yang Chan-mei's eyes were wet with tears
of grateful joy when she saw great leader Chairman Mao's
portrait. Holding her son's hand in her own, she told him:
"Son, it is Chairman Mao who has saved our family. We must
forever follow that old man, and forever follow the Party!"
Then, she straightened her clothes and headdress and made a
respectful bow to Chairman Mao's portrait. She said in a
whisper, "I wish you, my old friend, a long, long life!"

The wheelbarrow

In a corner of the yard of Cheng Ch'ing-yin, head of the Hsin-chuang Production Team of Pai-mu Commune in Ch'in-yüan hsien, there stands an old wheelbarrow covered with a mat which appears to the eye to have a history of at least thirty years. Whenever he is asked about the story behind his wheelbarrow, Cheng Ch'ing-yin replies with a deep sigh: "Ah! It's a long story. This wheelbarrow has borne the blood and tears of my family."

"I was born in Chang-ch'ing hsien, Shantung Province; I can't even remember the name of the village. I left my native place when I was only seven. I had heard my father say that we owned no land. My mother and elder brother cultivated a three-mou plot of land leased from a rich man, and my father worked for that rich man as a farmhand. Because there were so many mouths to feed, we never had more than one meal a day — we lived in poverty. Chang-ch'ing hsien was stricken by a drought in my sixth year. The naked ground stretched for a thousand li. There was no harvest. The five members of my household had to eat bark and wild vegetation. At that time, bark and wild vegetation were very difficult to find because

---

Ti Ch'iu, Ma An-jen, Sung Yen-chou, "Tu-lun-ch'e."

89

there were many poor people, and no one had enough to eat.
Children wailed from hunger; adults were so hungry that they
couldn't straighten their backs. We were on the verge of starving
to death. At his wit's end, my father borrowed several strings
of cash from our landlord and bought some kaoliang flour to
momentarily fill our stomaches. But it was those several
strings of cash that were the downfall of our entire family.
Our landlord was a black-hearted man. He exploited poor people by lending money at an exorbitant rate. If you borrowed
ten strings of cash from him, the interest was one string of
cash. Fearing that you would not pay your interest, he would
deduct it beforehand, and only give you nine strings of cash.
Month after month there was interest, and interest was added
onto interest. By the next year, those several strings of cash
of my father's debt had become more than ten strings of cash.
It was already December, but everyone in my family still wore
summer clothes. My father could not pay his debt. The landlord came every day to put pressure on us. My father was terribly upset and did not know what to do.

"On December 28, my second uncle rushed over to tell my
father: 'Elder brother, I heard the master say that you have
to clear up your debt before the end of the year. He's coming
tomorrow to collect the debt. He said that if you don't pay off
your debt he will seize you....' The whole family was terrified by the news. After much thought, we realized we had no
choice: we had to flee to a remote place.

"That night the northwest wind blew in gusts. We slipped
out of our home, fighting back our tears. Had there been the
slightest hope, we would never have left! My father pushed
this wheelbarrow. Fearing that it would make a racket, he
poured some water on the axle because we had no oil. My
mother, holding my two-year-old brother in her arms, I, and
even all our property (really nothing more than a shabby quilt,
a battered cooking pot, and three bowls) were crammed into
the wheelbarrow. My elder brother, only thirteen then, barefooted and wearing a pair of thin trousers, pulled the wheelbarrow. My mother put her nipple into my younger brother's

mouth because she feared that he might cry and our flight would be detected by the landlord's lackeys. The water on the axle of our wheelbarrow dried up after we had traveled five or six li. It began to creak and moan as if it were complaining about its heavy burden or about the injustice done to us. After a while, my elder brother dropped the rope from his shoulder and said in tearful dejection: 'I can't walk anymore. Father, how much farther? Where are we going?' My father also stopped pushing the wheelbarrow. He looked back and saw that no one was coming after us. He looked ahead and saw range after range of mountains far in the distance.

"'To Shansi. I've heard that Shansi is a province with high mountains and plenty of land, and that the people are few and kind. We can turn several mou of wasteland into farmland. If we work hard and make a living by farming, Heaven will never destroy our way of life.'

"Then he and my brother, one pushing, one pulling, picked up the wheelbarrow and we continued on our journey, in and out, up and down the mountains. At first we slept by the side of the road, then in derelict temples, and lived the life of mendicants.

"The third day after we set out was New Year's. And we stopped in a village. Homes of the rich people in the village were brightly lit up by lanterns and candles, and firecrackers popped all night long. Out of those black lacquered doors came men in red and women in green to make the cheerful rounds of New Year's visits to their friends. Their children played and watched the lantern parade. But we stayed in a derelict temple at the west end of the village, weeping, sighing, and trembling beside a dead fire. The firecrackers seemed to be exploding in our hearts. It was almost noon. My father looked at us as we sat there starving, and turned to my mother: 'You'd better take the children out to the village. Perhaps you can get your hands on some food if you meet some kindhearted people,' suggested my father.

"My mother carried my baby brother and my older brother and I followed her as we begged for food from door to door.

People in the homes with red silk lanterns hanging in front turned a cold shoulder to us and gave us nothing. Poor families who had little more than we were sympathetic but had no left-over food for us. We had almost nothing to show for our whole morning's efforts.

"Mention of begging makes my scalp creep. In begging for food, we had to call every man 'uncle' and every woman 'aunt,' no matter how young they were. Sometimes, after a whole day of going back and forth, we had only half a meal or no meal at all to show for it. We were just skin and bones, hardly looking like people at all.

"On January 6, we arrived at Wang Village in Tun-liu hsien, Shansi Province. It was already dark when we entered the village. Several people stood on the roadside. My father asked a man in a long gown for shelter from the cold. He gave my father a dirty look and went away. Later, an old shepherd named Tu, seeing our plight, led us to his sheepfold. There was no k'ang in the sheepfold, and we could see stars through the holes in the roof. But we felt warm, as if we were in a new house with a k'ang. We were heartily grateful to old shepherd Tu for his kindness. But when his master, a malevolent land-lord, found out that we were in his sheepfold, he came running in to tell us to leave the place. He reprimanded old shepherd Tu: 'This sheepfold is not yours. It's unlucky to keep beggars here just when we're beginning the New Year. And by the way, do you know what kind of people they are?'

"My father did not want to get old shepherd Tu into trouble and started pushing the wheelbarrow out. But the old man stopped him: 'You can't find any shelter in such cold at this time of night. Where can you go?' Indeed, we had no place to go. My father and old shepherd Tu entreated the landlord for mercy. Finally, the landlord allowed us to spend that night in his sheepfold.

"The following day, as soon as the day broke, the landlord came to drive us out of his sheepfold. Thank goodness, old shepherd Tu had found a disheveled grass hut for us, and we settled in.

"When spring came, and the leaves on the wheat plants were just turning green, and when everyone was busy spreading manure on the fields, the landlord who had driven us out of his sheepfold came to our shack.

" 'Old Cheng, have you had lunch?' landlord Tuan asked with false kindness.

" 'What is there to eat!' my father replied, getting angry.

"The landlord forced a smile onto his face.

" 'You've got to find some way.... You mean you'll do nothing until you and your family have starved to death?... Well, come over to my house and I'll give you a peck of corn.'

" 'Mr. Tuan, don't beat around the bush. Please, say what you want.'

" 'All right. My young son wants to visit our relative in Ch'ang-chih. All of our horse-drawn carts are off in Han-tan on business. I'd like you to run him over with your little cart.... For your service, I'll give you one peck of corn. Of course, I'll cover all the expenses on the trip.'

"My father thought that it would be better to get a peck of corn by running over to Ch'ang-chih than to beg for food in the village. So he accepted the offer. The following morning, the landlord's boy came over carrying two quilts with him, with which he lined my father's wheelbarrow. He then made a canopy out of a blue wool mat. He sat down, my father started pushing, and they were off. The road was muddy because of a steady spring rain for the last two days. Since the landlord's boy was a fat fellow, the wheel of the wheelbarrow sank deep into the mud. My father pushed the wheelbarrow with all his might, his back arched, and still it would hardly move. The landlord's boy sang a little song: 'I am a young master. Having had enough tea and a good meal, I am thinking about nothing but going through the wilderness to find some beautiful girls....' After what turned out to be a very easy trip, they reached Ch'ang-chih. The landlord's boy put up my father at a small inn and then disappeared for the whole night. The following morning, he came back to the inn and said to my father: 'Hey, Old Cheng, let's go home. It's closer by the shortcut.'

"Still a stranger in Shansi, my father thought it best to let the landlord's boy direct him. It was a tortuous mountain road. For ten li they passed through no villages. For twenty li they heard no dogs barking or cocks crowing. In the afternoon, they reached a mountain settlement with about thirty households. My father was tired and hungry, and he wanted to take a rest in the village before proceeding. The landlord's boy would not allow him to do so. As they argued, a man from a nearby customs checkpoint came to inspect the wheelbarrow. This checkpoint was set up to intercept contraband. The man turned the wheelbarrow over and found a small box underneath. This box was stuffed with opium and had been sneaked onto the wheelbarrow by the landlord's boy without my father's knowing it. The man from the checkpoint, without asking any questions, took the boy, the man, and the wheelbarrow into custody. A fat officer at the checkpoint invoked the 'law of the land' and charged my father with smuggling narcotics. My father could not prove that the box did not belong to him, and he was finally cast into prison.

"As for the real narcotics smuggler, the landlord's boy, he bribed the fat officer, who not only let him go free but also ordered a horse-drawn cart to take him home. Upon returning to the village, the landlord's boy told my mother that he had given my father ten yuan, that my father decided to stay at Ch'ang-chih to start a small business, and that he was not coming back. He also said that she would not get the peck of corn promised by his father! 'You can buy three pecks of corn for ten yuan.' My mother thought this very strange. After all, wasn't father a family man? She knew that something had happened to my father. She was a simple woman and all she could do was fret, weep, and say nothing for several days. Alas! Misfortunes never come one at a time. At this point, my baby brother starved to death. She hugged my baby brother and would not let go, crying and laughing hysterically and talking nonsensically to him. It was a long, long time before she finally began to come to her senses.

"We passed the days neither dead nor alive. One dark

September night, we suddenly heard the creaking sounds of a
wheelbarrow in the distance. My father had come home! How
happy we all were to see him! But my mother burst into tears
when she looked at him: his worn face was marked with slashes;
his hair was about three inches long; and his body was covered
with red and black bruises.

   "'Amitabha Buddha! You've come back.... If something
happens to you, I'll die also.... Where have you been? Why
do you look like this?'

   "'It's all the fault of that rich landlord and his boy,' said my
father. 'Do you know in what business that boy is? He is an
opium smuggler. We were stopped at the checkpoint in Shih
Village, and the opium was discovered. The landlord's son
was released because he bribed a fat officer at the checkpoint
with ten yuan. They made me a scapegoat and put me into
prison. They gave me nothing to eat. Many times I was brought
before the court and flogged.... However, there are also good
people in the world! When I was in the prison, I got to know a
guard at the checkpoint named Shih Te-fa. He too comes from
Shantung. He had been sold by a rich man into conscription.
He was mistreated by that fat officer at the checkpoint. He
also told me that he had seen me once in a derelict temple in
Li-ch'eng. I told him about the wrongs I suffered. He was
very sympathetic, and he was always trying to help me get out,
but he didn't have a chance to do so. A few nights ago, the fat
officer came back from a brothel dead drunk. The other guard
at the checkpoint had fallen asleep. Shih Te-fa quietly opened
the door of the jail and told me to follow him out. He had a
bayonet in his hand. He gave me another one and asked me to
help him kill the fat officer. Hating the fat officer as I did, I
immediately followed Shih Te-fa toward the fat officer's room.
When we two were at the door of his room, we heard him snoring. My heart beat fast and my hand trembled. After getting
into the room, I could hardly make myself stand still. Shih
Te-fa gave me a reassuring glance and went over to the bed.
Shih Te-fa clamped his left hand over the fat officer's mouth
and plunged the bayonet in his right hand into the fat officer's

breast. The fat fellow died without a sound. Then, Shih Te-fa
took me to the other guard's room. We put a towel into the
guard's mouth and bound his hands and feet with ropes. Shih
Te-fa wrote a note and put it on the body of the fat officer. He
told me that the note said: 'Killed by Shih Te-fa.' When we
were about to leave the checkpoint, he told me to take the
wheelbarrow with me. I said that I was not worried about my
wheelbarrow and I just wanted to get out of there! He said:
'Don't worry, there are only the three of us here, and we are
far from town.' I followed Shih Te-fa for a while, pushing my
wheelbarrow. Then, he parted with me. I asked him where he
would go, but he did not tell me .... By the way, did the landlord give you a peck of corn?'

"My mother shook her head and wiped away her tears.

"The following day, my father went to landlord Tuan for the
money for that peck of corn. As soon as he saw my father,
Tuan threatened him: 'Old Cheng, so you've escaped? Let's
go to town! Come on!' Fearing that this would implicate Shih
Te-fa in the killing of that fat officer at the checkpoint, my
father did not dare go. So he paid compliments to landlord Tuan
and left.

"Using his knowledge of my father's escape from jail as
blackmail, landlord Tuan forced my father to work in his paper
mill. In addition to work during the day, my father had to prepare pulp at night. He trampled on the mixture of waste paper,
wheat stems, and lime, and his feet and legs were burned by
the lime. Every day, he worked till midnight and he was so
exhausted that he could get no sleep. He overworked himself
into illness and his legs were badly swollen. Then, landlord
Tuan sent my father home and refused to give him pay on the
grounds that my father was not doing his job. My father was
sick for many months. In December, we pushed our wheelbarrow and fled to the mountains of Ch'in-yüan hsien.

"In Ch'in-yüan hsien there are many mountains and rocks;
there are many wolves, snakes, tigers, and leopards. There
are few people; there are few roads; there are few trees. My
father figured that because there were so few people, rich men

and government agencies would be few too. So we decided to come to Ch'in-yüan.

"Before we left Wang Village, my parents wanted to see my older brother, who was working in a blacksmith shop in Lu Village. The proprietor of the blacksmith shop was a rich peasant. My brother had been hired at thirty yuan for three years. By this time, he had been at the blacksmith shop for only a year. My parents wanted to take him to Ch'in-yüan, even if his one year's pay was forfeited, but the proprietor refused to let my elder brother quit or even visit us before our departure.

"It seemed that the twelfth month was a fateful month for us. We always fled hardships in the twelfth month. For rich people, New Year's was a time to enjoy their best food, wear their most beautiful clothes, and sit on their k'angs, snug and warm. For us, it was walking through endless snow-covered fields. The mountains in Ch'in-yüan are high. Wolves' droppings could be seen on the narrow twisting mountain trails. All we could hear was the creaking of our wheelbarrow. We had to unload things from the wheelbarrow when going down steep hills and carry both wheelbarrow and load when going up hills. And there was always the danger of slipping off the narrow path into the deep ravines below.

" 'Rich men would never come to such a mountainous area,' said my father when we reached Tiao-shao-ling. 'Children, look at how wild it is here. All we have to do is work very hard, farm well, and we'll be able to make a go of it. Heaven does not let even blind birds starve to death. Let's find a mountain hamlet and settle down there.'

"How were we to know that there was no sign of human habitation within ten li of here? As hungry and exhausted as we were, we could not find a hamlet, and the best we could do was bed down for the night in a mountain gulley. We huddled together in the black of night, terrified by the howling of wolves and the cry of leopards.

"The following evening we finally found a mountain village called Shih-ch'iao-kou.

"Shih-ch'iao-kou was a place where the soil was thin, the rocks were many, and there was no drinking water — a few families living on the side of a cliff. They had to bring drinking water from a well three to four li away. The slopes were so steep that even squirrels and cows would slip off them and fall into the deep gorges. The soil was sandy and gravelly and covered with thorns. After settling down, I began to tend the cattle of a landlord named Kao in Wu-pei-wa, ten li away.

"The following year, starving as he was, my father reclaimed a three-mou plot of slope land and planted corn and grain, which with intensive care grew tolerably well. Later on, my elder brother came too, and my baby sister was born. We were happy and worried: happy that we had a tract of land from which we could get a little food; but worried about supporting our suddenly larger family. We watched and waited in nervous anticipation for a good harvest. That autumn, a mountain landlord appeared out of the blue. He claimed that our reclaimed land belonged to him. Charging us with ruining the 'geomantic life' of his house, he seized our crop and threatened to evict us from the land. When my father entreated him for mercy, that son of a turtle kicked my father in the chest. Several days later, my father died from the injury. When he was dying, he called for my elder brother and me: 'I can't make it. I'm leaving you and your mother behind.... Children, never forget the cause of my death.' Then, he held my hand in his and said to me: 'From now on, your name will be Ch'ing-yin. The animosity of our family is vividly [ch'ing] stamped [yin] on your heart —'

"My father was dead. Since we had no money to buy a coffin for him, we wrapped his body in a mat of kao-liang stalk and buried him....

"My mother was bedridden with fever after my father's death. She had nightmares and lapsed into delirium. Not long after, she followed my father....

"With my parents dead, my older brother, my baby sister, and I were left behind. We lived in abject poverty. My baby sister cried of hunger all the time. My elder brother and I prepared corn gruel and put it into a small bottle for her to drink. She grew more emaciated, nothing but skin and bones. My elder brother went out to find some part-time jobs; I continued to tend cattle in Wu-pei-wa. There was just no way we could look after our baby sister. After long consideration, all we could do was give her away and hope that her fate would be better than ours.

"After this, we brothers managed to keep ourselves alive by working like horses. We did not marry or lead a human existence until the day liberation came.

"During the Land Reform of that year, a plot of land and a single-entrance cave were distributed to our family, and I was chosen as the leader of a people's militia unit. In the tumultuous revolutionary movement, landlords who had long sat on the necks of the poor were struggled down. I am sure I don't need to tell what all this has meant in the lives of the poor. Now, we live in new houses with tile roofs and glass-paned windows and have enough to eat and wear. Our children do not have to take care of landlords' cattle. Our hard work in cultivating the land owned by the people's communes is amply rewarded. This and the old society are two different worlds. That was Hell; this is Heaven!

"I am sure now that you can understand why I regard my wheelbarrow as a treasure. I roamed from Shantung to Shansi, from Tun-liu to Ch'in-yüan. My father and we brothers pushed the wheelbarrow whenever we went on our journeys. It was always with us. In the cold of winter it carried landlords' fuel; in autumn it was loaded with landlords' golden crops; it made squeaking noises under the burden of a landlord's fat son.... The wheel in front left a track behind: I cannot forget the past. So I still keep the wheelbarrow. Don't look down on it. In 1959 it played its part in socialist construction! When the 'East Wind Lake' reservoir was built, I fixed it up and oiled it and pushed it to the construction site. I said to my wheelbarrow: 'This time you should work harder. Don't be lazy!' Indeed, when I pushed it, it rolled smoothly and uncomplainingly; it did not make creaking noises as it once did when it was loaded with a heavy burden. I think that it works better than the wheelbarrows with rubber on their wheels. My wheelbarrow was outfitted with many small red flags, and when I looked at it, I was so happy that I sang Shang-tang folk songs* while pushing my wheelbarrow. Now, our country is developing, the people are living a decent life, and transportation has become modernized. There are more and more trains, automobiles, and airplanes. There are big carts with rubber wheels in our mountain commune. Nowadays, wheelbarrows are seldom used. I am thinking about building an exhibition house for my wheelbarrow and having those who are good at writing write the bitter history of my wheelbarrow so that in the future people will see it and hear about it and not forget what it represents.... By the way, I have forgotten to tell you about Shih Te-fa, who saved my father's life and killed that fat officer at the checkpoint in Shih Village. While he was alive, my father always worried about Shih. However, in the old society, how could he possibly learn of his whereabouts? After the liberation, I wrote letters and asked around. But his whereabouts was still unknown. In 1958, when I took part in the construction of the Tun-chiang Reservoir, I finally received a letter from a member of the Liberation Army saying that Shih Te-fa was a member of the military unit stationed in Pao-ting, Hopei Province, and that he had a family and had been promoted to captain!..."

---

*These are folk tunes from the region of Shang-tang in Shansi.

YEN CHEN-HUA

A funeral for a dog

The following is part of the family history of a poor old
farmer named Ch'in Ma-fu, a member of the Ch'uan-ti Production Brigade of the Ch'uan-ti Commune in Hu-kuan hsien.

Ch'in Ma-fu's home was at Hsi-po-kou in Hu-kuan hsien,
Shansi Province. More than sixty years ago, before Ch'in
Ma-fu was born, his grandfather took his parents to escape
to Hsi-po-kou because they could not pay their rent to the local landlord. After roaming from place to place, the family
finally settled down in a run-down temple in Ch'uan-ti Village.
Ch'in Ma-fu was born in 1912. He was given the auspicious
name of Ma-fu by his father, Ch'in Liu-chin, whose hopes
were reflected in the name "Ma-fu," meaning "good fortune
immediately." However, in the old, man-eat-man society, how
could man decide his own fate? Ch'in Liu-chin's family did
not get "immediate good fortune" just because his son was so
named.

For a month after they gave birth, women of rich families
were waited upon on their warm k'angs. But when Ch'in Ma-
fu was born, the Ch'in family "immediately" fell hungry. The
day after his birth, his mother had no choice but to go to the

---

Yen Chen-hua, "Wei kou pan sang-shih."

fields to find wild vegetation to prepare a bowl of soup for herself. Some kindhearted people told her: "You've got to get good rest for the first month after you give birth, or else you'll get sick." But did this poor woman have any choice?

Thereafter, after many years of backbreaking work, Ch'in Liu-chin reclaimed a seven-mou plot of barren land, but since there were so many mouths to feed, his family lived precariously. When Ch'in Ma-fu was seven years old, his family lived on the brink of starvation. Ch'in Liu-chin thought about sending Ch'in Ma-fu to tend sheep for a landlord, and said to him: "Son, your father has been sinned against for a generation. If I had any choice, I'd not send you to work for a black-hearted rich man. But I've got a big family to support. We can't sit idly by and wait for starvation...."

Before he was finished, Ma-fu already knew what he was getting at, and broke in reassuringly: "Father, don't worry. I'll do whatever you ask." Whereupon this lad of but seven years went to tend sheep for a landlord, struggling for enough to eat.

Seven years elapsed. He became a good and dependable shepherd who could handle any situation that came along. That year, he began to tend sheep for a landlord in his village named Li Ch'i-ts'ai. Li Ch'i-ts'ai promised to give him one string and 200 pieces of cash a month and free meals. But, "the meat was in the tiger's mouth, and power was in the man's hands." Ma-fu did not get even a single piece of cash from Li Ch'i-ts'ai after ten months of work. In the whole period, he got only about 2 pecks of rice from the landlord, which measured out to only 1.8 pecks when he got home. When winter came and there was snow everywhere, Ma-fu still wore only ragged pants and a tattered jacket. Every day, he drove the flock of sheep back and forth through the mountain gorges. In order to buy a cotton-wadded jacket for his mother, he asked for his pay several times. But every time, the black-hearted landlord Li Ch'i-ts'ai refused his request with: "The money isn't ready yet."

"Son, you'd better not count on your pay to get winter clothes.

You'll die of cold if you don't find a way," said Ch'en Liang-hsi, a farmhand working for Li Ch'i-ts'ai, to Ch'in Ma-fu after hearing that Ch'in Ma-fu's request for pay had been refused.

"We're poor and I can't afford the cotton-wadded clothes. Tell me, what can I do as long as he doesn't give me my pay?" said Ch'in Ma-fu.

Ch'en Liang-hsi said: "Since he treats you badly, you should treat him badly. Since he has refused to pay you for your work, you sell his sheep dog. Don't wait until you freeze to death."

Ch'uan-ti is a mountainous area where wolves abound, and wolves eat sheep. Rich men kept fierce and alert sheep dogs to guard their flocks of sheep. The richer the landlord, the better the sheep dog and the greater its value. Sometimes, the price of a good sheep dog was equivalent to that of many head of sheep. Ch'en Liang-hsi figured that Li Ch'i-ts'ai owed Ch'in Ma-fu at least the cost of a sheep dog, and that since Li Ch'i-ts'ai had tried to repudiate the debt, Ch'in Ma-fu had the right to enjoy the fruits of his labor. So he suggested to Ch'in Ma-fu the idea of selling Li Ch'i-ts'ai's sheep dog.

Ch'in Ma-fu followed Ch'en Liang-hsi's suggestion. The following day, he met a fur trader as he was driving the flock of sheep to pasture. He sold Li Ch'i-ts'ai's sheep dog to the fur trader for seven yuan.

Two days later, landlord Li Ch'i-ts'ai found out that his sheep dog had disappeared. He sent someone to bring Ch'in Ma-fu back to his home. Li Ch'i-ts'ai stood between his son Li K'o-i and his nephew Li T'uo-k'uei. With ropes in their hands, the two young men looked like demons.

"Ma-fu, I haven't seen my sheep dog in the past two days," Li Ch'i-ts'ai said angrily as soon as he saw Ch'in Ma-fu.

Ch'in Ma-fu did not utter a word.

"Why don't you tell me you lost my sheep dog?" pressed Li Ch'i-ts'ai.

"Speak out! If you don't tell the truth, you'll never live through the night!" Li K'o-i warned, even more fiercely than his father.

"You poor devil! I'll teach you a lesson!" said Li T'uo-k'uei, slapping his rope on a nearby table.

"I sold the sheep dog. But you people should be blamed. When I began to work for you, you promised to pay me one string and 200 pieces of cash a month. It's been almost a year now. You have given me only 1.8 pecks of rice, which is worth less than two strings of cash...," retorted Ch'in Ma-fu as he glared at landlord Li Ch'i-ts'ai.

He wanted to go on, but Li Ch'i-ts'ai exploded: "This has nothing to do with your pay. You have confessed that you sold my dog. A kid like you doesn't understand such things. I'll get your parents over here."

Ch'in Ma-fu told his parents that he had sold Li Ch'i-ts'ai's sheep dog. The whole family did not get a sound sleep that night.

The following day, word spread through the village that Ch'in Ma-fu had sold Li Ch'i-ts'ai's sheep dog and that he must forfeit his life for selling the dog to a fur trader.

When news that Ch'in Ma-fu's life would be traded for a dog's reached them, the family had a brief discussion. They decided that he should escape for his life. Poor Ch'in Ma-fu, just turned fourteen, wearing his thin clothes, left home in the cutting wind and walked through the snow-covered fields. This was the beginning of his mendicant's life of wandering.

Two days after Ma-fu's departure, landlord Li Ch'i-ts'ai sent one of his lackeys to the Ch'in house to demand the forfeiting of Ch'in Ma-fu's life for the sheep dog he had sold. Ch'in Liu-chin and his wife fainted away as if their heart had been struck by a ten-thousand-catty hammer. After reviving, Ch'in Liu-chin implored Li Ch'i-ts'ai's lackey for mercy: "Please, ask your master to pardon our silly child."

"I can do nothing about it. This is my master's order. I'm simply passing on his order," said the lackey, who was no less merciless than his master.

After the lackey left, Ch'in Liu-chin and his wife asked some of their relatives and friends to seek Li Ch'i-ts'ai's pardon for their son. But no matter how many went, each came back with the same story. Li Ch'i-ts'ai told them: "To strike the dog is to harm the master. Poor little devil Ch'in Ma-fu had

the nerve to bully me. If he can't bring back the dog, he must
forfeit his life for what he did."

In order to save their son's life, Ch'in Liu-chin and his wife
paid a number of visits to Li Ch'i-ts'ai to seek his pardon for
Ch'in Ma-fu. However, Li Ch'i-ts'ai was adamant in the face of
their entreaties. He told them: "If you want to save your son's life,
there are three conditions for making amends: first, call Ma-
fu back and have him mourn for my dog and escort its coffin;
second, give a party and accord a funeral to my dog; third,
stage theatricals for three days." Li Ch'i-ts'ai's demands
greatly disturbed the couple. They thought to themselves:
"That's more pomp for this dog than you gave even your own
parents. Obviously, he's ridiculing us." But what they said
to themselves, they dared not say out loud. Because of the
couple's entreaties, Li Ch'i-ts'ai reluctantly dropped his demand that Ch'in Ma-fu escort the dog's coffin. Instead, he told
Ch'in Ma-fu's parents: "Sell your land and bring all the money
to me. Then, I'll save your son's life." Ch'in Liu-chin and
his wife were about to make entreaties again when Li Ch'i-
ts'ai made a face, and his lackeys dragged the couple out of
his house.

The following day, Li Ch'i-ts'ai's lackeys came to the house
of the Ch'in family again.

"Has Ma-fu come back?" the leader of the group demanded
fiercely.

"No, not yet. I don't know where he is," replied Ch'in Liu-
chin.

"Then sell your land!"

"Land is our life. We'll be unable to sustain our lives if we
sell it."

"You don't want to hand Ma-fu over to us or to sell your
land, but Ma-fu has the right to sell my master's sheep dog?"
he said with perverse logic.

"Please, give us time and we'll find another solution."

"That is not our business," said the leader of the group
while taking a piece of paper out of his pocket.

The other lackeys closed in and forcibly put Ch'in Liu-chin's

right thumb into a red ink box and made a fingerprint on a prepared title deed. In an instant, Ch'in Liu-chin had lost six
mou of the seven mou of land he had struggled so arduously to
reclaim.

With the 210 yuan from the sale of Ch'in Liu-chin's land,
Li Ch'i-ts'ai gave a banquet with twenty-seven tables and
staged three days of Shang-tang theatricals.

More than two hundred relatives, friends, village elders, and
lackeys of Li Ch'i-ts'ai attended. A sixteen-course banquet of
eight main dishes and eight side dishes was held. Li Ch'i-ts'ai did
the honors of the table, playing the perfect host. He laughed
and talked loudly and gleefully as if a celebration were being
held. It was already dark after the banquet concluded. When
the sounds of gongs and drums came from the stage outside
the house, Li Ch'i-ts'ai and his guests went out to enjoy the
theatricals. Poor people in the village were indignant but
silent over this garrish display. They secretly cursed: "Some
day, you malevolent scoundrels who have done what you have
done to that family will die a violent death." Ch'in Liu-chin
and his wife clenched their teeth. Several times, when he
heard the beating of those gongs and drums, he was about to
rush on Li Ch'i-ts'ai and fight him to the bitter end. He was
restrained by his neighbors, who said: "He is rich and influential. You'll lose your life in vain if you fight him. Calm down.
Someday —"

The Ch'in family became poorer and poorer. Sometimes
they had no food at all. Ch'in Ma-fu's younger brother left
home to look for food to eat, and there was no word from him.
Ch'in Ma-fu's younger sister was sent to someone's home to
be brought up and married there. Ch'in Ma-fu, wandering
about in all kinds of weather, trying to stay alive, fell sick
with fever. He returned home. His mother wanted to help him
sweat out the fever. But they hadn't even one quilt. Finally,
she borrowed a big flat basket-tray and covered Ma-fu with it.
This helped him sweat out the fever. Fearing that landlord Li
Ch'i-ts'ai might murder Ch'in Ma-fu, Ch'in Liu-chin sent his
son to work as an apprentice for a rug weaver in a remote

place. For more than twenty years, Ch'in Ma-fu worked in various places, but he made only enough to feed himself and really could not do very much for his parents. Ch'in Liu-chin died amidst all this suffering and misery. When he was dying, he told Ch'in Ma-fu: "Never forget Li Ch'i-ts'ai. You must get revenge."

After liberation, Ch'in Ma-fu's family began to find "good fortune." During the Land Reform, landlord Li Ch'i-ts'ai was punished by the people's government in accordance with the law, and a house and a plot of land were distributed to Ch'in Ma-fu's family. Later, when the Party called on everyone to organize, Ma-fu was made the leader of the No. 1 Mutual As-sistance Team in Ch'uan-ti Village. When an agricultural cooperative was established in Ch'uan-ti Village in 1953, Ma-fu was the first to apply for membership in the cooperative. Now his family is living in comfort and peace. He has been elected the chairman of the poor and lower-middle peasant committee. This is truly a case of:

There are many new things in the new society,
The people have become the masters.
Class hatred and class sufferings must be remembered
    down through the ages.

The fight

I

Feng Ying-ts'e is a native of Chi-t'an Village, Kao-p'ing
hsien, Shansi Province, and a member of San-chia People's
Commune there. Her father was Feng Wu-ch'ou, and this family history must begin with the story of Feng Wu-ch'ou.

When Feng Wu-ch'ou was eight years old, his father, Feng
Chin-shui, was driven to his death because of his inability to
pay off the debt to a local landlord named Feng Shou-heng. His
father left behind a two-room house and a five-mou plot of land.
He also left behind Wu-ch'ou's ailing mother, his younger
brother, and his three younger sisters, and they passed the
days on chaff and vegetables.

One day in the twelfth month of 1922, a blizzard hit the Han-
wang Mountains and swept across the Tung-tsang River, over-
whelming the mountain area with its roar. Two children were
bent over picking out scrap iron in a heap of coal ashes near an
iron works on the northern edge of San-chia Village. They
were shivering from head to toe in the blizzard. They were
fourteen-year-old Wu-ch'ou and his younger brother Liu-erh.

Sung Kuei-sheng, Lang Chih-jen, "Po-tou."

110

"It's so cold! Elder brother, let's go home...," said Liu-erh, crying from the cold.

"Liu-erh, don't cry. Pick up a little more scrap iron. If we pick up more scrap iron, we can get money for a proper celebration of the New Year. Look at me, Liu-erh, I don't feel at all cold," Feng Wu-ch'ou tried to comfort his younger brother, waving his arms to show that he did not feel cold.

In fact, Wu-ch'ou's lips were blue and his limbs were chapped and bleeding. It was dark before the two boys stopped sifting out scrap iron, picked up their basket, and returned home.

Before they entered the door, they heard their sisters crying, "Mother! Mother!" They rushed into the house and found their mother lying on the k'ang gasping for breath. There was a puddle of blood on the ground near the k'ang which she had vomited.

"Feng Shou-heng came to call up our debt just now. He said that if Mother could not clear up the debt today, he would take our land at Pei-ko-wai. Mother entreated him for mercy, but that dog turned a deaf ear to her entreaties and threatened to take her to the Grand Temple and ring the bells. Then, Mother vomited blood —" said Feng Wu-ch'ou's younger sister.

Before his younger sister finished talking, Wu-ch'ou rushed to the k'ang and wept over his mother.

Feng Shou-heng was a villainous landlord of Chi-t'an Village. His sons and sons-in-law were either in business in the city or in the service of the puppet government. He employed many farmhands, manservants, and maidservants. He often boasted that the beams of all the houses in the village would shake three times if he shouted before the Grand Temple and that the leaves in the trees along the street would fall if he stamped his foot. All villagers had to call him the "Grand Master" and walk with their heads down whenever they met him. He tried in every way to seize others' property. Of the 200-odd mou of tillable land in the village, he had seized more than 150 mou. Of the 100-odd houses in the village, 70 became his property. However, he was hardly satisfied. He wanted to

make Chi-t'an Village his "everlasting and eternal" manor.
So he never missed an opportunity to seize land and houses
from the peasants. The three-mou plot of land owned by Wu-
ch'ou's family was contiguous with a large tract of land owned
by Feng Shou-heng. Feng Shou-heng would stop at nothing to
incorporate that plot into his own land. That year Wu-ch'ou's
father had borrowed twenty strings of cash from Feng Shou-
heng because he was sick and needed medicine. The interest
piled up and the three mou finally got into Feng Shou-heng's
hands. When the land, which had been his life, was gone, Wu-
ch'ou's father died. . . .

Hearing Feng Wu-ch'ou's wail, his dying mother opened her
lifeless eyes and touched his head with her dried and withered
hand and said: "Don't cry, child. Bear this in mind: never
ever borrow money from Feng Shou-heng. Never ever provoke
him. He is more vicious than a wolf or a jackal! . . . Your
father died of. . . ."

Wu-ch'ou's mother went on, wanting him to "take good care
of Liu-erh," and "take good care of everything." Then she
stopped and was silent. Wu-ch'ou thought that she had fallen
asleep. After a while, he fetched a cup of hot water for her.
She did not answer when he told her to drink the hot water. He
burst into tears, and his younger brother and sisters began to
weep bitterly. Hearing the children's cries, Aunt Wei, who
lived next door, rushed over. After touching the hard lips and
cold chest of Wu-ch'ou's mother, Aunt Wei knew that she had
already breathed her last.

It was the night of the twenty-third day of the twelfth month. When
Wu-ch'ou's mother breathed her last, landlord Feng Shou-heng was
seeing the kitchen god off to Heaven to report his "benevolence."

There is a saying, "Children of a poor family mature early."
Immediately after his mother's death, the fourteen-year-old
Wu-ch'ou seemed to become an adult. Carrying a small flickering lantern, he held a wake over his mother's corpse. When
he looked up and saw Feng Shou-heng's house towering in the
distance, and heard the firecrackers exploding in his courtyard, he became so outraged he tore chips out of the bricks of

the k'ang and bit his lips till they bled.

II

Feng Shou-heng burst into laughter when he heard the wail of Feng Chin-shui's children. That night, after much thought and calculation, he reached the conclusion that in the village only he and Kuo Chin-sung were rich enough to buy land from the peasants. Since Kuo Chin-sung was Feng Shou-heng's subordinate, he naturally dared not compete with him. That land of Wu-ch'ou's would slip into his hands as easily as meat into the mouth. All he had to do was sit back and wait. Feng Shou-heng's wife was stingy and venal. The following morning, she urged her husband to seize Feng Wu-ch'ou's three-mou plot of land.

"Ha, ha! A woman sees only the surface. Why don't we wait till Feng Wu-ch'ou comes to us for help? What's the hurry?" Feng Shou-heng said confidently, his evil eyes twinkling.

Feng Wu-ch'ou had to sell his land because he had no money for his mother's burial, because there was no food for his family, and because he had to pay off his father's debt to Feng Shou-heng. But clenching his teeth, Feng Wu-ch'ou thought to himself: "I'd rather sell our land to someone in a neighboring village than to Feng Shou-heng. I won't give him a pillow just because he wants to sleep!"

On the third day after the death of Wu-ch'ou's mother, Feng Shou-heng heard the news that Wu-ch'ou had sold his land to a man in San-chia Village. Raging with anger, he roamed all over the house constantly cursing: "Wu-ch'ou, you little monkey, see if this old man ever lets you off! See if you can ever escape my control!"

After all, Wu-ch'ou was only a fourteen-year-old boy! After his mother died, how could he take care of his younger brother and three younger sisters? During the day, Feng T'ung-te, Feng Shou-heng's son, often walked his big wild dog near Wu-ch'ou's door. Terrified of the wild dog's pointed teeth, the children dared not take one step out of their house. At night, the children huddled together and cried all night for their parents. Sometimes Aunt Wei came over to look after the children and comfort them. But she was hardly in a position to assume responsibility for them, being desperately poor herself and having to work.

Wu-ch'ou sold the three mou of land. He had a very small amount of money left after clearing his father's debt to Feng Shou-heng and paying the expenses for his mother's burial. Wu-ch'ou, still a boy, could not support a family of five with the scanty income from cultivating the two-mou plot of barren land at West Slope. Even a seven-foot giant could not have done it! Aunt Wei more than once advised Wu-ch'ou: "You can't do it, Wu-ch'ou, let your younger sisters escape for their lives." But the sisters wept when they heard this suggestion — they did not want to be separated from their eldest brother. Wu-ch'ou felt that a decision on this matter was beyond him.

Their hardships became greater and greater. By spring, Wu-ch'ou's family had nothing to eat or drink. Steeling his heart, he asked Aunt Wei to find three poor fiancés for each of his younger sisters, and he sent them to the houses of their fiancés.

After the departure of their sisters, Wu-ch'ou and his younger brother, Liu-erh, on the verge of starvation, wandered about doing odd jobs and living on wild vegetation, the bark of elm trees, and wheat chaff. Seeing that they were starving, Aunt Wei sometimes gave them pieces of bran bread. Feng Shou-heng's expression was wooden whenever he ran into Wu-ch'ou. He hated Wu-ch'ou for selling his land to a man in San-chia Village. Every day, Feng Shou-heng's wife sat on a stone block outside the door of her house and spilled invective against Wu-ch'ou. When Wu-ch'ou was angry sometimes and wanted to see Feng Shou-heng to appeal to reason, he was always stopped by Aunt Wei, who said: "Wu-ch'ou, don't go. Feng Shou-heng is like a man-eating leopard. You should avoid meeting him. Never provoke him. Have patience!"

However, the exploiting class never laid down the butcher's knife after you had made a concession to it. An unexpected calamity suddenly befell Wu-ch'ou.

It was the wheat-harvest season. One day, as Wu-ch'ou was threshing and winnowing wheat for a farmer, an excited boy rushed up to tell him: "Brother Wu-ch'ou! Hurry up! Feng T'ung-te is beating Liu-erh. He said Liu-erh stole his wheat. He has also set his big wild dog on Liu-erh!" Picking up a stick, Wu-ch'ou ran to his younger brother's rescue.

Feng T'ung-te was beating Liu-erh with a carrying pole. Seeing angry Wu-ch'ou running over, Feng T'ung-te immediately set his dog upon him. With all his strength, Wu-ch'ou hit the attacking dog with the stick, and it ran away with its nose bleeding. When Feng T'ung-te saw Wu-ch'ou strike his dog, he cursed him: "You leech! Now you've done it!" He tried to beat Wu-ch'ou with the carrying pole. A big fellow in his twenties, he thought that he could easily beat off Wu-ch'ou.

Wu-ch'ou slipped to one side, and Feng T'ung-te missed Wu-ch'ou by a couple of inches.

"Why are you beating Liu-erh?" Wu-ch'ou demanded angrily.

"Beating him? I'm going to pulverize you!" replied Feng T'ung-te.

At that moment Feng Ch'ou-hai, a good friend of Wu-ch'ou's, strode over with a big iron pitchfork in his hand. He said in a loud voice: "Feng T'ung-te, you dare to bully others!" Knowing that he was no match for Feng Ch'ou-hai, Feng T'ung-te ran away from the scene with his tail between his legs. Liu-erh lay on the ground. His head was bleeding, there were wounds all over his body, his clothes were torn, and his basket was smashed. Wu-ch'ou was heartbroken at the sight of his younger brother lying there. Ch'ou-hai helped Wu-ch'ou carry Liu-erh home.

That night, Liu-erh had a high fever and was in a coma. When he recovered his senses, he kept crying: "It hurts!" "Help me, Elder Brother!" "Help me, Mother!" Liu-erh's crying was like an awl piercing Wu-ch'ou's heart.

"My little brother! My good little brother!"

Looking at Liu-erh, whose lips were convulsed from the high fever, Wu-ch'ou remembered many things. Once, Wu-ch'ou was about to go out to carry coal in a blizzard. Liu-erh took off the shabby jacket which had been left to him by their mother and insisted that Wu-ch'ou put it on. Wu-ch'ou refused it, and Liu-erh was so upset he began to sob. Sometimes, Aunt Wei gave him a half loaf of bran bread, and he always waited for his older brother to return so they could share it. When there was not enough food, Liu-erh always insisted that Wu-ch'ou have the larger portion. He said that Wu-ch'ou must eat more because he was big and must work. When Liu-erh met adult poor people in the village, he always called them "uncle" or "sir." Villagers praised Liu-erh as a good boy who knew his manners. Wu-ch'ou also recalled that his dying mother had told him to take good care of his younger brother Liu-erh. He thought that if something happened to Liu-erh, how could he ever face his mother! He was heartbroken.

Liu-erh cried with pain for two days and two nights. Aunt Wei was constantly at his side. Finally, Liu-erh's brief, bitter life came to an end, and he left the evil old world.

Heartbroken, Wu-ch'ou remained in his bed for three days, and he wept so bitterly and long that he had no tears left to shed. Liu-erh's death taught him that in order to keep himself alive, it was no good to run away: he must stand up and fight such man-eating jackals and wolves as Feng Shou-heng and Feng T'ung-te.

III

Now Wu-ch'ou was all alone. He lived in poverty because of the poor harvest in the previous two years, and his existence was a bitter one indeed.

It is true that "the child who has been brought up in a poor family is made of tough fiber." Wu-ch'ou did not shrink back in the face of poverty and misfortune. Sometimes, he cultivated his land. Sometimes, he worked for others as a part-time farmhand or carried iron goods, coal, and earth for others — he could do any kind of miserable task. By the time he was nineteen, he was already a man of strong muscle and his hands and feet were big. He could carry a load of more than 200 catties for thirty li in a breeze. He could carry four honey buckets at one time, doing the work of two men. Using a specially made mattock which was large and heavy, he dug up the earth much faster than any of the other young men. He was straightforward in his speech and diligent in his work. When Aunt Wei asked him to carry water for her, he would fill her water vessel. When Uncle Li asked him to turn a mill for him, he would immediately pull off his clothes and turn the mill till midnight. Wu-ch'ou's grandfather had loved hunting and left behind an old shotgun which eventually fell into Wu-ch'ou's hands. Wu-ch'ou too loved this sort of thing and he became a good marksman. As soon as autumn came, and the ground was clean and the fields bright, he and Ch'ou-hai went to the Han-wang Mountains to hunt pheasant and hare. Ch'ou-hai chased the game, and Wu-ch'ou did the shooting. When he returned from the hunt, Wu-ch'ou gave his game to Aunt Wei and Uncle Li. He was liked by everyone in the village.

A few years older than Wu-ch'ou, Feng Ch'ou-hai was strong and stocky. His parents died when he was a little boy. He was a bachelor because he was too poor to take a wife. He and Wu-ch'ou were the best of friends. They made a good team in work and enjoyed talking with each other. For example, if Wu-ch'ou said: "Those rich people like to bully men of weak character; the more you fear them, the harder they press down on your head," Ch'ou-hai would say: "Rich men are honey-mouthed but black-hearted, and they deceive simple and honest people." When they worked together, they often ended their conversations by heaping curses on Vampire Feng Shou-heng to give vent to their chagrin.

And wasn't it so? Indeed, Feng Shou-heng was a vampire. Seeing Wu-ch'ou grow up to be a big, strong man, he began to think about hiring him. Feng Shou-heng knew that to have Wu-ch'ou working for him would be more useful than to seize the latter's three-mou plot of land. He also knew that Wu-ch'ou could do the work of two ordinary men and that he was a good marksman. Feng Shou-heng thought that he would ask Wu-ch'ou to cultivate land for him in the daytime and guard his warehouse at night and that he also would tell Wu-ch'ou to sell iron goods for him in the wintertime. Several times, Feng Shou-heng sent someone to convey his offer to Wu-ch'ou. But Wu-ch'ou would have nothing to do with it.

One day Feng Shou-heng met Wu-ch'ou on the roadside and made the same offer to him.

" 'Grand Master,' you'd better save your money! Besides, I don't deserve the 'honor' of working for you," said Wu-ch'ou coldly, walking away.

Feng Shou-heng was not discouraged by Wu-ch'ou's rejection of his offer. Instead, he sought out Kuo Chin-sung so that they could formulate a "plan."

Kuo Chin-sung was also a rich man in Chi-t'an Village. He looked like a kindhearted man, having a fair complexion and a drooping mustache. He was a capable man and was good at convincing others with his arguments. He was nicknamed "Second Fiddle" by the villagers because he often made vicious plans for Feng Shou-heng. After a few minutes' thought, "Second Fiddle" bowed to Feng Shou-heng and said: "No problem! No problem! Let me handle this matter...."

Kuo Chin-sung, who had always looked down on Wu-ch'ou, began to condescend to be nice to the latter. When he met Wu-ch'ou he would say: "Wu-ch'ou, have you had your lunch? Don't work too hard!" When he saw Wu-ch'ou eating wheat chaff gruel, he said with false kindness to the latter: "Little brother! This kind of food won't do. You'd better go to Grand Master for some food. Do you want me to go borrow some for you?" Every time he saw Wu-ch'ou digging, he told him: "Wu-ch'ou, stop digging. Tomorrow I'll ask Grand Master to lend you a draft animal to do the work." Like a yellow snake, Kuo Chin-sung entwined Wu-ch'ou.

That autumn, when Wu-ch'ou was helping someone carry grain, he was careless and a coarse hull of grain became lodged in his foot. It was imbedded so deep that he could not get it out. His foot hurt, and he had to go home supported by his co-workers. Aunt Wei tried everything to take the coarse grain hull out of Wu-ch'ou's foot. But it was not until she used her teeth that she finally got it out.

That afternoon, Kuo Chin-sung came to see Wu-ch'ou again, carrying something wrapped in cloth under his arm.

"Oh, Wu-ch'ou, how terribly your foot has been injured! Little brother! I just don't understand why you're so stubborn. If you listened to me, you'd have already taken a wife, not to speak of having shoes and socks to protect your feet from thorns," said Kuo Chin-sung, taking out a pair of new shoes from the cloth wrapper. "Grand Master heard of the injury to your foot, and he asked me to send this pair of new shoes to you. You shouldn't be ungrateful for his kindness!"

"His kindness! This reminds me of the story that a weasel showed its kindness to a chicken by paying it a New Year's visit," said Wu-ch'ou, pushing the shoes away. "I don't deserve such an 'honor.' I'm predestined to suffer from a foot injury. Nothing can help it."

"Wu-ch'ou, please accept this pair of shoes just for my sake. Don't let me lose face."

Wu-ch'ou grew angrier and threw the shoes to the floor.

"Kuo Chin-sung, you'd better give up your sinister scheme! I'd rather guard some people's graves than be the guardian angel of Feng Shou-heng's family."

Knowing that his plan would not work, Kuo Chin-sung bowed, put the pair of shoes back into the cloth wrapper, and left Wu-ch'ou's house in distress. Wu-ch'ou's firm stand toward Feng Shou-heng was highly praised by Feng Ch'ou-hai, who brought a pair of second-hand shoes for Wu-ch'ou that night.

IV

With the help of Aunt Wei, Feng Ch'ou-hai, and some other poor people, Wu-ch'ou took a wife from a poor family. Her name was Tu Tun-chieh and she was the daughter of poor peasant Tu Shui-jung in Ch'ih-hsiang Village.

Two years after her marriage, she gave birth to a girl, whom they named Ying-ts'e. Wu-ch'ou was happy with a wife and daughter, and worked harder. However, his family could not make a decent living from their two-mou plot of infertile land.

Not long afterward the Japanese imperialists occupied the city of Kao-p'ing. The Japanese garrison force in San-chia built a wall surrounding the town and gun emplacements on top of the wall. Chang Tzu-kao, Feng Shou-heng's son-in-law, became a district chief under the Japanese rule. Kuo Tzu-wen, Feng Shou-heng's adopted son, was made the head of the puppet garrison force in San-chia. As for Feng Shou-heng himself, he was the headman of Chi-t'an Village and at the same time in charge of the Maintenance of Order Society in the town. At this time he was truly rich and influential, and he got whatever he wanted. He sought every opportunity to frighten Wu-ch'ou into submission and always tried to find fault with Wu-ch'ou. One day, Wu-ch'ou's wife found a bundle of corn stalks in the street. Feng Shou-heng said that she stole the bundle of cornstalks from his barn. He threatened to bring her to the Grand Temple (where the village government was located at that time) to thrash her for the theft. When Wu-ch'ou's tax in grain was only a few days in arrears, Feng Shou-heng said that Wu-ch'ou should be taken to the Grand Temple and fined for opposing the grain tax. He colluded with his adopted son and son-in-law, the puppet garrison force, and bandits in perpetrating all kinds of evildoings. Wu-ch'ou and all the other villagers nursed an intense hatred for Feng Shou-heng.

There were three or four courtyards in Feng Shou-heng's villa. In addition to the main gate, his house had two side gates. In order to build two roads leading to these two side gates, Feng Shou-heng seized land owned by poor people. The hatred of all the villagers for him grew to a feverish pitch, but no one dared to argue with him.

"I'm going to see him" Wu-ch'ou said, furiously stamping his feet.

Ch'ou-hai restrained Wu-ch'ou and said: "Reason won't move him. Let's do something to him in secret."

That night Wu-ch'ou, Ch'ou-hai, and several other brave

young men initiated their plan of action.

Very early the next morning, when Feng Shou-heng opened the south gate, he found that the entrance was completely sealed off with several large rocks. Then a donkey coming out of the north gate sank into a pit that had been dug several paces away from the gate. The donkey became lame. Feng Shou-heng was so mad that he lost his appetite for the rest of the day. He thought to himself that this must be the work of Wu-ch'ou because no one else dared to take such actions. However, he had no evidence against Wu-ch'ou. Therefore, he sent for Kuo Chin-sung and discussed the matter with the latter over a pipe of opium.

A few days later Feng Shou-heng spread the rumor that a piece of canvas and ten catties of bean noodles in the Grand Temple were missing. Kuo Chin-sung also said that an incense burner in his house was missing. They said that there must be burglars in the village. Feng Shou-heng sent out his men to ferret out burglars. One day, Kuo Chin-sung burst into the Grand Temple with the lug of an incense burner in his hand. He said in a loud voice: "I haven't found my incense burner. But I've found the lug of my incense burner at the corner of the wall of Wu-ch'ou's house —" Before he could finish, Feng Shou-heng cut in: "Since you've found the lug of your incense burner at the corner of the wall of his house, then he must be the one who stole the incense burner and the canvas." Immediately he sent a few village policemen to arrest Wu-ch'ou, without a word of explanation, and take him to the Grand Temple.

The huge bell in the Grand Temple began to clang.

It was the practice in this place to sound the huge bell in the Grand Temple when a burglar or robber was arrested, and as soon as villagers heard the bell from the Grand Temple, each family had to send a representative to attend a meeting. Any family which failed to do so would be punished.

Wu-ch'ou was tied to a stone pillar at the entrance of the Grand Temple. At his side was a table, and a strong rope was hanging from the beam of the main hall. Kuo Chin-sung, Feng

T'ung-te, and several others stood there with whips, ropes, or clubs in their hands. The main entrance of the temple and doors of the offices in the temple were guarded by sentries. Seeing that Wu-ch'ou was tied to a pillar in the temple, the masses who came to attend the "meeting" put on a gloomy countenance and sat silently in the temple courtyard.

Wu-ch'ou was not frightened because he knew that he had not committed any offense. He thought to himself: "Although of course they are going to flog me, I'll expose Old Dog Feng Shou-heng's evildoings before the masses."

Before long, Feng Shou-heng, after turning his piglike head from side to side and seeing that everyone was there, stood behind the table at the entrance of the Grand Temple. He took a piece of paper out of his pocket and read a prepared statement before the participants at the meeting: "Feng Wu-ch'ou has committed theft. After a discussion, the village headman and hamlet leaders have made the decision that Feng Wu-ch'ou shall pay compensations for the loss of property and that he and his family shall be expelled from the village."

"You're telling lies. Can you produce evidence against me? How can you charge me with theft if you can't produce evidence against me?" Wu-ch'ou retorted, staring hard at Feng Shou-heng.

"Yes, I have evidence against you," said Feng Shou-heng.

Feng T'ung-te smiled and put the lug of an incense burner on the table.

"Here's the evidence against you!" said Feng Shou-heng, pointing to the lug.

"I'm the witness. I found the lug of my incense burner at the corner of the wall of his house," said Kuo Chin-sung, who had jumped up from his place.

"Nonsense! I'll tell you what really happened. You brought the lug of your incense burner from your home," said Wu-ch'ou, spitting at Kuo Chin-sung.

Kuo Chin-sung could find nothing to say and returned to his place.

"What kind of witness and material evidence is this? This

is a frame-up," the masses murmured.

Seeing the commotion in the meeting, Feng Shou-heng wanted to adjourn it. However, he controlled himself and said in a loud voice: "Since we have the testimony of a witness and material evidence, the accused shall be punished even if he refuses to confess his guilt."

"You should be the first to be punished for forgery of evidence and libel...," said Wu-ch'ou, not showing any signs of weakness.

"You're lying!"

"I'm lying, am I? I ask you, who murdered the whole family of Feng Ch'ang-shun?! Who insulted Li Ping-lan?! With the help of the garrison force, you squeezed money and grain from villagers, impressed villagers into military-coolie service, and seized land and property from others. What evil deed haven't you done?! Let me tell you, you swine, it is you who should be expelled from Chi-t'an Village!"

This exposure of his foul deeds had not been expected by Feng Shou-heng. Turning pale with anger, he ordered: "Hang him up and beat him!" Then, Feng Shou-heng's lackeys advanced on Wu-ch'ou and hung him from the beam. Although he was drenched in sweat and the ropes cut into his arms, he cursed Feng Shou-heng:

"You, Feng! Beat me if you want, but you'll have no peace if you don't beat me to death!"

"Beat him! Beat this son of a bitch to death!" Feng Shou-heng roared while stamping his feet.

Some of the masses watching this wept for Wu-ch'ou; others cursed Feng Shou-heng under their breath. When his wife rushed into the Grand Temple, Wu-ch'ou had lost his senses from the flogging.

V

When Wu-ch'ou came to, he found himself lying on a mound outside the village; his wife and daughter wept at his side, and their cooking pot and basins were on the ground. His wife

Tun-chieh told him that their house had been confiscated by
Feng Shou-heng as a "compensation" for the loss of the stolen
goods. Upon hearing this, Wu-ch'ou rose up from the ground
and picked up his shotgun. He wanted to fight Feng Shou-heng.

"What are you trying to do?" asked Tun-chieh, who held Wu-
ch'ou's arm.

"I want to fight the old son of a bitch," replied Wu-ch'ou.

"Please, don't go! His lackeys will help him. If something
happens to you, Ying-ts'e and I can't live on," said the weeping
Tun-chieh.

As Tun-chieh held her husband back, Ying-ts'e began to wail.
Wu-ch'ou also wept as he held his daughter in his arms.

Wu-ch'ou built a simple shed of kaoliang stalks on the
mound and also an earthen cooking range in the shed and made
this their temporary home. As soon as he and his family had
settled in, Feng Shou-heng sent a man to tell Wu-ch'ou that the
mound, a sacred place of the gods, could not be desecrated by
a burglar, and that Wu-ch'ou and his family must leave the
place immediately. Wu-ch'ou was so infuriated that for two
days he did not eat or drink anything. He thought about bringing a lawsuit against Feng Shou-heng. But he knew that he
would not win the lawsuit because there were many followers
of Feng Shou-heng in the local government. Wu-ch'ou also
thought about putting up a fight against Feng Shou-heng. But
he was sure that he would be outnumbered by Feng Shou-heng's
lackeys.

Suddenly, an idea crossed Wu-ch'ou's mind. He took his
wife and daughter to the temple of Kuan-ti [god of war] to
sound the sacred bell there.

People in Chi-t'an Village seldom paid homage to the temple
of Kuan-ti, but they went there to pray and sound the bell when
they could not redress their grievances. When the bell rang,
it startled the whole village, and in a few minutes, most of the
village showed up at the temple. They heard Wu-ch'ou making
a solemn declaration to the statue of Kuan-ti: "I, Feng Wu-
ch'ou, am falsely charged with theft. Today, I want to have
my grievance redressed before the villagers. Feng Shou-heng

devised the false charge against me. Oh, God of War, I pray
thee to display your divine efficacy by bringing death to his
family, sparing neither his fowl nor his dogs!"

It is true that "a thief has a guilty conscience." Kuo Chin-
sung overheard Wu-ch'ou's prayer at the entrance to the temple and immediately went to tell Feng Shou-heng. Feng Shou-
heng was beside himself with anger; he immediately sent his
lackeys to remove the sacred bell and incense burner from
the temple to Kuan-ti. He forced Wu-ch'ou to leave Chi-t'an
Village and at the same time warned villagers that anyone who
gave shelter to Wu-ch'ou would be charged with conspiracy.

Wu-ch'ou's back was against the wall. Steeling his heart,
he sold his two-mou plot of land and cleared his debts. He and
his family left Chi-t'an Village in tears.

VI

Wu-ch'ou and his family settled down in a ruined temple in
Nan-kuan in Kao-p'ing hsien, which is not far from Chi-t'an
Village. He worked for others doing odd jobs. He and his
family lived in poverty. His hatred for Feng Shou-heng never
left his heart. When he was with others he told them about it;
when he was alone he cursed. Therefore, people in Nan-kuan
knew about Feng Shou-heng's evildoings. Gradually, word of
what Wu-ch'ou was saying about him reached Feng Shou-heng,
and his anger was beyond description; he was constantly on
the lookout for opportunities to retaliate against Wu-ch'ou.

Poor people in Chi-t'an Village already hated Feng Shou-
heng, and Wu-ch'ou's sufferings intensified their animosity
toward the "Grand Master." However, they could only take
covert actions against him because he had power and influence
in Chi-t'an Village. In giving vent to their wrath, some villagers often threw rocks and tiles into his courtyard. One
evening, when Feng Shou-heng's wife was scolding a farmhand
in the courtyard, a rock came flying over the wall and hit her
in the head. Blood streamed down her face. Despite an intensive investigation, the rock thrower was not found. Feng

Shou-heng held a meeting to discuss a response with his son-in-law and his adopted son. They decided to retaliate against Wu-ch'ou for telling everyone in Nan-kuan about Feng Shou-heng's evildoings. Knowing that in July Wu-ch'ou would return to Chi-t'an Village to visit his friends and sweep his parents' graves, they falsely charged Wu-ch'ou with throwing the rock that injured Feng Shou-heng's wife. They also said that Wu-ch'ou had wanted to kill Feng Shou-heng with the rock but missed him and wounded his wife. By this false charge, they were trying to retaliate against Wu-ch'ou and suppress the "revolt" of the villagers.

One midnight, as Wu-ch'ou was dreaming, several men with rifles, who looked like members of the puppet security force or a group of bandits, broke down the door and burst into Wu-ch'ou's house. They aroused Wu-ch'ou and his wife and daughter from a sound sleep and took them away. As Nan-kuan is not far from Chi-t'an Village, Wu-ch'ou and his family were soon dragged into the Grand Temple in the village. Feng Shou-heng's lackeys immediately locked the gate of the temple. Feng Shou-heng himself ordered the flogging of Wu-ch'ou, trying to force him to confess his "guilt" for trying to kill Feng Shou-heng with the rock. Not only did Wu-ch'ou refuse to confess his "guilt," he swore wrathfully at Feng Shou-heng. No confession could be exacted from Wu-ch'ou after three days and nights of torture. Feng Shou-heng ordered the imprisonment of Wu-ch'ou and his family. In a secret meeting with Kuo Chin-sung, he decided to bury Wu-ch'ou, Tun-chieh, and Ying-ts'e alive, "to wrest out forever this thorn in his side."

Indeed, walls have ears. Feng Shou-heng's decision was overheard by Aunt Wei, who, since Wu-ch'ou's departure from the village, had worked as a maidservant in the house of Feng Shou-heng because of her inability to pay off her debt to him. She did not know what to do.

As it happened, the following day, Feng Shou-heng and his family went to worship at their ancestors' graves. He put Wu-ch'ou and his family in the custody of Aunt Wei and two other servants. That afternoon, Aunt Wei, in a collusion with

the two other servants, went to the Grand Temple. Wu-ch'ou
and his wife and daughter, with their hands tied behind their
backs, sat in the corner of a room, their bodies covered with
wounds. Aunt Wei untied their hands and gave them several
small loaves of wheat chaff bread she had brought for them.

"Aunt, I'll never forget your kindness. To me, you're as
kind as my mother was," said Wu-ch'ou between bites of the
bread.

"Aunt, is there any news? What will happen to us?" Tun-
chieh asked nervously.

"I haven't committed any crime. They can't punish me,"
Wu-ch'ou cut in.

Aunt Wei did not know what to say as she saw Wu-ch'ou's
simplicity and innocence.

"Aunt, when I was in town I heard that 'this' appeared in Fu-
shan Village," Wu-ch'ou whispered while making a sign for the
character "eight" [meaning Eighth Route Army] by spreading
his thumb and index finger widely apart [the character for
"eight" looks like an inverted victory sign]. "It is said that
they are taking vengeance on behalf of the poor people. When
they come here, I'll settle accounts with that old son of a bitch."
Wu-ch'ou's eyes twinkled with joy, and a smile flickered on
his face. Aunt Wei thought to herself: "He and his family will
be buried alive. Shall I tell him of the bad news? Maybe they
will collapse when I tell them the bad news." Finally, she
made up her mind and told Wu-ch'ou and his family about Feng
Shou-heng's plan to bury them alive.

Upon hearing the news, Wu-ch'ou's wife burst into tears.
Ying-ts'e, in her mother's arms, also wept.

"Wu-ch'ou and Tun-chieh, leave your child to me and run
away immediately. Let me deal with them," said Aunt Wei as
she embraced Tun-chieh and Ying-ts'e.

"No, we'll not run away. Aunt, they will punish you if you
let us escape," said Tun-chieh. Then she said to her husband:
"Please, you are her father. Take Ying-ts'e and escape for
your life. Let them bury me alive!... Take vengeance on my
behalf when Ying-ts'e grows up and the Eighth Route Army comes."

"My good children. Listen to your aunt. If you don't hurry, you'll be unable to get out of here!" said Aunt Wei.

Neither Wu-ch'ou nor Tun-chieh wanted to escape, as much as each urged the other to do so. They heard footsteps at the entrance of the temple. Wu-ch'ou quickly told Aunt Wei to tie their hands behind their backs again. Feng T'ung-te came in. After looking around, he said to Aunt Wei: "Watch over them. We'll kill you if any one of them runs away." After giving this warning to her, he went away, looking sideways at them.

On the evening of October 12, 1943, the bell at the Grand Temple in Chi-t'an Village clanged. The temple was brightly lit with lanterns and torches, and Feng Shou-heng's lackeys were running about like rabid dogs. All entrances to the temple were guarded by armed men. Whips and jute ropes soaked with water were on the ground of the main hall of the temple. As soon as the bell stopped clanging, Feng Shou-heng stood up from his seat behind a table.

"Wu-ch'ou, have you made up your mind?" he asked.

"Yes, I have," replied Wu-ch'ou.

"Then, confess your guilt!"

"I say that whoever threw that rock was a poor marksman. If it had been me, I would have dashed your brains out," said Wu-ch'ou.

"Shut up!" Feng Shou-heng thundered.

Feng Shou-heng tried to force Wu-ch'ou to confess his guilt.

Thinking that since things had gone this far, why fear anything, Wu-ch'ou said: "You're a traitor! You're not a man! You're a ravenous wolf! Maybe you can murder me and my family, but you can't murder all the poor people in the world. Feng, your days as a dog are numbered. The Eighth Route Army will soon settle accounts with you and these bandits of yours!" Wu-ch'ou cursed and spat at Feng Shou-heng.

Feng Shou-heng's face turned pale when he heard Wu-ch'ou say the three words "Eighth Route Army." He shouted in anger: "Beat him! Beat him!" In a second, whips, ropes soaked in water, and clubs fell on Wu-ch'ou's body, and he lost his senses. Feng Shou-heng ordered his men to dash cold

water over Wu-ch'ou. All he got out of Wu-ch'ou were curses.

"I'll kill you, you brat!" shouted Feng Shou-heng, clenching his teeth.

Hearing that Wu-ch'ou was going to be killed, the masses in the temple could no longer suppress their anger: "Wu-ch'ou is not guilty!..."

"Why do you want to kill people!..."

"If you want to kill him, you have to kill all of the villagers!"

"Feng Shou-heng, are you a judge?" Wu-ch'ou asked in a loud voice.

"What?"

"Are you the hsien magistrate?" Wu-ch'ou asked again.

"Why?"

"Since you are not a judge or the hsien magistrate, where do you get the right to murder someone?" retorted Wu-ch'ou.

The crowd in the temple burst into a frenzy of invective. Feng Shou-heng's fierce-looking lackeys, who held whips in their hands, could not suppress the crowd's indignation. After a glance at Kuo Chin-sung, Feng Shou-heng took a piece of paper out of his pocket and pronounced the sentence of death on Wu-ch'ou: "...Feng Wu-ch'ou has committed the crimes of endangering the public safety, disturbing social order, and collaborating with the Eighth Route Army. By order of my superiors, he and his family shall be buried alive!" Then, he pointed at them and ordered: "Take them away!" In an instant, pandemonium broke out. Lackey Kuo Chin-sung tried to drag Wu-ch'ou out of the temple but Wu-ch'ou kicked him to the ground. Wu-ch'ou swore at them: "You curs are nothing but a bunch of traitors and bandits. Maybe you can bury me and my family, but you can't bury all of the people in Chi-t'an Village!" Tun-chieh bit the hand of Feng T'ung-te as he was trying to take her away. Ying-ts'e wailed loudly and hysterically. Bearing the brunt of whips, Aunt Wei rushed to Ying-ts'e and embraced the young girl. The woman protested: "She is an innocent child. You can't bury her alive!" Li Hsiu-hai, Feng Ch'ü-fa, and some other poor people in the village rushed forward to help Ying-ts'e get out of the Grand Temple. Although

Aunt Wei was slapped by Feng Shou-heng on the face several times, Ying-ts'e was finally rescued.

There was great confusion inside and outside the Grand Temple. Feng Ch'ou-hai and the masses of the entire village blocked the main gate of the temple. Seeing that he was in an unfavorable position, Feng Shou-heng exchanged a few whispers with Kuo Chin-sung and then changed his expression and said: "We all live in this village. We don't like to do this thing. The sentence will not be carried out for the time being. I'll try to persuade my superiors to repeal the sentence." Then he ordered his lackeys to imprison Wu-ch'ou and Tun-chieh in the main hall.

After the meeting broke up and supper had been eaten, people in Chi-t'an Village began to go to bed. Ch'ou-hai and a group of his poor friends suspected that Feng Shou-heng was adopting a strategy of "delaying the approach of the enemy." With clubs in hand, they hid themselves in the Kuan-yin Pavilion and the fields at the northern end of the village. They wanted to go to the rescue of Wu-ch'ou and his wife even at the risk of their own lives.

Snowflakes danced in the cold wind, and everything in the fields was shrouded in gloom. They waited and waited, their hands and feet numb with cold. With the first cockcrow and the promise of dawn, they felt relieved that nothing had happened that night and went home.

Shortly before the dawn, Feng Shou-heng's lackeys tied the hands of Wu-ch'ou and Tun-chieh behind their backs and put rags into their mouths. Then, Feng Shou-heng and his lackeys took Wu-ch'ou and Tun-chieh to a previously dug pit and pushed the couple into it. When they had been half buried, the rags were taken out of their mouths.

"Is there anything you want to say?" Feng Shou-heng asked with a satanic smile.

"You shameless son of a bitch, go ahead and bury us. Soon you'll be buried by others," Wu-ch'ou cursed, scowling at Feng Shou-heng.

"Ying-ts'e, don't forget to take vengeance on behalf of your parents! —" shouted Tun-chieh from the pit.

In this way, Wu-ch'ou and his wife Tun-chieh were swallowed up by villainous landlord Feng Shou-heng and the evil old society.

The tragic news of the violent death of Wu-ch'ou and his wife was like a dagger stabbing in the hearts of their poor friends. In order to prevent Feng Shou-heng from laying his hands on Ying-ts'e, they sent the little girl to a safe place. Fearing that Feng Shou-heng might try to murder him, Feng Ch'ou-hai, Wu-ch'ou's bosom friend, left Chi-t'an Village in the night to escape for his life.

VII

Chi-t'an Village was liberated by the Eighth Route Army in March of 1945.

Those who had suffered under Feng Shou-heng stood up against him. And Feng Ying-ts'e stood up too! Feng Ch'ou-hai returned to Chi-t'an Village. Under the leadership of the Communist Party and the Eighth Route Army, all of the villagers engaged in revolution and struggle. They struggled down Feng Shou-heng and Kuo Chin-sung. The evil Feng Shou-heng was finally suppressed by the People's Government. The agricultural cooperative in Chi-t'an Village removed the bodies of Wu-ch'ou and Tun-chieh from the pit and buried them in graves. The villagers angrily stamped their feet while looking at the pit in which Wu-ch'ou and his wife had been buried alive. They wished that they could bury all landlords, scoundrels, and traitors alive in that pit.

"One man falls down, but millions of people stand up." At the ceremony of the burial of Wu-ch'ou and his wife, Feng Ch'ou-hai, Feng Ying-ts'e, Aunt Wei, and all the poor people in Chi-t'an Village who had suffered made speeches. They shouted that they would always follow the Communist Party and always follow Chairman Mao!

Wu-ch'ou and his wife fell down, outnumbered yet heroic in their struggle, but their good friend Feng Ch'ou-hai and their daughter Feng Ying-ts'e have stood up. Under the leadership of the Party, they have found out the correct way to carry out the struggle. Since the liberation, they have lived a happy life which was never dreamed of by Wu-ch'ou and his wife, but they have not forgotten the evildoings of the class enemies.

Yü-huang Temple in a blizzard

There is a Lu-ch'eng <u>hsien</u> in the Taihang Mountains. On Lu-i Mountain in southern Lu-ch'eng <u>hsien</u>, there is an ancient temple — Yü-huang Temple in Pei-chuang Village.

In the past, this temple was surrounded by tall grass and thorns. As soon as the wind blew, the moaning of the tall pines in the temple made the place gloomy and scary. The rich people of Pei-chuang Village seldom visited the temple. It was only vagabonds and beggars who would spend the night or pass the winter in it. No one knew when the temple was built or how many poor people had lived or died in it. So at that time people called it "temple of the poor."

Seventy-one-year-old Ssu Ta-jen, a representative of the poor peasants in Pei-chuang Village, in the old society lived in this temple for seventeen years after he became homeless as a result of exploitation by landlords. Every time he sees Yü-huang Temple he recalls his past sufferings and remembers his dire enmity.

Chang Mei-chen, Lang Chih-jen, Pi Yü-min, "Feng-hsüeh Yü-huang miao."

I

In the winter of 1930, a great blizzard made the desolate Tai-hang Mountains a boundless sea of snow. It was so cold that rocks cracked and birds and beasts vanished without a trace.

A man with a carrying pole was walking with unsteady steps along a winding path on towering Tan-chu Peak. He stumbled along, falling and picking himself up again, and cursed in the biting wind and freezing snow. This was Ssu Ta-jen.

Ssu Ta-jen was hurrying home to see his younger brother Erh-jen, who had been struck down by illness in the home of a landlord. Ssu Ta-jen was not just cursing the horrible weather. He was also cursing that vicious landlord, Sun Sheng-wu.

Sun Sheng-wu was a big landlord of Pei-chuang Village. A holder of the hsiu-ts'ai [degree] from the Ch'ing dynasty days, his mouth was full of quotations from famous poems and essays. He was calculating and vicious. He used all kinds of cruel devices against the poor, always trying to draw the very marrow from their bones. Erh-jen worked for him as a hired hand and was unable to bear the hardship he inflicted. Every day, he sent Erh-jen to work in the fields before the first cock-crow, and he wasn't even allowed to come back for lunch in the afternoon; he carried water and fed the livestock at night and didn't get to bed until after midnight. If he ate more than he was allowed, he would be severely scolded by the landlord's wife. If he did not work hard enough, part of his pay was forfeited; if the domestic animals became thin, again, part of his pay was forfeited. Most of Sun Sheng-wu's large landholding was at Hsi-ch'uan, which is not far from Pei-chuang Village. In order to keep an eye on his hands at work, he built a tall and wide wall in his backyard and often stood on it and watched them. If he saw a farmhand stop moving and straighten his back for a few seconds, he would cut his wages or forbid him to eat supper. From the start, Erh-jen thoroughly despised this old dog.

One day, when Erh-jen and several part-time hands were hoeing in the fields, they saw Sun Sheng-wu again standing on

the top of the wall. After a brief consultation with his co-
workers, Erh-jen raised his hand to heaven and said, "Let's
go!" The part-time hands, led by Erh-jen, returned from the
field, carrying the hoes on their shoulders. Sun Sheng-wu was
so mad that he came down from the top of the wall and paced
up and down his courtyard.

As soon as Erh-jen came in and laid down his hoe, Sun
Sheng-wu dragged him to his three-room living quarters in the
west wing of his house, and said savagely:

"A man who has been a part-time farmhand for only one day
would not do anything to damage the interests of his landlord.
You're hired by me as a farmhand on a permanent basis. We
provide you with free meals and living quarters. Why are you
giving me a hard time? Why have you led them back before
the lunch break?"

"It's very hot today. I thought you were telling us to come
back for a rest. Didn't you signal us with your hand?" replied
Erh-jen, pretending to be serious.

"When did I signal you! I was just fanning myself."

Hearing the argument in the landlord's west room, the part-
time farmhands came to the door to listen. As soon as Sun
Sheng-wu saw the farmhands come along, he stopped talking
and sat in his chair. He harbored an intense hatred against
Erh-jen.

After that, Sun Sheng-wu misused Erh-jen in every way.
Erh-jen began to suffer from stomachaches, and sometimes
the pain was so great that he could not go to work. Not only
did Sun Sheng-wu refuse to let Erh-jen get medical treatment,
the cruel landlord often forced him to work in the field when
his stomach was killing him.

Erh-jen's stomach pains worsened. Ta-jen and Erh-jen
lived in the same village. However, after quitting his work for
village headman Che Chao-ch'üan, Ta-jen did not have a steady
job and could not pay for medical treatment for his younger
brother. One evening, Ta-jen visited his younger brother in
landlord Sun Sheng-wu's freezing barn. Erh-jen was rolling
from side to side on his k'ang with pain. Ta-jen had no

choice but to go to Sun Sheng-wu to borrow money.

"Your younger brother has not yet cleared up his old debt. I'm afraid I can't lend him any more money. You'd better find some other way to get money for curing his disease," Sun Sheng-wu said in his best "eight-legged" essay style.

What could Ta-jen do? The following day, after much deliberation, he bought a picul of persimmons on credit and carried them to the market in a blizzard, with the expectation of making some money to get his younger brother cured.

On the morning of New Year's Day, when landlords' families were praying for good fortune, Ta-jen returned to Pei-chuang Village after walking through the heavy snowstorm for a day and a night. Upon entering the village, he came across Shen Hsiao-lai and asked the latter about Erh-jen's condition.

"Don't ask me about that. Go to Nai-nai Hall and then you'll find out the answer. What a New Year!" Shen Hsiao-lai said in anguish.

Ta-jen was shocked. Something must have happened. He asked Hsiao-lai to take care of his load and rushed toward Nai-nai Hall. Ta-jen squatted down and burst into tears when he saw Erh-jen's rigid body. The bystanders sighed with grief and wept.

As he was crying, Ta-jen suddenly discovered that Erh-jen's mouth was full of cotton floss, and there were cuts and blood on his back. He thought that his younger brother had been murdered by Sun Sheng-wu. Immediately his grief turned entirely to rage. He stood up and said to Erh-jen's corpse: "My dear brother, you've died a violent death! I'll settle accounts with Sun Sheng-wu, the son of a bitch, and take vengeance for your death." He wiped his tears and left in anger for Sun Sheng-wu's house.

When Sun Sheng-wu spied Ta-jen approaching, he said in a sad tone of voice: "Ta-jen, your younger brother's condition became worse after your departure. I sent for the doctor several times. But Erh-jen's disease was not cured. He died from the stomach pains on New Year's Eve. As you know, having a corpse in one's home on New Year's brings bad luck. I had no choice but to have his body taken to Nai-nai Hall."

"I'm afraid that stomachache was not the cause of his death. I think you murdered him!" said Ta-jen.

"What proof do you have!"

"There are wounds in his back and his mouth is filled with cotton floss."

As soon as he heard this, Sun Sheng-wu screamed at him: "Stop this nonsense on New Year's Day! Get out!

"All right, if you don't confess your guilt, let's go to the village office and talk about it," said Ta-jen, pulling Sun Sheng-wu.

"You poor devil, behave yourself! You can't intimidate me by dragging me to the village office. You go first, I'll be there later," said Sun Sheng-wu.

Here's what had happened earlier. On New Year's Eve, Erh-jen groaned with the stomach pains and he was bathed in sweat. Sun Sheng-wu thought to himself: "Erh-jen can do good work, but he is disobedient and troublesome. Now he has stomach trouble, and he is absent from work two days out of three. To cure his disease will cost money, and curing his disease will not cure his temperament." The thing he dreaded most was that Erh-jen would die on New Year's Day, bringing bad luck to him. Therefore he thought up an evil scheme. When he and his son entered the barn, Erh-jen was in a coma and all they could hear was his gasping. Sun Sheng-wu figured that Erh-jen would die from the cold in a half-hour if he and his son carried him to Nai-nai Hall. Sun Sheng-wu dug some cotton floss out from Erh-jen's shabby cotton-wadded trousers and stuffed it into his mouth to prevent him from crying. Then father and son, each holding one of Erh-jen's legs, dragged him to Nai-nai Hall. Erh-jen was in a thin jacket and his back was cut by the gravel on the road. Finally, he died from the cold.

Ta-jen ran to the village office to make the charge. Village headman Che Chao-ch'üan was notorious for his currying favor with rich men and his bullying of poor people.

"You're making a false charge against a good man. You know Erh-jen suffered from stomach pains. He must have been

wounded on his back when he fell over from the k'ang because
of the stomach pains. As for your claim that there was cotton
floss in Erh-jen's mouth, it is groundless nonsense," said Che
Chao-ch'üan with a serious countenance.

Just as he finished, Sun Sheng-wu came in and cursed:
"Ta-jen, I think you're trying to make a profit from your
brother's death. Well then, Chao-ch'üan, let's go to Nai-nai
Hall and take a look at Erh-jen's corpse. If Ta-jen's charge
against me is proved false, you'll have to punish him severely."

With that, they left the village office for Nai-nai Hall.

After they entered Nai-nai Hall, Ta-jen found that the cotton
floss had disappeared from Erh-jen's mouth. He knew that
someone had taken the cotton floss from his younger brother's
mouth. Che Chao-ch'üan angrily accused Ta-jen of making a
false charge against an innocent man. Sun Sheng-wu demanded
that Ta-jen be hung up and thrashed in the village office, but
because of entreaties from the masses, Sun Sheng-wu dropped
his demand.

Erh-jen had been murdered. And Ta-jen found himself accused of making a false charge against Sun Sheng-wu. His
grievance was not redressed. He was so enraged and frus-
trated that he fell on the ground and lost his senses. Sun
Sheng-wu and Che Chao-ch'üan left Nai-nai Hall cursing. A
few poor people there wanted to help Ta-jen up from the floor,
but there was nothing they could do. Just at that moment, Shen
Hsiao-lai came along and carried Ta-jen to Yü-huang Temple.

II

Shen Hsiao-lai was a few years older than Ssu Ta-jen. When
they were boys they cut firewood and begged for food together.
They were good friends. That year, hearing that Yü-huang
Temple was in need of a custodian, Hsiao-lai took the job. Although there was no pay, he was given the free use of the two-
mou tract of land owned by the temple.

That day, when he had been carried to the temple by Hsiao-
lai, Ta-jen fell sick from grief and frustration. For about two

months, Hsiao-lai never left his side, until Ta-jen's condition began to improve.

One day, Ta-jen, who had not completely recovered from his illness, picked up a pair of tongs and wanted to fight Sun Sheng-wu to the bitter end.

Hsiao-lai grabbed him and said:

"Ta-jen, don't be reckless! Sun Sheng-wu has many lackeys. You'll be outnumbered. Your family, four persons in all, came to Pei-chuang from Shantung Province. Your father died of exhaustion when he worked for his landlord, your third younger brother was sold, and Erh-jen was murdered. You're the only root left of your family. Who is going to avenge your father and brothers if something happens to you? As the common saying goes, 'One does not worry about a shortage of firewood as long as there are blue mountains.'"

Ta-jen saw the logic in Hsiao-lai's words. Grateful for Hsiao-lai's kindness to him, Ta-jen slowly laid down the tongs and said to his friend: "You are truly my benefactor. I'll do what you want me to do. I want to live long enough to see these rich men meet their downfall...." From then on, Ta-jen settled down in Yü-huang Temple.

As Ta-jen was still weak after his illness, he could not do heavy work. Hsiao-lai was poor and could not help Ta-jen. So, Ta-jen had to take odd jobs. When he was out of a job he begged for food by day and slept in Yü-huang Temple at night.

One day, village headman Che Chao-ch'üan came to Yü-huang Temple. When he saw Ta-jen he said: "I think you've had enough sleep these days. You're a man. It's a shame for a man to beg for food. I'll find some work for you." After saying this, Che Chao-ch'üan left the temple.

Ta-jen thought to himself: "Find some work for me! I worked for you as a farmhand and suffered much for it. I won't work for you anymore."

A few days later Che Chao-ch'üan sent for Ta-jen. As soon as Ta-jen entered the village office, a bankrupt landlord named Sun Fang-tse accosted him:

"Ta-jen, you have to thank the village headman for having

found a good job for you. You'll work as a harvest watcher."

Che Chao-ch'üan chimed in:

"Ta-jen, what do you say? Isn't it a good job for you? Sun Fang-tse will be the head of the group of harvest watchers."

Seeing that Ta-jen was not going to utter a word, Sun Fang-tse hurried on:

"Ta-jen, this is a really good job. There will be four harvest watchers. Your wages will be paid in grain, a ho of grain per mou and a sheng per 10 mou. There are 36 ch'ing of land in our village, which means that we can get 3.6 piculs of grain and each of the harvest watchers will have 9 pecks of grain. It'll be much better than begging for food."

Ta-jen knew that most of the land in Pei-chuang was owned by Sun Sheng-wu, Li Ku-tse, and a few other landlords, all of whom were villainous, and that they would break their promise after the autumn harvest or give him inferior or rotten grain.

"I'm afraid I can't do the work. You'd better find someone else for this job," Ta-jen told Sun Fang-tse.

Flinging his cigarette stub to the ground, Che Chao-ch'üan swore at him:

"Do you want to act against us? You live in Pei-chuang, you breathe in Pei-chuang, you eat the food of Pei-chuang, you sleep in the temple of Pei-chuang. What do you want to do, if you refuse to work for the people in Pei-chuang? If you don't want the job, you have to leave the village!"

"I don't care if I have to leave here. I can find a home anyplace!" retorted Ta-jen.

"I see you're a man who can't distinguish kindness from malevolence. It's very kind of the village headman to find such a good job for you. All right, tomorrow you watch the harvest!" said Sun Fang-tse, pushing Ta-jen out of the village office.

Ta-jen returned to Yü-huang Temple. Hsiao-lai told Ta-jen: "I'm afraid they will force you to take up the job. If I were you, I'd pay greater attention to the plots of land owned by poor farmers. A poor farmer who owns two or three mou of land can't afford any loss of crops."

Not long after Ta-jen took up the job of watching crops for

others, some of the corn crop was stolen from landlord Li Ku-tse's field. According to the practice in Pei-chuang Village, harvest watchers could not be held responsible for losses of crops. Furthermore, Ta-jen had reported the loss to Sun Fang-tse, the head of the group of harvest watchers, but Sun failed to do anything about it.

One day at noon, as soon as Ta-jen returned to Yü-huang Temple from the field, Li Ku-tse, with a stick in his hand, came into the temple to compel Ta-jen to make compensation for the loss of his corn crop.

"I've reported the loss to the head of the group of harvest watchers. I'm afraid you have to talk it over with him. This is not my business," said Ta-jen.

Li Ku-tse lifted the stick and was about to beat Ta-jen.

"You have the nerve to beat me!" Ta-jen thundered with his hands on his hips.

Knowing that he would be no match for Ta-jen, Li Ku-tse wanted to take Ta-jen to the village office to make his case. At this moment, Che Chao-ch'üan and Sung Fang-tse walked in.

Che Chao-ch'üan stared hard at Ta-jen and called him names. After whispering to Sun Fang-tse, Che Chao-ch'üan asked Ta-jen to pay five pieces of money as compensation for the loss of Li Ku-tse's crop.

"If you want a man, take me. If you want money, I haven't a penny!" said Ta-jen.

"Ta-jen, you'd better make the compensation. This has been decided by the village headman and Master Li. This is a matter of face," said Sun Fang-tse, taking Ta-jen aside. Then Sun Fang-tse said to Che Chao-ch'üan: "It's all set. Ta-jen will make the compensation."

"You make the compensation. I have no money!" Ta-jen said angrily.

"All right, I'll pay it if you have no money," said Sun Fang-tse smiling. Then, turning to Che Chao-ch'üan and Li Ku-tse, he said: "Let's go!"

The three left Yü-huang Temple.

After Ta-jen told him of this event, Hsiao-lai said indignantly:

"They're simply blackmailing! Let's find some way to deal with them." After a long discussion, the two hit upon an idea.

The idea proved effective. A few days later, Che Chao-ch'üan's younger brother stole some corn from a field owned by a landlord. Ta-jen and P'ang Chung (another harvest watcher) caught him and were about to take him to the village. The crop stealer lay down and refused to budge. After telling Pangchung to watch the crop thief, Ta-jen went to see the head of the group of harvest watchers.

As soon as he heard that it was the younger brother of the village headman, Sun Fang-tse feigned a stomachache and refused to show his face. Therefore Ta-jen angrily went to see Che Chao-ch'üan in the village office. Che Chao-ch'üan was not in his office. Several hamlet headmen in the village office held down their heads like scarecrows when Ta-jen told them of the theft. In a little while Che Chao-ch'üan came back. Ta-jen carefully reported the theft to him before the hamlet headmen. Just at that moment P'ang Chung rushed into the office and told Ta-jen: "Che Chao-ch'üan's younger brother waited till I let down my guard. Then he hit me with a sickle and fled."

Upon hearing that his younger brother had fled, Che Chao-ch'üan ordered Sun Fang-tse and some others to hang up Ta-jen and P'ang Chung.

At this time there were many villagers present in the village office. Before the crowd, Che Chao-ch'üan charged Ta-jen with making a false charge against a good man and ruining the reputation of his family, and he insisted that Ta-jen should give a party by way of apology.

Hanging in midair, Ta-jen swore at Che Chao-ch'üan: "Your younger brother stole the crop and you hang me up. You're crooked. You don't deserve to be a village headman. I won't give a party for apology. Kill me if you want!"

"Beat him! Beat the poor devil to death!" Che Chao-ch'üan shouted.

Che Chao-ch'üan's lackeys closed in on Ta-jen like tigers and wolves.

At this point, Shen Hsiao-lai stepped forward:

"Let's straighten out this matter. Flogging Ta-jen won't help us find out whether his report is true or not. There's a way we can do this. The ground is still damp because of the rain yesterday. Ta-jen and P'ang Chung were barefoot when they left Yü-huang Temple. I think we can get the answer if we check footprints left in the field."

"That's right. Check the footprints left on the ground!"
"Check the footprints," some poor people shouted.

Che Chao-ch'üan's younger brother had not dared come out after he had fled to home from the field. When he heard that Ta-jen had been hung up, he came to the village office and tried to "pour oil on the fire." But as soon as he heard the crowd calling for a check of footprints left in the field, he laid down his stick and was about to sneak out of the village office. But he was detained by some of the poor people. When he saw the look on his brother's face, Che Chao-ch'üan feared that he had not even changed his shoes. Thinking of a way to save face, he pounded his desk and shouted:

"Keep your hands off him! Since I'm here, he can't run away. Let P'ang Chung and Ta-jen down. Ssu Ta-jen, I want to make it very clear to you: if the footprints left in the field are not my younger brother's, I'll hack you to death!"

"I'm not afraid of you hacking me to pieces. But what will you do if your brother's footprints are found in the field?" Ta-jen retorted.

Despite his gruff talk, Che Chao-ch'üan was in a state, and sweat stood in beads upon his forehead. The hamlet headman knew the true story. They came to Che Chao-ch'üan's rescue.

Li Ku-tse spoke: "I'd like to make a suggestion to settle this dispute. Ssu Ta-jen stops insisting on checking footprints and the village headman drops his demand for an apology from Ta-jen."

Then he turned to Che Chao-ch'üan: "Village headman, you need not quarrel with the likes of him."

Ta-jen continued to insist that the footprints be checked. The crowd of poor people said in loud voices: "Don't be taken in!"

"Check the footprints if you're so brave!" "You don't deserve
to be called village headman!"

"Stop making noises! Go and check footprints if you want,"
said Che Chao-ch'üan to the crowd, but he was unable to look
them in the eye.

Che Chao-ch'üan sent some hamlet headmen to check the
footprints, but he did not go with them.

Many villagers went to watch the checking of footprints. It
was found that the footprints left in the field where the corn
had been stolen were those of Che Chao-ch'üan's younger
brother. The hamlet headmen could not but offer to mediate.
Ta-jen insisted that the Che family must give back the stolen
corn. Wearing a smile on his face and nodding his head, Li Ku-
tse assured Ta-jen that he would tell the Che family to do so.

III

From then on, Che Chao-ch'üan harbored a deep hatred
against Ta-jen. He no longer hired Ta-jen as a harvest watcher. In order to sustain his bitter existence, Ta-jen took up
heavy work for others and also took care of graves and did the
work of an undertaker and other such odd jobs. Rich men had
even more contempt for him when he took on such "low" profes-
sions.

One day Ta-jen went to see Li Ku-tse. Li Ku-tse refused
to let him enter his house on the grounds that a man who did
the undertaking work would bring bad luck to his family. Ta-
jen got mad and cursed: "You wait, when someone dies in your
family, I won't come even with an invitation.

Once, Li Ku-tse had a jealous quarrel with his wife, and
forced her to commit suicide by jumping into a well. It was a
deep well. For two days he tried to haul his wife's corpse up
from the well, but he couldn't do it. He sent for Ta-jen to
pull her up for him. Ta-jen refused to come. Li Ku-tse personally came to ask for help. Ta-jen thought to himself: "Li
Ku-tse is a miser. He'll not importune me with a request like
this if I charge a high price for my services." Thereupon, he

said that he wanted ten dollars [ta-yang] for the job. Li Ku-tse considered it for a moment and promised, "Fine, Fine." Ta-jen could not but go to his house to start the work. However, after the woman's corpse was hauled up from the well, Li Ku-tse broke his word and paid Ta-jen only three dollars. "Ten dollars is too much. Please, don't charge me so high this time! We'll hire you again next time." His words made bystanders burst into laughter. Some of them said: "Hire him again? When do you expect someone else in your family to jump into a well?" Others said: "Don't take the money. Throw the woman's corpse back into the well." There was nothing Li Ku-tse could do. He put his head down and went home.

The poor people in the village held their sides with laughter when they heard of this incident. They said that Ta-jen had given them an outlet for their anger. Che Chao-ch'üan and Li Ku-tse hated Ta-jen with an implacable hatred, but they could not speak of their hatred against Ta-jen before others.

In 1938 the Japanese imperialists occupied Lu-ch'eng hsien. Che Chao-ch'üan became the man in charge of the Maintenance of Order Society which was established under the Japanese occupation force and the local puppet government. With the help of the Sword of the Eastern Sea [Japan], he was all the more influential in the village. He "broke" those villagers who didn't go along with him before the puppets. Of course, Che Chao-ch'üan did not let Ta-jen off. He often sent Ta-jen to remote places on duty. Ta-jen avoided offending Che Chao-ch'üan to his face, but he secretly carried on his struggle against this traitor.

Like the pine trees in Yü-huang Temple, Ssu Ta-jen resisted the wind, frost, snow, and ice and waited for the coming of spring.

Lu-ch'eng hsien was liberated in 1945. Under the Party's leadership, Ssu Ta-jen, as did the other poor people, struggled down the landlords, had his greivances redressed, and obtained a house and a plot of land. This put an end to the miserable life of Ta-jen and Hsiao-lai in Yü-huang Temple. Ta-jen told everyone: "If it were not for the Communist Party, I would not have been able to live a happy life or get out of Yü-huang Temple."

CHIA CHIH-SHUN, AN LIEH AND LIEN CHÜN-HSIEN

Under the iron hoof of Japanese imperialism

Airing Grievances by Beating a Watchman's Gong

I am Ho Shou-i, a member of Pei-liu Production Brigade of Pei-liu Commune in Yang-ch'eng hsien, Shansi Province. I am now fifty-seven years old.

My ancestors suffered much, running small shops for rich people and doing odd jobs. My family had a shabby two-room house and a three-mou plot of barren land.

When I was nine years old, my family lived on the verge of starvation and our three-mou plot of land was seized by a landlord nicknamed "Sheep Knife."

My father went away to make a living and fell sick and died. Then my helpless mother, taking me and my younger sister, married Wu Yung-ch'ing.

Our stepfather was also a man leading a bitter existence. He had a twelve-year-old child by his former wife. He could manage to make a precarious living by cultivating several mou of land. However, things got worse now that he had three more mouths to feed and after he had paid off our debt of three piculs

Chia Chih-shun, An Lieh, Lien Chün-hsien, "Tsai Jih-ti ti t'ieh-t'i hsia."

148

of grain. My mother was in poor health. She often stayed hungry in order to let Shu-shu (which is what I called my stepfather) and the three children have a little more to eat. Sick from malnutrition, she had to stay in bed, and her condition became worse day by day.

One day when my stepfather and I returned from work in the fields, I heard my mother call out as we got to the door, "Shou-i! Sh — Shou — i!" I stepped toward her bed. She was out of breath. Her eyes were dull, and her face pallid.

"Mother! Mother! Wake up! Shu-shu and I are here. Wake up!"

When she heard my voice, she extended her withered hand and felt my face:

"Shou-i, from now on you should be obedient to Shu-shu — " Then, she turned to my stepfather: "I'm sorry I have to leave Shou-i to your care. My — child is your child. Shou-i is my former husband's — only son — For the sake of what we feel for each other, please let him be — brought up — in your home — "

Upon hearing my mother's words, I and my younger sister cried inconsolably.

"Don't think about such things. You'll feel better pretty soon," Shu-shu tried to comfort my mother as he wiped his tears.

"Mother, you mustn't die — " cried my younger sister, who pressed her face against my mother's.

My mother held my hand and my younger sister's and looked at us with wide eyes. She cried: "My — children!" Then she breathed her last.

My stepfather brought me up. I was already sixteen years old. On the evening of the first day of the tenth month on the lunar calendar, 1923, when I returned from the work in the field, I saw Shu-shu sitting in dejection by the door. I asked him what he was worrying about. He pointed to a brass gong on the table and told me: "The village office has assigned us to beat the watches tonight." In our village, the poor people had to take turns beating the night watches.

As soon as supper was over, the deputy headman of our village came to hurry us out to beat the watches. I wanted to do the job, but Shu-shu would not let me go because he thought I was too young to walk in the dark night. He wanted to go alone, but I wouldn't hear of it — he was already an old man and might stumble over something in the dark. My younger brother and sister also wanted to go. Finally, Shu-shu led the whole family out to beat the night watch.

Pei-liu was a big village with more than 500 families. It was more than one li between both ends of the village, and it took more than an hour to make the rounds. Therefore we had to start the second watch almost as soon as we had finished the first one. After following Shu-shu as he beat the night watches for three nights, I and my younger brother took over.

It was already cold. The north wind blew hard, and snowflakes danced and swirled. In shabby and thin clothes and wearing tattered shoes we had picked up, my brother and I trembled in the biting wind as we stumbled along the slippery, snow-covered road. In the darkness we ran into things with our legs and bumped into things with our heads. Our legs bled, and our heads were swollen. But rich people were sitting around fires, drinking wine, playing the finger-guessing game, and laughing heartily and lightly. I passed by the doors of rich people's houses while beating the watchman's gong. They scolded me for having spoiled their lively mirth by beating the gong too loudly. I thought to myself: "They seized our land and were the cause of my mother's death. Now, I am beating the night watches to frighten burglars away from their houses, but they think I beat the gong too loudly." I was so mad that I did not beat the watchman's gong when I passed by doors of rich people's houses. I wished that burglars would break in to their houses and steal all of their things. On the dark night of October 11 we did not beat the watchman's gong when we passed by the door of rich man Liu Wu-kuan's house. Who was to know that he was standing behind the door? He said in a loud voice: "Watchmen, come back here!"

My younger brother and I walked toward Liu Wu-kuan, and

he slapped me in the face twice. He warned me: "Next time, if you don't beat the gong when you pass by my door, I'll kill you."

On the following night, when we beat the third watch, I went up to Liu Wu-kuan's door: "Tong! Tong! Tong!... Tong! Tong! Tong!" I kept beating the gong. I thought to myself: "We brothers are suffering cold in the dark night. We won't let you have a sound sleep." As we expected, his household were aroused from their sleep by the beating of the gong. Fearing that they would come out and beat us, we hurried away.

The following morning, Liu Wu-kuan, a stick in hand, came toward our house in anger. My younger brother and I ran out to hide ourselves nearby. As he turned to leave, he cursed: "If I catch Ho Shou-i, the son of a bitch, I'll bury him alive."

That night, Shu-shu said: "Shou-i, rich men are worse than venomous snakes. They'll do vicious things to you. You'd better get out of Pei-liu Village and lay low for awhile."

Just then, Wu Ping-tzu, a native of our village and a saddler at the town of Chia-chuang in Ching-hsing hsien in Hopei Province, came back to look for an apprentice. Shu-shu left me to his care. In the middle of the night, Wu Ping-tzu and I left Pei-liu Village.

My stepfather and younger brother and sister saw me to the outskirts of the village. With tears in his eyes, Shu-shu said to me: "Shou-i, I'm sorry I can't keep my promise to your mother. Rich men have forced father and son to part; best that you go your way and I go mine!"

My stepfather's words made me think of my poor mother. My younger sister wept bitterly. I tried to comfort her: "Ch'i-feng, take Shu-shu home. I'll come back to see you next year." I did not know that this was to be the last time I ever saw her. My younger sister starved to death not long after I left Pei-liu Village.

Entering Hell

In 1944 I worked as a saddler in Wu Ping-tzu's shop at Chia-chuang Town in Ching-hsing hsien. On the early morning of April 18, I heard from afar the sporadic firing of rifles, the shouting of people, and the neighing of horses. I jumped into my clothes to investigate. As soon as I got out of my house I saw two members of the Japanese invasion army, wearing swords, come along. The two fellows burst into laughter and said in poor Chinese: "Young one, very very good!" A horrible picture flashed across my mind: "Filth!" I tried to get away, but one of the two soldiers hit me on the back with his rifle butt. I felt a violent pain and fell to the ground. Then the two bandits tied my hands up behind my back with a rope.

Several minutes later, I was brought to a place where a truck was waiting. There were already twenty-five other boys and men there, also with their hands tied behind their backs. They all looked angry. Then, a Japanese soldier with a sword ordered: "Put all of them into the truck!"

So that we couldn't escape, the Japanese soldiers tied us together with ropes. We were taken to the "Labor Research Institute" at the Ching-hsing coal mine.

We were terribly frightened when our truck entered the "Labor Research Institute." We had heard that the "Labor Research Institute" was a place where the Japanese imperialists carried out the political screening of captured laborers and where many captives had been killed.

We got off the truck. Then the enemy classified us into several groups and cast us into prison. Ts'ui San-hsiao, Fan K'e-chien, P'eng Shih-yüan, and I were imprisoned together in one cell. I knew Ts'ui San-hsiao well. He was a merchant in Chia-chuang Town.

During the first day of our imprisonment the enemy gave us nothing to drink or eat. I grew dizzy with hunger. I asked Chiao-li, the Japanese guard, for something to eat. "You can eat — !" he said, coming up to me and slapping me in the face three times. Then he went away, calling me names in Japanese. I was trembling with anger and wanted to fight this bandit to the bitter end.

That night, a Japanese soldier brought me and Ts'ui San-hsiao before the court. The Japanese interrogation room was as gloomy and horrible as the "Palace of the King of Hell." On the walls of the room were iron cages for steaming people; ropes were hung from the beam; a German shepherd was lying under a table; killers stood at the door, and there were "tiger stools," "pokers," "bamboo needles," "boots," and many other instruments of torture in the trial room. We shuddered with horror as we took them in.

The "interrogator" was a Japanese officer who could speak some Chinese. He clenched his teeth and fixed us with an angry stare. Pointing to those instruments of torture, he said to us: "Do you see those things?" I and Ts'ui San-hsiao were silent.

The angry "interrogator" stood up from his seat and seized Ts'ui San-hsiao by the collar.

"You're Eighth Route Army? Is everyone in the Eighth Route Army?" the Japanese "interrogator" asked in poor Chinese.

"I'm a merchant. I don't know who's in the Eighth Route Army," replied Ts'ui San-hsiao.

"You don't know? Damn it! Merchants are all no good. Who is in the Eighth Route Army? Speak! Speak!"

"I — I don't know — "

Before Ts'ui San-hsiao could finish his answer, the "interrogator" kicked him in the groin. Ts'ui San-hsiao cried out in pain and fell to the ground. A Japanese soldier came to Ts'ui San-hsiao and forced him to stand up. He held his groin and beads of sweat stood on his forehead from the acute pain.

"Ha-ha! You're in the Eighth Route Army? You won't speak?" the "interrogator" sneered.

Then he looked at Ts'ui San-hsiao's beard and eyebrows and gave the order: "Burn them!"

Immediately four Japanese soldier burned Ts'ui San-hsiao's beard and eyebrows with lighted cigarette butts and his hair with matches.

Looking at Ts'ui San-hsiao's head aflame, I felt a great pain, as if my heart had been ripped out.

Then the "interrogator" set a German shepherd on Ts'ui San-hsiao. When it heard "sic him!" the beast tore a mouthful of flesh from Ts'ui San-hsiao's calf and blood gushed from the wound. He lost consciousness. . . .

The "interrogator" pointed to Ts'ui San-hsiao, lying in a pool
of blood, and threatened me: "Do you see it?" I didn't say a
word.

"Who is in the Eighth Route Army? If you tell me, the Imperial Army will give you a reward," said the "interrogator."

I held my head high and did not look at the "interrogator."
He got mad and roared: "Beat him!" Four Japanese soldiers
threw me down to the ground and gave me a sound flogging. I
clenched my teeth and fixed the beast with an angry stare. He
ordered: "Bring the ladder here!" Several beastly Japanese
soldiers tied me to the ladder and poured dirty water into my
mouth.

I did not know how much dirty water they poured into my
mouth. I fainted away as they were pouring the second bucket.

When I recovered my senses I found myself in the cell. Ts'ui
San-hsiao was groaning beside me. I asked him how we had
gotten back to our cell. He didn't know either.

The following day Ts'ui San-hsiao had a high fever, and I
came down with malaria. I burst into tears when I recalled the
death of my poor father, mother, and younger sister and the
plight of my stepfather and stepbrother.

"Brother Shou-i, it's no use weeping. These vicious devils
will fail one of these days," San-hsiao tried to comfort me.
"Do you know that there are guerrillas and a hsien government
of the Eighth Route Army in the Western Hills in Ching-hsing?
They will take vengeance on the behalf of the poor people."

"How do you know this? I asked.

"A guerrilla commando spent a few nights at my house,"
San-hsiao whispered to me when the Japanese guard was out
of earshot.

Another day passed. San-hsiao's condition became aggravated. Yellowish blood oozed from the wound caused by the
German shepherd's bite.

It was April. But in the north it was still cold. At night, we
were numb with cold from the north wind blowing into the
prison cell through the iron bars. Shortly before the dawn, I
heard San-hsiao call out to me.

"Brother Shou-i, I know I'll die soon. If you go back safely,
tell my wife not to wait for me anymore and to go to the Western Hills to look for...."

San-hsiao breathed his last before he could finish.

Early on the morning of April·23, Chiao-li used the German
shepherd to drag San-hsiao's body out of our cell. The dog
was stopped by the prisoners in our cell. Su Yu-chien, one of
the prisoners, was a good boxer. He hit the dog with a heavy
blow, and the beast ran away from our cell vomiting blood.

"Who beat the dog? Confess your guilt!" Chiao-li thundered.

Nobody uttered a word. Then, Chiao-li said: "If you don't
confess, all of you will be buried alive."

More than thirty rifle-bearing Japanese soldiers led by
Chiao-li escorted us to an open field behind the prison.

Infuriated, Chiao-li shouted: "Each of you dig a hole in the
ground and each one will have to bury the other. The last one
will be buried by a member of the Imperial Army!"

Obeying Chiao-li's order, the Japanese soldiers used bayonets to force us to dig holes in the ground.

We looked at each other. Some of us set our teeth, others
clenched our fists. We stood there, looking angry. No one of
us began digging. Our enemies kicked us with their boots and
beat us with rifle butts, clubs, and whips.

After a whole day of digging, the holes were still not three
feet deep. It was already getting dark. Chiao-li ordered the
Japanese soldiers to push us into the holes. But we stood up
again. Chiao-li was infuriated and he kicked the prisoners
over into the holes one after the other.

When Chiao-li kicked at me, I caught his foot in fury and
dragged him into my hole. Immediately several Japanese soldiers pulled him out of the hole. Then they kicked me with
their boots and beat me with their rifle butts.

Chiao-li had been put to shame, and in his anger his eyes
opened as big as eggs. He swore at me: "This one is very,
very bad!" Then, he told the Japanese soldiers to put me in
the hole headfirst and bury me.

When I was almost completely buried, a Japanese soldier

ran to Chiao-li and whispered a few words into the latter's
ear. Chiao-li blew the whistle and ordered the Japanese soldiers to drag me and the other prisoners out of the holes. He
said to us: "It's very kind of the Imperial Army to let you live
for one more night." So, we were thrown into prison again.

I lay in the cold, damp corner of the cell, and my whole body
ached badly. Looking at the leaden sky through the bars and at
the dim light from a lamp hung on the wall of the cell, I recalled Ts'ui San-hsiao's violent death and the Japanese officer's plan to bury us alive and thought of what might happen
to us the following day. My heart was afire, and I clenched my
fists so tightly that my hands were wet with sweat.

Early the following morning, a truck came and stopped at the
gate of our prison. The Japanese soldiers escorted us out of
the prison. We thought that the time for our death was at hand.
Each of us fixed the Japanese soldiers with a cold and angry
stare. Some of us clenched our fists and were ready to fight
the Japanese devils to the bitter end.

After a while, Chiao-li, wearing a sword, came to us and
brandished his sword over our heads. He thundered: "It's very
merciful of the Imperial Army to allow you to go on living."
Then, he ordered the Japanese soldiers to tie us together and
lead us into the truck. We were watched by three Japanese soldiers led by Chiao-li.

The truck started out. None of us knew where we were going,
what we were going to do, or whether we would live or die.

In a few minutes the truck had left the "Labor Research Institute" at the Ching-hsing coal mine behind, and it headed in
a southeast direction at high speed.

About three hours later, the truck entered the "Labor Training Institute" in a camp at the south of Shihchiachuang. Immediately, we knew that we were going to be thrown into another prison.

The "Labor Training Institute" was a center where the Japanese imperialists were carrying out the enslavery education
and technical training for captured Chinese workmen. It was
a spacious compound and there were five rows of buildings in

which more than 3,000 prisoners were kept.

I was imprisoned in a building in the second row. There were over 300 prisoners in this building. The same Chiao-li was the leader of the guards who kept watch over the prisoners.

Life in this place was as bad as it had been in the "Labor Research Institute" in Ching-hsing. Each of us was given two small bowls of "dog food" a day. We suffered from dizziness caused by hunger. Those who were ill from want of food were sent to the "patients' isolation room" in a building in the fifth row.

All the prisoners called the room in the fifth row the "waiting for death room." Patients in the isolation room received no medical treatment and nothing to eat; they simply awaited death. Every day, twenty to thirty dead men were hauled out of the isolation room.

On the third day after our arrival at the "Labor Training Institute," Chiao-li told us to learn the Japanese language. I wondered why Chinese had to learn Japanese. I asked myself: "What is the use of learning Japanese? Can it be that when a man becomes a slave the language he uses must also be enslaved?"

The Japanese "class" began. A Japanese "instructor" read the twiglike Japanese syllabary which he had written on the blackboard and told us to repeat it. But no one in the class opened his mouth. The "instructor" tried several times to make us repeat the syllabary. All of us kept silent. He became mad and angrily walked toward two of the prisoners and beat them with a stick.

"You're dumb?" he asked angrily.

"We'd rather be dumb than learn Japanese," replied the two prisoners.

"Damn it! You want to be dumb, huh?"

The furious "instructor" ordered the Japanese soldiers in the classroom to hang up the two prisoners. In a moment, he had cut out the two prisoners' tongues with his sword.

I was extremely indignant at the brutal atrocity committed by the beastly "instructor." I was about to rush him and fight him to the bitter end. Ching Ch'ang-k'ai who sat next to me whispered to me: "You shouldn't fight him. We're unarmed. We can't beat an enemy who is armed with guns."

Ching Ch'ang-k'ai had been captured during the Japanese "sweeping up" operations in the liberated area. Because of his concern about us, we got along well with him and called him Big Brother Ching. His words were usually convincing. I began to realize that he was right when he told me not to clash with an armed enemy. I controlled my anger and waited for an opportunity to fight the Japanese devils.

Finally, an opportunity came. Fearing that we might break prison, our enemies took off our clothes and put the clothes outside the prison every night. We had to sleep naked in the cold prison. Many of us fell ill from the cold. One of our number went to Chiao-li to ask for clothes to wear at night, but Chiao-li refused and sent him back with a sound beating.

Big Brother Ching had a plan.

"He has rejected the request by one of us. Now let all of us go to him to make the same request. If he rejects our request, we'll refuse to eat. This is the tactic of the 'fast struggle.'"

The following day, we started the "fast struggle." Fearing that our death would bring damage to the "labor force" and that he would be reprimanded by the higher-ups for neglect of duty, Chiao-li agreed to let us sleep with our clothes on.

From victory in this struggle we learned a lesson: no matter how strong our enemies were, we could beat them as long as we were of one mind.

Hearts in the Motherland

Three days after the victory of our struggle, Chiao-li called us together and roared: "You laborers are going to work!"

Our enemies escorted us into a train. The whistle sounded, and the trains' wheels began to turn. Sitting in this "sealed jug" with all its windows shut, we asked one another: "Where are they taking us?" None of us could solve this "mystery."

After a twenty-four-hour journey we arrived in Tangku

Station. We were escorted to the port of Taku and forced to board a big ship flying a Japanese flag.

After an eight-day voyage we landed in Shimonoseki. We realized that we were already in Japan. We clenched our teeth and cursed under our breath....

Then, after another two days of riding on a train, we arrived at Sekiso Village in Aomori Prefecture, where we were forced to build a railway.

The construction site was enclosed within barbed-wire fences. All the supervisors were Japanese. They included Chiao-li, Matsuyama, Nobufuku, Kawakiho, and Ishijima. They could speak some Chinese. Each was more brutal and vicious than the next, and they kept five German shepherds to deal with us.

One day a prisoner went to defecate outside the barbed-wire fence. Matsuyama charged him with trying to escape and brought him back to the construction site. Matsuyama said before all of the prisoners: "Anyone who tries to escape is going to get this!" Several supervisors put the prisoner into a burlap sack and whipped him savagely, and then rolled him down a hill. Chiao-li then set the five German shepherds on the burlap sack. The beasts tore the sack open and devoured the prisoner's body. The other prisoners set their teeth when they witnessed this heinous crime.

Since the Japanese imperialist used the German shepherds to deal with us, we were determined to get rid of these beasts. One day, the Japanese supervisors took us to a mountain chasm to dig a tunnel. After digging a few score feet into the mountain, we discovered a big crack on the top of the tunnel. Rocks and clods of earth fell down from the crack. Big Brother Ching knew that a cave-in was imminent. He cried: "Let's get out of here! Hurry up!" We all rushed toward the entrance of the tunnel. But we were stopped by the Japanese supervisors. As soon as one prisoner stuck his hand out of the entrance of the tunnel, Ishijima cut three of his fingers off with a sword. We wanted to get out of the tunnel. Ishijima set the five German shepherds on us. These beasts attacked us, and blood streamed

down the bodies of more than ten prisoners. Ching Ch'ang-k'ai caught the hind legs of a German shepherd and threw it up in the air. He kicked the dog with full strength. The dog fell to the ground several feet away from him. All of the other prisoners used spades and rocks to hit the dogs. In a few minutes, all five of the German shepherds were dead. Just at that moment, the tunnel caved in. I and several other prisoners were caught by huge earth blocks. Thanks to Big Brother Ching and the other prisoners, our lives were saved. I was seriously wounded in the hip, and four other prisoners' legs were broken.

The railway in Hokkaido was opened to traffic on the eve of the Japanese imperialists' surrender. One morning, the supervisors told us to speed up our work because a train was coming through that afternoon.

Since I could not do the heavy work because of the serious injury to my hip, Chiao-li forced me to break rocks beside the railway. Seeing the supervisors take a rest under the shade of a tree, Big Brother Ching came over and laid down his baskets for carrying gravel. Pointing to the spikes fastening the rails to the ties, he told me: "I'm going to pull some of them out!" I nodded. He took the hammer from my hand and ran to a curve in the track which had already passed inspection. He loosened several spikes and swiftly returned to my side. He gave the hammer back to me and went away with his load.

That afternoon we spotted a column of black smoke in the distance. This was followed by the sounding of a whistle. A train roared by at full speed. In a few seconds, there was an ear-deafening sound near the curve of the railway as the train was derailed. Our hearts were thrilled with secret joy.

The Japanese bandits thought that we had something to do with the derailment because it took place near our work site. However, their investigation yielded no results. They intensified their guard over and persecution of us. More supervisors and more German shepherds were brought to the site.

In early September of 1945, a Chinese national who worked as an interpreter in the Japan railway authority communicated the news of the Japanese surrender to us. He also gave us other information about the Japanese surrender.

This happy news spread among the prisoners quickly. We were so excited that we could not sit quietly or sleep at night. Big Brother Ching had an idea: "Let's hoist our national flag in celebration of our Motherland's victory over Japan." We looked for cloth and thread, and some of us volunteered to do the cutting and sewing work. Finally, we came up with a Chinese flag.

The following morning, as soon as the east grew light, we ran to the flagpole. We pulled down the Japanese flag and hoisted the Chinese flag. We clapped our hands, and our eyes were wet with tears of joy. Chiao-li, Matsuyama, Ishijima, and some other supervisors came up to us, waving their clubs.

"You're not permitted to hoist that flag!" they thundered.

"China has achieved the victory. We'll hoist the Chinese flag!" we spoke with one voice.

As soon as they heard the news of Japan's defeat, they roared in fury:

"You want to cast away your lives? If you don't lower the Chinese flag, we'll set the dogs on you!"

Like a fence made of iron, the several hundred prisoners stood around the flagpole. Knowing that they were outnumbered, the Japanese supervisors dared not set their dogs on us. After circling around us several times, they went away with their German shepherds.

Once again our struggle ended in a victory!

Falling into Another Sea of Misery

I lived the life of a slave in Japan for fifteen months. After Japan's surrender, we returned to China on December 4, 1945.

We were overjoyed to be aboard the ship bound for China, and we all said that our suffering was over. We were looking forward to family reunions.

Our ship steamed into the port of Taku. Many warships flying the Stars and Stripes were in port. American soldiers and Chinese soldiers of the "Central Army" and the "Security

Force" could be seen everywhere in the port city. I was somewhat perplexed at the things I saw. I asked Big Brother Ching what these things meant. He did not say anything but shook his head. Judging from his gloomy countenance, I knew that his heart was heavy.

According to the arrangements made by the repatriation personnel, we arrived in Tientsin by train. At an office on the campus of Peiyang University, we got our "workers' repatriation cards" issued by the Kuomintang government. A Kuomintang official told us: "You can go to any place and nobody will stop you as long as you have the 'repatriation cards!'"

Nevertheless, we were stopped by some soldiers of the "Central Army" when we walked toward the gate of the university. We showed them our "workers' repatriation cards," but they hardened their countenance and did not even glance at our cards. They pushed us into a room and detained us there. When I realized what was going on, my heart sank.

One of us, a young man from Szechuan Province, went up to the officer checking identification cards and asked: "Why isn't this identification card any good? Isn't it issued by the government?" After adjusting his hat and inclining his head, the officer boxed the young man on the ears twice.

"You're simply unreasonable. What do you want us to show you, if this 'repatriation card' is no good?" the young man boldly retorted.

"Nothing is good except my whip!" said the officer, who picked up a whip and angrily flogged the young man with it. Blood oozed from all over the young man's body. Another man in our group went to the officer and angrily asked him: "By what right are you beating that young man?"

"This bastard wants to show his guts? Take him away and hang him up!" the officer ordered.

Two Kuomintang soldiers dragged him away, and we never found out what happened to him.

All these things gnawed at my heart. Big Brother Ching knew what annoyed me.

"We've fallen into another sea of misery. But we're not

afraid of them. We've still got the Eighth Route Army. Go seek help from the Eighth Route Army!" Big Brother Ching whispered to me after pulling me over to a corner of the enclosing wall.

"Big Brother Ching, I can't stand parting with you," I said in tears.

"We'll have the chance to meet again," Big Brother Ching tried to comfort me.

No sooner had he finished speaking than Big Brother Ching was taken away by the bandit Kuomintang soldiers. At the same time, over 100 repatriated laborers were impressed into military service.

They did not force me into military service because I was a cripple. But the soldiers of the "Central Army" took all of the little money I had. Hence I had to sell the clothes off my back in the dead of winter. When I arrived in Cheng-ting-fu, I saw two soldiers of the "Central Army" shoot two repatriated laborers to death in a narrow alley. I knew the two laborers because we were aboard the same ship when we returned from Japan. Their personal effects were taken away by the two soldiers.

As soon as I got off the train at the station in Shihchia-chuang, I was seized by soldiers of the "Central Army." At first they wanted to impress me into military service. When they found that I was crippled in the hip, they kicked me and called me a useless fellow. They took the money I had gotten by selling my clothes and forced me to leave Shihchiachuang.

What could I do? I begged for food on my journey and just kept on walking. Again I ran into the "Central Army." Because I dreaded encountering the "army of calamity," I dared not move during the day. I lived in temple ruins at night. One night I stayed in the ruins of a temple in Hu-lu hsien and was ferreted out by the "Central Army." I was violently beaten and detained. But I managed to slip my ropes and flee.

Indeed, lawlessness prevailed in the areas controlled by the Kuomintang. There was no way out for me. I remembered Big Brother Ching's words: "Go seek help from the Eighth Route Army!"

Seeing the Blue Sky

In the spring of 1946 for the first time I tasted the sweetness of life. I returned to liberated Chia-chuang Town in Ching-hsing, my second home. Barefoot and carrying a shabby bag and a stick to beat off dogs, I entered Chia-chuang Town. I was begging for food. Even now I cannot forget the kindness shown to me by the comrades from the work team of the People's Government in Ching-hsing who were sent by Chairman Mao to welcome me. Although it's been almost twenty years, I still remember that several women comrades helped me wash my feet and put on my new shoes and clothes, prepared food for me, and gave me medicine and injections. They helped me recover my health, which had been ruined by the Japanese bandits and the Kuomintang soldiers. With their help, I returned to my native place — Pei-liu Village in Yang-ch'eng hsien, Shansi Province.

After I returned, a house and a plot of land were distributed to me, and my life got better and better.

I was exploited, oppressed, bullied, and insulted by landlords, capitalists, the Kuomintang, and the Japanese imperialists. I became a slave who lost the basic rights of man. Now I am a real master and have seen the blue sky. I am living a happy life. Although I am old, I will still contribute my strength to the socialist construction of my motherland.

The "Millstone" shoes

Hsiao Ping-ch'üan is the deputy director of the Poor and Lower-Middle Peasants Cooperative in Hsiang-yüan hsien, a member of the Party branch committee in Chi-chia-ling Production Brigade, and the deputy director of the production brigade in charge of animal husbandry. Now forty-one years old, he is a veteran shepherd. He usually likes to wear a pair of patched nailed shoes. He still treasures two pairs of "millstone" shoes. Three soles are nailed to the bottom and the sides are braced with five patches. They are five times heavier than ordinary shoes, and they are all the heavier when wet with rain and mud sticks to their soles. His two pairs of "millstone" shoes have a twenty-year history. Though they are ungainly, they are called the "shoes of glory" by members of the production brigade. Now, let us tell the story of the "shoes of glory."

Hsiao Ping-ch'üan was born in Lin hsien in Honan Province. In 1928, when he was four years old, his family fled to Shansi because of a famine in Honan. They settled in Cheng-tao Village in Hsiang-yüan hsien, Shansi Province. At that time his family comprised his grandfather and his parents. His

---

Lien T'ai-i, Sun Shou-ch'u, "'Tun-tzu' hsieh."

grandfather was good at working land, his father was a skilled mason, and his mother was apt at needlework. Nevertheless, even this family of skilled workers could not support little Hsiao Ping-ch'üan. Therefore, Ping-ch'üan had to tend sheep for a rich man.

A Pair of Broken Shoes

In 1932 Ping-ch'üan, eight years old, began to tend sheep for a landlord named Ts'ui Shih-so at Tu Village, twenty or thirty li from Cheng-tao Village. It was agreed that the little boy would get no pay for his work but that he would have free meals at the landlord's house. Every day, Ping-ch'üan walked in paths covered with thorns. In summer he worked under the blazing sun as he scrambled over the burning rock slopes. In winter he trod through ice and snow in the biting wind. He hoped he could get a pair of thick-soled shoes to protect his feet from the cold and heat and the thorns. Not only did Ts'ui Shih-so not give him shoes, the landlord gave Ping-ch'üan only the most meager food and and the dirtiest water, so that he never had enough to eat. And he often scolded him. Eighteen months later, Ping-ch'üan, no longer able to endure, deserted the flock of sheep and fled back to Cheng-tao Village. He never again worked for landlord Ts'ui Shih-so.

Hsiang Ping-ch'üan loved his sweet home. But his family was so poor that he had to work. With the help of a relative, his grandfather and father found ten-year-old Ping-ch'üan a job tending sheep for a rich man named Wang Chin-fu in Chi-tui Village, a few li away from Cheng-tao Village. Ping-ch'üan did not want to go. His grandfather and father persuaded him to take the job by telling him that their home was not far from Chi-tui Village and that Wang Chin-fu's head shepherd was a kind man. His mother gave him a pair of heavily patched, thick-toed shoes, and she encouraged Ping-ch'üan: "Son, you'd better take the job! This pair of shoes will protect your feet from cold, heat, and thorns. Meanwhile, I'll make a pair of new shoes for you." Thus, Ping-ch'üan, wearing the heavily patched shoes, walked through Wang Chin-fu's main gate.

Wang Chin-fu was a rich man in Chi-tui Village. He loved his money and was unkind to others. He even scolded and beat his parents. So he was called "Little Cow." It goes without saying that he treated his shepherds badly, that he often slapped P'ing-ch'üan, head shepherd Hsi Ch'un-yüan, and their little companion Liu Ch'iu-shan in the face and gave them nothing to eat.

Every day, ten-year-old Ping-ch'üan followed head shepherd Hsi Ch'un-yüan as he drove the flock of sheep to field. Because of the rain, mud, and thorns, Ping-ch'üan's patched shoes were soon coming apart again. His feet were badly cut by thorns and he suffered a great deal. Hsi Ch'un-yüan was touched with pity for the boy. He found some hemp and nails and patched Ping-ch'üan's broken shoes. Ping-ch'üan wore the shoes for many years. With layer on layer of patches and nails, the shoes weighed six or seven catties when the sun was shining and double that on rainy days. They were so heavy that Ping-ch'üan could hardly move his legs, just as it would be if he were turning a mill. That is why people called his shoes the "millstone" shoes.

In the spring of 1938 the Japanese imperialists invaded Yü-tz'u and T'ai-ku in Shansi. Everyone was in panic as the flames of war came closer and closer to Hsiang-yüan hsien. Rich men and landlords began to pack up and hide their money and valuables.

One morning, Ping-ch'üan, in his "millstone" shoes, went to see Wang Chin-fu and asked permission to go home to get another pair of shoes from his mother. Wang Chin-fu was busy packing his things.

"You don't have to go home for shoes. My children have many shoes. I'll give you a pair later," said Wang Chin-fu with a forced smile.

Ping-ch'üan believed Wang Chin-fu and expected that the landlord would soon give him a pair of shoes. But he had to wait until after dinner before the landlord sent for him.

"I want you to do one thing for me tonight. If you do it and don't tell anyone, I'll give you a pair of shoes tomorrow," Wang Chin-fu said to Ping-ch'üan in a low voice.

"I'll do it for you if I can," replied Ping-ch'üan, who was bewildered, not knowing what the landlord wanted him to do.

"Oh yes, you can. I want you to carry things for me."

"Okay!"

For a whole night, Ping-ch'üan carried things for landlord Wang. After all the things had been safely hidden, the landlord gave Ping-ch'üan a pair of old shoes.

The following day Ping-ch'üan went to the sheepfold wearing the shoes which had been given him by Wang Chin-fu on the previous night.

"Hey! Buddy, where did you get this pair of shoes?" asked Liu Ch'iu-shan.

"The landlord gave them to me," replied Ping-ch'üan.

Liu Ch'iu-shan thought to himself: "The landlord never gives anything to anyone. Now he has given Ping-ch'üan a pair of shoes. Isn't it as if the sun had risen in the west?"

"Why did he give you a pair of shoes?" Liu Ch'iu-shan asked again.

Ping-ch'üan told Liu Ch'iu-shan how he had asked for leave and had carried the landlord's valuables to a safe place. Liu Ch'iu-shan did not say a word, but only sighed to himself for what had happened to Ping-ch'üan.

The first day of the tenth month on the lunar calendar was the day on which shepherds received their annual salary. With a rice sack in his hand, Ping-ch'üan's father hopefully entered the landlord's house. He told himself: "It will be good to have five or six pecks of rice. This will help tide us over the difficult period in winter." Ping-ch'üan's annual wage was seven pecks of rice. But Wang Chin-fu took out his accounts book and explained the various deductions for sick leave, etc. The landlord even had the impudence to charge Ping-ch'üan one peck of rice for that pair of old shoes. The seven pecks were reduced to practically nothing. Ping-ch'üan's father was dismayed.

"I'm not going to talk about all the other deductions yet. But I wonder if there is a mistake in the price of that pair of shoes.

Landlord, a peck of rice is quite something for us. I've never bought a pair of shoes for a peck of rice in my life," Ping-ch'üan's father complained.

"No mistake! If you don't believe it, ask your son about it," shouted Wang Chin-fu, getting red in the face and pushing the abacus aside.

Ping-ch'üan's father was so bewildered that he forgot to ask the landlord how the deductions were calculated. Carrying the small amount of rice in the sack, he went to look for his son.

"Ping-ch'üan, you've gone against your father! You paid a peck of rice for a pair of shoes without consulting with me!" said Ping-ch'üan's father.

At first, Ping-ch'üan didn't say a word, for he did not understand what his father was talking about. Then he hurriedly explained: "Father, I never paid a peck of rice for a pair of shoes!"

"You didn't buy them? The landlord said that you got a pair of shoes from him and he deducted a peck of rice from your wages...."

"I didn't buy them. He gave them to me...."

Ping-ch'üan proceeded to tell his father the whole story.

"Goddamn it! This landlord is really a fox. He is not satisfied with his exploitation of the poor. He has swindled money out of us with this pair of shoes. I'm going to see him to appeal to reason," Ping-ch'üan's father said angrily.

Ping-ch'üan's father hurried away, cursing Wang Chin-fu all the while. He entered Wang Chin-fu's house.

"Manager, you shouldn't do things against your conscience. You gave that pair of old shoes to Ping-ch'üan. But then you charged him a peck of rice for the shoes. Was my son not entitled to that pair of old shoes as a reward for the backbreaking work he did for you a whole night?" Ping-ch'üan's father said defiantly.

Wang Chin-fu was irritated by the remarks of Ping-ch'üan's father. He pounded his brass pipe on the table.

"Poor devil! Do you want to revolt? Your son wanted to go home to get a pair of shoes. The shoes provided by me saved him a trip. I did it with a good conscience. As for his work on that night, that was his duty. He must work for me as long as he gets pay and free meals from me. Your son must pay for the shoes. Now you are trying to repudiate a debt," Wang Chin-fu scolded Ping-ch'üan's father.

"If we were figuring the cost, a pair of old shoes is not worth a peck of rice!"

Landlord Wang's money was his life, and he had never given ground in such matters.

"Old shoes? How many old shoes do you have? They were new shoes that I had only worn twice. I paid 1.2 pecks of rice for them. Was it unreasonable for me to charge a peck of rice for them?"

Ping-ch'üan's father clenched his teeth. He was so mad that he couldn't speak.

"Get out! Stop your nonsense! If you think that pair of shoes is expensive, you can return the shoes to me. But they must be as new as they were when your son bought them. Then I'll give you back your peck of rice. If you can't make the shoes as new as they were, you'd better get out of her right away. I don't have time to talk about such silly things with you!" said Wang Chin-fu.

Ping-ch'üan's father left Wang Chin-fu's house in anger. He found his son and said: "Don't wear the shoes given to you by that old son of a bitch even if your feet fall off from the cold!"

Looking for the "Millstone" Shoes

When chief herdsman Hsi Ch'un-yüan and his companion Liu Ch'iu-shan found out what had happened to Ping-ch'üan, they were very sympathetic. They got together and started to fight the vicious landlord. They buried sheep's droppings collected from the sheepfold; they let sheep trample on and eat crops in the fields owned by the Wang family. However, crops continued to grow; poor people were as poor as they had been; rich people remained rich; and shepherds still had no shoes to wear.

Later, the three of them adopted a new tactic to deal with

Wang Chin-fu. They quit working for him. Hsi Ch'un-yüan and
some ten-odd families in the village made an arrangement
whereby the three of them would take care of the sheep owned
by the families. Although they were much freer than they had
been watching Wang Chin-fu's sheep, they could not change
their poverty status, and Chin-fu got others to tend his sheep.
They still had not found the correct way to oppose rich people.

In 1942 Ping-ch'üan's father became an intelligence-
communication worker at an underground liaison station operated by the armed struggle committee in Hsiang-yüan <u>hsien</u>.
Ping-ch'üan and his father received the Party education and
heightened their class consciousness and hence found the correct revolutionary way to fight the class enemy.

Ping-ch'üan's father had frequent contact with Li Ch'iang, a
member of the Chinese Communist Party and the staff officer
in charge of reconnaissance in the armed struggle committee
in Hsiang-yüan <u>hsien</u>.

A tall man with big eyes and bushy eyebrows, Li Ch'iang
was very adept at his work against the enemy. He demonstrated
his quick wits and courage in the famous Battle of Hsiang-yüan.
Before the battle, he had stayed seven days and nights at the
home of the magistrate of Hsiang-yüan. He adroitly dealt blows
against the enemy, and the enemy agents for miles around
trembled with fear when his name was mentioned.

Ping-ch'üan's father enjoyed a delightful conversation with
Li Ch'iang in their first meeting. When their conversation
came around to the problem of poverty, Ping-ch'üan's father
aired his personal and family grievances. He finished by saying with a sigh:

"We poor people cannot afford even a pair of good shoes.
Rich people are vicious; poor people have a bitter lot in life!"

"Old Hsiao, it isn't a bitter lot or bad luck. Oppression and
exploitation by landlords and rich men are the causes of poverty. You said you have no shoes to wear. Have you seen my
shoes?" asked Li Ch'iang, lifting his feet to show his heavily
patched shoes. Li Ch'iang went on, patting Hsiao on the shoulder, "Don't worry about having shoes to wear now. We'll have

enough shoes to wear in the future. Chairman Mao leads us poor people in making revolution to strike down the Japanese aggressors, to strike down the landlords, to liberate the whole of China, and to enable us poor people to secure power in our own hands. Today we don't have good shoes, but we can fight the enemy while wearing patched shoes. Tomorrow the poor will secure power in their own hands...."

"Can it happen?" asked Ping-ch'üan's father, half-convinced by Li Ch'iang's remarks.

"Why not? If we are united, we can fight the enemy to the bitter end and we'll succeed," Li Ch'iang explained.

Li Ch'iang went on to tell Ping-ch'üan's father many stories about Chairman Mao's role in the revolution, about soldiers of the Red Army who participated in the revolution while wearing straw sandals, about the situation in the liberated areas in northern Shensi, about the capability of the Eighth Route Army, and about the victories in the battles against the enemy. Ping-ch'üan's father nodded and his face beamed with joy. From then on, his back straightened and he puffed his chest out. Several days later, he was admitted to the intelligence team. Ping-ch'üan took part in guerrilla work under the guidance of the guerrilla team. He often carried intelligence messages for his father. Regardless of the weather, the dark of night, or the number of army checkpoints, he never failed in his assignments. He understood that the hard struggle today would bring happiness to the people tomorrow. This was why he could successfully fulfill his revolutionary missions in hardships and difficulties. He was no longer a shepherd fighting single-handedly against the class enemy. He was in the vanguard in the anti-Japanese war.

One autumn day of that year, Ping-ch'üan and Liu Ch'iu-shan were watching their sheep grazing on a hillside near Chi-tui Village. Suddenly, they saw some twenty puppet soldiers in yellow uniforms chasing five men in civilian dress. As they approached, Ping-ch'üan could tell that the five men in civilian dress were guerrillas. As the guerrillas ran into a ravine, the puppet soldiers were still far behind. Ping-ch'üan exchanged

a few words with Liu Ch'iu-shan, and they immediately drove
the flock of sheep to the "intermediate zone" to block the ad-
vancing puppet soldiers. In a few seconds, the twenty-odd puppet soldiers rushed to the hillside and surrounded Ping-ch'üan
and Liu Ch'iu-shan.

"Where are those men who were fleeing in this direction?"
the puppet soldiers asked.

"What do you want?" Ping-ch'üan said with pretended ignorance, all the while his heart throbbing with terror.

"Damn it! Don't pretend to be deaf. Tell me where those
men are. If you don't tell me, I'll shoot you to death," one of
the soldiers threatened.

Several puppet soldiers leveled their rifles at Ping-ch'üan
and Liu Ch'iu-shan. Ping-ch'üan thought to himself: "I'll never
tell you the whereabouts of the guerrillas. It would be more
difficult for you to get information from me than to fly to the
heavens."

"I don't know. I didn't see anyone come along," Ping-ch'üan
said calmly.

"I see you two don't want to go on living," said the puppet
soldier, knocking Liu Ch'iu-shan down with his rifle butt.

Ping-ch'üan went up to Liu Ch'iu-shan and tried to help him
stand up. Just then, another puppet soldier shouted in a hoarse
voice to Liu Ch'iu-shan, "Talk! Talk!" and he leveled his rifle
at Liu Ch'iu-shan's heaving chest.

"I didn't see them come along. Go ahead and kill me. I have
nothing to tell you," said Liu Ch'iu-shan calmly.

"We are shepherds and we know nothing but sheep-tending.
If you want to know how to take care of sheep, we can tell you,"
said Ping-ch'üan, jumping in.

The puppet soldier turned the barrel of his rifle away from
Liu Ch'iu-shan and toward Ping-ch'üan. He asked Ping-ch'üan
a few more questions. But Ping-ch'üan's answers were completely impertinent.

"Damn it! Tell me where the guerrillas are. If you refuse
to do so, you'll be shot to death on the charge of aiding the
bandits," said the puppet soldier.

Ping-ch'üan made up his mind: "In any case, to fall into the hands of these turtles is the same as dying. It would be folly to expect anything but the worst from them." He reiterated Liu Ch'iu-shan's words: "I don't know. I didn't see them." The puppet soldier slapped Ping-ch'üan in the face and hit Ping-ch'üan with his rifle butt as he kept repeating the same question. He asked and hit, asked and hit, over and over again.

Suddenly, "crack!" a rifle shot was heard. Ping-ch'üan thought the puppet soldiers had begun to fire at him and Liu Ch'iu-shan. But in a second he realized that the shooting was being done by the guerrillas who, having circled around and seen the spot the two shepherds were in, had opened fire to divert the puppet soldiers' attention from him and Ch'iu-shan. Hearing the rifle fire, the puppet soldiers let go of the two shepherds and ran off in the direction of the guerrillas. On the hilltop, the guerrillas killed and wounded many of the puppet soldiers. The rest threw down their rifles and fled in disarray.

Although Ping-ch'üan and Ch'iu-shan had been brutally beaten by the enemy, they were victorious in rescuing the guerrillas. The two young men were exhilarated and had just begun to round up their frightened sheep when Ping-ch'üan discovered that Ch'iu-shan had lost one of his shoes. Ping-ch'üan asked Ch'iu-shan: "Where is your 'millstone' shoe?" Ch'iu-shan looked down and burst into laughter. He held his sides as he roared. "Don't laugh at me! Where are your 'millstone' shoes?" Ping-ch'üan found that he too had lost his "millstone" shoes. They looked into each other's faces and burst into laughter again. Finally, they found their "millstone" shoes.

The Shoes of Glory

Under the leadership of the Communist Party, the people defeated the Japanese devils and obtained control over rich men. Poor people in the Taihang Mountain area came into their own in 1945.

In 1946 the Land Reform was carried out in Hsiang-yüan hsien. Hsiao Ping-ch'üan's family obtained a house and a plot of land. They no longer were bullied by landlords and rich men. Their sufferings in the old society were over. Under the leadership of the Party, Hsiao Ping-ch'üan joined the mutual aid team, the elementary and the advanced agricultural cooperatives, and the people's commune. He was transformed from an ordinary shepherd into a proletarian vanguard fighter. However, he never left the flocks of sheep. He was good at tending sheep. Because of the progress he made in his profession and the overfulfillment of production year after year, he became a famous model shepherd in Shansi Province.

In 1952 Hsiao Ping-ch'üan turned his attention to improving the breeding of sheep. He succeeded in developing a mixed breed of sheep which provides more wool of longer fiber and finer texture. In the last thirteen years he has already given the production team in Chi-chia-ling 280 head of sheep of the mixed breed. In the past, a sheep yielded only seven ounces of coarse wool a year. But now a sheep of the mixed breed provides three catties of fine-textured wool a year. As a result, the wool production of the production team has quadrupled, and its income has increased over five times. For years the production team in Chi-chia-ling has been awarded for its increased production.

But most important of all, Ping-ch'üan never boasts of his achievements or alienates himself from the collective. He still regards himself as a shepherd. One July day in 1962, Han Hsien-wen and some other shepherds drove the production team's flock of sheep to the meadow between Hsi-ni-kou and Ta-sha-kou. That afternoon, a storm broke out. Ping-ch'üan saw Han Hsien-wen, naked to the waist and barefoot, rounding up the flock of sheep in the storm. He took off his raincoat and rubber shoes and let Han Hsien-wen wear them. He braved the storm to join the other shepherds in rounding up the flock of sheep.

"Deputy director, please put on your raincoat and rubber shoes. I'm young. It doesn't matter if I get wet," said Han Hsien-wen.

"Don't take them off! You'll catch cold," Ping-ch'üan ordered.

It took quite a long time for the shepherds to drive the flock of sheep to a safe place. Finding that three sheep were missing, the shepherds volunteered to look for them.

"You've been busy all day. You need a rest. Make a fire to keep yourselves warm. I'll go look for the sheep. Anyway, my clothes are already soaking wet," said Ping-ch'üan.

Despite the shepherds' protestations, Ping-ch'üan went to look for the stray sheep. Running about in the storm for quite a long time, he found the three stray sheep and brought them back to the flock. When he came back, he did not dry his soaked clothes at the fire. Instead, he brought the wet and trembling sheep near the fire to keep them warm. As a result, the three sheep did not die of cold.

Ping-ch'üan is heart and soul for the collective. Since 1952 he has played a leading role in clearing away thorns, tending sheep, and making wicker baskets. Whenever he is not tending sheep, he is working together with other commune members in the field. He is devoted to the collective and production work. Whenever he goes to other places to buy domestic animals for the commune, he never asks for traveling expenses or a food allowance.

His heart becomes redder and redder and his revolutionary fervor is increasing in intensity. Proof of this is that he is constantly seen in a pair of patched shoes. As a shepherd boy, he suffered great hardships and could not afford even a pair of old shoes. Now he is deputy director of Chi-chia-ling Production Team. He can afford good shoes, even leather shoes. But he always wears a pair of patched shoes. He often tells others: "Good shoes will spoil your feet. Wearing patched shoes will harden your heels and help you stand firm on the ground."

When he is asked why he wants to keep the "millstone" shoes which he wore when he tended sheep for others in the old society, Hsiao Ping-ch'üan says: "The 'millstone' shoes remind me of my suffering, the suffering of the poor, and the class suffering in the old society. They also remand me of the importance of continuing the struggle and revolution. Meanwhile this pair of shoes will be handed down to my children and grandchildren and help to bring them up to be resolute revolutionary successors." This is why members of the production team in Chi-chia-ling have shown their respect for Comrade Hsiao Ping-ch'üan by calling his "millstone" shoes the "shoes of glory."

A woman farmhand

Every June, the Taihang Mountains area is overwhelmed by golden waves of wheat. Young men and women are active in the wheat fields. An atmosphere of joy prevails on the threshing floors....

On the threshing floor of San-chia-tien Production Brigade of Pa-kung Commune in Chin-ch'eng <u>hsien</u>, the harvested wheat piles up like a small mountain. An old woman whose hair is sprinkled with threads of silver picks up a handful of wheat and says with joy: "How good the crop is! I suspect that this is the best crop we've had in the last several years."

Twice late every night, this old woman comes to the threshing floor. In explaining why she does so, she says: "I know we have watchers here. But young people who are weary from a day's work will easily fall asleep. They heighten their vigilance when I frequently come to check them. Besides, it gives me peace of mind if I also do the watching...."

Who is this old woman? She is Wang Ch'un-lan, the people's representative of Chin-ch'eng <u>hsien</u>, a member of the Party committee in Pa-kung Commune, and deputy secretary of the Party branch in San-chia-tien Production Brigade.

Liu Kuang-p'u, Ch'en Fu-t'ung, "Nü ch'ang-kung."

Childhood

Wang Ch'un-lan's maiden name is Chao, and she was a
woman of Tung-pan-ch'iao Village in Pa-kung Town. Her father
worked a lifetime for landlords as a farmhand. When Ch'un-
lan, the third child, was born, her mother, lying on the k'ang,
complained: "Poor child, why were you born into our poor family? Enough! Enough!" Hence the father gave the newborn
girl the name "Kou" [enough].

Less than thirty days after the birth of little Kou, her father
died from overwork. Her ailing mother had to work to support
her three children. Three years later, Kou's mother died.

After the burial of their mother, the three children became
orphans; they had no relatives to look to. The fifteen-year-old
brother started to work for a man in Fu-shan; the twelve-year-
old sister was engaged to a young man and was to be brought
up in her fiance's home. Little Kou, who was barely four, became a maidservant in the house of a rich peasant named Wang
Mang-nü in Pei-pan-ch'iao.

"What's this about 'Kou,' 'Kou,' 'Kou'? Our family never
has 'enough' maidservants. From now on, her surname will be
Wang and her first name will be Ch'un-yeh," Wang Mang-nü
said in an authoritative tone. So Wang Ch'un-yeh, a child not
old enough to take care of herself, entered into this Palace of
Hell.

One day, Ch'un-yeh spilled urine from a chamber vessel
when she carried it to an outhouse from the room of Wang
Mang-nü's second daughter, Yü-niao. This made Yü-niao blaze
with anger. With owlish eyes, the young woman pinched Ch'un-
yeh hard on the cheek. Poor Ch'un-yeh trembled with pain, but
she dared not move for fear that she would spill the urine
again!

As soon as Ch'un-yeh entered the outhouse, she thought to
herself: "Chamber vessels! Chamber vessels! I have to clean
them every day. It'll save me a lot of trouble if I break this
chamber vessel." She instantly threw the chamber vessel
against a rock in the outhouse, and it was smashed to pieces.

Hearing the crash, Amah Li came in and asked Ch'un-yeh
what had happened. The little girl poured her heart out to
Amah Li.

Amah Li sighed and said: "Silly girl, rich people have more
chamber vessels than you can break. You have smashed the
chamber vessel, but you won't stop Miss Yü-niao from
urinating!"

This was but one of the many things little Ch'un-yeh suffered
in Wang Mang-nü's house for four years. Ch'un-yeh was almost eight years old. That year Miss Yü-niao had a baby.
From then on, Ch'un-yeh had to take care of the baby in addition to her regular work of making the fire, washing cooking
pots and bowls, and mixed coal dust with clay and water.

One day at noon, the members of the Wang family were having their lunch; Ch'un-yeh was busy mixing coal dust with clay
and water. Miss Yü-niao's baby made a mess in the bassinet,
getting it all over its diaper and panties. Miss Yü-niao threw
her chopsticks to the ground and pushed Ch'un-yeh into the
mixture of coal dust and clay and water.

"Scamp! You stop behaving yourself if I don't beat you. I'm
having my lunch. Why don't you take care of my baby? All
right, I'll let you relish the taste of my baby's excrement,"
said Miss Yü-niao, and she smeared Ch'un-yeh's face with the
dirty diaper.

Ch'un-yeh grew up quickly. But as her years increased, so
did her workload. She cooked for the farmhands in the early
morning, turned the mill in midmorning, cut grass at noon,
and took care of the cattle in the afternoon. Despite the hard
work, she was poorly fed and clothed and was often scolded
and thrashed. Her childhood passed in a boundless sea of
suffering.

A Villainous Scheme

Ch'un-yeh was already fourteen. The Wangs began to treat
her "kindly." They did not scold or beat her often, and they
allowed her to eat at the same table with the farmhands.

Ch'un-yeh wondered why these rich people had changed their attitude toward her. She did not know that Wang Mang-nü and his wife had conceived a diabolical scheme for her future.

One December evening, Wang Mang-nü and his wife sent for Ch'un-yeh.

"Ch'un-yeh, it's been over ten years since you came to our house. Now you've grown up to be a young girl. As the common saying goes, when boys grow up they marry, when girls grow up they become a wife. We've already found a husband for you...," said Wang Mang-nü, putting some money before Ch'un-yeh. "Buy some cosmetics with this 200 cash."

Ch'un-yeh did not utter a word; nor did she take the money. She knew that she had been sold to somebody else! Maid-servants could not avoid the fate of being sold as a commodity!

"Ch'un-yeh, you're a good girl. Don't worry, we'll treat you as our daughter. We'll do anything for your good. Your future husband is Chiao Ho-shang," said Wang Mang-nü.

"Chiao Ho-shang? The man who plays the female part in the opera?" gasped Ch'un-yeh.

"Yes, that's the one."

Chiao Ho-shang was also born to a bitter life. He was a good-looking man, and he loved opera from the time he was a little boy. He joined an opera troupe and began to play female roles. He was good at playing the part of Mu Kuei-ying in "Mu Kuei-ying Takes Command." Yet Chiao Ho-shang was a man of strong character. One time, an official of the hsien government visited his village and a rich man named Wei Kuang-yao in the village sent for Chiao Ho-shang's theatrical troupe to present an opera to entertain the honored guest. Wei Kuang-yao asked the troupe to present the opera "Ch'iu Hu Tests His Wife's Chastity" and wanted Chiao Ho-shang to play the part of Ch'iu Hu's wife in the opera. But he did not feel well that day.

"I can't sing in the opera today," said Chiao Ho-shang.

"Not sing? You want to revolt against me?" asked Wei Kuang-yao.

"I don't feel well. I just can't sing in the opera today."

"Damn it! Poor devil, you mean even I can't order you to sing in the opera? You'll learn a lesson from what you're doing."

Later, Chiao Ho-shang was expelled from the troupe by Wei Kuang-yao. He returned home and he and his mother led a precarious existence.

Ch'un-yeh thought to herself: "He is a man of mettle. It would be better to be his wife, no matter how hard our life is, than to stay in this inferno." A faint, wistful smile lightened her brooding face.

Wang Mang-nü knew from Ch'un-yeh's facial expression that she was willing to marry Chiao Ho-shang. He put the 200 cash into her hand. She took the money knowing that she deserved the reward because she had worked like a horse in his house for many years and that even a farmhand could earn many strings of cash a year.

Early on the morning of December 18, Wang Mang-nü's wife found an old dress for Ch'un-yeh and said to her: "Ch'un-yeh, the matchmaker is already here. Today is a happy day for you. Put on this dress and go to your future husband's house." Wang Mang-nü joined in: "Ch'un-yeh, go to your future husband's house. If the life in his house is hard, come back to us."

Ch'un-yeh did not say a word. She thought to herself: "Come back? Never. I'd rather die of poverty than come back to this Palace of Nightmares of yours!"

Hearing that Ch'un-yeh was about to leave, Amah Li rushed over from her room. She took a brass thimble off her finger and put it on Ch'un-yeh's finger: "I'm sorry I have nothing to give you as a gift. Don't forget me when you use this thimble...."

Wang Ch'un-yeh went to Chiao Ho-shang's house at San-chia-tien. After their marriage, the two young people grew to love each other. After about three months the busy days of spring planting drew near. One day, the couple enthusiastically talked about a plan to reclaim a barren slope at Chu-shan. But that night Chiao Ho-shang was in low spirits after coming back from outside. He did not eat or drink. Thinking that he did not feel well, Ch'un-yeh wanted to pick some <u>huo-kuan</u> (an herbal curative) for him. Chiao Ho-shang said that he was not ill. But Ch'un-yeh, suspecting that something was wrong with her husband, said:

"Ho-shang, we're husband and wife. Only you and your mother are dear to me. Don't exclude me —"

"Ch'un-yeh —"

"Ho-shang, why are you so upset?"

"It's not that I don't want to tell you. It's just that I'm afraid you'll worry if I do."

"Tell me what it is! It's not as if we had robbed or stolen things from others!"

"Ch'un-yeh, as you know, Wang Mang-nü is a notoriously stingy man in this area. Do you think he gave you away for nothing?"

"Do you mean? —"

"I had no money to offer him. He told me: 'Ch'un-yeh came to my house when she was only four. We've spent a lot of money to bring her up. I know you're poor. Just pay me eighteen strings of cash'!"

"Eighteen strings!"

"I said: 'Mr. Wang, eighteen strings of cash is reasonable but I — ' He cut in: 'I'm not dealing in human traffic. What I'm doing is for your good. You don't have to pay me right now. You can pay me when you have money.' But who would have thought today — "

"What about today?"

"Today, he sent for me. As soon as I entered his house he asked me: 'Chiao Ho-shang, you two are getting along well?' I replied: 'Mr. Wang, thank you for your kindness.' Then he said: 'Now that the amenities are over, I need the eighteen strings of cash.' I retorted: 'Mr. Wang, didn't you tell me I could pay when I had the money?' He hardened his countenance and insulted me by saying: 'You'll always be poor. Now, make your choice: work as a farmhand for me to clear up your debt with your wages, or pay me the eighteen strings of cash immediately!' ..."

Chiao Ho-shang bent over the edge of the k'ang and burst
into tears after he finished the story. Ch'un-yeh was so angry
that she felt as if flames had spurted from her eyes. She
thought to herself: "Wang Mang-nü, how vicious you are! How
many tears and how much sweat I shed when I was a maidservant in your house! Now you've played a trick on this honest man!..." But she controlled her anger and took a piece of
cornbread from the stove and gave it to her husband.

"Ho-shang, stop upsetting yourself! You haven't eaten anything today. You must be hungry. Eat this cornbread. Don't
worry about the eighteen strings of cash. We two have four
hands and we can work. We'll clear up our debt in a few years!"
Ch'un-yeh tried to comfort her husband as she wiped his tears.

In order to clear his debt, Chiao Ho-shang began to work as
a farmhand for the Wangs.

On the first night of Chiao Ho-shang's arrival in the Wang
house, Wang Mang-nü and his wife were lying on the k'ang
smoking opium. Wang Mang-nü was elated by his success. He
asked his wife: "How about this deal?" His wife poked him in
the thigh and said with a diabolical smile: "You're smart!
You've exchanged a young donkey for a mule!"

A Farmhand

As the common saying goes, misfortunes always come in
twos, calamities never happen one at a time. On the second
day of Chiao Ho-shang's arrival in Wang Mang-nü's house,
Ch'un-yeh and her mother-in-law were evicted from their
house by their landlord. Her mother-in-law became a servant
in the house of a rich man named Chao, and Ch'un-yeh began
to work for a landlord named Ch'ang in Li Village.

This landlord Ch'ang was a man with whom even a devil would
not want to deal. He wanted to hire Ch'un-yeh when he saw her
broad shoulders and big feet. He knew that she could do heavy
work. But he deliberately hesitated, stroking his moustache;
he said to Ch'un-yeh: "We need a farmhand, not a wet nurse.
You're a woman...."

"A woman? So what? I can do a man's work," said Ch'un-yeh boldly. She wanted the job to help her husband pay off the eighteen strings of cash.

She noticed a horse turning a mill. She took the horse away and turned the mill over twenty rounds at one breath.

"How about that? Mr. Ch'ang, I won't waste your food if you hire me," said Ch'un-yeh.

"Yes, you're strong. But I'm still afraid you can't do a farmhand's work," Landlord Ch'ang told Ch'un-yeh.

"I can do what a man does. A farmhand is a farmhand!" Ch'un-yeh said confidently.

From then on, Ch'un-yeh became a "woman farmhand" in the house of landlord Ch'ang. Every day, she got up before dawn and prepared breakfast and carried water. After breakfast she went to the fields and worked with the farmhands. She also brought lunch to them. At noon the farmhands took a rest, but Ch'un-yeh had to wash clothes and do the needlework. At night she fed the animals or turned the mill.

Although Ch'un-yeh exhausted herself with the work, she was poorly fed. The other farmhands had steamed bread and rice gruel, while she had to eat food for pigs. One day, Landlord Ch'ang discovered that she was eating some comparatively rich food she had taken from the pot. He smashed the rice bowl in her hand with a poker and scolded her: "Poor devil, a pig will put on fat if it eats rich food. What's the use of feeding you!"

Although Ch'un-yeh never had enough to eat, she had to work hard. Late one night, she was nowhere near finishing the work of grinding corn into flour. She knew that she would be scolded if she did not finish the work before morning. According to the practice in the landlord's house, domestic animals were not to be used to turn the mill after midnight. The practice was aimed at saving their energy for the following day's work in the field. Ch'un-yeh had to get the job done, but she was too exhausted to stand, much less turn the mill. She harnessed a draft animal and made it turn the mill.

The grinding work was finished that night. But the following day Landlord Ch'ang found that the draft animal was weak and could not do the plowing work.

"Who gave you permission to use a draft animal after midnight? Do you know how much one draft animal is worth?" shouted Landlord Ch'ang, slapping Ch'un-yeh hard twice in the face.

A draft animal was worth more than a human being! A draft animal must be well fed and allowed to rest, while Ch'un-yeh did not have enough to eat and had to work from morning to midnight. This was Wang Ch'un-yeh's life in Landlord Ch'ang's house for more than two years.

The third summer after Ch'un-yeh's arrival in Landlord Ch'ang's house was very hot. He and his wife fell victim to an epidemic. Sitting on the edge of the k'ang, Ch'un-yeh used a fan to keep the couple cool. She took care of them day and night and was not allowed to close her eyes. She would be beaten by Landlord Ch'ang's son with a bamboo pole if she was found dozing off, and many times blood oozed from wounds on her head.

Seven days later, Landlord Ch'ang and his wife recovered, but Ch'un-yeh fainted away from fatigue. Thinking that Ch'un-yeh was feigning sickness, Landlord Ch'ang gave her a sound beating and ordered her to leave his house.

Ch'un-yeh didn't budge. She took a stand, planting her feet firmly:

"Okay, I'll go! But give me my three years' pay!"

"Your pay? Ha! For three years, how much food have you eaten? How many clothes have you worn? The cost of food and clothing as well as boarding expenses have to be paid before you get your salary!"

So Ch'un-yeh did not get a cent for her three years' work!

Later, with the help of a friend, Ch'un-yeh got a job as a woman farmhand for another landlord nicknamed "King of Hell" Chang. She was bound and determined to save eighteen strings of cash to clear the debt to Wang Mang-nü. She would confront Wang Mang-nü and lead Chiao Ho-shang out of the Palace of Hell.

King of Hell Chang had three farmhands on a full-time basis

and a dozen others on a part-time basis. When winter came,
he sent all his farmhands home but asked Ch'un-yeh to stay.

"Ch'un-yeh, now that it's cold I've sent all my farmhands
home. I know you're homeless and your husband is working in
a landlord's house. Yours is a sad lot. You can stay here.
From tomorrow on, you shall have a buffalo and a cart and
you will do delivery work for me!"

Ch'un-yeh, a woman in her twenties, became a carter. Every
day, just when it was getting light and the northwest wind was
blowing, she went to the hamlet of Li and loaded up the cart
with coal and sent the coal to the Ta-yang Pottery Kiln. Then
she drove to Sung-chia-shan to pick up a load of ore, which she delivered to Lai Village. These trips covered sixty-five li a day.

On day at noon, Ch'un-yeh was driving the cart loaded with
coal toward the Ta-yang Pottery Kiln. The road was muddy
because the snow on the road had melted in the sun, and the
cart got stuck in the mud. The buffalo could not get the cart
out of the mud. Ch'un-yeh came down from the cart and pushed
the animal, but the cart could not be moved.

As she pushed the cart, a man driving a flat-bottom cart
came along. Without uttering a word, he helped Ch'un-yeh get
her cart out of the mud. When she wiped the sweat on her forehead and said "thank you" to the man, she found that he was
her husband, Chiao Ho-shang!

"Ho-shang! . . ."

"Ch'un-yeh! . . ."

They looked at each other, and their eyes swelled with tears.

"Ho-shang, don't feel sad. As long as there are blue mountains, we don't have to worry about firewood. We're still in
our twenties. After a few years' hard work, we'll be able to
pay off the eighteen strings of cash to Wang Mang-nü. Then
we'll live a happy life!" Ch'un-yeh tried to comfort her husband while fighting back her tears.

Many seasons had come and gone. Four years had passed
since Ch'un-yeh had started her work in King of Hell Chang's
house. Her annual wage was three strings of cash. She had already
saved twelve strings of cash and expected that in another two years

she would have enough. . . .

Who could have known that in the fall of that year Chiao Ho-shang would die of consumption. Ch'un-yeh's hopes were crushed. Aunt Liu, a kind woman in Li Village, told Ch'un-yeh: "You're an unlucky woman. You'd better use the twelve strings of cash to buy joss sticks and burn them in the temple of the guardian god of the city. By doing so, you can expiate the sins of your previous life."

"No! Aunt Liu, I've committed no sins. I want Chiao Ho-shang! I want Chiao Ho-shang. . . ," cried Ch'un-yeh.

Defiance

After her husband's death, Ch'un-yeh thought about commit-ting suicide. But she had to take care of her mother-in-law, who had become somewhat crazy because of her sufferings in Landlord Chao's house. Besides, didn't she want to take ven-geance? "I want to live! I want to live! One day this world is going to change!" Therefore she continued to work as a woman farmhand in King of Hell Chang's house. After working twenty-seven years as a woman farmhand — three years in Landlord Chang's house and twenty-four years in King of Hell Chang's house — she was now forty-three. Hard life through the long years had left her face wrinkled, and many silver threads ran through her hair.

It was an extremely cold winter. Ch'un-yeh still wore tat-tered and thin clothes which she had patched with a diaper of King of Hell Chang's baby by his concubine. The following day the landlord's concubine saw the new patch on Ch'un-yeh's jacket.

"You stole one of our things. You scoundrel, you'd better look into a mirror to see whether you are a human being to deserve the diaper," the concubine scolded Ch'un-yeh while boxing her in the face.

"Take the diaper off your jacket! Hurry up!" said King of Hell Chang, showering Ch'un-yeh's head with blows from a bunch of keys which he always carried.

Ch'un-yeh went to her bedroom. She took off the patched jacket and put on a thinner jacket. She brought the patched jacket before the landlord and said: "The diaper is on it. Here is the jacket. You wear it! I can stand the cold weather. See! Your wealth is increasing. I'm leaving!"

That evening, Ch'un-yeh left the house of the Changs. When she returned to San-chia-tien, her mother-in-law could not recognize her. The old woman did not know that her daughter-in-law was coming back to her until she heard Ch'un-yeh call out, "Mother."

"Ch'un-yeh, I hope you'll not go again," the old woman pleaded.

"I'll stay here, Mother. Even if we die, we'll die together," said Ch'un-yeh.

Aunt Kao, a nextdoor neighbor and also a woman with experience of hardships, offered Ch'un-yeh and her mother-in-law a shabby room and a two-_mou_ plot of wasteland.

The spring came. Ch'un-yeh had no seeds to start the spring planting. Some poor neighbors borrowed for her a peck of grain from a landlord named Chao Pu-lai, but she got only about 0.6 peck of grain after the sifting. Ch'un-yeh and her mother-in-law repressed their hunger and managed to get the two-_mou_ plot of land sown with seeds.

The harvest season was approaching. The two women's faces beamed with a joy that they hadn't felt for twenty or thirty years. It seemed that they could reap over 200 catties of grain.

Ch'un-yeh and her mother-in-law were threshing grain in the field. Landlord Chao Pu-lai and his lackeys came along. He said to Ch'un-yeh: "A good harvest, huh? Now, you'll be returning the grain you borrowed from me last spring?"

One of Ch'ao Pu-lai's lackeys took out an abacus and an account book from a large briefcase and handed them to him. Rolling up his sleeves, Chao Pu-lai looked at the account book and made some calculations on the abacus.

"According to the established practice, when you borrow a peck of grain you have to pay back 2 pecks of grain. You owe

me 4.8 pecks of rice. And you have to pay 4 pecks of rice for
taxes. So, you owe me 8.8 pecks of rice or 12 pecks of grain,"
Chao Pu-lai said to Ch'un-yeh.

Before Ch'un-yeh and her mother-in-law could say a word,
Chao Pu-lai ordered his lackeys to put the grain into sacks.
They took all of the grain away from Ch'un-yeh. Before Chao
Pu-lai left he told Ch'un-yeh that she still owed him 2.5 pecks
of grain!

Many other farmers in the village had the same experience
as Ch'un-yeh. Their entire harvest had also been taken away
by the landlord. The ten-odd families were in distress over
their food problem.

Suddenly, Ch'un-yeh jumped to her feet and brushed back
the tangled hair hanging about her forehead.

"It's better to revolt than to commit suicide! If a man tears
the dragon robe from an emperor he will be sentenced to death.
But he will not receive a more severe punishment than death
if he kills an emperor. Those who cultivate the land are entitled to harvests. Landlords never work in the field; they
never sweat; but they want to eat corn. No, they can't. Let's
get together! Let's reap the corn in the field over there!"
said Ch'un-yeh, pointing to the corn crop standing in a nearby
field.

With a shout the poor people swarmed over the field and
reaped the corn crop. Indeed, "when all people are of one mind
they can move Mt. T'ai." Chao Pu-lai and the other landlords
could not do anything about it because they knew they were outnumbered by the angry poor farmers.

A Red Heart

After the Marco Polo Bridge Incident on July 7, 1937, Yen
Hsi-shan, the ruler of Shansi, under pressure from the masses
to resist Japan, put forth the slogan "Resist Japan and Save the
Country" and established the "National Salvation Society." This
organization was in fact led by the Chinese Communist Party.
Under this organization, each hsien, district, and village

established such anti-Japanese groups as "peasants' salvation associations," "youth salvation associations," and "women's salvation associations."

Wang Ch'un-yeh was already forty-five. A meeting of women was called by the <u>hsien</u> authorities. She attended the meeting. Most participants in this meeting were poor women. This meeting was presided over by a capable woman. She talked of such things as "the liberation of women," "equality between the sexes," "overthrowing villainous landlords and gentry," and "overthrowing Japanese imperialism," all of which touched Ch'un-yeh's heart.

That same evening, Ch'un-yeh learned from others that the woman presiding over the meeting was Jen Hsiu-lan. The following day, Ch'un-yeh went to talk with Comrade Jen Hsiu-lan, from whom she learned many aspects of the theory of revolution. She was enlightened. That very year, with the help of Comrade Jen Hsiu-lan, she joined the Chinese Communist Party and changed her name to Wang Ch'un-lan.

After attending the <u>hsien</u> meeting, she organized the fifty-odd women in the village into seven teams. As a result, the women's salvation association was established in San-chia-tien.

Responding to the Party's call, Wang Ch'un-lan mobilized women to cut their hair short and unbind their bound feet. And she herself cut her long hair! In order to enable her to do heavy work, landlords had forbidden her to bind her feet. She looked at her big feet and said with a smile: "I was ahead of my time!"

At first, women in the village were rather hesitant about cutting their hair and unbinding their feet, and at the same time, landlords and rich people were spreading rumors about these matters.

"Don't be hesitant! You'll look neat after you cut your hair short," said Wang Ch'un-lan, caressing her short hair. "In the past, women suffered much when they bound their feet. Landlords and rich men thought that bound feet were beautiful. They wanted to make women their slaves!" She extended her feet.

"People laughed at my big feet and they said that a woman with big feet would be a barbarian. I'm not a barbarian. But I know I can do the work which women with bound feet can never do."

In a few days, twenty-seven women in the seven teams cut their hair short and unbound their feet.

For two years Wang Ch'un-lan was active on the "Resist Japan and Save the Country" front. She led women in San-chia-tien, Pei-pan-ch'iao, Tung-pan-ch'iao, Li Village and other villages in supporting the men at the front and wiping out traitors. She became a woman leader of Chin-ch'eng hsien, in Pei-ta District.

In 1939 the Yen Hsi-shan bandit clique staged the "December Incident" and pulled off their mask of "Resist Japan and Save the Country" and showed their anticommunist face. Thousands of Communists and progressive elements were arrested and then killed. Wang Ch'un-lan was also arrested and detained in the village office in San-chia-tien.

Like rabid dogs, puppet village headman Wei Kuang-yao and villainous landlords such as Wen Huai-te and Wen Shan-fu hung Wang Ch'un-lan up and tortured her.

"Speak! Who are the Communists ?"

"I don't know. I only know that you rich men are all traitors!"

"Damn it! You want to show your stubbornness ?"

"I'd not have been arrested if I were not stubborn."

Clubs, sticks, bamboo picks, irons, tiger stools ... they could inflict torture on revolutionaries' bodies, but they could not shake the proletarian fighters' revolutionary will.

Torture did not make Wang Ch'un-lan speak. The reactionary landlords set her free in order to ferret out and arrest all of the Communists working in the underground.

Wang Ch'un-lan practically had to crawl out of the village office. When she got home, her mother-in-law had already died.

"Strong wind reveals the strength of grass, and gold is refined in fierce fire." Wang Ch'un-lan was courageous and did not give in. She accomplished her delicate and important

missions. Under the Party's direction, she was involved in communication and liaison missions in the border area of the three
hsien of Chin-ch'eng, Ling-ch'uan, and Kao-p'ing. Many times
she sent the Party's messages to liaison points, traveling
through the mountains and going hungry. Many times she was
arrested by the enemy plainclothes police and almost beaten
to death. But Wang Ch'un-lan never thought about her personal safety!

One day, she ran across Comrade Jen Hsiu-lan.

"Ch'un-lan, are you having trouble?"

"No! Sister Hsiu-lan, didn't you tell me to march against
difficulties?"

"Right! The more difficulties there are the more you must
struggle and the more you must march on!"

"Sister Hsiu-lan, I have no money to pay my membership
dues to the Party. Here is a handful of soil from San-chia-
tien. Please, give it to the organization. This is a mere token
of my gratitude!" Wang Ch'un-lan said slowly, giving a small
sack of soil to Jen Hsiu-lan.

"I'll most surely forward this to the organization. This is
a revolutionary's red heart, the kind of heart our Party needs!"
said Jen Hsiu-lan, taking the small sack from Wang Ch'un-lan.

Spring Thunder

Chin-ch'eng was liberated in 1945. The feudal system which
had been in existence for several thousand years collapsed in
ruins! Wang Ch'un-lan emerged from an abyss of sufferings
and basked in Mao Tse-tung's radiant favor.

The first spring thunder rumbled in San-chia-tien: the Land
Reform began!

Poor tenant farmers in Tung-pan-ch'iao, Pei-pan-ch'iao,
Li Village, and San-chia-tien participated in public gatherings
to struggle against villainous gentry and landlords. Everyone
asked Wang Ch'un-lan to come forward and air her grievances.

Wang Ch'un-lan stood on a platform and told how her father

died of overwork in a landlord's house, how she started out as
a maidservant in a landlord's house when she was only four
years old, how she was sold by a landlord as a commodity,
how her husband died of overwork in a landlord's house, how
she worked as a woman farmhand for twenty-seven years....
She wept, and the masses also wept. Wang Ch'un-lan and the
masses struggled down villainous landlords Wei Kuang-yao,
Wen Shan-fu, Wen Huai-te, Chao Pu-lai, and King of Hell
Chang and rich peasant Wang Mang-nü.

The poor men and women wanted Wang Ch'un-lan to enjoy
the fruits of victory. They said: "Wang Ch'un-lan suffered the
most. She should be the first to enjoy the fruits of victory."

Holding her head high and walking with long strides, Wang
Ch'un-lan entered King of Hell Chang's house. In this very
house, what sufferings hadn't she experienced for twenty-four
years! Which corner or brick of this house had not been damp-
ened by her blood and tears.

Some villagers brought suits of clothes to Wang Ch'un-lan
and said: "Ch'un-lan, take your pick!"

Wang Ch'un-lan smiled. She looked through King of Hell
Chang's trunks. Finally, she found a piece of clothing under
his "Arhat" and showed it to the villagers: "If you want to
give me something, I'll take this jacket."

The villagers could not understand why Wang Ch'un-lan
wanted a shabby and heavily patched jacket instead of some of
the beautiful dresses. She pointed to a blue patch on the shoulder of the jacket and told them her sad story....

The Evergreen

Wang Ch'un-lan made great strides on the road of socialist
collectivization. She was always out in front in organizing the
mutual aid team, the primary agricultural cooperative, the advanced agricultural cooperative, and the people's commune.

After the establishment of the people's commune, all the
other members of the commune made Wang Ch'un-lan a "five
guarantees" member. Yet she organized several women, all

over sixty, into an "Old Mothers Team." She said: "It's still
early to 'guarantee' my livelihood. I'm healthy and energetic.
Why do I need the 'five guarantees'?"

In 1963 there was a heavy hailstorm when the ears of wheat
were beginning to fill out. Some cadres and commune members were disheartened. Wang Ch'un-lan went all over the
commune visiting families to encourage them:

"The people's commune is a fixture of the land hammered
out of iron. Can a cold rain crush the collectivized economy!
We should be prepared for natural calamities on the one hand
and ensure bumper harvests on the other!"

As soon as she had finished, Wang Ch'un-lan put on her
boots, rolled up the legs of her pants, threw away her walking
stick, and went to work together with the others in the fields.

One early morning this spring, when manure was being
spread in the fields, Li La-hai, the secretary of the Party
branch in the production brigade, was carrying two honey buckets to the fields. After leaving the village, he saw far in front
a broad-shouldered person moving quickly and carrying two
honey buckets. In the dim light he could not make out who it
was. But when the sun came up and bathed the fields in a golden
light, Li La-hai discovered that that bobbing grey head belonged
to Wang Ch'un-lan.

"My dear old woman, you don't have to work. If you stumble,
I'll be blamed for not taking good care of you!" said Li La-hai.

"La-hai, please, don't make a fuss! I start the work early
because I know that when they come they won't let me do it. I
try to get in a few loads before they get here."

Wang Ch'un-lan is a model worker in the hsien, the special
district, and the province. She was cited thirty-seven times for
her work. She was elected the people's representative of Chin-
ch'eng hsien in 1953. The members of the commune to which
she belongs call her the "evergreen of San-chia-tien."

Now she can often be seen working in the fields, on the road-
sides, and on the threshing floors. Looking at the silver hair
bobbing on her head, people feel great respect for her and feel
that she is growing larger in size and stature....

WANG HSI-T'ANG, LIEN PU-WANG AND YAO I-HSIN

The poor people's cave

There is a broken-down cave with three entrances at the foot of Mo-p'an Hill on the east bank of the Chang River. It is called the "poor people's cave."

The "poor people's cave," five to six feet high, seven to eight feet wide, and twenty to thirty feet long, had been shared for many generations by several poor families. The occupants of the cave were those who had been reduced to abject poverty because of the exploitation by landlords and rich peasants. However, the exploiting class called them "good-for-nothings" and "failures."

Since the liberation, the "poor people's cave" has been preserved as historical evidence of the exploitation of peasants by the landlord class. It has been completely restored and preserved by Hsiao-sung Production Brigade of Kao-ho Commune in Ch'ang-chih hsien as a tool for the class education of young people. On occasions of festivals, Comrade Li Yu-cheng, the secretary of the production brigade Party branch, stands before the cave the tells the masses stories about the "poor people's cave."

Wang Hsi-t'ang, Lien Pu-wang, Yao I-hsin, "Ch'iung-jen hsüeh."

The Heartbreaking Road

Early on the morning of May 5, 1943, a man of medium stature was helping an old woman along on her way from the temple
of the local deity to the "poor people's cave" northwest of
Hsiao-sung Village. A little over thirty, with an emaciated
face, the man carried a broken earthen vessel in his hand and
shabby quilt on his shoulder. They were Li Yu-ch'eng and his
mother.

For three generations, Li Yu-ch'eng's family had been living
in poverty. His grandfather left only a dilapidated shack to his
father. His father worked at the Te-t'ai-yung shop in Ch'ang-
chih hsien. Yu-ch'eng's eldest and second elder brothers were
farmhands working for landlords, and his third elder brother
was a mason. At twelve, Yu-ch'eng left home to work as a
part-time farmhand. This was a job without pay but with free
board. His family had pawned almost everything, from farm
implements to old, shabby clothing, to raise money. Finally,
they had nothing left to pawn.

When Yu-ch'eng was fifteen, his sixty-two-year-old father
vomited blood from overwork, and the capitalist he worked for
angrily drove him away. Yu-ch'eng and his four brothers looked
in vain for a doctor to cure their father's disease, which was
worsening. Then he and three of his older brothers carried
their father to "Ho-sheng Pharmacy" in Nan-chang to consult a
doctor. The doctor wrote out a prescription, but the family had
no money to purchase the medicine, and they could borrow none.
Yu-ch'eng thought about pawning their two hoes to raise the
money. When his father heard this, the old man said in a trembling voice: "Son, hoes are our tools of subsistence. Don't
worry about me! It's more important to sustain your lives." Yu-
ch'eng thought: "I know that the hoes are our very life, but they're
still not as vital as our own father." When his father fell into a
coma, Yu-ch'eng went out with the two hoes in his hands.

Their hoes had been pawned, and the money had been spent.
But this did not save the life of Yu-ch'eng's father. Rich people in the village called up debts to make preparations for the

New Year's celebration, while Yu-ch'eng and his family were worrying about money for the burial of their father. Yu-ch'eng and his three brothers needed money to buy a coffin for their father. Their mother could not be so unfeeling as to wrap her husband, who had undergone much sufferings in his life, with nothing but a mat in burial. Finally, she sold their dilapidated shack; but the money from selling the shack wasn't enough to buy a coffin. Her five children prostrated themselves before their ancestors' tablets, which were placed on a cupboard. Her eldest son said: "We're not impious. Please, allow us to move your tablets to another place. Let us sell this cupboard."

The brothers and their mother moved their ancestors' tablets and carried the cupboard to the market in the village. They sold the cupboard, and with the money they bought a coffin made of very thin boards and buried the old man.

The dead was already buried, but the living had no place to live. Where could a family of six go to live? At the west end of the village was a temple to the local deity. Nobody had ever lived in this temple because superstitious villagers believed that the dead made their reports in its dark recesses. Yu-ch'eng said: "Let's move into that temple. Poor people are not afraid of ghosts!" He got permission from the village authorities for his family to dwell in the temple after he promised to offer incense and make sacrifices to the local deity on occasions of festivals.

Yu-ch'eng's family, now a family of six, settled down in the deserted temple. The yard in the temple was overgrown with bush. They leased a two-mou plot of land from the temple's board of trustees and began to cultivate it. It goes without saying that a two-mou tract of land could not yield enough to support a family of six. Yu-ch'eng worked as a farmhand for a landlord in Wang-chia-pao, five li away. His second and third elder brothers also went away to make their living working for others. The young brothers tried their best to tide themselves over the difficult period, but a more difficult time was in store for them: in 1943 they were hit by famine.

At that time Ch'ang-chih and Hsiao-sung villages were occupied by the Japanese imperialists. Poor people in the village
had suffered much from the enemy atrocities of massacre,
pillage, and burning, but the famine made it even more difficult
for them to survive. Farmhands were out of work; begging for
food was entirely impossible. Yu-ch'eng's second and third
elder brothers lost their jobs and came back home. The five
brothers could not support their mother. Then in early spring,
Yu-ch'eng's youngest brother, Wu-yüan, died of starvation; his
third elder brother, Wu-sheng, escaped the famine to southern
Shansi; his second elder brother, Hei-tan, was kidnapped by a
dealer in human beings and never came back again. With the
other members of the family either dead or far away, only Yu-
ch'eng, his mother, and his eldest brother, Fu-yung, were left
in the temple to the local deity.

The famine got worse and worse. Leaves and roots were
eaten by the poor people. Yu-ch'eng's mother's eyes were
black and her face swollen and she gasped for breath. She
was on the verge of starvation.

Yu-ch'eng's brother was desperate because of his mother's
plight. One evening, he was standing on the roadside near the
temple, trying to think of a way out. The wheat in the field by
the roadside had already turned yellow. He found that some
wheat plants in the field had apparently been trampled by draft
animals. Thinking that the wheat plants would not grow anyway,
he picked six wheat plants in order to prepare some hot soup
for his mother to drink. Just then, however, he was apprehended by the landlord's lackey Liu Ho-pao. The landlord's
lackey dragged Li Fu-yung by the ear to the Grand Temple in
the village. Before Li Fu-yung could explain, village headman
Li Fu-yüan pounded on his desk and roared: "Hang him up!"
Immediately two village policemen tied Li Fu-yung's hands
behind his back and hung him up. Poor people in the courtyard
of the Grand Temple were indignant, but they dared not say
anything.

Li Fu-yüan clenched his teeth and swore at him:

"You poor devil, you simply don't know what is right and

what is wrong. You can eat bran and wild vegetation. Why did you steal a rich man's wheat crop? Speak! How much did you steal?"

Knowing that explanations or entreaties would not help him, Li Fu-yung remained silent. The village headman, nicknamed "Living King of Hell," nodded to the village policemen. They soaked ropes in water and flogged Li Fu-yung with them till there was blood all over his body. Then they let him down and threw him out of the Grand Temple.

After the beating, the village headman led two village policemen, who carried lanterns in their hands, to the temple of the local deity. As soon as they entered the temple, Li Fu-yüan swore at Yu-ch'eng's mother: "You poor devils are not contented with your lot. A temple is not a hideout for pilferers. Get out of here!"

One of the policemen dragged Yu-ch'eng's mother out of the temple; the other threw the quilt, cooking pot, and bowls out the door. They locked the door of the temple and strutted away.

Upon hearing the news that his family was in trouble, Yu-ch'eng rushed home. When he reached the temple, his eldest brother, who had already recovered his senses, was staggering along toward the temple. Looking at his unconscious mother, who had fainted, and his badly wounded brother, Yu-ch'eng felt as if his heart had been torn out. Trying to revive his mother, he propped her up to a sitting position. She clenched her teeth and closed her eyes. Fu-yung forgot the pain of his wounds and wept, embracing his mother. After what seemed an eternity, she recovered her senses. Tears streamed down her face when she saw her two sons. Mother and sons wept and talked together until they grew hoarse. What else could they do in that man-eating world?

As it was just growing light in the east, Fu-yung kneeled before his mother:

"Mother, Yu-ch'eng will look after you, and I'll find a place for us to settle down. As long as I'm alive, I'll not let these sons of bitches off!"

"Fu-yung, there's nothing for you here anyway.... But try

to come back soon, if you can," said his mother.

"Eldest Brother, don't worry about Mother. I'll take care of her. Be sure to let us know your whereabouts," Yu-ch'eng told his eldest brother, wiping away his tears.

However, Yu-ch'eng and his mother never heard from Fu-yung after he left.

Yu-ch'eng and his mother were left standing before the temple with no place to live. At this point, the "poor people's cave" came to Yu-ch'eng's mind.

When she heard his idea, Yu-ch'eng's mother wept and said:

"That's a cave for dead people. If we move into it, we'll never have a chance to come out alive. With my own eyes I saw that the families of Wang Ho-shang, Kao Fu-ch'eng, and some others all died in that cave. I'll never go in there."

"Mother, don't be afraid of that. We'll just stay there for several days. We'll move out when we find a place to settle down," Yu-ch'eng said to persuade his mother.

On the morning of the Dragon Boat Festival, when rich people had family reunions and enjoyed their tsung-tzu dumplings, Yu-ch'eng and his mother entered the "poor people's cave" with tears in their eyes and nothing in their stomachs.

A Cave of Bitterness

As soon as Yu-ch'eng helped his mother into the small, dilapidated cave, they found an old man and a young man lying on a heap of wheat stalks at the back of the cave. Yu-ch'eng looked for some broken bricks to make a simple k'ang at the left side of the cave. But soon he found that the roof of the cave on that side was about to fall down. So he went to a spot near the entrance to the cave and cleared and leveled the area with a broken bowl; he made a frame for a k'ang with some broken bricks, and laid some wheat stalks over the frame. Then he moved his mother onto the simple k'ang. Yu-ch'eng was sitting on a brick, absorbed in thought. The old man, named Li K'o-i, came over, and Kao Chia-ts'e's mother also came in from a neighboring cave. They said hello to Yu-ch'eng and his mother.

"Look at me, my life is going from bad to worse!" said Yu-ch'eng's mother, bursting into tears.

"Don't vex yourself, Aunt Li. We're all poor people. Look at where we live. We eat the food of pigs and dogs. My two sons have to share a pair of very shabby trousers...." Aunt Kao tried to comfort Yu-ch'eng's mother.

"I think either of you is better off than I. We shouldn't let worries get the upper hand," Li K'o-i cut in.

Seeing that time was wasting, and in order to take care of his mother, Yu-ch'eng, who had quit his job in Wang-chia-pao, went out to begin looking for part-time jobs in Hsiao-sung Village. After waking up the young man on the heap of wheat stalks, Li K'o-i, with a stick and a broken bowl in his hands, went out to beg for food. The young man, Li Yin-shun, was about eighteen years old. After looking at Yu-ch'eng's mother, Li Yin-shun picked up an ax and some ropes and without a word went out to cut firewood.

Now that Yu-ch'eng's mother was alone in the cave, she made a thorough inspection. She found that the sides of the cave were blackened with smoke and soot, and a small part of its top at the left side had caved in; there were holes on the ground, and the entrance was covered with a simple screen of corn stalks. Outside the cave were a few "stoves," each of them made of three bricks. Weeds grew at the entrance of the cave. In the cave there was no furniture at all, but there were broken cooking pots, bowls, burlap sacks, and rags. How could this be a place in which people lived!

In his begging, Li K'o-i got a handful of bran and a mouthful of scorched rice. Yu-ch'eng brought his mother a half bowl of rice gruel. She wanted to give some of the rice gruel to Li K'o-i. The old man refused to take it and went out to "prepare his meal." He got a basin of water from a nearby stream and put the bran and scorched rice in the water and cooked his meal. Then Li Yin-shun brought in a bundle of firewood and lay down on the heap of wheat stalks. Knowing that Li Yin-shun was hungry, Yu-ch'eng's mother gave him some of her rice gruel.

It was summer. It was scorching hot in the cave, and there were flies buzzing all around. Li Yin-shun got rid of them with some artemisia weeds, but they flew back into the cave again, as they always did.

Having prepared his "meal," Li K'o-i gave half a bowl to Yu-ch'eng's mother. He ate his share out of the cooking pot. A mixture of a handful of bran, a mouthful of scorched rice, some wild greens, and a basin of water — it could hardly be called a meal.

Aunt Kao came in. Seeing Li K'o-i's "meal," she said to him: "I have some elm bark flour. Next time, I'll give you some so you can put it into your watery food."

Yu-ch'eng's mother and Aunt Kao started talking about what had happened to their families....

Heart to Heart

After Yu-ch'eng's mother had settled in the cave, she fell ill with worry about her three sons far away, and with hunger, and she became confined to her k'ang.

Yu-ch'eng had to go to work everyday, so Aunt Kao took care of his mother. One day, Li Yu-ch'eng saved a half bowl of his gruel and wanted to bring it to his mother. But he was stopped by rich peasant Li Fu-hsing.

"Li Yu-ch'eng, you've had enough food at my house. Now you take food to your mother. I don't want to feed two persons in order to keep one to work for me!" Li Fu-hsing scolded.

"I saved this for my mother. I haven't had more than I'm entitled to. You don't have to say such an unpleasant thing to me," Li Yu-ch'eng retorted.

"If you save food for your mother, you'll not be able to work. From now on, you can't take food away from my house."

"Then you'd better find another man for the job!"

Li Fu-hsing did not say anything more. He knew that Yu-ch'eng was a good worker and that if he drove him into a corner, he would quit. So, after grumbling a bit, Li Fu-hsing went away.

Yu-ch'eng got home and heated the gruel which he had brought from Li Fu-hsing's house. He gave the porridge to his mother. She could only take two mouthfuls because she had no appetite.

It was getting dark. Old man Li K'o-i stumbled home. As soon as he came into the cave, he told Yu-ch'eng: "You... you wash the mud off these flour dumplings and heat them. Give them to your mother!"

After helping the old man to the back of the cave, Yu-ch'eng washed the mud from the dumplings. When he was making a fire to heat the dumplings, he heard Li Yin-shun cry: "Uncle, look at the blood on your leg!"

Li Yu-ch'eng came over and discovered that there were three dog bites on the old man's calf. Immediately he tore a strip of cloth from his shirt and wrapped the old man's wounds.

Li K'o-i had been looking for something good to eat for Yu-ch'eng's ailing mother. After a whole morning of begging, he got a half bowl of flour dumplings. He was attacked by two vicious dogs when he passed by the door of rich peasant Tung Hai-wang's house. He would have been killed if the two dogs had not been driven off by one of Tung Hai-wang's farmhands.

On the evening of July 16, 1943, the condition of Yu-ch'eng's mother worsened. She spit up everything she ate or drank. Her face was pallid. She could not speak clearly. Yu-ch'eng embraced his mother and wept. Li Yin-shun made a fire in front of the cave to keep mosquitoes away. Aunt Kao tried to comfort Yu-ch'eng's mother. Old man K'o-i, whose leg was badly swollen, lay off to the side, incessantly sighing.

Yu-ch'eng's mother moved her lips several times. She seemed to want to say something, but she could not utter a word. Then her mouth stopped moving. Realizing she had breathed her last, Aunt Kao told Yu-ch'eng: "You've got to think about her funeral."

What could Yu-ch'eng do? He wept over his mother's body.

Just at that moment, Wu P'ang-jen and Yüan Chang-so entered the cave. They were Yu-ch'eng's good friends and they had worked together for some time. They were coming to visit

Yu-ch'eng's ailing mother. But she had died shortly before
they came.

"Brother Yu-ch'eng, weeping won't help anything. You'd bet-
ger think about your mother's funeral. Do you have any plans?"
said Wu P'ang-jen, holding Yu-ch'eng's hand.

"I'm penniless. I've got to wrap her in a mat and bury her."

"No, you can't do that —"

"I have no money. What shall I do?"

"Don't worry! We'll find a way. We two will borrow some
money for you."

After a discussion, Wu P'ang-jen and Yüan Chang-so went
to borrow money to buy a coffin.

"Child, when rich people die they wear a dozen suits of grave
garments," said Aunt Kao, who was thinking about grave garments for Yu-ch'eng's mother. "Since you're poor, your mother
can't have many grave garments. But we can't let your mother
wear her dirty and shabby clothes to her grave."

"I'll put this sleeveless and collarless jacket on her," said
Yu-ch'eng, taking off his old jacket and covering his mother's
body with it.

"I have an old pair of trousers. I'll give them to your mother," Aunt Kao offered. She went and fetched them and put them
on Yu-ch'eng's mother.

The following day, Wu P'ang-jen and Yüan Chang-so carried
a coffin to the cave. Led by Aunt Kao, Yu-ch'eng and the others
put Mrs. Li's body into the coffin, lighted an "eternally bright
lamp," offered "sacrifices," and burned four sticks of incense.
After weeping bitterly for a while, they began to hold a watch
over Mrs. Li's coffin.

On the day of the burial, Wu P'ang-jen and Yüan Chang-so
came to help. All the people living in the "poor people's cave"
and thereabouts, twenty-odd people in all, dressed in mourning
for Mrs. Li and escorted her coffin to the grave. It was the
first time ever that people dressed in mourning for a dead person who was neither a family member nor a relative. Someone said: "Hey! Those beggars have become members of one
family!"

Poor Old Man

After his mother's death Yu-ch'eng was all alone. He liked
the people living in the "poor people's cave" and treated them
as his relatives. He decided to stay in the cave. During the
day he worked as a part-time farmhand for rich peasants. In
the evening he took care of the old man K'o-i. The old man's
wounds from the dog bites on his leg suppurated, and for a
long time he could not walk. During that period he was supported by Yu-ch'eng and Yin-shun.

Li K'o-i too had undergone much suffering. His parents
died when he was only eight years old. He tended sheep for a
landlord and was often scolded and flogged. The landlord did
not give him enough to eat. At eleven, he left the landlord's
house and started the life of a vagabond. Then Chang K'e-chien,
a big landlord of Su-tien in Ch'ang-chih hsien, hired Li K'o-i
as a farmhand. Chang K'e-chien did not look as vicious as
other landlords, but he was in fact more malevolent than all of
them. In order to make Li K'o-i work hard for him, he always
told the young boy: "If you work hard I'll bring you up to be an
adult and then find a wife for you." The young boy took his
word for it and worked like a horse. But he remained a bachelor after fifty-two years of work in landlord Chang K'e-
chien's house. He was driven off because of his old age when
he was sixty-four.

Li K'o-i returned to Hsiao-sung Village, but he was homeless. Somebody told him that there was a Catholic church at
Chiu Village in Ch'ang-tzu hsien that took in and cared for
old people. After several days' travel, he went to the home
for the aged run by the Catholic church. Nominally it was a
charity organization. But, in fact, it was far from that. During his stay there, Li K'o-i witnessed the inhuman treatment
of Chinese by foreigners dressed in religious garb. In fear
and indignation he left the Catholic church and returned to
Hsiao-sung Village again. He moved into the "poor people's
cave" and began to sustain his life by begging for food.

Old man K'o-i's leg wounds, under the care of Yu-ch'eng and

Yin-shun, were healed by winter. He could walk to the village to beg for food from door to door.

One dark night, it suddenly began to snow heavily. A strong wind drove the snowflakes directly into the "poor people's cave." Li Yin-shun could not stand the cold. He made a fire with hay and squatted by the fire to keep warm. Li Yu-ch'eng came in with a half a bowl of rice, and asked:

"Yin-shun, where is your uncle?"

"He went out to beg for food this afternoon. He's not back yet."

"You silly boy! Why don't you go to look for him?"

Li Yu-ch'eng scolded Yin-shun some more and then went back out. Yin-shun followed Yu-ch'eng out of the cave. They went in two different directions to look for the old man.

Li Yu-ch'eng took the road to Hu-chia-chuang. He found a mound covered with snow on a slope. He suspiciously poked at the thing with his stick. It was a man lying face down on the ground. Yu-ch'eng felt him and found him stiff, frozen to death. He knew it was old man Li K'o-i when he saw the scars on his leg. Tears began to stream from Yu-ch'eng's eyes....

The dwellers in the "poor people's cave" got together after Li K'o-i's body was carried back after midnight. Aunt Kao, along with her son Kao Chia-ts'e, also came over from their nearby cave.

"What shall we do about the burial?" Yu-ch'eng asked Kao Chia-ts'e.

"Of course, we'll try our best, but I'm afraid we'll not be able to buy a coffin for him," replied Kao Chia-ts'e.

"That's right," said Yu-ch'eng, turning this matter over in his mind. "I'll go to my landlord to get my pay and borrow some money to buy two large earthen vessels. By putting them mouth to mouth, we can use them as a coffin for the old man."

"That's what we'll do. Come on, let's lay the old man's body in the middle of the cave and burn four sticks of incense before it. We'll have to keep watch over his corpse to keep the rats away from it," Aunt Kao told the others in the cave.

The following day, Yu-ch'eng and some other men buried Li

K'o-i in a potter's field in the northeastern part of Chao Village.

Because of the serious famine that year, that winter was much colder than in previous years. Nine persons living in the "poor people's cave" died of starvation and cold. Life there became even more difficult.

A Steel Needle

The following summer, people in Hsiao-sung Village were busy harvesting the hemp crop. There was a shortage of manpower because many people had left the village during the previous year's famine. But the work of harvesting and soaking hemp must be done in time. As the common saying goes, "You can ruin a pondful of hemp in the time it takes to drink a cup of tea." Especially landlords and rich peasants who had plentiful hemp crops needed farmhands badly.

Early one morning, rich peasant Li Fu-hsing sneaked into the "poor people's cave."

"Hey! Get up! Get up! The sun is already high," said Li Fu-hsing as he approached Li Yin-shun.

"What's the hurry?" Li Yin-shun said with indifference.

"You're sleeping on a busy day! Come help me harvest the hemp crop."

"Maybe you're busy, but I'm not. I want to sleep today."

"I'll give you double pay and free noodles for lunch."

"You'd better go away. I won't work for you even if you put gold ingots before me!"

"You've turned down my kind offer. You'll be sorry for what you're doing."

Li Fu-hsing left in anger. As soon as he left, Aunt Kao came in.

"Child! You've got to find food to fill your empty stomach. Now that you can easily find a job, you'd better go out and find something," Aunt Kao advised Yin-shun.

"I'm sick of these fellows. I'd rather starve than work for them," said Yin-shun, who quickly sat up when he saw Aunt Kao come in.

"Even if you don't work for them, you've got to find something for your stomach!"

With a tattered basket in hand, Li Yin-shun went out to pick some wild vegetation.

Li Yin-shun was a solid young man. Like a steel needle, he would be broken rather than bent. He became an orphan at five and was brought up by his grandmother. He began to harbor an intense hatred against landlords and rich farmers when he was a boy. At ten, he began to work at a brick kiln owned by rich peasant Li Fu-hsing. One day, when Li Yin-shun was bending over to pick up some bricks, Li Fu-hsing's little son jumped on his neck and beat his buttocks with a whip. The little boy cried: "Giddup! Giddup! Little horse!" Li Yin-shun was furious. He shook himself violently and threw the boy to the ground. The little boy picked up a brick and hit Li Yin-shun on the head. Li Yin-shun gave the boy a punch on the nose, causing a nosebleed. Squealing like a pig, the boy ran home.

In a moment, Li Fu-hsing came to the brick kiln, his face burning with rage.

"You bastard, why don't you do your work? Why do you go around beating up people?" shouted Li Fu-hsing, kicking Li Yin-shun.

"You ask him who started it. He rode on my neck and hit my head with a brick. If he is a human being, am I not?" Li Yin-shun retorted.

"Son of a bitch, you've got the nerve to talk back!" Li Fu-hsing roared, kicking and beating Li Yin-shun.

"Your son is full of it and you're full of it. I won't work for you anymore," Li Yin-shun cried as he struggled against Li Fu-hsing. Finally some workers at the brick kiln ran over and pulled them apart. Li Yin-shun's mouth was full of blood. He quit the work in the brick kiln and went home, saying he would never again work for a landlord or a rich peasant.

After that, Li Yin-shun supported his grandmother by cutting and selling firewood. After his grandmother's death, he moved into the "poor people's cave." Two years earlier, old man Li K'o-i had moved into the "poor people's cave." They lived together like relatives, and Li Yin-shun treated the old man as his uncle. The old man lived by begging for food. He would always share the begged food with Li Yin-shun. When Li Yin-shun got money from selling firewood, he would always buy some baked cakes for the old man.

After Li K'o-i's death, Li Yin-shun wept every night and was not in the mood for work during the day. One day, he went into the hills to cut firewood. He was exhausted. On his way to the "poor people's cave," he felt dizzy and was covered with cold sweat. He staggered toward a big locust tree and leaned against it. Then, just as he was dying, he scowled in the direction of Li Fu-hsing's house.

A Kindler

In the end, the grievances of an eternity must be redressed. Black clouds cannot hide the sun forever. It always grows light after a long night.

Those who lived in the "poor people's cave" could no longer sustain their lives. They only hoped that the sun would shine through very soon.

On a September day in 1944, a man from Hu-kuan dressed in peasant garb came to the village, carrying a hoe on his shoulder and a bag attached to the handle of the hoe. He reached the "poor people's cave" just as it was getting dark. He introduced himself to the residents of the cave. He told them that his surname was Kuan. When they saw that he was a man who had suffered much, like themselves, the residents of the cave talked freely with him. Inevitably the conversation came around to the problem of poverty. He said: "We poor people will soon come into our own. Reduction of taxes and interests has already been carried out in the old base in Hu-kuan...."

Kao Chia-ts'e, Li Ch'iang-ts'e, Li Chin-wang, and the others did not understand what he meant by the reduction of taxes and interests. When they asked Old Kuan to explain, he told them many things about the revolution. While everyone was enjoying the free and easy conversation, Li Yu-ch'eng silently squatted in a

corner of the cave, listening but not talking. Knowing that Li
Yu-ch'eng's mind was occupied by something, Old Kuan spoke
plainly to everyone: "I too am a farmhand, and I want to be
your friend."

As Li Yu-ch'eng listened, he realized that Old Kuan always
spoke the language of the poor people and that the visitor had
large and calloused hands. Then he began to talk in a warm
and friendly way with Old Kuan.

Old Kuan left for Ch'ang-tzu hsien shortly before the dawn.
At his departure, he took out two suits of old clothes from a
bag and asked Li Yu-ch'eng to give them to those who needed
clothes badly.

Four or five days later, Old Kuan visited the "poor people's
cave" again. He brought about three pecks of corn for the residents of the cave. Now Yu-ch'eng was sure that Old Kuan was
no ordinary farm worker.

"I'd like to go with you. I can't live on here...," Yu-ch'eng
told Old Kuan.

"No, you should stay here and organize the poor people to do
a little work for the anti-Japanese government. Once the Japanese aggressors are driven out, our day will be at hand," said
Old Kuan.

Old Kuan left behind the spark of revolution in the "poor people's cave." This cave became a base for the Party's underground activities. Li Yu-ch'eng heightened his class consciousness and became a revolutionary activist in Hsiao-sung Village.
He organized the dwellers in the "poor people's cave" and farmhands Wang Lin-ts'e, Wu P'ang-jen, and Li Tu-ts'e in the village into a revolutionary team to participate in underground
activities, transport food for the anti-Japanese government,
collect intelligence, strike at the enemy, and support revolution.

At one point, a unit of the Eighth Route Army was stationed
at the "poor people's cave." Li Yu-ch'eng and some of the
others suggested suppressing a few villainous rascals and traitors
to deal a blow to the enemy. Whereupon Tung Hai-chin, the
deputy headman of Hsiao-sung Village, was suppressed by the

Eighth Route Army. As a result, the "poor people's cave" became a thorn in the enemy's side.

One morning, village headman Li Fu-yüan led some village policemen to the "poor people's cave."

"Get out here, all of you! I know you want to revolt," Li Fu-yüan roared.

"No, we won't leave here. You can't intimidate us with threats," said the residents of the cave defiantly.

"Who collected intelligence for the Eighth Route Army?" asked Li Fu-yüan.

"We don't know," replied Li Yu-ch'eng angrily.

"This is simply lawlessness! Well, we'll teach you a lesson," Li Fu-yüan threatened.

However, Li Fu-yüan found that the situation of the moment was unfavorable to him and he retreated from the cave.

Li Yu-ch'eng knew that the enemy would take other steps against the residents of the cave. He began to send them out on patrol.

As had been expected, early one morning Li Fu-yüan led a company of the puppet troops into Hsiao-sung Village. The cave residents had quickly hidden in a safe place outside the cave before the puppet soldiers came. The enemy encircled the "poor people's cave," but they found no one in it. They smashed some broken cooking pots and bowls in the cave and left without accomplishing anything.

Ch'ang-chih was liberated in the fall of 1945. This put an end to the miserable life of the poor people in Hsiao-sung Village. The residents of the "poor people's cave" moved into big houses that had been owned by landlords and rich peasants and that had been built at the expense of poor people. The poor people in the village stood up.

Comrade Li Yu-ch'eng is the secretary of the Party branch in Hsiao-sung Production Brigade of Kao-ho Commune in Ch'ang-chih hsien. This production brigade is one of the advanced agricultural units in Shansi Province. Its production has increased yearly. Hsiao-sung Village used to be plagued

with food shortages. But now it is a village with surplus grain.
Many new houses have been built in the village. Families in
the village have more food than they can consume. Joy has re-
placed suffering; poverty has been expelled by affluence. An
atmosphere of prosperity prevails in Hsiao-sung Village.

The "poor people's cave" has become a reminder of the past.
The place where poor people suffered so in the past has been
turned into an orchard and a pasture. Li Yu-ch'eng, deeply
fearful that "when the scars are healed, the wounds are forgotten," relates the story of the poor people to everyone so
that they will always keep these tales in their hearts, and they
will become a tradition that is never forgotten!

Revolutionary mother Pao Lien-tzu

Pao Lien-tzu, a native of Lu Village, Chien-chang Commune, Wu-hsiang hsien, Shansi, is sixty-three years old this year. She is tall, with an oval face, and she walks briskly. Were it not for some streaks of gray at her temples, no one would guess that she is an old woman past her prime.

This fine woman member of the Communist Party is a Wu-hsiang hsien people's representative and a juror of the hsien court. The hsien regularly calls her to attend this or that meeting. People say that since she is so old and has such dainty feet, she should go by cart. But she won't do anything of the kind, and taking her own baggage and provisions, she starts walking. From Lu Village to the center of the hsien is a distance of some forty or fifty li, but she covers it without even a single stop for rest. She arrives at and attends her meetings punctually; and after the meetings she hurries back on the same day. She is truly an "Old Woman of Iron"!

To explain why she has been called "Revolutionary Mother," the story must start with the year 1940.

Chang Feng-ju, Li Chih-k'uan, Liu Chung, "Ke-ming ma-ma Pao Lien-tzu."

A Good Mother to the Eighth Route Army

In 1940 Japanese troops invaded and occupied Tuan Village, an important town west of the city of Wu-hsiang. They turned the town into a large bastion, and every two or three days, guided by Chinese traitors, they would make raids along the P'an(-lung)-Wu(-hsiang) highway to burn and slaughter. The Eighth Route Army guerrilla forces would regularly attack the enemy here. In response to the call of the anti-Japanese government, Pao Lien-tzu led the women of her village in making shoes for the soldiers, mending army uniforms, hauling food grains, and standing watch; they kept so busy day and night that they often even forgot to eat.

By 1942 the enemy had become more and more savage in its "extermination," "fixed-point extermination," and "annihilation" campaigns against the anti-Japanese bases of the Taihang area. As a result, the anti-annihilation campaigns of the army and the civilians in the bases were also intensified. At that time, Pao Lien-tzu had already become chairman of the Women's National Salvation Association, taking a lead in all kinds of work and performing with great distinction.

One evening in April, violent bursts of gunfire were heard from the banks of the Cho-chang River. The Eighth Route Army and the guerrillas once again came out to attack the devils that were launching an "annihilation" campaign. Lu Village was only seven or eight li from the Cho-chang River, and when they heard about the enemy situation, everyone went into the fields. Pao Lien-tzu busied herself putting together the army shoes that had been delivered by the women of her village in order to move them somewhere else for safekeeping. As she was doing this, she heard a knocking on the door. Thinking that it was the enemy surprising her, she quickly hid the shoes and went to open her door.

"Old woman, don't get scared. I'm from the Eighth Route Army...." A tall soldier dragged himself across the threshold. He was talking in the dialect of an outsider, which made him sound all the more feeble and exhausted. His face was pallid and covered with dark, heavy whiskers.

Pao Lien-tzu hastened to help him onto the k'ang. While she
added some firewood to her stove to heat a kettle of water, she
asked him about news from the front and learned that his name
was Chao Teng-shou; he was a veteran Red soldier in the
Eighth Route Army and had just been wounded and separated
from his unit as he fought with the devils on the banks of Cho-
chang River.

As the water came to a boil and Pao Lien-tzu was about to
wash Old Chao's wounds, she heard a banging at the front gate,
accompanied by cursing and shouting. She immediately concealed Old Chao in the cave used to store the ashes of her
k'ang, covering his body with two bundles of straw and wood,
and closed the lid of the cave.

Before she could open her gate, it was kicked in, and two
yellow dogs with rifles and fixed bayonets entered the courtyard. They slapped Pao Lien-tzu on the face brutally, demanding threateningly: "Has any wounded soldier of the Eighth Route
Army run into your house?"

Pao Lien-tzu pretended that she did not understand their
words. Standing on the cave's cover, she said: "Officer, would
you like to eat some baked cakes?"

"Wounded soldiers! Wounded soldiers of the Eighth Route
Army! Damn it, who said anything about baked cakes?"

"Let's go. Let's not waste our time with this stupid old
woman!" Shouting and cursing, the two yellow dogs moved on
to several compounds on the west side of the village to continue
their search.

After the enemy departed, Old Chao emerged from the cave,
and seizing a chopping knife, was about to leave immediately.
"Mother, as soon as dawn comes, the enemy will come to
search again, and you will become implicated...."

Mother Pao grasped Old Chao's hand and said she would not
let him go no matter what might happen.

Late that night, the militia helped Mother Pao take Old Chao
to a cave in a desolate spot. Every day she would cross ravines
and climb hills to fetch rice and water for Old Chao and

apply medicines and dress his wounds. She made oil cakes
with the white bread which was too precious for herself to consume and cooked egg-drop soup with the eggs laid by her
home-bred chickens.

After a few days under her meticulous care Old Chao's
wounds had healed, and he wanted to rejoin his unit. As he left,
he said, his eyes brimming with tears: "Mother, you are truly
a good mother to the Eighth Route Army! After I return to the
front, I'm going to kill a few extra devils as a reward for you!"

In 1943 the enemy implemented the policy of "nibbling away"
in the Taihang region, thus putting many "nails" [blockades]
into the P'an-Wu highway and cutting up the base east of Wu-
hsiang into southern and northern sectors. Lu Village was located in the southern sector, and Mother Pao's cave became
the communications center between the southern and northern
sectors.

One evening in the early winter of that year, rain was falling
incessantly, mixed with a damp snow: it was very cold. Militiamen stationed mobile sentinels on top of Mother Pao's cave.
Suddenly, through the sea of rain and snow appeared a tiny
shadow approaching over a tortuous trail behind the mountain.

"Who is it? Halt!"

"Me, I'm No. 105...."

"No. 105" was Little Ch'en, an intelligence member of the
Eighth Route Army in the northern sector. When Mother Pao
heard this number, she opened her door to greet him. It really
was Little Ch'en! His clothes were soaking wet, like a chicken
that has been dropped into a bowl of soup; his round, plump face
was frozen blue. Mother Pao lost no time in helping Little
Ch'en take off his clothes, and she asked him to wrap himself
in her warm quilt. Yawning with fatigue, Little Ch'en briefed
Mother Pao with the intelligence that the enemy entrenched in
P'an-lung and Hu-mang-ling was planning to come to the southern sector to seize grain. In turn she told him about the
situation in the southern sector. At the end, Little Ch'en said:
"I must go back as early as possible tomorrow."

"The weather is bad and the road is slippery. Why not rest

for a day or even half a day!"

"No, I can't. The leaders have asked me to return tomorrow; I still have an important task to perform!"

Mother Pao felt sorry for Little Ch'en. She took out a handful of dates, hoping these would allay his hunger, but he had already fallen asleep and was snoring. So she put the quilt over him and even pulled a tattered blanket from under her own children and placed it gently on Little Ch'en's body. She built a fire to cook, and to dry Little Ch'en's clothes.

"He must go back tomorrow, and yet it is raining and snowing; he is wearing such thin, unpadded clothing. This won't do...." While Mother Pao was thus pondering, she looked at Little Ch'en's face, which had turned a healthy red. She picked up the dried clothing and, as she was listening to the howling, sharp winds outside of her cave, she lit her small oil lamp, carefully pulled off the cotton bedding that covered her children, took pieces of cotton from the padding, and stuffed them into Little Ch'en's single-lined clothing, and then sewed it up stitch by stitch. She was apprehensive that Little Ch'en might discover what she was doing, and whenever he turned over, she would extinguish her oil lamp, only to continue her sewing after he was fast asleep again.

As dawn broke, all the denizens of the neighboring caves arose, and the commotion woke Little Ch'en. He stood up and, as he was putting on his clothes, how startled he was to find that his single-lined garment had been transformed into a padded one. Then he turned and noticed that there were shreds of cotton at the corners of the padded quilt used by the three little sisters, and Mother Pao was napping beside them. It became clear to him.

He put on his padded clothes, thinking that the cave dwelling of this mother of the Eighth Route Army was warmer even than his own home.

After the Japanese surrender in 1945, and even before the people of China could begin to smile, the Kuomintang reactionaries attempted to usurp the people's fruits of victory and immediately unleashed a frantic attack on the liberated areas.

The Battle of Pai-chin began. Our army captured the strong-holds of Ch'in hsien and Tuan Village in succession, and the battle raged violently. Stretcher bearers brought a steady stream of casualties from the front. A front-line hospital for the Eighth Route Army was set up in Lu Village. In a temple on the west side and in civilian homes — wounded soldiers were everywhere. At the height of the battle some four hundred wounded soldiers lived in the village. In Mother Pao's compound more than forty wounded soldiers filled the two mud rooms and three caves.

Every day at the first crowing of the roosters, Mother Pao would jump up from her bed to lead her own three daughters and the women of the entire village to the big temple and the various homes to look after wounded personnel. Before leaving them she would take the dirty clothes of these wounded personnel to her home to launder and dry, bringing them back the next day. In the evenings the women and militiamen would take turns at sentry duties. Mother Pao went up and down the hills and slopes to patrol, to bring water and clothes to the sentinels, and whenever she caught someone napping she would wake him and caution him to be alert.

She loved the wounded more than she did her own children, and they in return loved her more than they did their own mothers. When the front-line hospital for the Eighth Route Army was established in Lu Village she personally saved the lives of scores of seriously wounded personnel, and so she was hailed by the Taihang Region Party Committee as the honored "Revolutionary Mother."

On the front lines and in the rear areas, everywhere her deeds were legend. In the Eighth Route Army, all the men and women fighters respected her and addressed her intimately as "Mother."

In August 1945 a seriously wounded case was brought in from the Ch'in hsien front line. His head was wounded severely, and his right shoulder bone was cracked. Three operations had been performed on the way, but because of excessive loss of blood, he was in a coma when he was carried into the village. The hospital performed emergency operations to save his life, and later Mother Pao volunteered to take this seriously wounded man to her own home for recuperation.

The doctor said that the patient must have absolute quiet, and before the sutures of the head wounds were removed, he absolutely must not be moved in any way. Mother Pao neatly piled up all the beddings in her household. She felt them and decided they were not soft enough. So she brought out a piece of white cloth she had woven with her own hands, and with the help of her three daughters, she sewed the cloth into a cover, which was stuffed with wheat stalks. This made a mattress that was thick and soft and springy. She placed the mattress on the beddings, and then very gently helped the wounded man lie down on it.

Flies abounded in summer, making it impossible for the invalid to lie still and quiet. Mother Pao cut pieces of paper which she wrapped on jute stalks to make a fly brush. She told her oldest daughter to sit by the patient day and night and use the brush to drive away the flies. The daughter was as iron-hearted as her mother, and even in the depth of night when she was napping, her hands would not stop swinging the fly brush. Needless to say, the mother and daughter took every care for the man's personal needs, including his bowel movements.

When this wounded man first arrived, he developed a high temperature. The doctor said he must perspire in order to diminish his fever. Since the hospital had used up even such drugs as aspirin, Mother Pao went out into the field to gather some peppermint and bramble, and from a neighbor she borrowed ginger and scallion; then she boiled all this together into a soup for him to drink in order to induce sweat. His arm was swollen as huge as a melon, and for lack of medication, it soon began to deteriorate. Mother Pao then gathered leaves from peach trees. Wrapping them in white cloth, she crushed the leaves to squeeze out some bitter greenish juice, which she used to wash his wounds.

When he first arrived, the wounded man's chin and lips were inflamed, and when a spoon was used to feed medicine or food to him, he would suffer excruciating pain as the spoon touched his swollen lips. Mother Pao, simulating the feeding of swallows, would first place the food in her own mouth, and holding her mouth to his, feed him one mouthful after another.

To enable this wounded man to regain his health sooner, Mother Pao gave him her entire stock of eggs. After that, she killed her beloved hen in order to feed him. She had saved two silver dollars, a silver bracelet, and some cotton clothes, all of which were hidden underground, and now she went to a neighboring village to exchange them for chickens and eggs for the patient. In the process, she went all over nearby Jen Village, Cheng-chia Hamlet, and Ch'i-tung-kou. After about a month of her meticulous care and nursing, the wounded man gradually began to improve.

The doctors and nurses of the hospital considered it a miracle that a man so critically wounded was able to regain his health.

One day, when this wounded man was chatting with Mother Pao, he mentioned that as a boy he had liked to eat ears of corn. Mother Pao remembered what she had been told and whispered to her youngest daughter to quietly haul from her field some thirty ears of young corn. She boiled the corn in a large kettle and gave it not only to this wounded soldier but also to other wounded men in order to give them "a taste of something new." Thereafter they no longer dared to mention such things to the old lady for fear that she might make a fuss again.

But in spite of this, Mother Pao was still able to learn another secret from them on another occasion. It was midnight already, with a heavy rain pouring down outside. This wounded man felt somehow disturbed and could not fall to sleep. Talking with another patient, he said that since he had been wounded, he had not smoked even once, and now he would not know how cigarettes tasted. This casual remark fell on the ears of Mother Pao. Pretending that she was going out to check the sentries, she went everywhere to look for cigarettes. Although she ran through the entire village, she failed to find any. Later, someone told her that he had seen some cigarettes on the shelves of a certain peddler at Hsiang-shui-wen Village, which

was about four li from Lu Village. Braving the heavy down-
pour, she hiked to Hsiang-shui-wen, eventually buying a pack
of cigarettes. After returning home, she gave the cigarettes to
the wounded men, and lied that she had seen the cigarettes
when a militiaman was smoking and had asked him for a pack.

This was how Mother Pao served the wounded of the Eighth
Route Army wholeheartedly, treating the fighters as if they
were dearer than her own kin. Truly, if you wanted a star,
she would go to heaven to pick one up for you!

Three months later, this seriously wounded soldier was
about to be released from the hospital. It was only then that
Mother Pao thought of asking for his name.

"My name is Tu Kuei-pao," he said affectionately, "my home
is in Ch'ing-hsü hsien in central Shansi. My mother died under
the mistreatment of a landlord...Mother Pao, so now you are
my mother!"

"My son, it does not matter, since we are all bitter melons from
the same vine.... My father, like your mother, also died at the
hands of his landlord. If it were not for the Eighth Route Army and
the Communist Party, how could I, who was reared as a small
maidservant in a landlord family, be where I am today!..."

She went on to tell Tu Kuei-pao about her own family background.

Bitter Seeds Grown on a Bitter Plant

"My name is Pao Lien-tzu, because it is true that both my
father and mother had bitter lives, and from the bitter plant
was born this bitter seed, me...." Whenever Mother Pao
talked about her background, this was how she would start.

Pao Lien-tzu was born in 1901 into the family of a hired
peasant at Chien-chang Township on the banks of the Cho-chang
River (about seven or eight li from Lu Village). At that time,
her family owned only two mou of barren, sandy land which
yielded practically no crops. In such abject poverty, her parents could not but sell their services to the notorious landlord
of the township, who was dubbed "No. 2 Magistrate."

The real name of "No. 2 Magistrate" was Pao Ping-hsü, an arch despot who could devour human flesh without spitting out the bones. He connived with officialdom, maintained his private court and prison, recklessly bamboozled and looted other people's properties, and often harassed the poor by illegally apprehending and trying them in his private court and jail. He had no less a stern demeanor than did the country magistrate, and so the people dubbed him with that title. When the birth of Lien-tzu was drawing near, No. 2 Magistrate still forced her mother to turn the rice mill. Born prematurely, Lien-tzu was tiny and thin, and she could not even cry. It was only after her mother had carried her at her bosom for some time that the baby uttered its first cries.

Lien-tzu's mother survived on grain husks and coarse vegetables. In addition, she overworked herself. How could she have sufficient milk to feed her daughter? Thus, Lien-tzu merely nibbled at her dried-up breast, whimpering and crying. There were some poor brethren who pitied her; some gave her a handful of beans, and some gave her a few measures of rice. But this little bit of grain lasted only a few days, and so about four days after Lien-tzu's birth, Lien-tzu's mother went again to perform such tough chores as laundering and pig-feeding for No. 2 Magistrate.

It was with much sweat and tears that Lien-tzu's mother raised her to the age of five or six. One day, she summoned Lien-tzu and said: "My child, no matter what our family has to do to eke out a living, we still don't have enough for all of us. You'll have to go out to beg for rice...." From that day, Pao Lien-tzu began her life in the township as a beggar.

In the autumn of Pao Lien-tzu's twelfth year, her father began to spit blood as a result of physical exhaustion from some tough jobs he had performed for No. 2 Magistrate. As he was dying, he stared at the members of his family for a long time, unable to utter even half a sentence. Lien-tzu's mother borrowed some wooden boards from her neighbors, with which she made a thin coffin. When the cask was being carried out for burial, it fell all of a sudden, along with the broken bones of the deceased. Pao Lien-tzu, who was escorting her father's coffin, was greatly frightened and cried loudly. Her mother said: "Death is like the extinction of an oil lamp; let the dead be buried like this!" But the relatives and neighbors said unanimously: "He has suffered all his life when alive, and how can we let him be buried without any clothes on his body?!" They all joined to offer some money to buy a piece of mat to wrap him in, and thus Lien-tzu's father was buried.

After the father's death, the family became so poor that there wasn't even any rice to cook. People came to demand payment of loans and rents, one after another. Lien-tzu's mother would keep silent all day long. One evening, after Lien-tzu had been in bed for quite some time, she noticed that her mother was still sitting up on the edge of the k'ang, as if she were demented. Lien-tzu had fallen asleep by midnight, but later she thought she heard the door creak, and when she opened her eyes she discovered that her mother had vanished. Crying and shouting, she jumped from the k'ang and ran out of the door. A shadow was walking in front of her toward the river, and she hurried to catch up, finding her mother at the bank of the river. She held her mother's legs tightly, pleading: "Mother, I'm scared. Hurry up and come home!"

Her mother seemed totally oblivious of her, and it was a long while before she said tearfully: "Child, your mother's heart feels like a ball of fire, and I'd like to cool myself somewhat on the river bank." Lien-tzu, seeing the roaring waves of the great river which shimmered with a pale light in the gloom, became more and more frightened. Her whole body trembled, and holding her mother's clothes tightly, she wept: "Mother, Mother, let's hurry back. From now on, I won't ask you again for anything to eat. I won't ask you for anything to eat...."

When the mother saw that her dear daughter was crying like a baby, her heart softened. She took her daughter's arm, and they went slowly home.

Thereafter the mother resolved that she would never enter the black gate of No. 2 Magistrate. During the winter she did some odd jobs — spinning cotton, weaving cloth, sewing, making soles — to earn enough for food to survive on. Lien-tzu continued to beg from door to door.

On the twenty-ninth day of the twelfth lunar moon, Lien-tzu's mother husked the two pints of wheat which she had earned with a whole winter's hard labor, and told Lien-tzu: "Child, I am going out to turn the millstone so that when New Year's comes the day after tomorrow, we can eat some white wheat sticks for a change."

When Lien-tzu heard this, she could not express her delight. Her mother picked up the wheat and started for the door, and Lien-tzu followed close behind.

Before she reached the door, it was kicked open with a resounding crash. Wearing a black hat, a long gown and a short jacket, and carrying a water pipe in his hand, No. 2 Magistrate walked in officiously. He was followed by a lackey by the name of Kuo, who carried on his shoulder several money belts.

Putting on a long face and staring fiercely at the wheat in the bamboo shovel, No. 2 Magistrate said: "You have grain, why won't you pay your rent and your debts?" As he was saying this, the running dog had already produced an abacus from his money belt; he fingered it noisily and said to her finally: "Principal plus interest, you owe four piculs and five bushels of grain for rent, and thirty yuan in back debts."

"Mr. Kuo — you — you must have miscalculated! There is only one and a half picul of grain in arrears, and her father repaid the old debt a long time ago."

No. 2 Magistrate shouted angrily: "You dirty widow, if you don't believe it, why don't you dig out your dead husband and ask him!"

When Lien-tzu's mother realized that he couldn't be reasoned with, she entreated him: "Lord and master, the two of us, mother and daughter, are really too poor to pay back!"

The lackey looked at Lien-tzu and said sneeringly: "You can't pay? It's all right. Let your daughter serve the Old Mistress in place of paying back your debt!"

No. 2 Magistrate pulled on his water pipe, and the, blowing out the smoke, said: "Since the beginning, you have brought up

this girl depending on me for the food you eat. It is therefore
reasonable for her to serve as a slave girl in my house!" As
he was talking, he nodded to his lackey, who immediately
dragged Lien-tzu out. When her mother tried to stop him,
No. 2 Magistrate kicked her to the ground, and then casually
walked out with his hands behind his back.

Entering the black gate of No. 2 Magistrate was tantamount
to entering the gate of hell. That compound was gloomy and
deep, and even during broad daylight, Lien-tzu would feel a
spooky fright.

The "Old Mistress" mentioned by the running dog was none
other than No. 2 Magistrate's wife, who was known as "Tigress." The Tigress gave orders throughout the day: she sent
the regular workers and the day laborers into the fields to
plant; she ordered slave girls and maidservants to run mill-
stones and wash vegetables; she dispatched her lackeys to collect rents and give out loans. She was No. 2 Magistrate's ac-
complice in oppressing and exploiting the poor. With her cru-
elty and cunning, she deserved the nickname of "Tigress."
Thus No. 2 Magistrate agreed to let Lien-tzu serve this Tigress.

Taking orders from the Tigress, Lien-tzu performed a continuous round of chores — cleaning tables, sweeping the floor,
fetching tea, pouring water — and no sooner had she finished
than the Tigress would ask her to massage her back and make
opium. What Lien-tzu was most apprehensive about was preparing opium for the Tigress. If the opium was raw, it was no
good; if it was burned, it was no good; and if the opium juice
dripped away, it was even worse. If anything she did failed to
meet with the Tigress's approval, the Tigress would either
beat and scold her, or use her opium stick to stab her. In only
a few days, Lien-tzu's hands were covered with needle wounds.

One evening, Lien-tzu was again preparing opium for the Tigress. Because of overexhaustion from her daytime work, she
could not help dozing off while she was cooking the opium. The
opium became overheated on the lamp and burst into flame.
When the Tigress saw this, she pulled out the opium iron and

hit Lien-tzu with it. Lien-tzu cried out in pain, but the Tigress only cursed her viciously: "Dead slave girl, see if you nap again!" Poor Lien-tzu felt an agonizing pain on her face, but she dared not cry openly in the presence of the Tigress.

It was long past midnight when Lien-tzu returned to her dark room. She could no longer sleep, and she resolved to run away to her own family. She slipped out to the outer courtyard and was about to open the gate when two watchdogs charged at her, barking ferociously. Lien-tzu dodged to one side, and because the dogs were chained, she was not bitten. She then turned to the workroom in the rear, planning to escape by a small door, unaware that it was locked with a heavy padlock. She looked at the wall, so dark and so tall that she would have no chance even if she could fly. She tried to rest for a while in the room used to store fodder, figuring that at the break of dawn when the small door would be opened, she could sneak out. As she was thinking, she fell asleep in the fodder room.

On the next morning when Uncle Feng, an old hired laborer, came to feed the livestock, he discovered Lien-tzu sleeping there. He woke her up and asked why she was there. Lien-tzu told him through her tears: "Big uncle, I ... miss my mother. . . ." She begged Uncle Feng to save her. Just then they heard the Tigress shouting from the hall:

"Lien-tzu, you dead slave girl! Where have you been and why didn't you come to empty the chamber pot!"

Uncle Feng told Lien-tzu to hurry up and serve her Old Mistress. After Lien-tzu had gone, he went immediately to loosen up the hay and restore it to its original shape.

Later, the Tigress complained that Lien-tzu was not clever enough for her. She took in another slave girl and had Lien-tzu serve her son and daughter-in-law. The younger mistress was also a notorious shrew; because of her yellowish face and mean heart, people dubbed her "Little Hornet."

During the day, Little Hornet had Lien-tzu wash clothes. In the home of a rich man there is an abundance of grain and also an inexhaustible supply of laundry to do. Little Hornet had a baby that she was still nursing, and an endless number

of diapers had to be washed everyday. When the laundry was piled up, it would reach higher than Lien-tzu. She had to scrub and wash, scrub and wash, with the result that Lien-tzu's hands became blistered and broken, and when she touched the clothes, the pain became excruciating. Nonetheless she had to launder. After a whole day of torture, she had to rock the cradle for the baby in the evening and feed Little Hornet's elder son, who was about fourteen or fifteen.

As for this rich older son of Little Hornet's, Lien-tzu felt a deep hatred for him. Not only did she have to feed him rice and clean his nose and mouth, but oftentimes he wanted to make her into a donkey on whose back he would ride to school.

What was "ride donkey to school"? It meant that Lien-tzu must crawl on the ground to simulate a "donkey" so that the boy could ride on her back, whipping and shouting as he went to school. This scion of the rich man, though only fourteen or fifteen, was as fat and tough as a pig: Lien-tzu was two or three years younger, lean and frail, so you can imagine how she felt about "riding donkey to school"!

One day, after laundering for a whole morning, Lien-tzu felt so exhausted that her arms and back seemed to crumble. She had not yet swallowed a mouthful of rice when Little Hornet's elder boy clamored that he must "ride donkey to school." Lien-tzu was so tired and hungry that she thought she should go after her meal. Little Hornet said angrily: "Have you become deaf? You are more and more disrespectful. You won't even answer the young master when he calls you!" Lien-tzu dared not delay anymore, and so she crawled on the ground, with the rich brat riding on her back flamboyantly, whipping her and shouting, "Run!"

The threshold of the landlord's house was high, and outside the gate there were five or six stone steps, which made it very difficult to crawl or climb! Lien-tzu paused to catch her breath, and for this she was beaten and kicked by the young master. How easy it was for him to ride her to and from school. By the time they got back, what rice was left had been eaten by the watchdogs.

In the evening, Little Hornet gave Lien-tzu a large pile of clothes to unthread and wash. As she was using scissors to unthread, the landlord's little brat came back from school. He went to his mother to accuse Lien-tzu of being too lazy, not carrying him carefully, and trying to purposely tumble him. When Little Hornet heard the accusation, she scolded Lien-tzu angrily: "If you should try to injure this life root of our family, even if you had a thousand poor lives, you wouldn't be able to pay back!" As she fumed, she grasped an iron pick from the fire basin and threw it squarely at Lien-tzu. Lien-tzu immediately ducked to avoid the pick, but in the process her left eye was inadvertently hit by the scissors she was holding. Blood gushed out and she fainted. Little Hornet said sneeringly: "You deserve it! You deserve it!"

After one of Lien-tzu's eyes was blinded, she was chased by Little Hornet into the kitchen to make the fire, cook rice, fetch water, feed the dogs, and sweep the courtyard. One day, Lien-tzu went to wash rice, and although she did a good job, Little Hornet tried to find fault, charging that she did not wash it thoroughly. When Lien-tzu argued back, Little Hornet became enraged and swore at her: "When one raises a dog, at least it can still bite. What's the use of keeping such a rice pail as you?" She summoned her lackey and told him that Lien-tzu was disrespectful of her master and asked him to tie her on a pillar and flog her with a leather whip. Lien-tzu was beaten terribly; there were wounds all over her body, and blood was everywhere. But this did not satisfy Little Hornet's sadism, so she poured saltwater over Lien-tzu's wounds. Lien-tzu was in horrible pain and she cried out pitifully. After this beating, Lien-tzu fell ill, developing a high fever. After several days, she became so emaciated that she no longer looked like a human being. When the rich master saw that there was no more oil to be squeezed from her, he kicked her out for good.

When Uncle Feng carried Lien-tzu back to her own home, she was near death. At midnight on the fifth day after her return, Lien-tzu fell into a coma. Her mother thought she was dead and carried her out to bury her. But when she reached

Pan-kou-li, she touched her daughter, and feeling some warmth left in her body, took her back home again.

Lien-tzu was on the k'ang for more than three months and was fortunate enough to escape death. But her left eye had become blinded permanently because of the injury from the scissors.

When she was fourteen, Lien-tzu went to a poor peasant family in Lu Village to become a child wife. Wang Tan-hai was ten years older than Lien-tzu, but he was honest and industrious, and he treated her like his own sister. The couple shared their poverty and hardships, and they lived on harmoniously. When her husband went out to work as a regular or day laborer, or when he stayed at home to plant a few mou of barren ground, she would always do her household chores diligently. In the spring she would carry a hoe to reclaim wasteland: in the summer she would go out to pick up ears of grain; in the autumn she would hire on as a farm laborer to earn some grain; in the winter she would stay home to spin and weave. These chores kept her busy from morning till night. She would often say: "As long as I have two hands that are not idle, even if the times become harder and more arduous, I will go on enthusiastically."

Although the couple would get up before dawn and get to sleep late at night, spending every minute and every second on labor, there were all kinds of exploitation, such as land rent, taxes, and usurious loans. Like all other poor people, they tried everything to make ends meet, but there was no escape for them. When the first daughter was born, they just managed to cope: but when the second and third daughters came in succession, they became so poor that there was no respite at all.

"When would the poor people see the light of a new day? Must the two sisters, Ch'eng-chü and Lan-chü, forever live with the fate of beggar and slave girl and be like Lien-tzu, who suffered all her life?..."

As a result of hard labor and constant worries, although Lien-tzu was not yet forty, she already looked very pale and old. They were just about at the end of their rope when the light of dawn appeared on the Cho-chang River, illuminating Lu Village, and the gloomy and chilly home of Lien-tzu.

In the spring of 1938, when peach and almond trees were blooming along the stream, the Communist Party's Eighth Route Army came to the Taihang Mountains.

The First Spring

"The Eighth Route Army has arrived!"

"Yes, I heard that this is the Red Army from North Shensi...."

"There are also women soldiers! Look, isn't that soldier with long hair peaking out from under her army cap a woman?..."

Group after group of army units wearing uniforms of coarse cloth entered Lu Village, as people welcomed them enthusiastically, talking excitedly among themselves. The women were especially interested in the Eighth Route Army's female soldiers. No sooner had these units entered the village than they dispersed, some writing posters, others conversing with the villagers, and still others vying with each other in carrying water and sweeping courtyards for the local people. On a grinding stand stood a short and plump woman soldier, explaining the reasons for resisting Japanese aggression and calling for national salvation. She was surrounded by a large crowd. Lien-tzu went over to hear what she was saying:

"...with cooperation between the army and civilians, our strength is inexhaustible. Although the Japanese aggressors have airplanes and cannons, we are not afraid of them, and we will defeat them!..."

Lien-tzu squeezed into the crowd in order to look at the woman soldier closely and hear her refreshing talk clearly.

"...There will be strength with organization.... Women want to join the Women's National Salvation Association for the purpose of saving China, defeating Japanese imperialism, and seeking liberation.... Women will no longer be abused, and poor people will no longer be poor!..." Every word went right to Lien-tzu's heart. Her mind brightened; her eyes sparkled, and it seemed to her that even the sky above her had suddenly become more brilliant.

From that day on Pao Lien-tzu was a member of the Women's National Salvation Association. She would attend meetings and sing songs all day long, thus gradually coming to understand many of the revolutionary reasons for resistance against Japan and national salvation. From that day on she began to unbind her bound feet, cut her long hair short, and give vent to her accumulated grievances of the past several decades.

On the stony path beside the creek which she must have treaded many thousand times before, she would visit every family to carry out propaganda and organization work among the women. It seemed to her that in this valley with its mountains and ravines she was for the first time hearing the singing of birds, seeing the blooming of flowers, and appreciating the idyllic scenery of springtime, with its green mountains and clear waters amidst pink peach blossoms and lush willow trees. It was indeed a great year, one in which heaven and earth and the people changed!

Not long thereafter, she was elected unanimously as chairman of the Women's National Salvation Association. She joined the women in making army shoes, ration bags, and smoke pouches. She not only produced more but was also adept and expert at what she did. Whenever she found some women who failed to meet the demands of quality and quantity, or who used straw paper instead of rags to make soles, she would sort out the inferior items and reject them. Some women thought that she was too serious, and would say sarcastically: "This is merely dealing with requisition, and not...." But before they could finish their remarks, Lien-tzu would tell them solemnly: "Since shoes are being issued at the front seasonally, one pair must last three or four months. How long would a pair last if it was made in such a slipshod way? Since we are now making shoes for our own army, how can it be compared with coping with the requisition of Yen Hsi-shan [the governor of Shansi] before?" When they heard this, they began to make soles more solidly, and they would even embroider some words on the shoes, like "Endeavor to kill the enemy" or "Protect the motherland."

Thereafter Lien-tzu busied herself selflessly in nursing the
wounded soldiers of the Eighth Route Army. In 1945 Japan
surrendered. When the bandit troops of Chiang Kai-shek and
Yen Hsi-shan attacked the liberated areas, a number of militiamen in Lu Village responded to the call of the Party to join
the Eighth Route Army and fight Yen's bandit troops. Lien-tzu
also resolutely sent her second daughter, Lan-chü, who was
only fourteen, to join the army. Because she had no sons, she
earned high praise for sending her daughter to enlist. She
was also praised by others for the inspiring story of "earning
a son in her old age."

The reader may recall that when she was nursing wounded
soldiers she made every effort to save Tu Kuei-pao from his
near-fatal wounds.

After Tu Kuei-pao had rejoined his unit, he took part in several battles and then was wounded again. In July of 1946, when
his unit was being reorganized in Hopei, the leadership decided
to let him retire from the army to take up another vocation.
When Tu was leaving, the instructor said:

"Comrade Kuei-pao, do you plan to return to your old home
in Shansi?"

"Yes."

"Isn't your home in Ch'ing-hsü? That place is still in enemy-
occupied territory."

"I still want to go to my home."

"Won't that be too dangerous?"

"No," said Kuei-pao. "Comrade instructor, I want to go
back to my other home to visit my mother."

When he mentioned his "other home," the instructor understood him completely. He said happily: "Right, you should go
back to see your revolutionary mother." Chao Teng-shou, who
had lived with Tu Kuei-pao in Lu Village, also joined the conversation, saying: "Please give my regards to the revolutionary
mother."

Tu Kuei-pao returned to the little mountain hamlet of Lu
Village on the banks of the Cho-chang River.

Among Tu Kuei-pao's friends in Lu Village were Chang

Liu-hai, who was the veteran secretary of the Lu Village Party branch; Chang Ta-sheng, who was originally the village head but was now director of a brigade; and Jen Ken-sheng, who was director of pensions. They all came out to welcome him as one of their own, and said: "Old Tu, why don't you settle down in our village here?" Liu-hai's wife was especially enthusiastic. She said: "Old Tu, please stay here. If you can't cook, please eat in our home; I'll wash and mend your clothes when they need laundering and mending...."

Liu-hai pushed his wife's shoulder, telling her to look at the expressions of Mother Pao and Ch'eng-chü. She understood, laughed, and said no more.

What happened thereafter needs no elaboration. Tu Kuei-pao became secretary of the Lu Village Party branch, and he and Ch'eng-chü had three sons. Mother Pao would cheerfully tell anybody she met: "Even I, who did not have my own son, have one now, and even grandsons! This is a result of the radiance of the Communist Party and Chairman Mao!"

In the winter of that year, the resounding Land Reform movement began. At the struggle meeting against Pao Lien-sheng (No. 2 Magistrate had already passed away; Lien-sheng was his son), a big landlord of Chien-chang, the first to go to the platform to make accusations was Mother Pao Lien-tzu.

She spilled the waters of her bitterness and redeemed the blood debts of several generations. In another struggle against a despot landlord by the name of Wang, who was dubbed "King of the Ravine," they had some difficulty in mobilizing the masses at first. It was Mother Pao who took the lead in exposing his criminal history. She said finally:

"...I must also expose another crime of this crooked fellow. A few days ago, when he found out that the wind was not blowing in the right direction, he stealthily presented a bag of grain to my old man. How sweet were his words! He said: 'Wang Tan-hai, Wang Tan-hai, we are brothers from the same father, and how can we split the Wang character into two halves? Please don't bear any grudge if your younger brother has not treated you properly.' I and my husband immediately asked him to take back that bag of grain. I then said to him: 'There was one time when at year's end we wanted to borrow some grain from you to pass the New Year, why didn't you realize then that my old man and you were brothers from the same father? Why did you try to take advantage of our hardship to get our few mou of barren land and also to take my daughter as a slave girl to pay off our debt?' "

When the masses saw that Mother Pao had disregarded the ties of brotherly kinship to struggle against him, they also vied with each other in exposing the King of the Ravine's various crimes in oppressing poor people and conniving with the enemy and the puppets. Finally, they demanded that the government punish this despot landlord in accordance with the law.

During the Land Reform, Mother Pao proved very resolute in struggle, but when the fruits of struggle were distributed, she suggested that the better land and some of the more valuable properties be given to such poor and lower-middle peasants as Wang Shuang-feng, Chang Kuei-chih, and others. She declined any portion for herself. Everyone said: "In that case, we give you a cotton-padded coat so you can wear it to attend meetings." She replied: "I would attend them even though I had no cotton-padded coat." She insisted that this cotton garment be given to Chang Kuei-chih. The latter said: "Since you are so old, it would be warmer for you to wear it. I work in the daytime and rest after dark — I won't feel cold." She said: "I can spin and weave myself, and so I can get what I want. But you are single, and who would make it for you?" After many polite refusals, it was decided that the garment be given to Chang Kuei-chih.

During the Land Reform, Mother Pao was totally dedicated to the Party and did everything in accordance with the directives of the Party. Landlords and rich peasants regarded her as a thorn in their side. One evening, she went out to attend a meeting of poor hired peasants. As she was leaving her gate, a "bang" was heard, and a huge piece of rock fell just behind her. It was followed by a series of "bang, bang, bang" and more rocks fell. Mother Pao felt panic at first, but when she turned her thoughts to the Party and the masses, she regained her strength. She advanced boldly, cursing loudly:

"Dog thing, if you have guts, come out! Let me tell you this: if you kill me, there would still be the Party and thousands and tens of thousands of masses who will get revenge for me!"
That bad egg dared not make a move and ran away stealthily.

In these past several years, Mother Pao has been truly loyal to the Party; she feels deeply that it was the Party that saved her, pointed out the direction for her to struggle, and gave her inexhaustible strength. Whatever the Party has asked her to do, she has never avoided any hardships and never complained. In these years she has kept a secret wish that she would not divulge easily, though in 1949 she told a comrade who was a Party member. It was one day that year that she received news that moved her to unprecedented excitement and elation. It was impossible for her to calm herself, and she was moved to tears — her application for Party membership had been approved; her ambition of many years was fulfilled.

On the Road to Struggle

After she joined the Party, Mother Pao's awareness was greatly enhanced and her revolutionary resolve became stronger.

When the first mutual aid team in Lu Village was formed, her husband became head of the team and she became the deputy head. When the primary cooperative was founded in 1952, she was the first one to join it, and she exercised an exemplary influence in the movement to accumulate fertilizers. In 1956 the cooperative became an advanced cooperative, and Mother Pao was elected deputy director. At the critical time of drought during spring planting, she went all out to persuade cooperative members to dig irrigation ditches and drill wells; as a result, production was increased and everyone calmed down. In 1957 the Party issued an appeal for afforestation. Starting with the premise of long-range benefits, Mother Pao mobilized the masses to plant some 1,500 pine trees, 10,000 willow trees, 1,200 walnut trees, and 1,000 pear and apple trees on the South

Hill, the North Hill and in the ravines.

She listened to the Party, and she followed the Party closely, holding high the great banner of agricultural collectivization. She stood at the forefront in the struggles against nature, against feudal superstitions, and against conservative and backward ideology. She maintained a high degree of vigilance against the sabotage of class enemies.

Following the switchover to communes in 1958, an unprecedented harvest was garnered in agricultural production, thus bringing tremendous joy to the members. However, at mealtime one day, Mother Pao heard that someone was spreading rumors on the street alleging that "the more that is produced, the more will be the requisition for public grains so that, in the end, the toilers will have labored in vain."

Mother Pao felt that such sentiments were wrong. She immediately reported what she heard to the branch Party headquarters so they could investigate the rumor. They found out that it was Chang Huai-pi who started the rumor, and so the case was handled immediately.

There was a time when the following rumor was making the rounds of the village: "When a comet appears in the heavens, it means fighting will rage on earth." Where did this rumor originate? Mother Pao went among the masses to investigate and discovered that it was spread by Chang Huai-pi, who was a member of the so-called "Return-home Taoists" that had escaped apprehension. Later, the leadership also handled this case.

Mother Pao was a juror of the hsien People's Court. When these two cases were tried by the court, she attended personally. On behalf of the laboring people of Lu Village, she held the official seal of the proletarian dictatorship, thus bringing to bear ruthless dictatorship against the class enemy.

In the winter of 1963, another capitalist evil wind was blowing.

Someone said: "There is not much to gain from winter production. Our brigade might as well assign one or two persons to run a business. It won't be difficult for one person to make two thousand yuan each month, and two can make four thousand yuan."

Another fellow joined in, saying: "It is true. There is great profit to be made by using grain to make noodles. Let's do it."

When Mother Pao heard this, she said resolutely: "Nothing doing! Ours is an agricultural commune, not a business commune. Unless agricultural production has been consummated, no business can solve the basic problems. Is there a shortage of chores to be taken up in winter? Land should be fixed up; conservation should be undertaken; fertilizers should be accumulated ... all to lay a good foundation for increasing farm production."

No sooner was this said than it was immediately done. She led the women to fix up the land. During a single winter some sixty <u>mou</u> of land were repaired and improved. The current crop of corn was growing exuberantly and sturdily.

Even last year someone was saying: "There is no war now, and no gunshots can be heard. Everybody remains in the commune, each one with his own share, and so how can there be class struggle?"

When Mother Pao heard these words, she said disapprovingly: "You must have looked at the wrong scale! Although landlords have been overthrown, their ideology has not. These monsters and ghosts, with their pointed heads, try to stir up a storm whenever there is some trouble and want to recover the seal of power. Not only is there class struggle now, but if one is careless, one will be victimized by the class enemy."

Thus, under the teaching and guidance of the Party, Mother Pao has permanently grasped the principle of class struggle, watching at all times the conspiracy and intrigues of the class enemy. In all kinds of storms, she has never gone astray; moreover, she has managed to educate the masses of her village in a timely fashion, thus enhancing their class awareness. She is like a pillar standing firmly in the middle of a stream, stemming the crosscurrent of capitalism.

Mother Pao has stood in the forefront not only in the various political movements and class struggles, as befitting the honorable title of a Communist Party member, but she has also been a model in managing her household diligently and frugally and in educating Communist successors. She is truly an "old woman of iron" who becomes more Red as she grows older.

Though Mother Pao's household has many members, the labor force is short. The village knows that she is in a difficult situation because her family is an army family (her daughter Lan-chü is enlisted), and Kuei-pao is a crippled serviceman who has taken up a different job. Thus they are entitled to pensions, and whenever relief grains and funds are distributed, there is always some for her. But she always declines. Nor will she accept any wage points. She says: "I have not yet become seventy or eighty, unable to move about, and so why should I accept relief! Give relief to some other families!"

Although Mother Pao is advanced in age, she is a veritable "old woman of iron" and can handle any chores in the fields. Except when she goes to the hsien to attend meetings, she never misses work. When labor accounts are settled each year, she always has completed at least 200 labor days, and once reached 220. Last year, when she returned from the field, her legs were swollen. Her elder daughter, Ch'eng-chü, was apprehensive that she might hurt herself, and so she said: "Mother, you are so old, but you won't stop working with your hands or feet. What can we do if you get sick? Moreover, since we live better now, why don't you enjoy yourself for a few days? However, Mother Pao paid no attention to her daughter's advice. On the next day, she went to the field as usual.

In the past several years, the village has had bumper harvests continuously. In her home, the granary was full of grains, but she treated a bumper year as a lean one, and the whole family lived frugally. She would often say: "I'd rather let a small stream flow permanently, than cause the river to stop flowing."

Kuei-pao's elder son, Chi-hsiang, is seventeen this year, and he attends middle school. Once he returned home and said to his mother: "Other middle school students are dressed so well, but although I am so old now, I have never worn a pair of good pants —" He said it rather embarrassedly, hoping that his mother would buy a pair of corduroy pants for him. When Mother Pao heard it, she said emotionally:

"My son, you must know how lucky you are as you are now. When I was of your age, not to say that I had not worn anything of refined cloth, but even my dresses of coarse cloth were ragged and patched up. By the time I was nineteen, I hadn't yet worn a new garment. During the day I wore trousers like a lantern, and in the evening my bedding was like one made of spider web. Now you have single garments, double-lined garments, a student uniform of blue khaki, and you are still not satisfied, and you still want —"

When Chi-hsiang heard this, he was moved to tears, saying: "Mother, please don't continue. I know everything now."

But Mother Pao never misses an opportunity to educate this successor, and so she continued painfully: "My son, although we are leading a happy life, we must never forget our pains just because our scars have healed. What we must do is not to speak of food, clothing, and enjoyment, but to think constantly about the distresses of our predecessors, about how your mother's left eye was blinded, about how your father's right arm was broken, and about how your aunt marched in the army in the Taihang Mountains when she was only fourteen, and as a result of the march, her feet were afflicted with huge bloody boils. The mountains and rivers of we poor were not easily come by!"

OFFICE OF THE FOUR HISTORIES COMPILATION COMMITTEE
OF THE LING-CH'UAN *HSIEN* CCP COMMITTEE

A shepherd becomes a college professor

August 15, 1958, was a beautiful day. The entire faculty and
student body of Shansi Agricultural College were dressed up
neatly, as if they were involved in some happy occasion. They
formed a long line and proceeded jubilantly to the railway station in T'ai-ku to greet Ning Hua-t'ang, dressed in a pair of
mountain boots and coarse clothes, who, as a specialist in
herding sheep, had been invited by the college to take a post
as professor in the department of animal husbandry.

Ning Hua-t'ang, who had been despised as a "filthy shepherd"
in the old society, stepped to the college's platform amidst thunderous applause! He accepted the college president's letter of
appointment and Professor Lü Hsiao-wu's framed testimonial,
which stated: "We wish to study from you and make you our
teacher." At that moment, he felt that his blood was boiling,
and he was overwhelmed by many different emotions. All past
events and memories flashed before him. After a moment of
shock, he suddenly turned toward Chairman Mao's portrait on
the wall to make a deep bow, and his eyes brimmed with tears.

Chung-kung Ling-ch'uan hsien wei pien ssu-shih pan-kung-
shih, "Fang-yang-kung tang-le ta-hsüeh chiao-shou."

In the first lecture, he did not discuss shepherding techniques, but instead talked about his own bitter past.

I

My name is Ning Hua-t'ang, and I am forty-eight years old this year. My home was at Wa-yao-shang Village in Ling-ch'uan <u>hsien</u>, Shansi Province. I have herded sheep for forty years, and for more than twenty years I suffered hardships.

For four generations, my ancestors herded sheep for land-lords, and each generation was so poor that there was not a single tile to cover the roof and not a single plot of land to stand on. My grandfather used to be a husky fellow, but because he herded sheep for a landlord, his back became hunched, and he was afflicted with many ailments. He coughed a good deal and would spit up half a bowl of saliva mixed with blood. My father herded sheep for landlord Chiang Kuei-sheng, but after a year of hardships, he could no longer support my aged and bedridden grandfather. One day, when the family had already gone without rice for three days, it seemed that my ailing grandfather would starve to death. Father had no choice but to borrow two <u>mou</u> of barren land that belonged to my aunt's family and pawn it to Chiang Kuei-sheng. Though the land was worth eighty strings of copper cash, this heartless Chiang Kuei-sheng gave him only half the amount. My father used this money to buy three bushels of maize, with which he cooked a meal for my grandfather after he returned home. As they were just about to eat, the deputy village head and the head of the <u>lu</u> [comprising twenty-five families] came in, scolding him viciously:

"You won't pay back your tax grain, but you yourselves seem to eat comfortably!"

My father asked: "What kind of tax do I owe you?"

Counting them off on his fingers, the head of the <u>lu</u> said: "Head tax, land tax, house tax, road tax, tax for the birth of a baby, tax for marrying off a daughter —"

My grandfather said: "No baby has been born into our family;

nor have we married off any daughter; moreover, we don't
even own a single <u>mou</u> of green land. What taxes can we owe?"

The running dog who was head of the <u>lu</u> would not tolerate
any argument. He seized the maize from my father. My father
begged him to allow the family to keep it, but all he got for it
was a kicking. Grandfather was so angry that, holding onto his
rice bowl, he cursed bitterly: "My god! What kind of a world
has this become? Why don't you open up your eyes and say
something for the poor?" As a result of his rage, grandfather
became even more sick.

The situation became so hopeless that my father went to consult my mother: "Since we are at the end of our resources,
we'll have to sell our young daughter. This would save her life,
and moreover, we could buy some grain to sustain the family!"
When my younger sister heard this, she was so terrified that
she wept and cried out. My elder brother suggested: "I am
older. It would be best to sell me!" I said: "My brother has
grown up and can support Father. I think you should sell me!"
When my parents heard this, their crying became even more
agonizing. Mother said: "Children, all ten fingers are con-
nected to the heart of your mother, and all of you are a part of
my own flesh. I cannot part with any of you; I cannot sell you!"
With the help of some of our poor brethren we managed to get
enough grain to feed ourselves and sustain grandfather's life.
After some five months, the deadline came for the redemption
of our pawned land, and if the land was not redeemed, it would
be lost. Uncle and Aunt and some of our poor friends managed
to scrape together forty strings of cash to redeem the land.
But Chiang Kuei-sheng compounded the interest and demanded
eighty strings of cash. Cocking his melonlike head and staring
with his viper's eyes, he said, between puffs on his water pipe
and sips of his Dragon Well tea:

"This forty strings of cash is only enough to pay the interest.
You have to bring another forty strings to redeem the land!"

God! Wasn't this the same as killing the poor? Well, let him
kill us. With no land to plant crops, it would be impossible to survive anyway. Moreover, this land had been borrowed from our aunt.

Our family had to beg from relatives and friends and borrow from here and there in order to raise another forty strings of cash to give to Chiang Kuei-sheng. But that heartless Chiang Kuei-sheng took out the mortgage paper and said:

"The deadline of the mortgage has been exceeded by one month, so you can't redeem it anymore."

It happened that Chiang Kuei-sheng was intending to link these two mou of land belonging to our aunt to his own larger plot of land, and he tried every means to prevent its redemption. Consequently he altered the mortgage term from six months to five months.

My father said: "On my piece of paper it clearly says six months!"

But Chiang Kuei-sheng replied: "My own paper says it is for five months!"

When my father returned home, he told the story to some of the poor neighbors, who said in unison: "Let us go to the hsien court to sue that son of a bitch who is being so unreasonable!"

When the case reached the hsien government, the corrupt bureaucrat there declared: "Your paper is not bona fide; only the Chiang family's is genuine."

My father still wanted to argue, but instead he was given fifty floggings with a wood plank, and he had to limp all the way home. Since Chiang Kuei-sheng and the magistrate were sworn brothers, how could a poor man win such a litigation? Chiang Kuei-sheng was like a fox which borrowed its might from a tiger, and so he ran amuck in the entire village, and the poor people there called him "Locust Chiang" behind his back.

My mother had already been sick, and as a result of this episode, she died of indignation. When grandfather saw that the future was so bleak, he committed suicide by hanging himself with a rope. Though grandfather had worked hard all his life, all he left father was a shepherd's staff.

After burying grandfather, my father realized that we could not survive in Wa-yao-shang Village. So he took the three of us — me, my older brother, and my younger sister — away from the village where we had been born and raised. He said: "We'd rather starve to death in some other place; we must leave this place which is dominated by the Chiang family!"

Though he said this, it was in fact by no means an easy thing for a poor family to leave its own native place! When we had walked a long way and the village was no longer visible, father couldn't help but turn his head to look back nostalgically.

Not long after we had left, a violent wind began to blow, and a huge snow fell, enveloping the landscape. It became dark. There was no village before us; there was no inn we could stop in; we had no shelter. From Shansi to Honan there are thousands of mountains, and the road was treacherous. We walked a whole day without anything to eat, and we were hungry and exhausted. The biting wind lashed our emaciated faces like a sharp knife. Icy snowflakes penetrated our ragged clothes. We were so frozen that our teeth chattered. We were both hungry and cold, crying for our mother and father. When father heard us crying for mother, it again reminded him of his painful predicament.

"Children, what use is it to call out to your mother now? She died a long time ago in a fit of anger!..."

Just then, a big fellow came up. He looked and looked at us and then inquired: "Why don't you walk on?" My father said spiritedly but without strength: "Ha! As refugees far from home, where can we go! If we drop dead on the street, the street will bury us; if we die on the road, the road will bury us. A wolf's mouth will be our grave, and a dog's stomach will be our coffin!"

This fellow quickly took off his ragged cotton-padded jacket to wrap about my sister, and then told my father: "Old man, you had better bring your children to the small mountain temple up ahead for a night's shelter!"

Staring at the stranger, my father couldn't help asking him: "Young brother, where are you from and where are you going?"

He replied: "I am a native of Kuan-yeh-p'ing, and I am taking a trip to the mountains. Where are you going?"

As we were thus talking, we entered the mountain temple.

We learned that his name was Lü Chen-te, and he was a shepherd for a landlord of Kuan-yeh-p'ing named Wang K'uei-feng. There was truly a kind of professional rapport, as well as the sympathy of one poor man for another. When he learned that my father was also a shepherd, he became all the more friendly with us. He quickly burned some wood and straw to build a fire to warm us. Then he produced three pieces of wheat bran cake for us children. Father declined several times, but Chen-te said:

"The children are small; it doesn't matter if an adult gets a little hungry."

My father was so grateful that he said tearfully: "Children, remember, it is Master Lü who saved you."

On the next day, we followed Master Lü to Kuan-yeh-p'ing, where we settled into a small temple. He also arranged for my father and elder brother to begin to tend sheep for Wang K'uei-feng, who was Lü's landlord. Though I too wanted to be a shepherd along with father, the landlord thought I was too young and would waste his rice, so he refused to accept me. All my sister and I could do was go out to beg.

II

One day, my sister and I went to a tall house where a fat, baldheaded old man was sitting in a chair outside the door. As we approached him he suddenly took his long smoking pipe and struck me several fierce blows on the head, hurting me terribly.

I said to him: "It's all right if you won't give me anything, but why hit me?"

He swore at me: "I've never seen you two bastards — you don't even know the rules of begging!" As he was saying this, he called an old yellow dog to bite us until our skins were broken and blood gushed out.

After we had returned to the temple, some of the poor uncles and brothers who were also beggars taught us:

"Children, there are some rules even in begging rice; keep

at a distance of three feet in winter, ten feet in summer, and
stay near the door at other times. If you walk too near, the
heartless rich folks will think that you are too dirty, and they
will beat you."

Alas, there are so many rules even in begging! Thereafter
these poor uncles and brothers vied with each other in exposing
the stingy habits of that bald-headed rich man (whose name was
Chao Liang). We were all so aroused that Master Lü made a
suggestion on how we could punish him. After our plan was
made, we sneaked into Chao Liang's wheat field late at
night, and when the watchman was not looking, we set fire to
the stacks of wheat. In no time at all several piculs of wheat
were burned. We felt we had avenged ourselves, and said:
"Come on and bite us again, you son of a bitch!" My father
was timid, and after he had heard what we had done, he worried for a long time. My elder brother had always been reti-
cent, and after we burned the rich man's wheat stacks, he became even more quiet. Nonetheless, I was unafraid, thinking
that "he deserved the burning."

When I went out begging, I always passed a private school.
I could see the rich men's children carrying their handsome
book bags, walking and dancing to attend school. How splendid
it was to be able to read and write! I pouted, saying to father:

"Father, I also want to read books!"

He said sorrowfully: "Stupid child, you don't have that kind
of luck! Our family has tended sheep for generation after generation; who knows how to handle a book?"

I was naive, and so I demanded: "No, I must study! I know
how to hold a book. I want to study!"

In fact, my father didn't want to tell me I couldn't study. But
all he could do was to try to comfort me with words which he
well knew could never come to pass: "Good child, when I have
some money, I'll let you study."

I was elated, thinking that there was bound to be a day when
my father would let me study. Nevertheless he only turned
his back to wipe his eyes. How eager I was then to study,
though I was not even allowed to cross the threshold of a school.

Sometimes I would stand outside the gate of that private school, listening surreptitiously to the students reading. After some time I could also read a few sentences.

One day, the teacher asked a student to recite, and the student started: "Chao...Ch'ien...Sun...," and was unable to finish. I finished for him, reciting: "Chao Ch'ien Sun Li, Chou Wu Cheng Wang," and as I finished, I tried to run away. But they felt insulted and all rushed out to chase me, beating and scolding:

"You dirty shepherd, still you dream of studying. You are really an insult to scholars!"

They seized the writing brush that I had found somewhere and then threw it away. Nonetheless I still wanted to study. Since I did not have paper and pen, I tore down some red paper scrolls from rich men's homes or picked up some waste paper, and used burned charcoal as a pen to write and draw pictures.

III

After that, landlord Chao Liang investigated everywhere to learn who were the "criminals" who had burned his wheat stacks. My father was afraid that there might be an incident. Also, as the landlord Wang K'uei-feng was making deductions from his wages, life there became impossible. Thus he took us and fled to Hui hsien, to a place called Yeh-chuang, and there he tended sheep for the Yüan family's Eighth Young Master, who was a distant relative of the great landlord and warlord Yüan Shih-k'ai. I was nine years old then, and so I went to tend sheep together with my father, running in the mountains all day long. When the weather was cold, and my hands and feet became frozen and bruised, I would carry a lamb to warm my hands and face. The little lambs seemed to understand, and they would run to me to let me carry them.

By the time I was eighteen or nineteen, because I had spent so much time herding sheep in the mountains, seeing more rocks than human beings, I became more of a loner and more stubborn. My father realized that herding sheep would get us

nowhere. He arranged with the young Master Yüan's bookkeeper to rent him five mou of land, agreeing to pay an annual
rent of five piculs of grain, and paying forty dollars in advance
as a deposit. However, after he had paid three years' rents in
grain the bookkeeper refused to return the rent deposit when
father asked him for it. I was enraged. Like a young cow undaunted
by a tiger, I went to the young Master Yüan, when he came to
inspect the sheep, to accuse his bookkeeper. I told him that his
bookkeeper should not use a large bushel measure with a double
bottom to take in rents, and then a smaller bushel measure to
measure out rents he was paying others.... It was the fault of
my own ignorance. I didn't realize that the bookkeeper was his
master's lackey. Young Master Yüan not only refused to return
the deposit money demanded by my father, but he also tied me
to a tree and gave me a sound beating. Nonetheless I was in-
transigent, and the more he beat me, the more I cursed him.

He said: "You are such a dirty shepherd — how many heads
can you have? How dare you disturb the earth over the head
of the god, or scratch the itch on a tiger's head!"

I replied: "Don't you talk reason at all?"

As he beat me, I continued to curse him. The vicious landlord then used some bamboo sticks to pinch my fingernails.
(You can see that the scars are still there!) When my father
heard this, he immediately went to the landlord to beg for pardon. His request was in vain! As a result he did not get back
any money, and the land was also taken away from him!

Yeh-chuang was no place for poor people either. Thus we
went to Ta-ssu-yao to tend sheep for another landlord named
K'ung Hsiang-lin.

One day a little lamb stepped on my bowl of bitter vegetable
soup, spilling it all over. Picking up my sheep's staff, I was
about to beat the lamb with it. The little lamb merely stared
at me, bleating pitifully, and my heart softened. I thought:
"Why should I vent my anger on you? You are just like me,
and when you have grown fat, the landlord will kill you to eat.
No, you are perhaps better than I, because you still have thick
wool and won't be cold. In my case, ever since my grandfather's

generation we have endured hunger and cold, floggings and
scoldings, and in the end we won't even have a single strand
of wool. You still have your mother, but I?" When I thought
of my situation, bitter tears brimmed in my eyes. After thus
crying, I suddenly turned my thoughts, remembering what Master Lü had told me. What's the use of crying? Tears cannot
avenge! Let's fight the sons of bitches!

My father made another decision: if it was impossible to
rent land, then buy it. If it is bought by someone named Ning,
then it should belong to someone named Ning. However, where
could we get money to buy land? My father went to see K'ung
Hsiang-lin several times, trying his best to seek his help. As
a result, K'ung-Hsiang-lin agreed to lend him 100 dollars,
but he asked my father to tend sheep for him for six more
years so that he would pay his debt with labor. Since
father was determined to build his own source of livelihood,
he was willing to endure the hardships for six more years, so
that after he had his own land, he would no longer have to tend
sheep for the rich. With the 100 dollars he had borrowed,
plus whatever savings he had accumulated during the last
few years, father bought four _mou_ of barren land from
K'ung Hsiang-lin. From then on, father and son would rise
early and go to bed late, tending sheep, on the one hand, and
farming those four _mou_ of land we had just bought, on the other.
Our days passed with hard work and hope. Our sheep grew fat
and strong, and the land also promised to be fertile. However,
who could have known that when the six years were up K'ung
Hsiang-lin would tell us that with interest, father's debt had
reached a total of 240 dollars. Thus, instead of acquiring some
land, he had incurred a bellyful of debt. He couldn't even run
away, and must forever tend sheep for K'ung Hsiang-lin to pay
off his debt.

I was so infuriated by this incident that I went to Master Lü
to inform him. He explained that this was how the poor became
poorer and the rich made their fortune. From then on, I understood that it was impossible to kowtow to the rich; one could only
struggle against them, if not openly, then secretly, using trickery!

IV

With this setback my father gradually came to realize that
it was very difficult for the poor to create any enterprise of
their own. Thereafter he was no longer so diligent in tending
sheep for the landlord. Nonetheless, with a view to guarantee-
ing his rice bowl, he did his best to teach me the techniques of
sheepherding. I really admired my father's and Master Lü's
skills. Even if a sheep were rolling and bleating pitifully, sick
to the point of dying, after they treated it, it would immediately
get up and romp and prance. I resolved to study the techniques
hard and thoroughly. I thought that one day I would raise many
sheep, so that all the poor people would be able to wear sheepskin coats and eat mutton! When father was giving injections
to sick sheep, I would drop everything to observe him closely.
I would use a small stick in place of a needle, and watch closely
how my father applied his needle. I remembered what kind of
needle to use for which disease, where to insert the needle,
and how many needles to use. I also learned from my father
how to collect medicinal herbs. I could also distinguish between a kind of sedge grass that could poison sheep and a kind
of grass known as peng-lu which served as an antidote. In my
little sheepfold I kept herbal drugs, needle bags, and medicine
bottles. When the landlord saw these things, he would scold me:
    "You spend all day fooling with these things instead of tend-
ing sheep properly! What can a dirty shepherd like you accomplish? Even if the emperor held an examination to recruit
scholars, such a shepherd as you wouldn't be selected as the
top scholar!"
    As he was saying this, he dumped out all the drugs, needle
bags, and medicine bottles which I had worked so hard to collect.
    Father became more senile and feeble as time went by, and
it became more difficult for him to climb slopes and scale
mountains. One day, as he was tending sheep on the mountain,
some routed Kuomintang stragglers came along. They tried to
take the sheep so that they would have mutton to eat. My father

did his best to protect the herd, but in the end they succeeded in seizing a dozen or more. When father came back that evening, the dog landlord wouldn't give him any supper; moreover he flogged him severely with a leather whip. I was going to rescue my father, but several of the landlord's lackeys used force to deter me. My father was so advanced in age and so sick, how could he stand such a severe beating? Before they were finished, he was dead on his feet.

After murdering my father, the landlord still wanted to beat me. I was not to be abused so easily, and I told him boldly:

"Since the sheep were seized by Kuomintang troops, and since I didn't slaughter or eat them, why should you beat me? When my father tried to protect the sheep for you, he was beaten with the rifle butts of the bandit soldiers of Kuomintang. His legs were injured because of this, yet you beat him to death. We herded sheep for you in wind and rain, and even when we were sick with exhaustion, we still tended sheep for you. My father became old, but your sheep grew fat. While you have grown fat with good food, we starved and became emaciated. Since you have beaten my father to death, I must fight it out with you!"

I was thinking then that since I would die even if I knelt before his dragon bed, I might just as well kick the life out of this dragon prince. Thus I tore loose from the lackeys, and leapt over to confront the dog rich man. I seized his leather whip and broke it in two, and threw it into the courtyard. I made a great ruckus, thereby attracting many of my poor brothers to rush over. When the dog landlord realized that the situation was bad, he angrily walked away into his house. My poor brothers advised me to sue the son of a bitch landlord. I remembered that Master Lü had told me that in a world where the rich held the seal of power, a poor man wouldn't win even though all the truth was on his side. Therefore I thanked these poor friends for their good intentions and bore my vengeance in my heart. Tearfully, with the help of these poor brothers, I buried my father. I vowed that thereafter I must let K'ung Hsiang-lin realize that the taste of me, Ning Hua-t'ang, was bitter and pepperish!

From then on, I intentionally prevented the sheep from drinking water for several days at a stretch. Thus, while their stomachs dried up, they outwardly looked rather fat. One day, the dog landlord came over to watch me as I was feeding salt to the sheep. I intentionally did not fry the salt thoroughly, and threw the salt powder on a large boulder along a rivulet. At noontime in summer, the sun broiled like a fire basin, making the water in the rivulet steaming hot. I then drove my herd of sheep down a steep slope, making them very hot and thirsty; before they could catch their breath, I let them eat the salt that had been left on the boulder. Then I drove the herd to the water's edge. Because the sheep had not drunk water for many days, no sooner did they see the water than they drank as greedily as they could. Thus in a short while the sheeps' stomachs became so full that they cried from pain. I tried to say to them jokingly: "You have eaten enough and drunk enough, why do you still yell?"

By afternoon all the hundred-odd sheep were dead! When the dog landlord saw this, he shouted to me angrily: "What did you do to them?"

I said to him calmly, word by word: "Master, you have seen with your own eyes that they ate salt and drank water. The sheep were not thin, and I have done my best to herd them so that each was robust and strong. If they wanted to die, what could I do to stop them? What shepherd would not want to raise good sheep!"

I had anticipated that the dog landlord would make trouble for me, and so I had asked some of my poor brothers to come over to help me out. No sooner had I finished than these poor brothers picked up my argument:

"It is true that if sheep wish to die, no man can stop them."

"Which shepherd wouldn't hope to have good sheep!"

"Since it is not Hua-t'ang that killed the sheep, you shouldn't put the responsibility on Hua-t'ang!"

The dog landlord gave them a dirty look, unable to say anything. Anyway, since he was such an ignorant dog, it was

possible to deceive him with anything technical. He wanted me
to pay him back for his sheep, but I refused, insisting: "It is
not I who strangled the sheep. I won't repay you!"

V

At that time my younger sister Yin-hua was already sixteen.
She did all kinds of chores in K'ung Hsiang-lin's house — washing clothes and cooking for the family's old lady and daughter,
looking after babies, cleaning chamber pots. She got her meals,
but was paid no wages, and what she ate consisted of leftover
rice and vegetables, often sour and spoiled. Sometimes she
did not even get enough rice to eat. It goes without saying that
she would often be scolded and beaten. One day, the landlord's
wife asked my sister to wash clothes on the river bank. A piece
of rock dropped suddenly from the bank, injuring her hands and
legs. Drenched in the river water, she felt such acute pains on
her skin that she couldn't continue laundering. However, if she
failed to wash the clothes, she would not be given food; moreover she would get a beating. So my sister kneeled on the river
bank, crying as she washed, and when she could no longer continue with the chore, she rested there. She returned after the
laundry was done. The landlord's wife checked the clothes. Because some spots were not clean, my sister got a beating. As
her hands and legs had been bruised by rocks, the pain became
so great that she could not fall to sleep that night. She made
some noise. The landlord's wife chastised her for waking her
up, and again gave her a harsh beating.

On the evening of the very day the hundred-odd sheep were
bloated to death, the dog landlord noticed that my sister's legs
were so swollen that she could no longer serve him. He therefore secretly sold her to a peddler of human beings. When my
elder brother learned that our sister had been sold to someone
in Hsuchow, which was about 1,000 li away, he immediately
went to look for her. On his way he was seized by Kuomintang
troops to serve as a conscript laborer, and he was never heard
of again.

My father was beaten to death by the rich man; my sister was sold by the rich man; my brother was captured by Kuomintang troops. I was left all alone, and my hatred grew more and more intense.

When it was almost time for the Ch'ing-ming festival [early April], and the sheep were giving birth to their lambs, it snowed suddenly. When it was time to nurse the lambs, I stood aside and paid no attention to them. Both sheep and lambs were bleating in confusion, trembling in the snow, and running and stumbling. When the dog landlord failed to locate me, he had no choice but to call a new hand. This novice could not handle the sheep properly. The mother sheep were glutted with milk and crying in pain; the lambs were hungry for milk, and couldn't find their mothers. If a lamb approached the wrong sheep, it would get kicked. The snow fell harder and harder. The dog landlord became desperate, and there was nothing he could do. So, you had the guts to beat my father and sell my sister, but you can't milk the lambs. In less time than it takes to finish a meal, your sheep will be swollen to death and your lambs would be starving! So you wish to find Grandfather Ning! He has long since departed to another world! He will no longer serve as the docile ass for K'ung Hsiang-lin!

VI

All waters return to the sea in the end. Leaving the K'ung family, I returned to Wa-yao-shang Village in Ling-ch'uan hsien. Anyone who has learned to herd sheep will not give up his shepherd's staff, and so I resumed shepherding.

The poor brothers asked me: "For whom are you going to herd sheep?"

I replied: "Chiang Kuei-sheng!"

"Do you still want to work for him?" they asked. "Haven't you forgotten how your grandfather and mother died? Maybe you were still too young then and you didn't realize it."

"I know all," I replied. "When father was still living, he told me everything!"

Someone retorted: "In that case, you must call anyone mother
that has milk!"

I told my poor brothers somberly: "What I've come to do is
shave this conical head in order to avenge my family and to
vent the anger of the poor! From now on I hope you will help
me."

They said unanimously: "Good. If you can exterminate this
locust, we'd all thank you. We can't allow him to oppress the
poor of this area!"

The last time Chiang Kuei-sheng had seen me, I was a mere
boy of seven or eight. Now I had grown to twenty-eight or
twenty-nine, tall and strong. He thought: this donkey has again
come back to pay his debt to me. The grandfather owed me a
debt, and now the grandson is here to repay it. He accepted
me, agreeing to pay a wage of twelve yuan a year.

Thus I again tended sheep for Locust Chiang. The sixth day
of the sixth moon on the lunar calendar was a festival for shepherds. On that day, it was incumbent on the employer to count
the sheep, settle the accounts, and "give bonuses" to shepherds.
All shepherds looked forward to this day. Nonetheless, by noontime that day, Locust Chiang had not prepared any good food,
but instead spread out dead sheepskins one after another until
they filled the entire courtyard, and then he asked me to explain the causes of the sheeps' death. Locust Chiang was more
shrewd than K'ung Hsiang-lin, and so it was more difficult to
struggle against him. Pointing at each piece of sheepskin, he
said:

"There are threads of blood on this piece, which means that
the sheep died because you failed to bleed it. So, you should
pay me five dollars. This piece has blood spots on it, showing
that the sheep died because you killed it with rocks. Another
five dollars you owe me. This sheep died of snakebite, which
was due to your negligence. Another five dollars —"

In short, he conjured up some reason for the death of each
sheep in order to deduct from my wages, and after the accounts
were settled, I still owed him ten silver dollars after herding
sheep for one year.

I remembered all my new grievances and old hatreds and vowed that I won't be a man if I could not overcome him.

That autumn, I drove the entire herd of sheep to the old river ditch. I asked several poor brothers to help me stop the herd and hold up the sheep's tails, thus allowing the autumnal wind to blow into their stomachs through their anuses. After half a night's work, the entire herd became afflicted with stomach trouble.

Early the next morning, when Locust Chiang came out and saw that the ground was covered with fallen leaves, he chanted, shaking his head: "After the nocturnal sounds of wind and rain, how many flowers have fallen?"

I thought: "You need not be poetic. Although I cannot write poetry, I know that after the autumn wind, a good many sheep have perished!"

Thus, after three days, almost all the hundred-odd sheep had died. Locust Chiang was adept at finding fault, but this time he could not discover the cause of death. He came to ask me. I knew that he was superstitious, and so I said:

"It is because a cold autumn wind came in the night. This is the will of heaven!"

He was genuinely scared into believing that the death of the sheep was the punishment of heaven. He hastened to slaughter a pig, lighted strings and strings of firecrackers, and kneeled down before some incense sticks to pay respects to the god of the sheepfold. He also engaged a good theatrical troupe to perform for three days, beating loud cymbals and dainty drums. He did not know that the god of the sheepfold was none other than Ning Hua-t'ang; what a joy it was for the poor brethren to have the chance to attend three days of entertainments.

VII

Late one night as I was fast asleep in Sheep Grass Temple, I heard suddenly someone call my name: "Ning Hua-t'ang! Ning Hua-t'ang!" I went out to see who it was and found a stranger.

He said in a friendly way: "Big brother, don't be afraid. I am also a poor fellow and my name is Lang Erh-hu. You must have known Master Lü Chen-te. It was he who asked me to come look you up."

I thought: "Right, if not, how could he know that my name is Ning Hua-t'ang?" He began to talk to me, and holding my hand, he made the character eight, saying:

"This [meaning the Eighth Route Army] will soon be coming. They are coming to deliver the poor from their sea of bitterness. Hereafter please make an extra effort. Tonight I will ask you to guide my way. Is it all right?"

I said: "Okay, I will do my best if it is within my power!"

From then on, people constantly came to ask me to serve as a guide. I was so happy that I wanted to laugh.

Late one night, someone again called my name and I thought they wanted me to be their guide. I hurried out. But before I could see their shadows, several men jumped on me, using ropes to tie me up. I thought that my role as a guide for the Eighth Route Army must have been discovered. But that was not the case. It turned out that Locust Chiang had learned that I had pretended to be the god of the sheepfold. He dipped some rope in water and beat me severely, asking me to pay him back for his sheep. I'd have let him beat me to death without even asking for pardon. He then said that I connived with the Eighth Route Army and he wanted to put me to death. It was at this critical moment of life and death that rifle shots were heard from hills to the east. I thought to myself that my savior the Communist Party had come. Locust Chiang immediately stopped his beating and detained me in a small hut. That night, the Eighth Route Army really entered the village, and I gained my freedom.

VIII

With liberation, I really emerged from the sea of bitterness. The Party led the poor to stand up and struggle against the landlords. I and the other poor united and seized all the treasure

of gold and silver hoarded by the dog landlord Chiang Kuei-
sheng, dividing it among ourselves. A house and some land
were distributed to me, and I no longer had to worry about
food and clothing. They also helped me to get married, though
I was already over thirty then. Now my daughter is already
fourteen, and my son is six. I must use all my expertise in
herding sheep to do my job successfully. When I tended sheep
on the mountains, it was originally a familiar road that I had
tread day and night. But it seems to be a new road that I am
covering today. I feel that the mountain has become more beautiful than before! The flowers on the trees are also more fragrant! As I drink water from the streams, it tastes so much
sweeter! Even the birds sing better! I've been unbelievably
happy! After I was admitted to the Party, I became even more
zealous in tending sheep! The experiment to produce twin
lambs was successful, and it has even become possible for
sheep to deliver four or five lambs!

During the decade and more since liberation, I have done
some of the things I am expected to do in tending sheep for the
cooperative: the birthrate and life expectancy rate of newborn
lambs has increased 95 percent or more; the herd has grown
from the 40 of six years ago to 467 head at present. At meetings in the provincial capital, they all dubbed me a "sheep expert." In point of fact, what accomplishments have I made? If
there were any, it was entirely due to the Communist Party,
because without the Party, even if there were ten Ning Hua-
t'angs, they would not have survived on earth. Now that you
teachers and students ask me to be a professor, I really do not
have anything to teach you. I must learn from you all. That's
all.

Another round of thunderous applause resounded through the
auditorium of Shansi Agricultural College.

In September 1958 Ning Hua-t'ang went to Peking to attend
the First National Congress of the National Scientific Workers
Association. After the conference a commemorative photo-
graph was taken of him with Premier Chou. The conference

presented him with a Hero brand fountain pen, bidding him to
study assiduously. He remembered that while he lived in the
old society, he had no means to attend school, and he was
beaten when he went stealthily to listen to others who attended
classes. They even took away his rotten writing brushes.
What a difference between heaven and earth!

Now Ning Hua-t'ang serves as director of the Ling-chuan
hsien sheep farm. Shansi Agricultural College has also sent
Professor Lü and two assistants to help him write books, of
which Ning Hua-t'ang's Sheepherding Experiences and Three
Hundred Songs and Ballads on Sheepherding have already been
completed and published. After his articles were published in
various newspapers and periodicals, he received scores of
letters from readers. Even overseas Chinese have written him
from afar to congratulate him, saying: "... You are the glory
of our Party, our motherland, and our laboring people!"

P'EI FENG, LI CHIH-K'UAN, CHANG FENG-JU AND LIU CHUNG

A poor blacksmith becomes a master of the country

Master Sang, whose given name is Yün-chiao, is fifty-one years old this year. The son of a blacksmith, he followed his father from one place to another. From his childhood he was fed the bitter water of class oppression and class exploitation; the old society drove to their deaths seven members of his family.... In 1945 the Communist Party saved his entire family. Now he is the head of the welding group of the United Factory in Wu-hsiang <u>hsien</u> and an honored labor model.

Three Generations Gripped by Poverty

Sang Yün-chiao's native home was in Tuan-kou Village in Lin <u>hsien</u>, Honan Province. For three generations, starting with his grandfather, his family was so poor that they could hang up their empty kettle like a cymbal or drum, and even the rats were so starved that they had to chew bricks. From the time of his great-grandfather, they served the big landlord

P'ei Feng, Li Chih-k'uan, Chang Feng-ju, Liu Chung, "Ch'iung t'ieh-chiang ch'eng-le kuo-chia ti chu-jen."

267

Yang Lao-p'ei like draft animals.

Rich Yang lived in Yao Village, about eight li from Tuan-kou Village. He owned some one thousand mou of the best land; his family's wealth was worth probably tens of thousands of strings of cash. His pens were full of pigs and sheep, and he had many horses and mules. He employed scores of lackeys; these plus his hired laborers and maidservants must have made his house-hold number more than a hundred persons. His family also operated stores, pawnshops, and kerosene companies in such places as Kaifeng, Paoting, and Taiyuan.... At that time most of the poor people there, like the Sang family, were serving Rich Yang as hired laborers and tenant farmers generation after generation.

Yün-chiao's great-grandfather for his entire life had served Rich Yang as a hired laborer; but he earned nothing; on the contrary, at his death he owed an "open-ended debt" to Rich Yang. Even by the time of Yün-chiao's grandfather there was still no choice but to serve in the Yang family, and moreover, his grandfather began to learn the chores of a blacksmith diligently.

One New Year's Eve, after the day's work was done, my grandfather begged Yang Lao-p'ei:

"Master, father and I have served as regular laborers for your Yang family for a total of eighty years. Since tomorrow is New Year's Day, won't you be kind enough to give me some money to buy salt!"

He must have spoken eight bagfuls of sweet words before the rich man consented to give him enough money to buy five ounces of salt. At the salt shop the salesman said: "The price of salt has risen at New Year's time." The money for five ounces of salt bought only four ounces, wrapped in a small bag no bigger than a fist.

At that time Rich Yang operated a salt shop which monopo-lized the business and controlled salt prices, and it cost ten catties of maize to buy a catty of salt. Salt was as expensive as silver; how could poor people afford it! Throughout the year the Sang family could get hardly a taste of salt. On New Year's Eve, as grandfather brought this small bag of salt back home, he said on crossing the threshold:

"Look! What is this?"

My grandmother stared, asking with surprise and joy: "Where did you get the money to buy salt?"

Grandfather explained everything, and the whole family came to look at the salt, as if they had found a treasure; they were delighted beyond imagination.

Grandmother dropped some salt into the vegetable paste, asking the children to taste it and inquiring: "Is it delicious?"

Yün-chiao's third uncle was already six years old, but it was still the first time that he had tasted salt. He said, pursing his lips and shaking his small head: "Ah! It is good to eat! It's wonderful!" He finished half a bowl of the vegetable soup, and insisted on eating some of the salted vegetable paste.

Grandmother said: "Tomorrow, on New Year's day, let's put some salt on the rice so that the entire family can eat a delicious meal."

After lunch, Yün-chiao went out with his grandfather to grind bran; second uncle and grandmother went to the river bank to wash clothes; third uncle was left at home to watch the door. After a while, second uncle became so hungry that he couldn't stand it any longer. So grandmother asked him to go home first and warm up the vegetable paste still left in the pot, and to go ahead and eat it with third uncle.

Second uncle hurried home, carrying some wet leaves to build a fire to cook the "rice." While second uncle was stooping to blow on the fire, third uncle had already climbed up to the pot; using a broken ladle to scoop up the leftover paste, he ate a mouthful, scrounging a bit of salt with it, then another mouthful, scrounging another bit of salt. By the time second uncle had built a bright fire and the pot was hot, third uncle had already finished the leftover paste, and the small bag of salt was almost entirely gone. Second uncle did not even have a mouthful of the leftover rice to eat. When second uncle hurried away to look for grandmother, third uncle was seized by such a terrible thirst that he drank an enormous amount of cold water.

At dusk, as the adults hurried home after a busy day of work, they saw that third uncle had collapsed beside the kitchen stove, with white foam streaming from his mouth; he had already died from the burning effect of the salt.

After Yün-chiao's third uncle's death, Yün-chiao's grandmother was so aggrieved that she became seriously ill. She had to see a doctor and buy medicine, thus creating more debts to the master. The family passed the Yüan-hsiao festival [fifteenth day of the first lunar month] in great distress. Yün-chiao's grandfather realized that the family could not go on like this, so he had to send second uncle, who was only seven years of age, to herd sheep for Rich Yang.

One summer, while second uncle was driving his herd of sheep to the river bank to drink, he was caught by surprise when the herd went into the field beside the stream to nip rice sprouts. When Rich Yang learned about it, he accused second uncle of negligence and careless shepherding. Second uncle tried to argue with him, and so the master summoned some of his lackeys to hang second uncle from an ash tree and to flog him right and left with leather whips. By the time the hands of the lackeys had become exhausted, poor second uncle had breathed his last.

After Yün-chiao's grandmother thus suffered one calamity after another, she became so mad that she would vow determinedly: "Rich Yang, Rich Yang, you have killed three members of my family. Though I can't get revenge myself, my children and grandchildren will sooner or later settle accounts with you!"

The next year Yün-chiao's grandfather became ill from accumulated grievances; he had received a beating from Rich Yang and was then pushed into the snow to freeze there. Before he died, he called Yün-chiao's father to his side, saying tearfully: "Son, I can no longer live on — Yang Lao-p'ei is a man-eating wolf, and hereafter you mustn't serve that son of a bitch as a hired laborer!" Having said this, he closed his eyes.

After grandfather's death, Yün-chiao's father swore: "Even

if I die, I won't enter Rich Yang's door!" Thereafter he began
to work as a blacksmith, wielding the huge iron hammer which
was left by grandfather, carrying on his shoulders the bag of
his blacksmith trade as he walked through villages and alleys.
After several years of hardship, he was still unable to pay back
the "open-ended debt" owed to the Yang family.

It was a year of spring drought and autumn flood, and there
was no harvest at all. The whole family had nothing to eat or
drink, and everybody was terribly emaciated; their eyes were
so deep in their sockets that they looked like wine cups. It
seemed that it would be impossible to survive. Yün-chiao's
father thought: "I couldn't make a living with a hoe, and now I
can't make a living wielding a hammer either. In this cursed
place I have suffered enough and had enough frustrations. A
living man must not be swollen to death because he can't piss!
The world is large, and I can't believe that a big fellow like me
can't find a way to survive!" He took a look at the broken hut,
through whose broken ceiling he could see daylight, and the
dilapidated stove which for days had not seen a kitchen fire.
He became so angry that he used his hammer to smash the
broken earthenware pot, and told Yün-chiao's mother: "Let's
go! Let's run for our lives!"

Difficult to Survive Wherever They Go

In the thirteenth year of the "Republic" [1924], Yün-chiao's
father carried his blacksmith bag and led his wife, sister, and
brothers, four in all, to drift and beg, finally reaching Liang-
ma Township in Tun-liu hsien, Shansi Province. After working
for some time as a blacksmith, he still could not support his
family. It was only when he had reached the end of his rope
that he went to a landlord named Liang, dubbed "Sitting Tiger,"
to rent five mou of barren sandy land and three dilapidated
shacks used to watch the rice fields, paying an annual rent of
eight piculs, five bushels.

Yün-chiao's father was also good at farming. The entire family would rise before dawn and finish work by midnight, bleeding

and sweating, and they thus made it through the first year without mishap. In the second year, drought was followed by flood,
and by autumn they had harvested only nine bushels of maize.
After the harvest, Sitting Tiger came with his servants and
lackeys, and the sons of bitches acted like bandits, turning
everything topsy-turvy and looting all the grain. And Sitting
Tiger threatened them:
    "You, Sang, you still owe me seven piculs of rent grain, and
you must send them in before year's end!"
    Yün-chiao's father pleaded: "It is such a disastrous year
this year and I really can't do anything!"
    Glaring with his cone-shaped eyes, Sitting Tiger said: "Who
cares whether there was a disaster or no disaster, you have
to pay your rent!"
    Some poor brethren came to plead for mercy: "Master,
please let these refugees go."
    Sitting Tiger was unmoved: "If you pity him, then you pay
the rent for him!"
    Finally, after much pleading by the poor people, Sitting
Tiger agreed that the full rent could be paid up in the ensuing
year. That night the whole family planned to run away, but
when they reached the west side of the street, they were turned
back by the nightwatchman who patrolled the street and beat a
drum to announce the watches. Consequently they remained to
serve as beasts of labor for Sitting Tiger. Yün-chiao's father
went on performing odd jobs during the day and hammering
iron beside the furnace at night, thus paying back the debt to
Sitting Tiger after five years of toil. Yün-chiao's father realized that it would be impossible to make a living there, and he
canceled his tenancy. Yün-chiao's mother said: "Since we can't
live by running away from home, we may just as well die at our
own home!" Thereafter they drifted back to their native place
in Honan....
    On the day after New Year's, Yün-chiao's father came home
saying: "My son, I learned that there may be some odd jobs to
be found in Taiyuan in Shansi. Let's go and try."
    After considering it Yün-chiao said: "Good." But where

could they get the traveling expenses ? They were obliged to borrow eight dollars from Rich Yang so that father and son could make the long trip. On the way they dared not buy food when they were hungry: nor did they dare to drop in at inns in the evening. They begged for rice along the way, and hiked for half a month before they finally reached Taiyuan. After running around for a whole night, calling on friends and acquaintances, they finally succeeded in securing contractual work with the "San-hsün Shop," a blacksmith shop.

The proprietor of that shop, called Niu Ch'ang-heng, was a rake who like gormandizing, visiting prostitutes, and gambling; his two rat eyes were full of evil designs. His two eyebrows came together, and even when nothing was happening, if his fat torso trembled, it would bode something tragic. He treated people the way one tightens screws on a plate, one turn tighter than another. Yün-chiao and his father came there to make kitchen knives; according to the average daily output, the best craftsmen like them, with their hands moving incessantly, could make five large kitchen knives, or less than eight sets of smaller knives. Nonetheless, the proprietor stipulated that each should turn out eight large kitchen knives, or twelve sets of smaller ones, and wages would be deducted if they fell short of the quota.

In the sultry summer it was almost impossible to endure the sweltering heat beside the furnace, hammering with the heavy hammer. One time, Yün-chiao and his father had worked a whole day soaked with sweat and with nothing to drink. Their throats were itching with thirst as if they had been scratched by the claws of a cat. Yün-chiao seized an opportunity to go into the kitchen. Before he could scoop up a bowl of water and drink it, the proprietor came over, shouting loudly:

"Who has asked you to come here to drink water?" He followed this immediately by giving Yün-chiao a whipping with a rattan stick. "No wonder you can't produce a few knives in a whole day — you're lazy! This is terrible. I mustn't allow your father and you to violate the rules of my shop! "

It was in this manner that the entire day's wages of the father

and son were deducted. Yün-chiao's father became so enraged that he went to see Proprietor Niu and told him:

"Even though my son has missed his work by drinking water, why should you also deduct my wage?"

The proprietor said stubbornly: "When the son errs, it is usually the fault of the father. So it is reasonable for me to deduct your wage."

Although Yün-chiao's father was exasperated, he was afraid to antagonize others, and he swallowed his grievance passively.

Yün-chiao and his father did their best to perform their tasks, baring their backs all the year round, and getting hurt by the sparks of molten iron that sprayed over their bodies. Although they toiled sixteen hours a day, they still couldn't meet the quota of knives prescribed for them. They would bring their kaoliang bread and maize cakes to the furnace side, so that they could get a few bites when it was time to eat. With the passage of time, they became constipated, and blood dripped from their dried mouths. This, coupled with lack of sleep at night, made them gravely ill. One day, as Yün-chiao's father was forging iron, he was suddenly seized by a spasm, and he collapsed onto the ground. When Yün-chiao saw this, he cried pitifully. Luckily some fellow workers came over to help; someone took his pulse; others helped him bend his legs, thus enabling Yün-chiao's father to gradually revive. In that gloomy old society, even though you happened to be a man of iron, how many nails could you make!

After they finished their work in the twelfth lunar month, father and son went to see Proprietor Niu to settle their wages. The latter looked at his ledger and said: "You were short three knives on the eighth day of the fifth moon; rejects were produced on the second day of the seventh month...." He went on working on his abacus and concluded that 160 dollars must be deducted from their wages. That left 40 dollars, but the son of a bitch would give them only 30, saying that the other 10 dollars had to be kept as "deposit money," since he was afraid that they would not come back to work anymore the next year.

On the sixteenth day of the twelfth lunar month, snowflakes

were dropping from the sky, and the drifting snow buried them up to their knees. Yün-chiao followed his father out of Taiyuan. They walked in the snow, leaving footprints with each step they took, hiking and shaking — how distant seemed their native region!

On the ninth day snow fell more heavily; severe northwesterly winds cut through to their bones. By dusk they had climbed to the top of the Taihang Mountains. The mountains were high and the winds were strong. Their hands and feet were frozen into numbness. By midnight their shoes and feet had been frozen together. When the two of them, cold and hungry, came across a temple to a mountain god, it was not difficult for them to decide to go in. Yün-chiao's father groped around with his hands, finding an iron incense pot and a cymbal stand. He grasped the pot and smashed the stand, breaking it into pieces which he used to build a fire. The broken pieces of wood were soon consumed by fire. He looked around, but he couldn't find any wood or hay. He discovered that the sacrificial table was also made of wood which would make good firewood. Yün-chiao's father used his hammer, and with a few strokes broke the table into pieces. Thus, the fire became more vibrant, lighting up the entire temple. Father and son dried their wet clothes. Their bodies felt much warmer, but they became more and more famished. In the bright light of the fire, Yün-chiao's father noticed that the mud idol of the mountain god seemed to be glaring at them angrily, exposing its teeth and its fierce visage, exactly like a landlord or a rich man. As Yün-chiao's father stared at the mountain god, he became more and more indignant.

"Mud idol! Mud idol! You have been pretentious and affected, helping the rich cheat us poor people. We have become so poor already, and yet you still won't give us a decent look!" He spat on the idol, turning it over in order to sit on it, and dried his shoes and socks.

Yün-chiao and his father followed the tortuous mountain trail as they walked on....

It was on the twenty-ninth of the twelfth month that they

returned to Tuan-kou Village. Yün-chiao's father and mother told each other what had happened during that year of separation and then discussed what they should do with the thirty dollars. On the second day, Yün-chiao brought twenty dollars to the market, and spent four dollars to buy a few feet of cloth to make a bed cover. He then went to buy grain, but he was shocked when he asked the price. A few days ago, the price of millet had already risen to forty dollars a picul, but on that day, it had suddenly gone up to eighty dollars. He immediately used the money that was left over to buy two bushels of millet and hurried home. As he approached the hut he suddenly heard shouting from the house, followed by his father's voice.

"Master, I have already spent my money; I still can't repay the debt. Wait —"

"Damn it, the poorer you are the bolder you become. You embezzled my money to go to Taiyuan; you made money there, but you won't pay your debt. How unreasonable!" There was a loud thumping on the rim of the k'ang. "If you won't pay back, I won't pardon you!" So landlord Yang Lao-p'ei had come again to demand payment of the debt.

When Yün-chiao heard the fracas, his anger rose from the soles of his feet to the tip of his head. In his haste he forgot to conceal the millet and the cloth, and he strode through the door. When Yang Lao-p'ei saw Yün-chiao return, he smiled sinisterly: "Good child, I see that you have made a fortune this time, since you have cloth and grain. Now come and pay your debt!"

Yün-chiao said angrily: "What fortune? We will all soon be murdered by you blood-sucking devils."

Yang Lao-p'ei jumped up with anger, hitting Yün-chiao on the face and ordering his lackeys who stood beside him: "Search the place!"

The lackeys went to search everywhere; they found the ten dollars concealed in the ceiling of the hut, and seized the cloth and millet brought back by Yün-chiao. Yün-chiao's mother and his wife begged in unison:

"Master, please be kindhearted. This little bit of millet is for us women to make some congee to pass the New Year!..."

Yün-chiao held the bag tightly to himself, refusing to let it go. Yang Lao-p'ei used his horsewhip to flog Yün-chiao soundly, but Yün-chiao still refused to yield. At last one of the lackeys kicked Yün-chiao in the head, knocking him to the floor. He was whipped by Yang Lao-p'ei a dozen strokes or more, until he was unable to rise. Then they seized the money, cloth, and millet and went away merrily.

With No Place to Go They Ascend Taihang

The road became narrower, and the days became harder. After autumn the Japanese aggressors struck here, and the Kuomintang reactionaries, conniving with the enemy, came out to burn and loot and kill everywhere. By 1942 this was aggravated by the four scourges of "flood, drought, locust pestilence, and T'ang (T'ang En-po, a reactionary KMT warlord)," which combined to oppress the people, who were becoming ill and dying; wolves and tigers were literally running wild in packs, and the skeletons of the dead were everywhere.

One day, Yang Lao-p'ei led some Kuomintang bandit troops to Yün-chiao's home to demand grain and firewood. When his family couldn't produce them, the bandit soldiers and Rich Yang tied up Yün-chiao's sick father, then hanged him upside down onto a tree and beat him severely with wet whips. Yün-chiao was so angry that he wished he could bite some of the bastards and kill them, but he was being held by several bandit soldiers and couldn't move an inch. Then Rich Yang and a bandit soldier had a private talk, and they detained Yün-chiao in the hut. When Yün-chiao heard the hissing sound of whipping and his father's agonizing cry of pain, he could no longer contain his vehemence. He was trying to crash the door when he heard a bandit chief speaking to his man: "Watch him closely; don't let him escape!" Yün-chiao surmised that the enemy wanted to conscript him and so he dared not linger any longer. He opened the rear window and fled into the forest....

Yün-chiao took refuge for several days in the mountain fastness.

At dusk one day, he went home stealthily, only to learn that his father had died of serious injuries on the very day he had taken flight. They all cried pitifully, realizing that it was no longer possible to remain there. They discussed how to run away. At dawn, Yün-chiao carried two baskets supported by a bamboo pole, one basket containing his son Feng-ch'i, and the other basket containing his daughter Mei-hua. His wife carried a broken bamboo basket in one hand and a willow cane in the other. Yün-chiao's mother and his younger brother, Yün-lung, escorted them to the Bitter Water Spring which was in the foothills of the Taihang Mountains.

Looking at her grandchildren in the vegetable baskets, his mother said carefully: "Yün-chiao, I've heard that the Communists and the Eighth Route Army are in the Taihang Mountains and they treat poor people generously. Please go there to look for them...."

In the tenth month the mountains were chilly and the water was cold. Yün-chiao and his wife walked hurriedly along the rugged mountain trail, fearful of pursuit.

They hiked for five days to reach Hung-ti Pass in P'ing-hsün hsien, Shansi. A "massive sweeping up" operation by Japanese troops was currently underway, and there was a sea of fire in the village. Turning toward another ravine, they encountered some people who were dressed in plain clothes but carried swords and rifles. Yün-chiao did not know who they were, and was about to turn back when a man with a gun greeted him: "Fellow countryman, don't be afraid. We are the Eighth Route Army!"

When Yün-chiao learned that it was the Eighth Route Army, he was so elated that he became speechless. There was a long pause before he could say: "I — I have been victimized by rich men and the 'calamity troops,' and so I have fled when I could no longer live in my home. I — I wish to join you!"

Fighters of the Eighth Route Army gathered around in a circle and told him warmly: "The situation is still very tense now, and so we won't stay here too long. For the time being, you'd better get settled in with some fellow countrymen in this area.

The war of armed resistance will soon end in victory. After
the Japanese imperialists have been defeated and the landlords
and despots have been struggled down, poor people will stand
up and live a good life." One fighter took from his shoulder a
small bag of fried noodles and gave it to Yün-chiao, saying
"You'd better take this to cope with the next day or two. There
is a mountain search party of the devils somewhere in front of
you. Take shelter quickly in the ravine. We still have to carry
out our mission!"

After leaving the fighters of the Eighth Route Army, Yün-
chiao took their advice and went into the village. He contacted
some local people, and with the assistance of the local Peasants' Association chairman, settled his family at Hsin-an Village in Lu-ch'eng. After half a month he got a letter from his
maternal uncle informing him that not long after he departed,
Yang Lao-p'ei led the "calamity troops" to his home. They
burned his house; his mother had since died of starvation.

The hateful landlord Yang Lao-p'ei thus added a new blood
debt to Yün-chiao!

The Communist Party Comes with the Spring

In March 1945 willow trees turned green and the peach and
almond trees blossomed, announcing the real spring to the
Taihang Mountains. One day, after returning from a meeting
in the local district, the chairman of the Peasants' Association
said to Yün-chiao: "Old Sang, our anti-Japanese government
has set up a cooperative at Huang-niu-ti and is looking for a
blacksmith to make farm implements. Why don't you contact
Director T'ien."

Yün-chiao was most delighted at this news. When he returned home at noontime, he consulted with his wife and decided to call on Director T'ien at Huang-niu-ti.

T'ien Ch'üan-fu, about forty years old, was director of the
cooperative. A peasant, he was honest and simple. Holding
Yün-chiao's hand, he said, smiling: "Great! You folks from
Lin hsien are adept at hammering iron; this is too wonderful.

For one day's work making tools, we will give you four catties of millet and if you have any difficulties, we will help you solve them. Is this all right?"

Yün-chiao kept replying: "Fine. Fine. Fine."

When Yün-chiao moved his family to Huang-niu-ti, Director T'ien had already found a house for him. There was a new mat on the k'ang, and a fire was built for him to cook rice. Director T'ien helped him unpack his things, and asked him to rest a while first. But he was so excited, how could he rest? When the furnace had been set up properly and the fire burned brightly, he began, asking his wife to help him, and the big and small hammers started swinging noisily.

T'ien Ch'üan-fu was a veteran member of the Communist Party. From the time that Yün-chiao's family moved to Huang-niu-ti, besides showing every concern about the livelihood of the entire family, T'ien would also frequently explain to him some of the reasons why the poor had to pull themselves up. Yün-chiao's class consciousness was thus steadily enhanced. Grateful to the Party and Chairman Mao, he would put his heart into every farm implement he made and delivered into the hands of his poor brothers. His craftsmanship quickly earned the praise of everybody.

In August of that year, no sooner had the Japanese imperialists surrendered than the Yen [Hsi-shan] bandits thrust into Shang-tang. They gained a foothold at Hui-tzu Township, and every few days the bandits would come out for "sweeping up operations." The people said: "These 'No. 2 devils' are just as bad as the Japanese devils, and we must punish them severely!" Yün-chiao also hoped that the militia in the village would kill some No. 2 devils for vengeance. However, he noticed that the militia, carrying their rifles, would scatter each time after they had protected the masses to move to some other place. They never fired any shots.

At noontime one day, Yün-chiao went to see Wang Shuang-hu, who was the village's ordnance director, to find out what was the matter.

Wang Shuang-hu told him: "All the fourteen rifles they have

are so old that they either can't fire at all, or can fire one shot only."

Yün-chiao said: "Old Wang, please bring me one rifle and let me check it."

The ordnance director brought over one with the words "Made in Han-yang" inscribed on it. Yün-chiao immediately did some "surgery" on it. He turned the gun over and over in his hands, touching it and examining it, but he couldn't see any problem. Then he carefully dismantled its mechanism, "diagnosing" each part and each screw. After four or five hours, he still did not find the trouble. Later he polished and lubricated the parts and assembled them in the original way, but after trying the gun, it still refused to work. He spent a whole night probing, but he couldn't find the cause. The next day, he again turned it inside out, and suddenly discovered that there was no pushing device in it and that the screw was also loose. He made a new pushing device in accordance with the original pattern and tightened the screw.

He couldn't find any other defects, and so he brought the rifle to the director: "Old Wang, let's load it and try to fire it!"

Wang Shuang-hu gave him a bullet, and when he tried it, it really fired. Wang Shuang-hu patted Yün-chiao on the back affectionately, saying: "Old Sang, you really have the spirit of endeavor!"

After repairing the first rifle, Yün-chiao became all the more zealous. He then worked the next five or six days and nights overhauling all fourteen rifles, all of which became workable again. A few days later, the militia used the rifles repaired by Yün-chiao to lay a brilliant ambush along the Han-tan-Ch'ang-chih highway, wiping out some thirty Yen bandit troops and capturing a light machine gun. The news of victory soon spread through the entire district, and the director of the all-district military committee went to see Yün-chiao personally and said to him: "Master Sang, your merit is really most remarkable! I have already studied the matter with the district committee and decided to ask you to set up a small ordnance repair shop." Yün-chiao immediately agreed.

After the opening of the ordnance repair shop, Yün-chiao worked even harder, staying in the shop all hours and even forgetting to eat and sleep. He repaired and rebuilt many kinds of weapons: rifles, grenade throwers, and field artillery.... Whatever he handled, the broken ones were all repaired, and the defective ones all became crack weapons again.

One morning Yün-chiao told Wang Shuang-hu: "I wonder when I can use a weapon I have repaired myself to match strength with the enemy!"

Wang Shuang-hu replied: "Good, if you want to kill the enemy, you don't have to worry about finding a chance!"

And sure enough, the opportunity came! Once, when he and five militiamen were covering the masses evacuating Hun-ling Village, they killed a dozen or more enemies and saved the lives of the entire village population.

This small ordnance repair shop that Yün-chiao operated supported the militia guerrillas effectively and had a great impact in the renowned Battle of Shang-tang.

A Poor Blacksmith Becomes a Master of the Country

After the liberation of the whole country, Sang Yün-chiao was transferred to a larger factory. Later, with a view to supporting industrial construction in the mountain regions, he came once again to the machine factory in Wu-hsiang hsien. Now his entire family lives happily. His son, Feng-ch'i, and his daughter-in-law are both shock troopers on the agricultural front; his elder daughter, Mei-hua, and son-in-law are "five-good" commune members; his second daughter, Chin-hua, is attending primary school and is a "three-good" student....

He often says: "Water has its source and a tree has its roots. Now that I am living such a happy life, how can I forget the favors of the Communist Party and Chairman Mao, and how can I but work diligently!" He is the kind of man who does what he says. Last year, for instance, during the period from July to September, he and his fellow workers utilized waste copper and scrap iron to make such farm implements as

circles for handcart seats and handy hoes, thus supporting agricultural production and saving some one thousand dollars of
capital funds for the state. In ordinary times whenever he
sees a bit of scrap or a piece of charcoal, even if it is as tiny
as a screw, he puts them into a neat pile. Since the Great
Leap Forward, Sang Yün-chiao has been appraised annually as
an advanced producer. Last year he was judged by the People's Congress of Shansi as a "five-good" staff member and
worker.

An honorable family of miners

"Veteran miner Wang Man-hsi has retired!" This news quickly stirred the entire village.

When old Man-hsi, who had just reached the age of sixty, returned to his home, the young people vied with each other to greet him, and surrounded him in the house.

The newly painted parlor had been redecorated by the young people. On the mantlepiece were placed a large clock and a new teapot, with its cotton-padded cover to hold in the warmth, complete with cups. On the large k'ang were piled cotton bedding and woolen blankets. There was a new screen for the k'ang, painted brightly with colorful designs, thus adding a warmth to this neat room. It was no wonder that no sooner had the young people entered, than they joked with Mother Wang: "Mrs. Wang, look at this house which is decorated so elegantly. If one did not know better, one would think this must be someone's bridal suite."

"Bridal suite!" Mother Wang laughed. "We have never lived in a bridal suite! When we were young, none of the young fellows in the vicinity of Tung-wang, Hsi-wang, and Wei Village in Ch'ang-chih could get married, to say nothing of having a bridal suite."

Kai T'ien-wen, Ch'en Fu-t'ung, "K'uang-kung shih-chia."

285

Pointing to a side lantern used by miners in the old society that was hanging on the wall, a mischievous youth said to Mother Wang jokingly: "Mrs. Wang, look how bright this newly installed electric light is! Why do you still hang this old thing here? Such a black ugly thing, and even the iron hook is still attached to it! It really does not match at all! If my grandfather had not told me about it, I'd think it was a chamberpot!"

Everybody laughed after hearing this. Old man Man-hsi, who was then sitting in his chair, jumped up, and taking the side lantern in his hands, said: "In the old society, when miners went down into the shaft, they used two kinds of lanterns. The haulers used a lantern which was put on the head, and it was called a head lantern; the coal cutters used the lantern hung on the colliery wall, and it was called a side lantern. These lanterns burned vegetable oil, and rags were used as wicks. Don't look upon this as a side lantern but as Mrs. Wang's 'trousseau.'"

No sooner had the old man finished than Mrs. Wang continued: "True, this was my trousseau; moreover it was the heirloom of our Wang family also." Mrs. Wang took the lantern from old man Man-hsi and held it in her own hands. The old lady became solemn as she continued:

"To say that this is an heirloom is by no means false. Under the light of this lantern men of our old generation shed plenty of tears and lost enormous amounts of blood and sweat! This side lantern is the living witness to the miserable life of us coal miners! As you all said this was a 'trousseau,' let me start with the story of the trousseau...."

I

"No one would want their daughter to marry someone in Tung-wang and Hsi-wang. Day and night one would be worried. When one took a day off on the first and fifteenth of the month, he'd take off a pile of blackened clothes." This was a folk ballad that was prevalent in our area in the old society. This was because our Wei Village was close to the Shih-ch'i-chieh colliery, and most of the villagers went out to work in the mines. The work of a miner was hard; he would make very little money, and accidents were frequent. Thus people would often say: "It's only when one is down and out that he'd go down to work in a mine." Because of this, no girls within an area of twenty or thirty li would marry here. Even the daughters of our own village would like to marry outsiders; who'd want to be the wife of a "black coal miner"? As time passed, people concocted this ballad, and it became quite popular.

In the year when I turned thirteen, I became engaged to Man-hsi. Man-hsi and I were born in the same year. He went into the mine with his father when he was thirteen.

One night, I asked my mother quietly: "Mother, why did you ask me to be engaged to a miner?"

My mother sighed, and then told me: "Good daughter, for many generations our family has worked in the mines, and Man-hsi's family has also worked as miners for generations. Now consider, if you don't want to marry a miner, and a girl in that family also doesn't want to marry a miner, then no miner would get married. Except for being poor, what miner lacks a good character? You have also known that this boy Man-hsi is honest, kindhearted, and courageous, his only fault being that he is quick-tempered. When you go to his house, though life may be somewhat hard, they won't mistreat you...."

Of course I knew these things, because Man-hsi and I had grown up in the same village. He was a very sensitive young man, afraid of neither heaven nor earth, and he would dare to swat the fly perched on the tiger's head. When he was small there were some young fellows who wanted to bet with Man-hsi, daring him to go into the Patron Saint Temple at midnight and fill the mouths of the mud idols with some wild vegetables. If Man-hsi accepted the challenge, they would invite him to eat fried cakes on the next day.

Man-hsi said: "Not only will I invite them to eat wild vegetables, but if you want me to cut off their heads, I'd dare do it!"

So these fellows really cooked a pot of wild vegetables and brought it over. That night, the moon was shrouded in clouds

288 The People of Taihang

and it was dark, and a person couldn't even see the five fingers
on his own hand. Man-hsi took the earthenware pot, saying:
"Wait and see!" He then followed the mountain path up
into the temple. He even stopped his breathing, and groped
around, and whenever he located the head of an idol, he filled
its mouth with wild vegetables. However, when he came to fill
the third idol's mouth, something strange happened. No sooner
had he given the idol one mouthful than that fellow swallowed
it immediately, and then it was followed by another mouthful,
and then he could hear the sound of the food being digested.
Although Man-hsi was brave, he felt himself trembling. Why?
Could there really be ghosts? He couldn't believe it! After
calming himself down, he continued to fill the mouth of that
fellow, and all of the food was swallowed immediately.

Man-hsi became furious, and holding the pot, he said: "I
think you must be out of luck today, and now that you have met
me, I must smash you to death and see who is more powerful,
you or I —"

Before he could finish his sentence, that fellow could stand
it no more. Laughing loudly, he said: "Good Man-hsi, you
really have guts. Now we concede to you!" For it happened
that this was a boy sent over by those who had challenged Man-
hsi to play a trick on him.

Frankly there was not another fellow like Man-hsi in our
village. So I did not argue with my mother anymore.

During the autumn harvest the next year, my mother had a
miscarriage. My father was then in the mine and hadn't been
home for several days. The whole family did not have anything
to eat for three whole days. On the second day after her miscarriage, my mother climbed down from her k'ang.

"Little Ying-tzu, you stay home to look after things while I
go out to pick up some stray grain so that I can cook some
soup after I return."

"Mother," I pleaded, "you are sick, so please wait at home
and let me and my younger brother go out for you."

Mother replied: "You are too small, and others might abuse
you!"

"Abuse me?" I said. "I am also more than ten years old, and if anyone dares to abuse me, I'll fight him!..."

When my mother failed to dissuade me, she took me and my younger brother along to go out together to collect a stray harvest.

That year there were many poor people, and there were many people looking for a stray harvest. The three of us braved the wind and sandstorms, and after some difficulty we picked up a few tassels of corn. After returning home, mother became so weak that she felt a chill all over her body, and her face was as pale as a sheet of paper. At midnight, I sensed that mother was not the same as in the old days. However, inexplicably, she seemed to be spirited and was rather talkative. She called me to light the side lantern that had been left by our grandfather before his death, and put it at the head of the k'ang. Then, summoning me to stand beside her, she faced the dim lantern, opened her sunken eyes, and touched my younger brother, who had just fallen asleep. She fingered the hair on my forehead, and tears streamed from her eyes. Grasping my hands, she said:

"Little Ying-tzu, I am finished. When I think of you two, my heart is more agonized than if it had been stabbed by a knife.... You are just fifteen and your brother is only nine, and who should you depend on from now! Little Ying-tzu, it is not that your mother's heart is cruel. It is rather this world won't let poor folks live!... After you go to Man-hsi's family, your mother won't be worried, but it'll be hard on this child —"

My mother barely managed to turn over to caress my brother, saying: "Child, you have been born into the wrong family. Let Mother take another look at you —" After she said this, she went to lie down and told me feebly: "Little Ying-tzu, go heat some water for your mother."

When I brought the hot water to the k'ang, my mother had closed her eyes. I called her a few times but could get no response; I pushed her and she wouldn't move. In her eyes were tears.

The autumn wind lashed through cracks in the wall. The dim

light danced in the chill wind.

From afar came the barking of dogs.

I pushed open the door and saw a torch approaching from a distance. I called, "Father," and strangely, Father really had returned.

"Little Ying-tzu, why aren't you in bed? Good daughter, your father has bought four catties of corn flour to make paste. Your mother is pregnant, and we must be careful —" Father did not know that Mother had had a miscarriage and that she had —

"Father —" I fell into his arms. What words could I use to tell the old man?

After mother's death, father's temperament underwent a great change. He wouldn't say a thing all day long. Although there were only I and my brother, the meager amount of grain earned by father was still insufficient. I had to go out to pick wild vegetables, which we cooked together with the grain, to sustain myself and my brother. My brother was also understanding, and he would go out early in the morning to pick up coal. When he returned at noon, he would first rub the lid of the pot, and if it was hot, he would wait to get something to eat; but if the lid was cold, he would immediately carry his baskets out again.

In July of the next year, my father contracted typhoid and could no longer go down into the mine. Some uncles who used to work in the colliery with father chipped in a few hundred dollars for my father to get medical treatment, but his illness, instead of improving, became more serious. On the night of July 19, father again asked me to light that side lantern. Why should he ask me to light it? I couldn't help but tremble. . . .

"Little Ying-tzu, good daughter, your father's health is no good, and so I can't take care of you. This lantern was used by your grandfather, and it has also guided your father for several decades. . . . It has been drenched with the sweat and blood of your grandfather and your father! In the last two years I was afraid that I might lose it, and it was too precious to be used! This time your father does not have even a single cent or half a catty of rice to leave to you. I have only this lantern; good daughter, take good care of it...."

II

After my parents' death, my brother became dependent on me. Some of the uncles who used to work in the mine with father would sometimes give us some money and grain. Man-hsi's mother also came to see us often, and she asked me to go over to live in her house. Nonetheless, as we were all so hard up how could I bother others?

Before we knew it winter was upon us, and many of Man-hsi's fellow workers suggested to him that he get married. Some of them would say to Man-hsi's father: "We poor people do things in a poor man's way, and we all help each other in times of distress!" Others would say: "This girl Ying-tzu is really one in a hundred. Who cares about the saying 'No one would want their daughter to marry someone in Tung-wang and Hsi-wang'? Isn't a fine person like Ying-tzu engaged to be married to a miner?..."

His enthusiastic fellow workers chipped in, 50 here, 100 there, until 2,000 strings had been collected. This amount was nothing in the eyes of the mine owner, but in the hands of the poor, it was no small sum. If we should accept the gifts, we knew their money did not come easily, and which family did not have a wife and children to support? But if we declined, the fellow workers would be displeased. One fellow became angry with Man-hsi, accusing him of not treating them as part of his family. Finally Man-hsi had no alternative but to accept the money, which he handed over to his mother.

After discussing it with his fellow workers, Man-hsi's father decided to set the wedding date on the twenty-third of the twelfth month. Man-hsi's mother used the 2,000 strings of cash to make a cotton-padded dress for me and to buy some odds and ends. On the wedding day, it would be necessary to invite our fellow workers to come over for a visit. Although we miners were too poor to prepare a feast, it would be

necessary to get a few catties of wine and fry one or two dishes
of food. But where could we get the money?

Taking advantage of his youth and robust strength, Man-hsi
would take on "consecutive shifts" every day. To take on consecutive shifts meant to work another shift after the regular
one was finished. At that time each shift lasted twelve hours.
Working in the mine depended entirely on physical stamina.
One would be exhausted after taking one shift, and so how could
one work continuously for twenty-four hours? However, to support their families some miners were obliged to take up two
shifts or even three consecutive shifts....

In order to make some more money for the marriage, Man-
hsi began to undertake consecutive shifts without telling his
mother. On the twenty-first day of the twelfth month, after
leaving a few hundred coppers with his mother, Man-hsi went
out to work again. He volunteered to take up three consecutive
shifts. The tactic of mine owners at that time was truly cruel.
In order to induce workers to take more shifts, the wage for
consecutive shifts would be raised a little higher. For instance,
while the wage for one shift was 180 coppers, one would get
400 coppers for two consecutive shifts, and 900 coppers for
three consecutive shifts. To Man-hsi 900 coppers seemed to
be an impressive figure. Since his fellow workers had been so
enthusiastic, how could he treat them coolly on the wedding
day?

On the twenty-first, when the cashier heard that Man-hsi
would take on three consecutive shifts, he immediately took a
few silver dollars to the counter. Holding the silver dollars in
his hand, he said: "Good boy! Your pay is ready! Let's agree
beforehand. When you report for three shifts, you must take
three shifts! If you can't fulfill them, it will be counted as one
shift in pay. I know that in your Wang family one generation is
tougher than the one before, and if you can say it, you can do
it!" As he was thus speaking, he took out a silver dollar, turning its edge toward his mouth, blowing a mouthful of air onto it
energetically, and then listening to the sound of vibration by his
ear. It was said that this was a tactic to test whether the silver

dollar was genuine or counterfeit. In point of fact, he was merely using this trick to lure the workers.

At that time, Man-hsi said: "All right!" He put on the head lantern and fastened the "fetter" rope on his back, and then went down into the mine shaft.

No sooner had he reached the shaft than a fellow worker came to tell him: "Man-hsi, why are you so stubborn? The day after tomorrow will be your big day, and though we are poor, you must make some preparations, such as sweeping the house and polishing the kitchen. We advise you for your own good; why should you turn a deaf ear to us?"

An older worker said: "Since you have come down, you might as well get to work. But work only one shift, and then go home after that!"

"Yes, Big Uncle!" Man-hsi began to work together with the others.

When the first shift ended, Man-hsi, under the pretext that he was going to the toilet, hid himself. After the others had left, he began the second shift....

By dusk on the twenty-second, as Man-hsi was beginning his third shift, he became dizzy and weak; cold sweat was pouring off him like rain, and even such a strong fellow as he, who was like a vibrant dragon and a living tiger, could hardly stand. His friends advised him to climb out of the shaft. Just then the foreman came by. The workers said to him: "Third Boss, Man-hsi is sick. Please let him go."

The foreman smiled sinisterly, exposing his yellow teeth: "Nowadays, workers have their freedom, and if he wants to go, then let him go! Nonetheless, we do things according to the rules. Since he has not fulfilled his three shifts, she should be paid for one shift, which is 180 coppers! Go, ask the cashier to settle the account!"

"One hundred and eighty coppers?" Man-hsi used his whole strength to stand up. He thought that he should get 900 coppers for three shifts, and now after he had completed two shifts, it was still 180 coppers! Biting his lips he said: "See, if I can't complete three shifts, I won't be worthy of the Wang family's posterity!"

The foreman said disdainfully: "The money is in the counting room, and unless you have completed three shifts, don't ever think you'll get 900 coppers!"

"Nine hundred coppers! I won't settle for 899! Wait another half day and see if you don't bring it docilely to me!" He immediately stumbled back into the coal deposit, put on his "fetter" rope, and began to haul. After the foreman had left, worker friends asked Man-hsi to sleep. Man-hsi said: "I won't sleep. I am young, and it won't matter if I take on another shift!" Later, when he could no longer refuse their advice, Man-hsi rested for a while. Even Man-hsi himself did not know how he managed to get through the third shift....

Early on the morning of the twenty-third, Man-hsi reached the exit of the shaft only with the assistance of his fellow workers. He claimed the 900 coppers, and with a trace of a smile, challenged the cashier: "Mr. Cashier, Wang Man-hsi has not even cheated fifteen minutes of the shift."

Nine hundred coppers, earned with blood and tears.

As he entered his house, Man-hsi collapsed onto the k'ang....

The big day, this was my big happy day with Man-hsi!

By noon the next day Man-hsi was still unconscious. His mother called, "Man-hsi." He replied, "I'll do it!" and sprang up suddenly, rushing toward the door and pulling down the ragged bedding from the bed.

I said quickly: "Man-hsi, please wake up. This is your home...." After quieting himself down, he began to come around slowly.

"Ying-tzu, did we all drink some wine yesterday?"

What could I say to him? When our friends saw Man-hsi collapse with exhaustion on his bed and become unconscious, how could they have the heart to drink? I had to tell him: "When they saw that you were ill, they asked me to take good care of you and then left...."

When he was working those consecutive shifts, Man-hsi had lost his own head lantern. After resting for two days at home, he took the side lantern left by my father to go down into the shaft. I also found a piece of bamboo to make into a stick with which to scrape sweat. I don't have this gadget now, but at that time it was indispensable to the miner. He could put it under his cap, to use it to scrape sweat, or as chopsticks....

III

In the year I turned twenty-two, I gave birth to my first baby. No matter how poor we were, the family was happy and harmonious. On the day the baby became one month old, Grandfather carried his little grandson and said smilingly: "Good, here is another generation of little miners!"

In the twelfth month of that year, my father-in-law injured his back while working in the shaft. At that time, when someone was crushed to death, the "old official price was 12,000 strings of cash," but if one was injured, the mine owner not only would do nothing but also would kick you out and make you go home....

On the twentieth day of the twelfth month, my father-in-law's injury became worse, and my mother-in-law cried and fainted many times. Man-hsi was working hard in the shaft and did not return home. That morning, after nursing my baby, I went out, trying to find some friendly worker to take a message to Man-hsi asking him to bring back some money for my father-in-law to see a doctor. I had not walked too far when Man-hsi returned to the village full of anger.

Upon returning home, he dumped the side lantern on the table, waking the baby.

I asked him: "What has happened to you?"

From under his cap, he took the sweat-scraper to scrape the coal dust from his face, and said: "I know that Father's injury has become more serious in the last two days, and so I took on several consecutive shifts. Today I did not feel well, and so after one shift, I went up. I figured I could get some money to bring home. When I reached the counting room, I asked the cashier to pay me. That fellow said, smoothing his whiskers: 'Wang Man-hsi, in this shift, you hauled thirteen baskets!'

"I said: 'What? Big Cashier, I hauled nearly sixteen baskets. How do you get thirteen only?'

"He grunted through his nose: 'Wang Man-hsi, it isn't one or two years that you have worked in this mine, so why should you pretend to be ignorant? Let me tell you clearly: the old boss, in order to see that everyone can celebrate the New Year, has increased the wages for the twelfth month, paying 300 coppers for each shift! Nonetheless, in the final analysis, you miners must also think about the proprietor. Throughout the four seasons of the year, how enormous are the expenses of the entire mine! Today, you did in fact haul sixteen baskets of coal. Nevertheless, the cashier has deducted three baskets. One basket goes to the owner so he can invite guests and make gifts; one basket goes to me to reward the care I have taken as cashier; one basket goes,' he pointed toward the Taoist temple through the window, 'to the purchase of incense to worship Lao-tzu! Let me tell you this. When you produce fully sixteen baskets, the wage will be 300 coppers; now that you have hauled only thirteen baskets, which is three baskets short, for each basket short, 40 coppers is deducted, which makes 120 coppers of deduction. Then there is added a tool fee of 30 coppers, so the total deduction should be 150 coppers from the 300; what you should get is 150 coppers net! Come, take the money!'

"I said: 'Big Cashier, my father has been seriously injured!'

"He said: 'It's good if you realize that your father has been seriously injured. Think for yourself, wasn't your father injured because he incurred the displeasure of Lao-tzu?'

"I said: 'Big Cashier, it will be New Year soon!'

"He thrust his abacus on the counter and said: 'New Year, New Year! You know only that you have to celebrate the New Year. Do you think that the old boss doesn't have to celebrate the New Year, and that I, the cashier, don't have to celebrate the New Year? Moreover, won't this Lord Lao-tzu also have to celebrate the New Year?'

"As he was saying this, he shouted louder and louder. I could not stand it any longer and so I said: 'They call you Big Cashier. This increase of wages to help us celebrate the New Year is

what you yourselves have dreamed up! If there is no increase,
we can make 180 coppers a day, but after the increase, it comes
only to 150! How come the words uttered by your yellow
mouth and white teeth aren't even worth a fart!'

"This really got that fellow mad: 'Good kid, you dare to scold
people!'

"What if I scolded you?' I said. 'I'd even like to beat you!'

"Like a mad dog he jumped at me: 'Damn it, Wang, you'll
taste this old man's toughness!'

"I tell you, Ying-tzu, were it not for the fellow workers who
pushed me away, were it not for the sake of my father, you,
and the baby, I'd have fought it out with him to see who lived
and who died. Anyway, to cut off the head would leave only a
hole, but at least it would let them know that while we are poor,
we can't be insulted and abused!"

As Man-hsi and I were still talking, some fellow workers
came in. When they found out that Man-hsi had not gotten his
money and that my father-in-law was seriously ill, they again
chipped in to give money so that he could see a doctor. In this
way my father-in-law's life was saved. Nonetheless, after he
had made a slow recovery, he remained hunchbacked.

IV

With his hunchback, father-in-law could no longer work in
the mine. The burden of supporting the entire family fell onto
Man-hsi's shoulders. After a few years, our first son, Ch'iu-
ch'eng, was already fifteen. One morning in spring, Ch'iu-
ch'eng wiped clean his father's side lantern and said: "Father,
won't you give me this lantern? You could find another one;
today let me follow you into the mine!" When Man-hsi heard
his request, he said, after pondering for a while: "Good, son,
you are ambitious and deserve to be the posterity of the Wang
family!"

Thus one more little miner came into our family.

As people have often said, blessings never come in twos,
but disasters never occur alone. After father-in-law became

a hunchback and could no longer work in the shaft, Man-hsi's
right leg was also injured soon after Ch'iu-ch'eng followed in
his footsteps to work in the shaft.

This was the seventeenth of the third month on the lunar calendar. Early one morning, when I was carrying my bamboo
basket to go out to pick wild vegetables, Ch'iu-ch'eng led some
fellow workers who were carrying Man-hsi through the door.
I could only hear him gritting his teeth and see pearls of sweat
as large as beans dripping down his coal-black face....

Here's what had happened on the night of the sixteenth: Man-
hsi and Niu Yung-so of Tung-wang Village went down into the
shaft together. When Man-hsi detected some strange sounds,
he said: "Yung-so, the ceiling boards are no good." Before he
could finish his words, some "dumplings" fell down. They were
trying to get out of there when there came a sudden "bang" and
the legs of both men were buried by the ceiling boards.

Ch'iu-ch'eng, who was then hauling coal, rushed over, calling,
"Father!" Man-hsi straightened his body and said: "Never
mind, dig quickly." It was fortunate that the area of the collapse of the ceiling was not too large, and after the energetic
digging of several fellow workers, the two men were rescued.

Yung-so's injuries were not too serious, and he managed to
stand firm after limping for a while. Man-hsi was supported
by Ch'iu-ch'eng, and after he manged to stand on his left foot
and was about to step on his right, he suddenly felt that that
leg was as heavy as a thousand catties, and said hurriedly: "Ch'iu-
ch'eng, put the lantern lower and let me see."

Man-hsi bowed his head to look and found that all the toes
on that foot had been twisted backward. He said involuntarily:
"It's bad!"

A fellow worker hurried over: "Let me rub it!" He held
Man-hsi's right foot to adjust it, but because he was worried
and did not apply his strength evenly, the bones were not set
properly. Man-hsi felt such an excruciating pain that he
clenched his fists and pressed his head against the coal wall....

The crowd hastened to carry Man-hsi under the shaft entrance, hoping to bring him out of the mine. It was then that

the No. 2 foreman entered the shaft and asked: "Why are you in such a panic instead of hauling coal? What are you doing here?"

Ch'iu-ch'eng couldn't endure any more and, pointing to his father, who was prostrated on the ground, he said angrily: "See for yourself...."

The No. 2 foreman raised the shiny brass stick he was holding and thrust it against Ch'iu-ch'eng's chest: "What does this matter? I knew about it the minute it happened!" He pointed toward Man-hsi and said: "Leave him here, and wait for dawn to take him out of the shaft. Hurry up and haul coal!"

One worker defied the No. 2 foreman: "Number two boss, Man-hsi's foot has been fractured, and he can't bear the pain!"

"Listen! He's not uttering a single word. You aren't the hookworm in his stomach; how do you know that he can't en-dure it?"

"Number two boss, please touch his tattered shirt and see how soaked with sweat it is. He's a tough guy and won't complain. Don't even you know this?"

"Don't argue anymore. Anyway, he couldn't leave the shaft now! Anyway, will his pain stop if he leaves the shaft?"

All the while more and more workers were coming over, and they insisted that they must help Man-hsi out of the mine. When the No. 2 foreman sensed that the situation was critical, he said: "All right, in consideration of your demand, you can use some ropes to pull him up!"

"Ropes? His injury is so serious that it would be very diffi-cult to use ropes; he must sit in a basket!"

"Sit in a basket? If he should sit in a basket, it would ac-count for a loss of several hundred catties of coal. Don't you even understand this simple arithmetic?"

"Number two boss, if you won't allow him to sit in a basket, we'll all stay here to attend to him...."

Thus they all insisted that they wouldn't leave. When the No. 2 foreman saw that the workers were numerous and insis-tent, he realized it wouldn't serve any interest to delay further. Thus he changed his mind and said: "All right, write it off to the bad luck of the owner, write it off to the bad luck of the owner. Go up quickly! Go up quickly!"

. . . .

In order to heal Man-hsi's illness, I would go outside of the village to pick wild vegetables early in the morning; at night I would spin cotton by the light of the moon; during the day I would help my neighbors by doing sewing chores. . . .

One night, when Ch'iu-ch'eng was home on a break, I said to him while I was spinning: "Son, I've had a talk with your grandfather and father, and we've decided that from tomorrow you shouldn't go down into the shaft anymore. We can suffer together, and die together. Now when you go down into the shaft, the entire family worries. . . . As I see it, it is better that you tend sheep for some landlord, even though you'd make less money —"

"Mother, all crows are black. Landlord and mine owner have the same heart. Though it is more grueling to work in the mine, the income is higher compared with herding sheep. Didn't you often tell me that my grandfather and maternal uncle were persecuted by their landlords so cruelly that they had no choice but to become miners? Moreover, Father has been hurt, and the family has more expenses —"

"Son, please don't say any more; listen to your mother. Don't go down into the shaft! My heart is breaking for your sake!"

Ch'iu-ch'eng, like his father, was a stubborn fellow. Although he agreed then that he would no longer go down into the shaft, before dawn on the next day, he sneaked out with his side lantern and went to work. This time he dared not come back, and after getting his pay he'd ask some friend to bring some money home. . . . To tell the truth, the entire family of some eight or nine mouths depended entirely on his support.

Though Man-hsi's injury steadily healed, his right leg was crippled and he walked with a limp.

With his crippled leg he could no longer work in the mine, which to Man-hsi was a tremendous blow. "No, I can't be crippled, and I must still go down into the shaft! I can't leave such a heavy burden on my child alone!"

In those days he would get up from his k'ang at dawn. From Wei Village to Huang-chan and from Huang-chan back to Wei Village is a distance of five or six li, and he'd make several round trips in the morning. I did not know what he was doing. One day, he strode in, his head drenched with sweat. My mother-in-law asked him: "Man-hsi, your leg is crippled, and you are recuperating at home. Why must you still walk to the east and then to the west; isn't this just inviting trouble for yourself! Son, you're a full-grown man now and should be more understanding!...."

After hearing this, Man-hsi became more serious: "Mother, think for yourself. How can our whole family depend on Ch'iu-ch'eng alone? By walking and drilling myself diligently, my bones could become more flexible and I might get well sooner...."

In this manner Man-hsi stayed home for some thirty or forty days, and then he limped to the mine.

When the cashier saw that this crippled fellow had returned, he hastened to look at Man-hsi's leg: "Why, I see that this leg is no good."

"No good?" Wasn't this lightning out of the blue sky! If he really wouldn't allow him to work in the shaft, how then could his family survive? Man-hsi became wise in this crisis. He stooped, put his feet together, and jumped abruptly a distance of several feet. "How is it, Mr. Cashier, not crippled?"

The cashier was still skeptical. Taking advantage of the fact that Man-hsi was just barely managing to stand firmly, he kicked with all his might at Man-hsi's leg! Fortunately, his kick landed on Man-hsi's left leg; if it had hit the right one, no matter how tough the man might have been, he would not have been able to stand it. Thinking that he must work in the mine, Man-hsi endured his pain and stretched out his right leg, asking: "What do you say, Mr. Cashier, do you still want to test this one?"

"Good, Wang Man-hsi, you are tough! I give you permission to go down into the shaft!"

Man-hsi crawled from the bottom of the shaft to the coal deposit, and immediately, he found that both legs were hurting
him....

In 1939 the Japanese invasion army occupied the Shih-ch'i-
chieh colliery. They lived in San-chiao-yüan, ostentatiously
lording over the villagers. They built seven large watchtowers
around the colliery, and in each tower Japanese soldiers were
stationed and machine guns were mounted. Every three or five
days they would go out into the surrounding countryside to
"sweep up." Though the miners wearied themselves with a
long day's work, all they could earn was one or two catties of
kaoliang flour. If anyone should happen to antagonize the foreman in the shaft, the latter would immediately accuse him before the enemy of "conniving with the Eighth Route Army," a
crime punishable by beheading or being shot to death. One
time some of the fleeing workers were captured by the enemy,
and they were all killed by machine-gun fire. The enemy also
called some fellow workers to witness the massacre and said
arrogantly to them: "If anyone tries to run away again, he will
be mowed down by machine gun like them!"

The family became further aggrieved when Man-hsi and
Ch'iu-ch'eng found life in the colliery more and more intoler-
able. The whole family, old and young, were often starving
with empty stomachs and sunken eyes. The second son died of
typhoid, and the fourth daughter broke her leg and died before
our eyes.... Being a mother, I couldn't allow my own flesh
and blood to die of hunger, and so I sent my youngest daughter
to a Catholic church....

V

It was the Communist Party and Chairman Mao that saved
us from the abyss of the well of bitterness. I, Wang Ying-tzu,
the daughter of a miner, like millions and millions of my sisters in China, saw the blue sky again after the dark clouds had
lifted!

Since liberation my hunchbacked father-in-law has had a

happy old age. Owing to the Party's concern, Man-hsi's leg injury received thorough treatment. In 1946 he joined the organization gloriously, thus becoming the first Communist Party
member in our family. The Party has also promoted him to the
post of director of the colliery. Thus a miner, who for generations had been despised as "coal black," for the first time became master of a coal mine. Like Man-hsi, the other workers
all loved their own colliery warmly. During the time of reha-
bilitation of production, for many days and nights the workers
defied fatigue and hardship to overcome one obstacle after another. At that time, when Man-hsi noticed that there was no
water tank in the shaft, he personally led three cadres to work
for more than ten days straight. After digging some forty feet
of bottom coal, they found a piece of rock measuring about
twenty feet in length. Man-hsi smiled as he saw the rock. He
wielded his iron pick to smash the rock, causing sparks of fire
under the terrific impact: "Let's see who is tougher, you or I!"
    Someone said: "This segment of the project is most difficult!"
    Man-hsi again raised his iron pick, saying: "If there is a
tiger, there must be a Wu Sung, and if there is difficulty, there
must be a hero! When the water tank is overhauled and safety
is ensured, the extra coal that is produced as a result will belong to the working class itself!"
    Li Ts'ai-kuei, who was the man in charge of safety, said:
"Director Wang, you have worked yourself into exhaustion for
several days already. Better go up and have a rest. Please
don't worry, because even if you aren't here, we can guarantee
that it will be done properly!"
    Out of habit, Man-hsi reached up to touch the sweat-scraper
he was carrying under his cap. It was then that Ts'ai-kuei
pointed to the white towel hanging on his own neck.
    "Why is it that you can't give up that gadget! We have plenty
of white towels now!"
    When he heard this, Man-hsi also laughed. One veteran
worker said jokingly: "Director Wang, you seem to be taking
on consecutive shifts this time again. Do you want to get married another time?"

Man-hsi smiled broadly: "Right, consecutive shifts! I am willing to work consecutive shifts all my life for socialism!"

It is true that unless one has eaten the bitter plant, one won't know its bitterness. Who would appreciate the sunny road of today if he has not trod the dark roads of the old society! Now, of our three children, two have joined the Party, and they all have their own families. Ch'iu-ch'eng already has become a grade seven dynamite-setter. Everyone lauds us as the "Honorable Family of Miners" and admires our happy life, full of children and grandchildren. True, how can a person like me, who has come through a vast sea of bitterness, not sincerely thank our Party and our brilliant leader Chairman Mao? Whenever I think of the past, my heart fills with zeal. I am sixty-one years old this year, and yet I have been evaluated as a "five-good" commune member. In the Wei Village Brigade of Huang-chan Commune in Ch'ang-chih Municipality, fellow members say that the older I am, the more Red I become, and the longer I live, the more youthful I become. What can I say? I often look toward the city of Peking and say heartily: "Chairman Mao, Chairman Mao, can you imagine the sentiments of a miner's daughter? Can you find the time to come here to see our life of today?..."

The day that "no one would want their daughter to marry someone in Tung-wang and Hsi-wang" has gone forever. Today, how blissful it is to be the wife of a miner!

Now all miners are using carbide lamps in the mine, which are not only bright and clear but also safe! Nothing like this side lantern, which is heavy and dirty; even when it is lit up, it gives no more light than a firefly! Nonetheless, we still hang it on the wall. We look at it every day and remember it at all hours; we never want to forget that part of our life in the past....

About the editor

Sidney Leonard Greenblatt is an assistant professor of
sociology at Drew University. He received his M.A. in
political science from Columbia University and a Certificate
from Columbia's East Asian Institute. Under the auspices of
Fulbright-Hays and the Contemporary China Committee,
Professor Greenblatt spent two years in Hong Kong and
Taiwan engaged in research on organizational change in China.
  Professor Greenblatt is a contributor to Robert A. Scalapino,
ed., Elites in the People's Republic of China (University of
Washington Press) and has presented a number of research
papers to conferences on contemporary China. He has been
Editor of Chinese Sociology and Anthropology since its
inception in 1968.